A Memory of Violets

Also by Hazel Gaynor

The Girl Who Came Home

A Memory of Violets

A Novel of London's Flower Sellers

HAZEL GAYNOR

wm
WILLIAM MORROW
An Imprint of HarperCollins*Publishers*

This book is a work of fiction. The characters, incidents, and dialogue are drawn from the author's imagination and are not to be construed as real. Any resemblance to actual events or persons, living or dead, is entirely coincidental.

HarperCollins books may be purchased for educational, business, or sales promotional use. For information please e-mail the Special Markets Department at SPsales@harpercollins.com.

FIRST EDITION

Designed by Diahann Sturge

Library of Congress Cataloging-in-Publication Data has been applied for.

ISBN 978-0-06-231689-9

15 16 17 18 19 OV/RRD 10 9 8 7 6 5 4

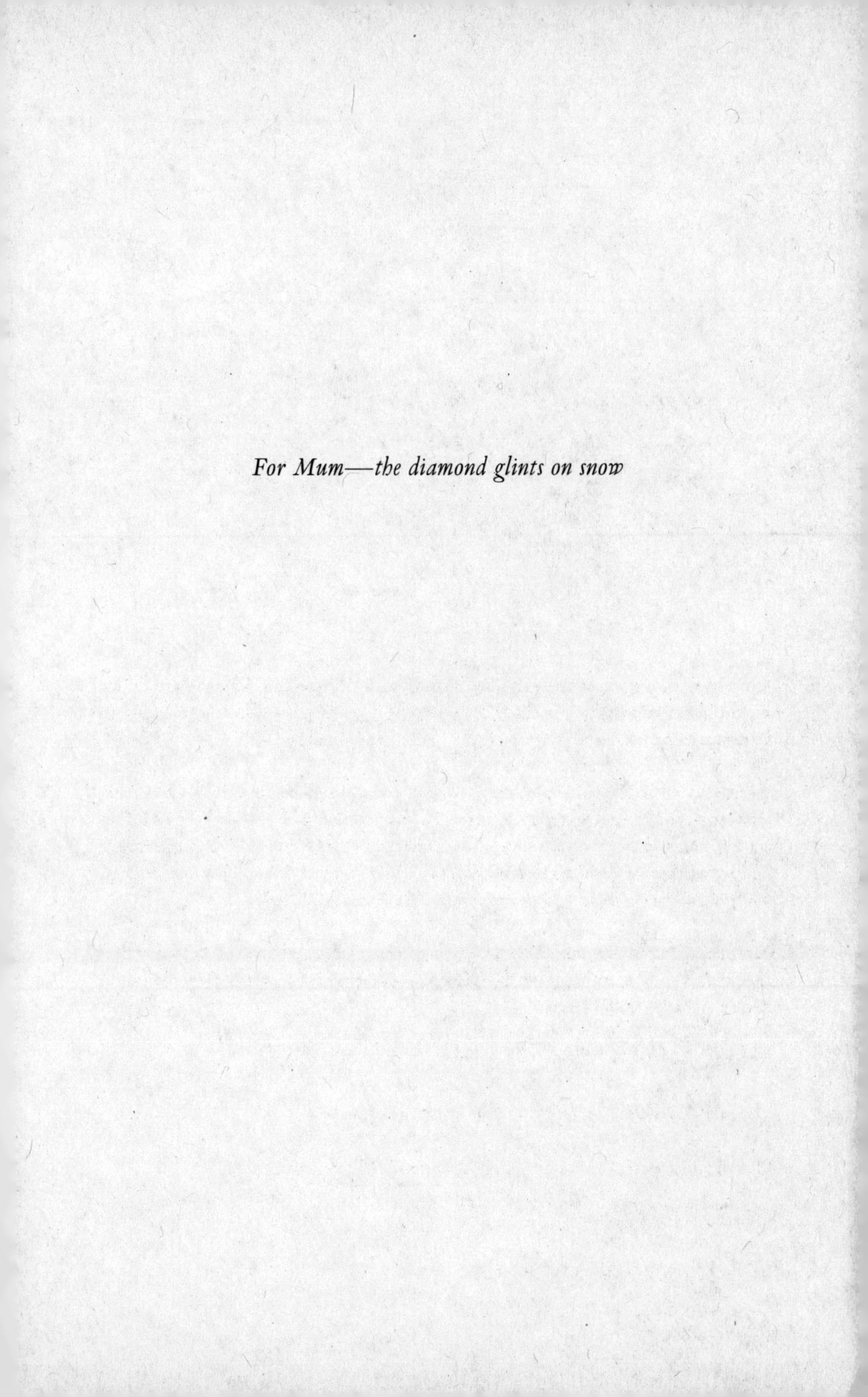

For Mum—the diamond glints on snow

The difference between a lady and a flower girl
is not how she behaves, but how she's treated.

—George Bernard Shaw, *Pygmalion*, 1912

For there is no friend like a sister
In calm or stormy weather;
To cheer one on the tedious way,
To fetch one if one goes astray,
To lift one if one totters down,
To strengthen whilst one stands.

—Christina Rossetti, "Goblin Market," 1862

Not what we have, but what we use;
Not what we see, but what we choose—
These are the things that mar or bless
The sum of human happiness.

—Clarence Urmy, "The Things That Count,"
inscribed at Woodbridge Chapel in memory of John Groom,
founder of the Watercress and Flower Girls' Mission

A Memory of Violets

Prologue

London
March 1876
Florrie

Mammy once told me that all flowers are beautiful, but some are more beautiful than others. "Same with babies," she said, 'cause I was after saying that little baby Rosie looked like a rotten old turnip, what with her face all purple and scrunched up. "All babies look like rotten old turnips at first," Mammy said. "She'll be all smoothed out by Lady Day. You wait and see."

She was, too. All smoothed out. After turning into a real pretty little thing she was then, 'specially with that hair. Red as the flames in the costers' smudge-pot fires.

"Sure, there's no denying the Irish in that one." That's what Da said. Don't think he ever spoke about Rosie again. Barely noticed her, other than to let out a roar at her or give her a wallop when she was after bawling too much. Awful mean to Little Sister, so he was, so I gave her all the love I could find in my heart, to try and make things nicer for her, like.

Truth be told, I loved little Rosie Flynn from the very first minute I set eyes on her—even with her squashed-up turnip face. I'd never had nothing of my own, not until Little Sister was born—my very own sister, what had lived. Not like them other poor babies what had been born all blue and quiet. Like wilted violets after the frosts, so they were. But not little Rosie. Pink as a carnation she was, bawlin' good 'n' proper in her vegetable-pallet cradle, and there I was, smiling at her like a great eejit. Loved her to bits, so I did.

When Rosie was small, Mammy'd throw her into the shallow with the stock money and we'd head off to Covent Garden in the soot-black dark. You've to get to the Garden good 'n' early, see—four or five o'clock—so as to get the pick of the best blooms after the shopkeepers have bought their stock. We'd leave our cold, stinking room at Rosemary Court and walk by the light of the gas lamps, Rosie's little turnip face peeping out o' the basket and Mammy striding along like a great ox. "Keep up, will ye, Florrie Flynn," she'd shout over her shoulder. "For the love of God, it'll be Christmas before we get there at this rate." And I'd gallop along behind, clinging to her skirts so as not to get lost or snatched away by one of them bad men what takes little children and teaches them thievin' and such—like the natty lads. Unsteady as a tune on a hurdy-gurdy machine, so I was, going up and down, up and down, my good leg dragging my bad one along as best it could. Awful painful it was, for me to walk. My leg won't grow proper, see, 'cause of the polio I had as a baby. I've an old stick for a crutch, but it's about as much use as a frozen water pump.

While Mammy bought the stock for the day's sellin'—a shillin' for a dozen bunches—I'd coo at Rosie and sing songs to make her smile. She liked "The Dawning of the Day" the best. Mammy'd buy whatever blooms was lookin' the prettiest and smellin' the sweetest. "It's the sweetness what sells the flowers, Florrie, sure it is," she'd say. "The sweetness what sells 'em." Most days, it'd be violets, primroses, or moss roses. Sometimes it would be stocks or wallflowers if they were in, or maybe pinks and carnations. I liked the spring months, when the oranges were in. We'd do better on the oranges than the flowers, and the smell of 'em was something else. All in the shallow it would go, so as little Rosie was covered from head to toe in lovely, sweet blooms. Reckon she'd have stayed in there forever if she could. Better'n smelling that stinking sewer and them fish heads and cabbage leaves all rotten, and the flies buzzing round.

We'd sit then with the other flower sellers, round the columns at St. Paul's Church, across from the covered market. Mammy an' Maudie Brennan would chatter away, about Ireland's green fields and the smell of the turf fires, while we tied up our bunches and buttonholes by candlelight. Mammy'd do the tying and I'd pass the blooms. We'd tie them with the rush—we got that for nothing—then we'd add the leaves around the violets and primroses, and add the paper last, on the bunches that needed it. Mammy said I could make ten bunches of violets from thin air! I could, too, separating the flowers and fluffing them out. Then we'd sell 'em for a penny a bunch, and I knew me an' Rosie might get a penn'orth of pudding that day from the pudding shop on the Strand. Them great fat raisins never tasted so nice as after a hard day's selling, sure they didn't.

Off we'd go then, Mammy, Rosie (in the basket), and me, hawking our flowers round the streets and at the railway stations and the theaters up the West End—they're always good for trade—and the Covent Garden theater, what brings the ladies and gen'lemen out in their hundreds in the evenings.

"Two bunches of violets," we'd cry. "Sweet violets." "Buy y'r primroses. Two bunches a penny." "All a-blowin', all a-growin'." That's what you'd hear the sellers cry when the primroses were in and then you'd know it was spring for certain. And when the summer came to an end, it'd be "Lavender—sweet lavender!" and then the east wind'd start blowing for snow and the frosts'd come and the blooms'd wither up before you'd even sell a one of 'em. That's when we'd start sellin' the cresses. "Worter-creesss! Worter-creesss!" we'd cry, and you'd know that the winter'd arrived and then things'd get awful hard.

Freezing to make your fingers turn blue that water was, at the pump where we'd wash the cresses. I'd start wailing with the cold, my feet all frozen against the cobbles. "Stop y'r bawlin', Florrie Flynn," Mammy'd say, "and puff them cresses out. Y've to make 'em look bigger so as the ladies'll buy 'em." So I would stop bawlin' and puff out the cresses and we'd sell those what weren't frozen and then we'd go back to that stinking room in Rosemary Court. I'd sing little Rosie to sleep, her in the vegetable pallet and me on the tatty old mattress on the floor. Miserable, so I was—cold and afraid and with an ache in my belly from the hunger. But when I saw Rosie's little face smiling at me, I knew it would all be right come the morning, 'cause things don't seem so bad when someone smiles at you, sure they don't.

But that were all before the cholera came and took Mammy away.

I miss her, so I do. Maybe she couldn't teach me to read nor write, but she taught me all the tricks of the market: how to gather the dropped walnuts for the fire, how to walk behind the fish barrows to catch a slippery herrin' or two, how to tie the buttonholes and tussie-mussies. Taught me everything I know, so she did.

Things is different now, 'cause it's just Rosie an' me does the sellin', and we can't go too far, what with me on my crutch and Little Sister to be mindin' like I promised Mammy I would.

"Oh, please buy my flowers, kind lady. Tuppence a bunch. Oh, please do." That's what we cry.

Sometimes the ladies buy an extra buttonhole from Rosie, or pay the price of two bunches for one, what with her being so small and thin looking. "A penny, my poor girl, here's three halfpence for the bunch," they say, and they always tell her what lovely red hair she has, and she smiles, even though she can't see those pretty faces smiling back at her. Lives her life in the dark, so she does. Poor little Rosie with her useless eyes.

When the rains come and the ladies ain't out, or the fog comes down so thick it'll choke ye, and when the frosts come and the flowers is all frozen, we don't sell nothing. Them are the nights when we don't go back to Rosemary Court, 'cause I know that Da'll beat me till I'm lavender, for certain. So me an' Rosie sleep in a doorway, or under a market barrow, and my teeth ache with the cold and I hold Rosie's frozen little hand in mine. We get as tight together as we can, so not even so much as a rose petal could fit between us, and I remember my promise to Mammy and say a prayer that the flowers won't be frozen the next day and that we might get a bit of meat in our bellies if we're good girls.

And then we wait for the morning to come and the flowers to arrive.

Just me an' Little Sister. Waiting in the dark.

"Don't let go, Rosie," I whisper. "Don't let go."

Part One

Purple Hyacinth (*Hyacinthus orientalis*)

Please forgive me.

London
September 1876

Dear Mr. Shaw,

I hope you will forgive me the irregularity of writing to you without a formal introduction, but I cannot rest until I have filled this page with words of enthusiastic admiration for your work with the blind and crippled flower sellers. It is a most noble and honorable cause, sir, most noble and honorable, indeed.

I was fortunate enough to see a glorious display of the girls' flowers at the Guild Hall this very day and must admit that I was quite taken aback! The ability of these young girls to produce such realistic copies of so many varieties of flowers—using only fabric—is quite, quite remarkable. If it is not impertinent of me to say so, it is even more astonishing when one takes into account the dreadful physical afflictions which blight their young bodies. That such delicate beauty can be created by those who have known only hardship and depravity is most admirable.

A very helpful young girl kindly told me all about the Training Homes for Watercress and Flower Girls ("the Crippleage") that you have established in Clerkenwell. She informed me that you have some fifty girls housed there under your care, all of whom have been saved from a life of poverty selling flowers and watercress on the streets. She explained how they have been trained to make the artificial flowers in the workrooms of a nearby chapel.

I also read, with much concern, your recent note in The Christian Magazine: *"The Plight of London's Orphans." It is shocking to learn of the dreadful conditions these poor little souls are living in and I am certain that many readers will respond to your appeal for additional funding for the wonderfully named "Flower Village" orphanage in Clacton.*

To conclude, Mr. Shaw, I find myself so moved and affected by the bravery of the flower girls and the plight of the orphans that I wish to make a donation to your cause. I hope that the enclosed sum of one hundred pounds will assist you in your plans to construct a "Babies' Villa" at Clacton, to house the very youngest orphans, whose pitiful existence must surely stir the soul of even the most hard-hearted of men.

I hope you do not find me discourteous at all in wishing to remain anonymous.

Yours in admiration,
"Daisy"

Chapter 1

England
March 25, 1912

She was already some distance from home when it first occurred to Tilly Harper that she might be running away after all. "*Running away! Running away! Running away!*" the pistons shouted as the wheels clattered and rattled along the tracks. It was as if the train could read her thoughts, calling out her secret to the armies of sunlit daffodils that swayed in perfect unison at the edges of the lush green fields. "*Running away! Running away! Running away!*"—the words coming faster and faster as the fireman shoveled more coal into the blazing furnace, pushing Tilly farther away from what was and closer toward what might be, in London. Running away, or running toward? She wasn't entirely sure.

Lulled by the rhythmic motion of the train, she leaned her

head wearily against the cool glass of the window, glad to have secured a seat at the platform edge of the compartment. She was quite sure she could easily fall asleep if only the knots in her stomach would unravel, and the glass would stop juddering against her cheek, and the boxes and trunks would stop shifting around in the luggage rack above her head, sending a steady flurry of dust-fall into her lap. She sighed, sat upright, adjusted her skirts against the upholstered seat in the hope that they wouldn't be too creased when she arrived, and glanced, for the tenth time that day, at the letter in her hand.

Dear Miss Harper. I am pleased to confirm your appointment to the post of Assistant Housemother at Shaw's Training Homes for Watercress and Flower Girls, Sekforde Street, Clerkenwell . . . Crochet caps and white aprons will be provided. Please supply a coarse apron and bib, a holland apron for bed making and dusting, and plain cotton gowns for morning wear . . . Please report for duty on the twenty-fifth day of March, at your earliest convenience . . . May the Good Lord grant you a safe and comfortable journey. Sincerely yours, Mrs. Evelyn Shaw.

It was Tilly's mother who had first learned of Mr. Shaw's workrooms in London, after she'd seen a display of silk flowers at a church fete in Keswick. "Quite brilliant replicas of the real thing," she'd announced on her return home, "and all the more so for having been made by blind and crippled girls. You should write to this Mr. Shaw, Matilda. I believe they are looking for domestics to assist with the running of the homes the girls are housed in. You've the right sort of experience, after all. Doesn't she, Esther?" There was no apology for the cold manner in which she'd said this. Tilly understood that none was needed. Her sister, Esther, had merely stared blankly at her across the gaping chasm of the kitchen table before cutting herself another slice of bread. The matter wasn't discussed again. Tilly had sent her letter of application, attended an interview, and here she was, halfway to London, to start her new position. Running away? Perhaps.

With each turn of the wheels, each blast of the whistle as they entered another dark tunnel, she sensed the distance growing between herself and the dramatic Lakeland mountains and fells that had framed the twenty-one years of her life—Helvellyn, Skiddaw, Scafell—the places that had comforted her when nothing, and nobody, else could. They felt far behind her now, obscured by the mellow mist of a bright spring morning, a morning that seemed almost capable of erasing the dark shadows that lurked around the muddy edges of her life. "That Harper Girl," the people of Grasmere called her, a dismissive title by which she had been defined since the age of fourteen, when one reckless moment had changed everything. The passing of seven years and countless attempts to atone for her mistakes had made little, if any, difference to who Tilly Harper was, or might have been.

"*Running away! Running away! Running away!*" The train continued with its relentless chatter, sending startled rabbits bolting for cover into their burrows and birds fleeing from the hedgerows in a blur of dun and black against the clear blue sky. Tilly jumped at the screech of the whistle as the guard acknowledged a group of excited children who were balanced precariously on the struts of a gate, disregarding their mothers' words of caution in their efforts to get a better glimpse of the locomotive. She smiled as small, enthusiastic hands waved to the disinterested passengers, the rush of passing air blowing hats and bonnets off their young heads.

Part of her wanted to wave back. She lifted her hand a few inches before feeling foolish and returning it hastily to her lap. But how she envied their innocence, their ability to find excitement and joy in such a simple thing as a passing steam locomotive.

It wasn't so long ago that she'd shared in their childish enthusiasm, running beside the fence at the edge of the field, grasping Esther's hand to pull her along behind, laughing as they tried to outrun the approaching train: the low rumble of the engine; the distinctive *phut*, *phut*, *phut* of the smoke rising from the funnel, just visible above the tree line; the audible humming of the tracks signaling its approach long before the locomotive appeared.

"Here it is, Esther! Look! Here it comes! Here it comes! Run, run . . ."

Tilly remembered it so clearly: the thrill as the rush of air tugged at their bonnets and sent their petticoats flapping around their knees; their hands covering their ears against the deafening noise as the carriages rushed past—one, two, three, four, five; the acrid smell of smoke filling their nostrils; their squeals of excitement whisked away on the wind. And if they were lucky, the one thing they were waiting for—the haunting cry of the whistle as the driver acknowledged their excited waving. Then silence, as the great black engine and its mulberry carriages disappeared around the bend into the distance and to the mountains beyond, a few smudges of soot on their cheeks and the swaying of the long grass the only signs that the train had ever been there.

"All tickets please." The conductor's arrival distracted Tilly from her thoughts. "All tickets," he called as he slid back the compartment door.

His loud voice and sense of authority triggered a great rustling of coats and much standing up and sitting down as Tilly and her fellow passengers rummaged in ever-deepening pockets and dark, unyielding corners of handbags and purses, searching for their tickets. Tilly handed him her single-fare ticket to London Euston. He didn't even look at her as he clipped a small hole into the bottom and handed it back to her.

"Refreshments from the platform vendor at Crewe and Rugby," he said, yawning as he spoke.

She wasn't sure whether the information was specifically directed at her or to the compartment in general. "Thank you," she replied. "I will be glad of some tea." She smiled, maintaining her resolve to be pleasant to everyone she encountered. *Every interaction is a chance to erase a piece of the past*, she reminded herself.

The conductor ignored her, finished checking the tickets from the other passengers, and moved on to the next carriage, where, Tilly suspected, he would repeat the same procedure with the detached disinterest of a man who has been doing the same job for far too long. She vowed never to become as bored with anything, no matter how often she had to repeat it.

As the passengers gradually settled themselves back into their dozing and newspapers, and mothers resumed hushed recitals of nursery rhymes with their children, Tilly returned her ticket to her coat pocket and took out her book. Opening it to the page where she had earlier draped a thin, lilac-colored ribbon as a marker, she read only a couple of sentences before her mind started to wander. She closed the book again, placing it on her lap, her gloved hands resting on top—one gently over the other, as her mother had shown her. "Just because you're in service to the ladies, Matilda, doesn't mean you can't dress and behave like one when you finish work for the day. You would do well to pay closer attention to your sister. *She* knows how to behave properly, even without . . . well . . . just pay more attention to her." Tilly was tired of paying attention to Esther. It was all anyone ever did.

"So, is this an end or a beginning?"

Tilly glanced up from her lap to see a smartly dressed elderly lady sitting opposite her. Vivid blue eyes were fixed firmly in her direction, an arched eyebrow anticipating a response to the question. Tilly squinted against the glare of the sun as it reflected off a delicate silver locket that hung from a slim rope of pearls around the woman's neck.

"I'm sorry. I'm not sure I understand."

"Is this the end of your journey, or the beginning?" the woman repeated, dabbing at the corners of her eyes with a pretty lace handkerchief. Tilly wondered whether she was upset or a stray eyelash was bothering her. She noticed a cluster of shamrock leaves stitched into one corner of the handkerchief, admiring the intricate needlework and knowing that she would never be able to produce anything as neat, no matter how much her mother chided at her to take more care.

"I usually find, with trains, that people are either heading back home at the end of a journey or are just leaving home at the start of a new one," the woman continued. "Depending on how much one likes one's home, I suspect it can make quite a difference to how much one is enjoying the journey." She chuckled to herself.

Tilly smiled, finding the woman quite enchanting. She spoke in an accent Tilly couldn't place. It had an unfamiliar lilt: Irish, or French, perhaps? It only added to the woman's charm, wherever it had been formed.

"I suppose so. I'd never really thought about it like that," Tilly said.

"Oh, yes. It can make quite a difference to a person's manner, you know, whether they're coming or going." The woman crossed her ankles, folding her arms across her chest, just as Tilly's nana did when she was settling herself in for a conversation. "I'm guessing, with all your fidgeting and sighing and opening and closing that book of yours, that you're at the beginning stage. Going, as it were. Starting something you're not quite sure of. Hmm?" She raised a quizzical eyebrow again.

Tilly remembered her now. She'd boarded the train at Preston, accompanied only by the captivating scent of damask rose, her skirts crinkling and rustling as she'd settled into her seat.

"Mrs. Marguerite Ingram," the woman announced, holding out a gloved hand. "Very pleased to make your acquaintance, Miss . . ."

"Harper. Miss Harper. Matilda. Tilly, actually. Miss Tilly Harper."

Mrs. Ingram smiled, shook Tilly's hand, and turned her attention to the fields beyond the window, closing her eyes against the bright sunshine that streamed through the glass.

Tilly considered the question. Was this an end or a beginning? Since receiving confirmation of her new position at the Flower Homes, she'd always thought of her move to London as an end, an end to all the years of guilt and remorse. Finally, she was escaping her past. Some might call it running away, but all she knew was that, in London, she wouldn't have to be "That Harper Girl" anymore. She hoped she could be herself again, *the girl with the wind at her heels and a storm blowing in her heart*, as her father used to say. But she couldn't explain any of that to a stranger.

"Well, yes. I suppose I am at a beginning. Of sorts," she conceded. "You?"

Mrs. Ingram opened her eyes. Tilly noticed how her face had clouded, the attractive pink blush in her cheeks faded. She looked at Tilly for a moment, the inquisitive sparkle in her eyes dulled, before returning her gaze to the window, as if searching for an answer among the latticework of hedgerows and fields beyond.

She sighed. "That, my dear, is something I am afraid only my daughter can decide."

Chapter 2

England

March 25, 1912

Tilly shuffled awkwardly in her seat. Her corset was digging into her ribs, and her skirts rustled as she fidgeted. She wished she could stand up and walk around, wished she could get some fresh air. Her fingers worried at a button on the cuff of her coat. She was unsure what to say, already regretting engaging in this conversation with Mrs. Ingram.

She'd never really mastered the art of gossip and small talk, having been the subject of most of Grasmere's gossip for a long time. Even before Esther's accident, she'd never been very good at joining in with groups, finding the intricacies and etiquette of idle chitchat awkward and uninspiring. She preferred to retreat to the privacy of the lakes and mountains with her box of pastels and sketchbook. They were the only companionship she needed. Outside, in nature, she was free to express her thoughts and emotions in pictures that were worth a thousand of her mother's nonsensical words. In more recent years, when she'd worked in service as a housemaid at Wycke Hall, the home of the local gentry, she'd become numb to the tedious conversations she overheard while going about her business, finding neither interest nor intrigue in the petty troubles of Lady Wycke and her tiresome daughters.

Many considered Tilly withdrawn, rude even. The simple truth was that she felt adrift, uncertain of herself, so that she had neither opinion nor comment to add. She busied herself instead with her chores: blacking the fires, scrubbing the hems of the ladies' dresses, running the bed linen through the mangle, washing the steps, sweeping the floors, and beating great clouds of dust from the Turkey rugs, as if she might set herself free along with the spiraling dust motes, if only she could beat hard enough.

"Although," Mrs. Ingram continued, drawing Tilly back from her thoughts, "with today being Lady Day and the start of a new quarter, I suppose we should *all* be thinking about new beginnings, shouldn't we, especially after that dreadful winter. My goodness—I've never known cold like it. I sometimes felt as though I'd set out to the South Pole along with Captain Scott and his men!"

"It certainly was a cold one," Tilly replied, remembering the icicles that had hung in thick shards around the doorway of their small stone cottage, as if her father had forged them in his blazing furnace and placed them there for decoration.

"I can't abide the winter months—or the autumn, for that matter," Mrs. Ingram continued. "Far too dark and miserable. Thank goodness for the spring, I say. It does wonders for a person's spirits to feel the sun on their face. Brings us all back to life. No wonder the daffodils look so jolly!"

Tilly only smiled. She couldn't entirely agree.

"It's as if the weather got inside you the day you were born," her father said with a chuckle, his chestnut eyes sparkling in the reflection of the water as they sat by the edge of the lake. They were sharing a piece of delicious, still-warm gingerbread from Sarah Nelson's little shop in the village. Tilly rolled her tongue around her mouth, collecting every last crumb from her lips as she rested her head on his broad shoulder. "We'd never seen a storm like it that night—all raging wildness and dark clouds rushing across the sky. I'd say a piece of it got inside you all right, Tilly Harper."

Perhaps he was right. She'd always been drawn to the later seasons of the year, reveling in the wild autumn winds that sent the leaves skittering down the lane and tore the trees up by their roots. While everyone else in the village complained about blocked roads and there being no food for the cattle or the local Herdwick sheep, Tilly enjoyed the drama of the first frantic snowstorms of winter, jumping into the deep, wavelike drifts that hugged the walls of their home.

She knew her father admired her tempestuous, free spirit, that he encouraged her lust for adventure and love of the outdoors. It was *his* passion for the countryside that became her passion, *his* wonder at the soaring peaks surrounding their home that became her wonder.

It couldn't be more different with her mother, who, as the wife of the local blacksmith, set higher standards for her daughters than those set by the more "ordinary tradespeople."

She found Tilly's wild temperament a source of constant disappointment. They clashed. They argued. "For goodness' sake, child. Couldn't you take a brush to your hair occasionally?" she would chide. "Oh, honestly, Matilda. You've muddied your petticoats and boots again. Why can't you walk around the edge of the fields like a normal person, rather than running straight across them? Why can't you be more like your sister?"

Why can't you be more like your sister?

Dear, darling Esther. As clear and light as the perfect spring morning she was born on. The little sister Tilly had longed to love and care for. The little sister she had grown to envy and despise. Somewhere deep inside, she'd always sensed a storm was coming.

"Listen, Esther! A train! Let's try and outrun it. Come on. I dare you."

"Are you traveling all the way to London for your beginning, or do you disembark en route?"

Tilly was so lost in her memories she'd momentarily forgotten where she was. She felt the color rise in her cheeks, as if she'd spoken her thoughts out loud and Mrs. Ingram had overheard.

"I'm traveling all the way to London," she replied.

"First time?"

"No. I've been once before."

Tilly recalled how nervous she'd felt when making the same journey just a few months ago, how she'd watched the same landscape flash by, covered then by a soft blanket of snow. She remembered how she'd fiddled with the same button on the cuff of her coat, wondering how her interview would turn out. It went well, as it happened, much to the surprise of her mother, Lady

Wycke, and herself. With the exception of her father, nobody had ever really expected—or hoped for—much of Tilly Harper. Perhaps she didn't deserve their expectations or hope. Perhaps she deserved their forgiveness and understanding.

"So, what takes you there this time?" Mrs. Ingram asked.

Tilly coughed. She was uncomfortable to be having such a personal conversation, aware that the other passengers were listening as they feigned interest in their novels and newspapers. All the same, there was something undeniably compelling about Mrs. Ingram. She was different from other women Tilly had encountered; her charming accent and the rich scent of damask rose that drifted around her were tantalizing hints of another world, a world to which Tilly knew she would never belong. Apart from anything else, Tilly was quite glad of the distraction from the butterflies turning somersaults in her stomach.

"I'm taking up a new position," she replied.

"How wonderful. Good for you. Anywhere nice?"

Tilly wasn't sure whether the Flower Homes should be described as "nice." "Purposeful" or "functional" would perhaps be more appropriate.

"Well, *I* think it's nice. I'm to be assistant housemother at Shaw's Homes for Watercress and Flower Girls in Clerkenwell. I don't suppose you know of it. Most people outside London don't."

A sudden rush of air filled the carriage as the locomotive hurtled into a tunnel, the glass rattling dramatically in the windows. Tilly glanced at Mrs. Ingram, noticing the faintest flicker of a smile that played at the corners of her mouth. Tilly smiled back. The noise of the whistle and the reverberations of the carriage made it impossible for them to continue their conversation without shouting, which neither of them wished to do. They both turned their eyes to the window.

Tilly stared at her reflection, her image caught between the dark tunnel walls and the thin pane of glass that cocooned her inside the carriage. She studied her petite button nose, her large almond eyes, her round cheeks and narrow chin, staring without blinking until the image blurred. Once again, she was reminded of how unlike her sister she was in appearance. While Esther was porcelain skinned and fair haired, like their mother, Tilly's cheeks were reddened from too much time spent outdoors in inclement weather, her hair an unruly mass of russet curls.

Who are you, Matilda Harper?

She frowned at herself, fiddling with her hair to secure the stray curls that had escaped from her hat. It was new, bought for the occasion at her mother's insistence. "If Lady Wycke is kind enough to pay for a second-class train ticket, the least you can do is dress yourself properly."

Another rush of air, as sudden as the first, brought the locomotive speeding out of the tunnel. Like a ghost, Tilly's reflection disappeared, set free to roam forever among the verdant fields and sapphire sky. She wished she could be liberated as easily.

"Would you care to tell me about this flower girls' home you'll be working in?" Mrs. Ingram asked. Sunlight flooded the carriage again, settling on the silver locket that nestled against the nape of her neck. "It sounds like a most interesting place, and we've plenty of time to fill before we reach London."

Tilly took a deep breath, resigned to the fact that she was now well and truly engaged in conversation. She began to talk, recalling everything she had been told at her interview by Mrs. Evelyn Shaw.

"I suppose the simplest way to describe it is as a charity. It was started nearly fifty years ago by a Christian preacher and philanthropist, Albert Shaw. He took pity on the crippled girls selling flowers and watercress to make a living. It's a hard life—many are destitute and starving. He established a room near Covent Garden flower market where the girls could get a hot drink and something to eat, but he soon realized he needed to do more to make any lasting difference.

"He'd heard of the growing popularity of silk flowers being imported from Paris—the wealthy ladies like to use them for decorating their homes." Tilly paused, wondering whether Mrs. Ingram was one such "wealthy lady," but she didn't react, appearing to be unfamiliar with the concept. Tilly continued.

"Mr. Shaw saw an opportunity to teach the crippled girls to make the silk flowers themselves and provide housing for them while they were in training. This takes them off the streets and gives them a year-round occupation that isn't dependent on the seasons, or the weather. They make violets, primroses, and daisies for Mothering Sunday, and buttonholes for the announcers at Christmas—oh, and St. George's roses. They've established quite a reputation through their exhibitions. They even decorated the Guild Hall for the grand mayoral banquet in honor of the King and Queen of Norway some years ago. It's almost impossible to tell the artificial flowers from the real ones. Honestly. I've seen them."

Mrs. Ingram smiled warmly, her head angled slightly to one side, her eyes looking at Tilly but not really seeing her, lost in distant thoughts.

Tilly read the silence as boredom. She shuffled in her seat. "I'm talking too much, aren't I? I'm very sorry."

"Oh, no, no! Not at all. It's fascinating. You obviously have a great interest in your new place of work. Please, do carry on. Tell me, what will your responsibilities be?"

"I'll be working under the housemother, and together we'll

manage the general running of the house—cleaning, cooking, and washing—and I'll also help with the care of the twelve girls. There are six houses in total, each with a dozen girls. Each home is named after a flower. I'll be living and working in Violet House. The workrooms used to be in a chapel nearby, but a new factory has just been opened because there's such demand for the flowers."

Tilly was surprised by how much she was enjoying the opportunity to talk about her new position. She had barely spoken to her mother about it, other than to reassure her that it was a reputable organization, run by Christians. It was liberating to chat with somebody who knew nothing about Tilly's past. Mrs. Ingram had no reason to judge her, or to look at her, the way her own mother had whenever she'd mentioned the crippled girls she'd be working with.

Mrs. Ingram leaned forward. "And tell me, dear," she said, "in what way are the girls crippled?"

There was no hint of embarrassment or discomfort in her voice. Most people Tilly knew didn't care to talk about the cripples, finding it an impossibly awkward topic of conversation, something only whispered about on street corners or behind closed doors.

"Their afflictions vary. Some don't have full use of their hands after suffering from polio as infants. Some were born blind or developed problems with their eyesight after the scarlet fever. Others lost arms or legs in factory accidents. Without the full use of their limbs they can't be employed in domestic service. Selling flowers, or begging, was all they could do—until Mr. Shaw came along."

"I don't mean to appear insensitive," Mrs. Ingram continued, leaning even farther forward, sending a delicious burst of rose perfume drifting toward Tilly, "but how do they make the flowers without the use of arms or hands—or the benefit of eyesight? It seems to me an impossible task."

Tilly smiled. "Honestly? I have no idea. But they've somehow found a way. During my interview for the position, Mrs. Shaw explained that they've adapted quite remarkably. She told me the girls seem to instinctively take to the work, forming the leaves and petals of even the most delicate flowers with relative ease."

"It's really quite something. Isn't it?" Mrs. Ingram leaned back, her head resting against the top of the seat. "Still, I imagine it can't be the easiest of circumstances to work in—with cripples, I mean. I suppose it requires some sort of training—or experience?"

Tilly glanced at her hands. "Not really. Experience in domestic service was the main requirement for the position, although I suppose an understanding of the girls' physical limitations is helpful."

A sudden rocking of the train as it rounded a bend caused a momentary lapse in their conversation. Mrs. Ingram grabbed the edge of her seat.

"My goodness! These trains are unpleasant, aren't they? I simply cannot understand the fascination with them. I'd much prefer to travel by horse and carriage, even if it does take longer."

Tilly disagreed. She was enjoying the sensation of speed, of the distance growing between her and her Lakeland home. The sooner she got to London, the better.

"Well, I have to say, I admire your spirit, Miss Harper. It sounds like you'll have your hands full. There can't be many young women who would put themselves into such demanding circumstances. Good for you, I say." Mrs. Ingram paused, rummaged in her coat pocket, and produced a small paper bag. "Mint imperial?"

She offered the sweets in a manner that implied they were some sort of antidote to the impossible task Tilly was about to undertake. Tilly took one, smiling weakly, wondering whether she was up to the challenge of the "demanding circumstances" of her new position after all.

Appearing to have completed her interrogation into Tilly's future employment, and unable to speak with a mouth full of mint, Mrs. Ingram took to gazing out of the window again, her eyes fixed firmly on the passing countryside. Tilly did the same, allowing herself to relax into the soothing, rocking motion of the train as the fields gave way intermittently to towns and cities where great chimneys peppered the horizon, sending plumes of black smoke snaking up between the white clouds.

Narrowing her eyes against the glare of the sun, Tilly watched Mrs. Ingram as she twisted the lace handkerchief around and around between her fingers. She wondered what Mrs. Ingram had meant about its being up to her daughter to decide whether her journey was an end or a beginning. Tilly wondered whether she wasn't the only passenger the train was accusing of running away; perhaps others had secrets as well.

It had been an early start, and Tilly's eyes soon grew heavy in the warmth of the sun now streaming through the carriage window. How long ago it seemed since she'd woken in the lavender light of dawn, lying in the bed she had slept in since she was a young child. How long ago it seemed since she'd stood in the doorway of their humble cottage that morning, taking in the beautiful landscape as her breaths were carried toward the mountaintops in a dewy mist. She shivered at the memory of Esther's blank expression, at the sensation of her mother's reluctant embrace, which had sent a far greater chill through Tilly's bones than the cool morning air that surrounded her.

She rested her cheek against the window, her ears tuning, once again, to the rhythm of the train . . . *running away*, *running away*, *running away* . . . As she fell into a restless slumber, the memories, which lurked always at the edge of her thoughts, awoke in her mind and rushed eagerly into her dreams . . .

The hooves of the ponies thundering over the soft grass; the dark, brooding mountains ahead, cast into shadow; a pheasant taking to the skies, startled by their approach.

Laughing and calling to each other; the thrill of the chase. Her idea.

"Look after your sister and don't go too fast," her mother said. "Remember, Esther isn't as confident on the pony as you are."

"Yes, Mother."

"And don't go too near the railway tracks."

"Yes, Mother."

A flash of brilliant purple and blue from a damselfly dancing in front of her; the sweet, heady smell of the gorse and heather, intensified by the earlier sun. It was late in the day. They had stopped to pick lavender. Her idea.

"Don't be late back. You know how the light plays tricks on your eyes at dusk."

"Yes, Mother."

A thick, swirling fog descending rapidly from the mountaintops. The strange hue of twilight. A flash of white rabbit darting into the grass beside her. A nervous snort from Esther's pony. The shriek of a kestrel circling above.

"Shouldn't we be making our way back, Tilly? The fog is getting worse."

"Shhh. Listen, Esther! A train! Let's try and outrun it."

"But, Mother said . . ."

"Come on. I dare you."

Chapter 3

London

March 25, 1912

As the motor cabdriver navigated his way through the alarming assortment of traffic converged at the junction of King's Cross and Pentonville Roads, Tilly gazed in stunned silence through the small window. It was the lack of color that struck her the most; the drab, muted tones of gray upon gray, as if all the other shades had been painted over or forgotten about. The bright yellow daffodils and the ever-shifting shades of blue that graced the lakes of Westmorland had never felt farther away. As she worried at the buttons on her high-collared blouse, she wondered how she would ever feel at ease in this vast, colorless place, wondered when she would next take a breath of clear, fresh air.

Frowning at the sight of a wretched young boy sweeping the

road, she recalled Mrs. Ingram's parting words: "I think you and London are going to get along quite well, Miss Harper. She may look like a rotten old crone at first, but she scrubs up as fine as any lady when you really get to know her! Just give her time." Tilly hoped Mrs. Ingram would prove to be correct.

As the train had made its final approach to Euston Station, Tilly and her fellow passengers had stared out of the windows, struck by the unfamiliar sights that heralded their arrival in London: the soaring factory chimneys spewing out thick black smoke like immense just-extinguished candles; the grimy tenement housing that hugged the railway line; the cloying smell of soot and sulfur that drifted through the compartment window, which Tilly had secured shut with the leather strap. The clear blue skies that had accompanied Tilly for most of her journey had soon disappeared beneath the gloomy fog of industry, wispy clouds replaced by the billowing smoke that gushed from the train as it crept slowly to a stop beside the platform.

As the guard opened the compartment door, Mrs. Ingram wished Tilly a fond farewell. "It was very nice to meet you, Miss Harper, and fascinating to hear about your place of work. I sincerely wish you—and the girls—the very best of luck."

As she'd stepped onto the platform, Tilly saw the lace handkerchief fall from Mrs. Ingram's hand. "Oh! Mrs. Ingram! Your handkerchief!" she'd said, picking it up and handing it to her.

"Goodness! Thank you. Thank you very much. I'm quite attached to that handkerchief. I should have been most sad to lose it. A reminder to us both, perhaps, to take better care of the things we treasure the most."

Collecting her own trunk from the luggage car, Tilly had watched, then, as Mrs. Ingram embraced an elegantly dressed younger woman on the platform. "My dear Violette," she'd heard Mrs. Ingram say. "It's so good to see you! It just isn't natural for a mother to go so long without seeing her daughter."

Tilly had smiled as Mrs. Ingram was engulfed by three children. Her grandchildren, Tilly presumed. One, she'd noticed, walked with the aid of a crutch.

"WOULD YOU HAVE THE TIME?" she asked, leaning forward in her seat so that the driver might hear her above the din of car horns and the rumbling wheels of wagons and handcarts and the lilting cries of hawkers.

"Four bells and all's well," the driver shouted in reply. "I'll have you there in no time, Miss."

Tilly thanked him and settled back into her seat, several church bells chiming the hour as she did, as if to confirm the time, in case she had doubted him. The wheels of the car juddered beneath her as they bounced along the uneven roads.

Happy to let the driver concentrate on navigating through the traffic rather than chatting, Tilly settled her gaze outside. She was fascinated by the motorcars swarming over the road like an army of black ants. She stared at all the unfamiliar sights: street sellers pushing handcarts piled high with precarious mountains of vegetables; the muffin men carrying great trays of muffins on their heads and ringing their handbells to attract attention; groups of smartly dressed newspaper vendors calling out the day's headlines; knife grinders, bootblacks, match sellers, flower sellers—the streets were crowded with people shouting their wares, walking easily among the hansom cabs, trams, motor buses, and carriages.

Buildings hugged the streets in every direction, the shop fronts covered with huge boards advertising soap, meat, stout and ales, coffee and tonics. Posters and billboards promoted the suffragette newspaper as well as glamorous-sounding theater shows at the Olympia and the Palace. One proclaimed the terrifying experience of the Chamber of Horrors exhibit at Madame Tussauds. Tilly stared in wonder at it all, noticing the thick fog that cast a strange yellow light over everything and everyone, making the scene look almost unreal. She was about to ask the driver what the Chamber of Horrors was when he had to swerve suddenly to avoid a stationary hansom cab.

"Of course, you'll have heard the story of the girl who died there," he announced, seemingly unconcerned about the collision he had just avoided.

Tilly leaned forward so she could hear better. "I'm sorry. What girl? Where?"

"At the Crippleage. You did say that's where you're going, didn't you? Shaw's Crippleage?"

"Yes. Yes, that's right."

"Irish girl. Sad, really."

Tilly was confused. Why did everyone insist on talking in riddles today? "Somebody died there? What happened?"

"Say she died of a broken heart. Missed her sister, see."

"Her sister? But where was her sister?"

"Ain't nobody knew—not a soul. She didn't like to talk about it, what with her being so sad about it all the time. Heard she'd been taken to the workhouse, or taken in by a gang of pickpockets. Something unpleasant, anyway."

"That's very sad."

"Not uncommon in those days, though, Miss—still ain't. There's men taking girls off the streets all over London. Teach 'em a life of crime they do—show 'em how to take the gentlemen's pocket watches and the ladies' purses. They take the crippled kids 'cause nobody would suspect a cripple of stealing, now, would they?"

Tilly was shocked by the driver's tale. "And how old were the sisters?"

"Only young. Don't think the littlest would have been more than four year old when she went missing. I was just a young coster lad back then—before I started with the hansom cabs and the hackneys and now this contraption. I knew them two girls from the markets. Never saw a day when they weren't together, trudging around barefooted, selling their scrawny bunches of violets and primroses and watercress. Broke the older girl's heart it did when the little one went missing. That's what they say anyway. 'Course, I never seen her since." He paused to concentrate on making a difficult right turn across the continual stream of traffic.

Tilly tugged again at her blouse, wishing she could undo the top buttons. Or was it her corset that felt like it was choking her? She wriggled and fidgeted in her seat, her breaths coming quick and shallow. She didn't like the feeling of being hemmed in, unable to see any farther than the next corner or beyond the rows of shops that stood like soldiers, shoulder to shoulder, blocking any view of what might lie behind.

"That's the funny thing about sisters, ain't it," the driver continued. "Some can't stand the sight of each other and some can't bear to be apart." He chuckled to himself. "Strange things, families, eh?"

Tilly stared blankly ahead. "Yes. I suppose they are."

They both fell silent again as the motorcar weaved down a series of dark, narrow side streets. Tilly thought about the two sisters. She thought of Esther; saw her perfect porcelain face through the cottage window, her sea-green eyes staring directly into Tilly's and yet looking past her, through her. It was unnerving the way she did that, as if she were peering into another world, as if it were her eyes that had failed her, not her legs.

"That were just before Mr. Shaw took her to the orphanage in Clacton," the driver continued as the cab emerged onto a larger road again. "Spent her childhood down there and come back to work in the Crippleage to make the flowers when she was old enough."

"And what happened to her then?"

"Not sure, to be honest, Miss. Think she spent the rest of her days making the flowers. That was all. Seemed to be the only thing she cared about. Died there some years ago, as far as I remember. They say she never got over losing her little sister."

Tilly was unnerved by his revelations that someone had died at the house she would soon call home. "What a sad story," she said.

"Most of 'em are, though, Miss, ain't they? Any worth the tellin'." He had to stop talking as a dramatic coughing fit gripped him. Tilly instinctively put her hand to her mouth. She'd heard how easily disease was spread in London.

"At least the elder sister was taken in somewhere safe."

The driver nodded. "I suppose so." Recovering himself, he continued. "Does a wonderful thing, Mr. Shaw. Like a living saint he is, giving all them poor girls a home to live in and an occupation. Still," he added, lowering his voice a little, "you'd feel sorry for 'em, wouldn't you?"

"For who?" Tilly held her hand over her mouth and nose as a nauseating stench of sulfur, rotting fish, and manure filled the cab.

"Well. You know. People like *them*." He lowered his voice further so that Tilly had to strain to hear him above the noise outside. "The blind and the cripples. Can't think of nothin' worse than not being able to walk or see. Think I'd rather die than live like that. Need your wits about you in London, Miss—'specially round St. Giles or Spitalfields—riddled with disease and criminals. The houses there ain't fit for the rats to live in, and it's certainly not safe to walk about alone. It'd make your eyes water, Miss, if you saw how some people live. Well, let's hope you never need to be visiting *them* parts of the city, eh!"

Tilly pulled her coat closer around her as the motor cab bumped over cobbles, jolting her from side to side. She looked again at the fog that clung around the chimney tops, casting everything into a haunting half-light and giving the impression of evening time. How was she, a naïve blacksmith's daughter from the country, ever going to manage in this sprawling, dangerous metropolis? The London she'd read about in stories and seen depicted in the newspaper reports commemorating the King's coronation last summer bore no resemblance at all to the gray misery of Farringdon Road. There were no tree-lined malls here, no grand parks, no majestic statues or shimmering fountains. All she could see was poverty, slum housing, and the remnants of another busy day in the markets. Life was cruel for the people who lived here, she could see that. She felt the knots tighten in her stomach.

After turning off Farringdon Road and driving along a little farther, the driver began to slow the motor. "Well, here we are then, Miss. Sekforde Street." They turned a final corner. "Cor blimey! Looks like someone's expecting you an' all!"

Tilly gasped at the sight before her, pressing her nose up against the glass window. "Oh, my goodness!"

"A sight for sore eyes that is! Well, I never." The driver whistled through his teeth as he stepped out of the motorcar and walked around to open the door for Tilly. He helped her step down from the cab and lifted her trunk onto the street, both of them unable to take their eyes off the sight that greeted them.

Tilly handed him a shilling and thanked him.

"God bless you, Miss."

He tipped his cap and stepped back into the motorcar.

Vaguely aware of the engine firing up and the cab rumbling off down the street, Tilly stood motionless on the cobbles, gaping at the sight in front of her.

Flowers.

Flowers, everywhere.

Garlands and garlands of flowers decorated the entire street; draped around the windows on all three floors of the terraced houses; crisscrossing the sky above her, suspended on invisible wires, giving the impression that they were floating there by themselves. Flowers were draped over window boxes and framed the doorways of every house. Roses, geraniums, daisies, lilies, carnations, orchids—every conceivable type of flower was represented in the display, and every single one, Tilly knew, had been made by hand.

A small crowd had gathered to gaze at the astonishing display of color: vivid blues; regal purples; soft, candy-floss pinks; strawberry reds; vibrant lime greens; sun-bright, buttercup yellows; rich oranges; and creamy, vanilla whites. Tilly's eyes were unable to take it all in, her mouth unable to suppress a smile of sheer delight. It was as if someone had poured a box of paints onto this one street, leaving nothing with which to brighten up the drab gray of the rest of the city she had just passed.

"Wonderful, isn't it."

Tilly turned to see a woman next to her, three children scampering around her skirts. "It's magnificent," she whispered in reply.

"If only they could open a new factory here every day," the woman said, smiling. "How bright our days would be then! Are you visiting one of the girls?" she asked, noticing the trunk at Tilly's feet.

Tilly felt a glow of pride flush her cheeks pink. "No," she said. "Actually, I work here."

"Well, God bless you, love. It's wonderful work those girls do. God bless them all."

The woman called her children to her and continued on her way.

Taking a moment to smooth her skirt and adjust her hat, Tilly turned to walk down the street, her eyes darting from left to right and upward to make sure she didn't miss any of the fabulous displays. She strode purposefully toward Violet House, passing the low iron railings that ran along the fronts of all the houses on the street. She read the names that had been etched into a stone lintel above the door at the front of each: Bluebell, Rosebud, Primrose, Orchid, and Iris. She remembered taking such hesitant steps along this same street just a few months ago, but something was different today; she walked a little faster, stood a little taller.

Reaching Violet House, she pushed open the wrought-iron gate. It squeaked a welcome. Her heart pounding in her chest, she walked along the short pathway of red and gray diamond-patterned tiles leading to a neatly varnished front door. Each small footstep felt like a great stride—away from one life and toward another. She stopped in front of the leaded glass panels of the door and placed her trunk at her feet. Her hand poised over the brass knocker, she paused for a moment and took a long, deep breath. It had taken twenty-one years and a seven-hour train journey, but on this quiet London street, Tilly Harper felt, for the first time in her life, that she was, very definitely, at the beginning.

Chapter 4

Violet House, London
March 25, 1912

She was greeted by a large, red-faced woman who filled the narrow doorway with her ample frame and sizable arms.

"Well, you must be our Miss Harper. You're very welcome!" the woman enthused, a broad smile spreading across her face, accentuating her general roundness. Tilly took the hand that was offered to her, shaking the plump fingers firmly. "Come in, come in! Mrs. Pearce is my name. Harriet Pearce," she continued, still shaking Tilly's hand vigorously as she half dragged her inside the door and then into the passage.

"Very pleased to meet you, Mrs. Pearce," Tilly replied, wincing as her trunk banged off the edge of the door. "And what a wonderful greeting. The flowers are beautiful!"

"They are indeed. Quite the spectacle. On account of the new factory opening. We didn't decorate the entire street just for you, I'm afraid!" Mrs. Pearce laughed at her own joke as she closed the door. "Did you have a good journey? My, what a long distance you've traveled. From the Lake District, aren't you? You must be exhausted. Are you hungry? You must be hungry. Let me take that for you," she added, grabbing Tilly's trunk and hoisting it easily to one side of the narrow passage, despite its considerable weight.

It was like being met by a whirlwind. Tilly wasn't sure which question to answer first—or whether any answers were required at all, since Mrs. Pearce seemed quite capable of conducting an entire conversation with herself. As she chattered on about the noise of the locomotives and the disappointing quality of the items available on the refreshment trolleys, Tilly took the opportunity to look at her new home.

The passage was pleasantly lit by the pale afternoon sunlight, which had briefly penetrated the fog and shone through the leaded panels in the door. The walls were decorated with pretty tulip-patterned wallpaper, the vivid reds of the flowers set against a rich background of green and gold. It gave the impression of a field of tulips stretching from one end of the house to the other.

Looking down the long passage, Tilly admired the highly polished floors and banisters, which shone like glass. Someone had been very hard at work, she could tell. She caught a glimpse of a room to the right, which she presumed to be the parlor, and could see the scullery at the very back of the house. Just inside the door was an umbrella stand, and on the wall to her left hung a large beveled mirror, reflecting the light of a small hall lantern and making the passage feel larger than it was. Catching a glimpse of her reflection, Tilly adjusted her hat and rubbed at a smudge of soot on her cheek.

"I'm the housemother next door at Number Five. Rosebud," Mrs. Pearce said. She had hardly paused for breath. "Unfortunately, we've had quite the turn of events these last few days, and poor Mrs. Harris, the housemother here, finds herself with a broken leg!"

"Goodness. That's terrible. I hope she'll be all right." Despite her words, Tilly could think only of the repercussions Mrs. Harris's injury would have on her.

"Yes, it's dreadful bad luck—not to mention, awful timing. The poor woman. But never mind, these things are sent to try us!" Mrs. Pearce chuckled to herself good-naturedly as she took up a corner of her white apron, using it to wipe her hands, which were covered in flour. "Anyway," she continued, "she asked me to step in and show you the ropes until she's back on her feet. Oh! Hark at me. 'Back on her feet!' My, oh, my!"

Tilly's heart sank. How was she ever going to manage on her own, in an unfamiliar house, with unfamiliar routines and twelve girls to look after?

Mrs. Pearce didn't notice the look of shock on Tilly's face, or if she did, she chose to ignore it. "So, we'll just have to carry on without her and do our best! Won't we, girls?" she added, raising her eyebrows and winking at Tilly.

Following the direction of Mrs. Pearce's gaze, Tilly heard giggling and shuffling coming from the room behind her. Turning around, she was met with the sight of a dozen eyes staring back at her.

Mrs. Pearce leaned forward. She was so close that Tilly could feel the warmth radiating from her flushed cheeks. "Of course, we call them all 'girls,' but some of them are as old as me! Eyes in the back of your head. That's what you need round here," she whispered.

Tilly smiled weakly, her nose balking at the sour smell of body odor that accompanied Mrs. Pearce's every movement. She shifted her weight from one foot to the other. She felt awkward, unsure of what to do with herself. She wished someone would produce a pile of sopping laundry for her to mangle, or a carpet to beat or a fender to blacken—anything, just as long as she could do something useful. She was determined to prove herself here, determined to show that she was worth more than the people of Grasmere gave her credit for. The sooner she could get started on that, the better.

"Now, girls," Mrs. Pearce continued, turning to speak to the staring eyes and placing her hands firmly on her hips. "Don't gawp like that. I'm sure you've all seen new staff members arrive, and I'm quite sure Miss Harper doesn't need an audience inspecting her after such a long journey." This comment produced more barely stifled giggles.

Mrs. Pearce turned back to Tilly. "Always fascinated by the arrival of a new member of staff," she muttered. "Hopefully they won't give you too much trouble."

"Trouble?"

"Oh, nothing serious. Just childish pranks. The usual."

Tilly smiled nervously, wondering what "the usual" consisted of.

Finding it hard to ignore the increasingly loud whispers behind her, she decided it would be best to make her introductions and get it over with.

"Hello, everyone," she announced to the gathered eyes. "I'm Tilly. I'm really happy to be here." As soon as the words were out of her mouth she wished she hadn't spoken. She'd intended to sound confident and assured, but her voice sounded small and meek, even in the narrow entrance hall. She didn't sound authoritative or useful, let alone like someone who should be entrusted with the welfare of a houseful of blind and crippled girls.

"Hello," a dozen voices replied politely. The words were followed by more giggles.

"Now, girls, you're to leave Miss Harper—Matilda—to settle into her room and don't be causing her any difficulties. She'll start her duties tomorrow morning, and not before. So don't be bothering her to mend this and fetch that, d'you hear? We've enough on our plates as it is, what with Mrs. Harris out of action and Mr. Shaw's announcement expected this evening."

Tilly watched as Mrs. Pearce did a quick head count of the girls gathered around the door ". . . nine, ten, eleven . . . and where's Buttons?"

"Hiding. Again!" one of the girls replied. She spoke with a strong Yorkshire dialect. " 'aven't seen 'er since lunchtime."

Mrs. Pearce sighed. "Very well. I'll look for her when I have Miss Harper settled. Now, off you all go," she added, clapping her hands as if she was rounding up chickens. "We've to be in the chapel for six o'clock."

"Yes, Mrs. Pearce," the girls replied, before drifting back into the room, leaving the doorway empty.

"They're not a bad lot really. You'll soon get used to them. Now, follow me. I'll show you to your room and then I'll make you a nice cup of tea. No doubt you're gasping."

Before Tilly could say anything, Mrs. Pearce had grabbed the heavy trunk and was striding off up the stairs, reeling off a list of information and instructions as she went. Tilly grabbed her smaller carpetbag and raced after her, trying to take everything in.

"Coal hole's under the stairs. Scullery's at the back of the house—there's a range and a copper for heating water for washday and the occasional bath. You'll be familiar with all that, I presume?" Tilly didn't get chance to reply before Mrs. Pearce continued. "Lavatory's at the back of the scullery. Backyard's out the back. Washday's Monday, as usual."

As Tilly followed Mrs. Pearce up two flights of stairs, she wondered how the girls without legs ever managed. She didn't get a chance to ask.

"Bath's in the off room at the end of the landing there. There's another tin bath in the yard." Tilly tried to keep up—physically and mentally—as Mrs. Pearce reeled off the daily routine without stopping for breath. "The girls sleep in dormitories in the front and middle bedrooms, six to a room. They go to the workrooms—or factory I suppose I should be saying now—from eight till six, Monday to Friday. They're expected to make their own beds and help with the washing up after each meal. And mind they do. You'd think some were afraid of water the way they try to sneak off. They're free to do as they wish on Saturday afternoons and Sundays, though we encourage them to go to church at least once. Some of them could do to be going many more times, if you ask my opinion, but it's not my place to say.

"You'll have eight shillings a week to run the house. It's not much, granted, but a good housemother will make those eight shillings work as hard as the girls do at making their flowers. I prefer to do all the washing myself rather than send it out—leaves you a bit extra for food that way. I've always been very proud of the fact that my girls have margarine and dripping all week and butter on Sundays. When I'm bent over the washtub scrubbing those bedsheets and dresses, I remind myself of how good that butter tastes. The ache in my arms doesn't seem so bad that way.

"The weekly menu is written down in the housemother's

book—fish on Wednesdays, roast mutton on Sundays, suet pudding on Saturday. You can come to the markets with me for the supplies until Mrs. Harris is back on her feet. Don't worry. You'll soon get the hang of it all."

Tilly's mind was reeling but, despite Mrs. Pearce's relentless chatter, there was an air of starchy efficiency about her that Tilly warmed to. She was clearly used to being in charge, to having her instructions paid attention to, and although the unpleasant odor she produced every time she moved was an unfortunate addition, there was something quite charming about her.

Much to the relief of Tilly's exhausted ears, the exertion of the upstairs climb eventually rendered Mrs. Pearce incapable of speech, apart from when she stopped occasionally to call for Buttons. Other than this, the only sounds as they made their ascent were the rhythmic *thud*, *thud*, *thud* as the heavy trunk bumped crossly off each step and the *swish* of Mrs. Pearce's skirts as they jostled for position over her substantial rear.

Tilly's eyes wandered from left to right as they passed closed doors, the tulip-patterned wallpaper following them to each new floor of the house, her boots squeaking against the oilcloth floor.

"Does the cat go missing often, Mrs. Pearce?" she asked as Mrs. Pearce called for Buttons again. "Ours was always going missing at home. We'd find her in cupboards or down the back of the dresser. They can sneak into all sorts of tiny spaces, especially if they're chasing a mouse. Mittens was a great mouser."

She heard giggling behind her and realized they were being followed.

"Oh, Buttons isn't a cat!" Mrs. Pearce cried over her shoulder, without stopping or turning around. "Buttons is one of our girls, and—like your cat—she has a particular knack for disappearing."

"Oh! I see."

Finally they reached a white-paneled door on the third floor of the house and Mrs. Pearce stopped. "Now, this is your room, Matilda." She gasped, her face flushed with color as she tried to catch her breath. An attractive leaded skylight above the doorframe allowed just enough light onto the landing to prevent it from being entirely gloomy.

"Wonderful. Quite the climb, isn't it?" Tilly wasn't even breathing heavily.

"Not so much of a climb as a stroll for a fit and healthy young lass like you!" Mrs. Pearce leaned against the doorframe. "If I didn't already know you were from the mountains, I could probably have guessed. You're not even breathing heavily. Look at me—I'm practically dead!"

Tilly laughed. "Well, *I* wouldn't usually be carrying a heavy trunk up the mountains. Oh, and actually, I use the name Tilly." Mrs. Pearce looked at her, confused. "It's short for Matilda."

"Oh. Right. Yes. Very well then. Tilly it is. Now," she continued, pushing the door open to reveal a neat, sparsely furnished room, "this will be your room." She stood in the doorway while Tilly walked in. "I'll leave you to unpack. Mrs. Harris's room is down the corridor to the right, but, well, I suppose that doesn't matter with her not being here."

"Not here?" Tilly turned, surprised to hear this. "Not here—at all?"

"No! Didn't I mention it? I was sure I had. How silly of me. She's gone to stay with her sister in Brighton to convalesce. 'No use to us lying around here with your leg in plaster. Much better off by the seaside'—that's what I told her. 'The fresh sea air will heal that bone faster than you can say pease pudding,' I said. She went two days ago—in a motorcar no less, sent by her nephew. He's quite the gentleman, by all accounts."

Tilly felt her face pale.

"Oh, don't worry, dear. You won't be entirely on your own. I'll be around as much as I can, to help out—and you'll soon get the hang of everything. You look like a competent enough young woman. I can always tell a hard worker when I see one. You can feel it in their hands. That's why I always give them a good shake when I first meet a person."

Tilly wished she could feel as confident about her abilities as Mrs. Pearce did. Her mind was in a whirl. *Twelve* girls to look after on her own. How had Mrs. Ingram described her new position? "Demanding circumstances." Mrs. Ingram didn't know the half of it.

"We'll be heading to the chapel for six o'clock," Mrs. Pearce said as she rubbed at the door handle with the edge of her apron, hovering around the entrance to Tilly's room, neither stepping inside nor leaving.

"Oh, yes. I meant to ask—if I'm not intruding," Tilly said. "You mentioned that Mr. Shaw has an important announcement to make this evening. Are there to be some changes made?"

"No idea. Although," Mrs. Pearce whispered, "I did hear a rumor that he received a letter from Queen Alexandra recently. Perhaps we're to be making some flowers by royal appointment! Imagine that!" Her hands flew to her cheeks, like a small child on Christmas morning.

"Really? Goodness, that would be quite something, wouldn't it?" Tilly had always had great admiration for Queen Alexandra, especially for the dignified manner in which she'd tolerated her husband's scandalous behavior and many mistresses, a matter that had been discussed and debated at great length by the ladies at Wycke Hall as they sipped their tea or played a game of bridge.

"Well, I suppose we'll find out soon enough anyway," Mrs. Pearce continued, still fluttering around the doorway like an indecisive moth. "We'll meet in the kitchen and make our way together from there. Your caps and white aprons are in the wardrobe," she added before turning on her heel and disappearing.

Closing the door behind her, Tilly placed her carpetbag on the bed and glanced around the room. It was pleasant enough, if a little cramped; a neat efficiency about the room that her mother would have approved of. A pale light crept in through the narrow sash window on the right, casting everything in a yellow hue. Lace curtains framed the window, and a small vase of dusky pink roses and purple violets stood on the windowsill. They gave off a wonderful aroma. A small rosewood writing table in the window alcove was well positioned to catch the best of the meager daylight. Tilly planned to do her sketching there.

An iron bedstead stood against the wall on the left. It reminded her of her bed at home. She walked over to it, running her fingers across the white fan-patterned counterpane, wondering whose patient hands had knitted the intricate pattern. A pastel blue candlewick blanket was folded neatly at the foot of the bed. She sat on it, her boot kicking the edge of the chamber pot beneath her as she bounced up and down. The mattress felt good and firm. The bed linen had a freshly laundered smell—she'd know the scent of Sunlight carbolic anywhere.

A gas lamp and a Bible had been placed on a lace doily on top of a nightstand to the right of the bed. A blue-and-white bowl and ewer stood on a washstand just behind the door, and a fire had been lit in the small grate, giving a much-needed warmth to the room, which, Tilly felt, would otherwise be cold and drafty. At Wycke Hall, Lady Day signaled an end to the fires being lit in the rooms until the cooler autumn months returned. She was glad they didn't appear to follow that custom in Violet House.

Walking over to the window to look out at the street below, Tilly noticed that the flowers in the vase were made of silk. "Of course!" she whispered, her fingers brushing the dusty surface of the delicate, hand-painted petals. They were shaped and molded so perfectly, it was hard to believe they weren't real. She picked up one of the dainty stems, admiring the veined leaves and detailed workmanship that had gone into the construction. It was so lifelike she almost bent her face toward the petals to breathe in their perfume. She wondered, briefly, where the scent of violets was coming from, if not from the flowers, but the arrival of the rag and bone man distracted her. She leaned forward to watch as he trundled along, his days' collection clattering noisily as he bumped his cart over the cobbles and cracks in the road. His face was darkened with filth, his trousers and coat tattered. Tilly listened as he called out in a thick East London accent, "Bones! Any old iron! Bones! Any old iron!" She'd never seen, nor heard, anything like it. He stopped at the end of the street, lit a cigarette, and took a rest as he leaned against a lamppost.

Draping her coat over the chair at the writing table, Tilly turned back to the room, bending down to undo the buckles on the leather straps of her trunk. She took out her beloved sketchbook and pastels first, placing them neatly on the writing table. She opened the sketchbook, flicking through the pages she had already filled with her drawings: sweeping Lake District landscapes; rough sketches of wildflowers; a detailed study of the buttercups and cowslips that grew in the fields and fells around the cottage; the mountains reflected in Lake Windermere and the lake at Grasmere. Turning back to the first page of the book, she read the familiar inscription:

October 2, 1900
To my darling Tilly, on your tenth birthday.
There is no greater gift than an empty page.
With much love,
Daddy

Running her fingers over the looping, sprawling handwriting, she thought about the man who had written these words. It had been such an unexpected surprise: not only the gift of the sketchbook and pastels but that *he* had chosen them and had written the inscription himself. It was a surprisingly tender gesture that had struck her at the time and had stayed with her ever since. Although he was a kind and gentle man, her father was not usually one for sentimentality. Perhaps he'd known. Perhaps he had sensed what was to come.

"I miss you, Daddy," she whispered. "I miss you so much."

Shivering from a cool draft that was coming through a gap in the window frame, she draped her coat over her shoulders as she checked that the sash window was fully shut. It was. She closed the sketchbook, the scent of violets intensifying briefly as she did, and returned to her trunk.

Kneeling down beside the trunk, she looked at the drab assortment of work clothes she had brought, sighing as she thought of the elegant outfits worn by Mrs. Ingram and her daughter, Violette, and many other ladies she had seen at the train station. How she longed to wear a dress of silk or chiffon; a dress to dance in, rather than to clean floors in; a dress to catch the attention of an admirer—a would-be husband, perhaps. Among her many other flaws, Tilly knew that her failure to receive a proposal of marriage was a cause of great disappointment to her mother. "You would do well to observe your appearance as closely as you observe those wildflowers. Sketching harebells will not find you a husband, Matilda, of that I am quite sure." She thought of her mother's words as she considered her plain country-girl clothes, the fabric cut and stitched by her own hands.

Bundling several garments in her arms, she walked to the wardrobe, lifting the brass latch and allowing the heavy doors to swing open. She hung up her two cotton day dresses and shook out her large holland apron and the coarse apron she would need for dirty jobs: cleaning the fire, sweeping the floors, and emptying the chamber pots. She brushed her hand over the starched fabric to smooth out the creases.

Next, she lifted out her shifts, drawers, corsets, and petticoats, giving them a good shake to free them of the soot and dust accumulated from the train journey before she set about refolding them. She had done this so often for the Misses Wycke when they returned from some outing or other. That it was her own clothing she was now unpacking and refolding sent a rush of nervous excitement tumbling in the pit of her stomach.

As she bent down to remove her shoes from the trunk, her eye was drawn to an untidy pile of blankets bunched together at the back of the wardrobe. Years of domestic service instinctively urged her to straighten and refold them. Kneeling down in front of the wardrobe, she reached into the back, her fingers grabbing one of the blankets. As she pulled, it fell to one side, and she found herself face-to-face with a young woman.

Chapter 5

Violet House, London
March 25, 1912

Her screams brought Mrs. Pearce thundering up the stairs. "Miss Harper! Oh, Good Lord. Miss Harper, is everything all right?" She burst into the room, her face purple with anxiety and exertion.

Tilly stood motionless in front of the wardrobe, a blanket hanging limply from her hands. Beside her was a very short woman, not more than four feet tall. She wore a simple black cotton dress with a white apron tied around her waist. A small spray of violets was pinned to her dress at the chest, and she clutched a neat posy of pink and purple silk freesias in her hands. Her hair was curled and pinned up around her face. She stared at Tilly with wide nut-brown eyes. Everything about her was childlike, and yet her face had the features of an adult's.

"Ah, I see you have found our missing Buttons." Mrs. Pearce folded her arms across her chest as it became apparent to her what had happened. "Fancy, frightening Miss Harper like that," she chided, leading Buttons firmly toward the door, "and what with her only just arriving. Barely opened her trunk, I shouldn't wonder. Must have thought she was seeing ghosts! Never seen the likes of it. Really, I haven't. Suppose you were trying to avoid going to chapel again, eh? I'm so sorry, Miss Harper. You must have got an awful fright. Sit yourself down on the bed. I'll fetch the smelling salts."

Tilly had recovered a little by the time Mrs. Pearce stopped talking. "Oh, no. Really, there's no need. I'm fine. Just a little surprised."

Her words fell on deaf ears as Mrs. Pearce bundled Tilly over to the bed, wafting the edge of her apron vigorously in front of her face.

"I only wanted to say hello," Buttons protested, aware that she was in trouble. "I wanted to give Miss Harper the flowers, to welcome her. I must have fallen asleep." She looked at Tilly with the innocence of a child as she handed her the posy of freesias. "I didn't mean to give you such a fright, Miss. Harper."

Tilly folded the blanket she was still clutching and laid it on the bed beside her. She took the flowers, her hands shaking a little.

"I know you didn't mean to frighten me. And thank you very much for the lovely flowers. It was a very kind thought." She was relieved to feel her heart rate slowing. "But I will admit that you surprised me! Moth balls I might have expected to find in the wardrobe—certainly not a person!"

"Goodness me! I shouldn't wonder if you had to spend the rest of the evening in bed with the shock," Mrs. Pearce muttered, turning a steely gaze on Buttons. "And it was *very* silly of you to hide in such a place, young lady. I hope such nonsense won't be happening again."

Buttons gazed at the floor, a sullen expression clouding her face. "It won't."

Mrs. Pearce winked at Tilly as she continued to speak to Buttons. "Mrs. Harris may be out of action, but she warned me about these games of hide-and-seek you're partial to. Now, come along. It's time you were dressed for chapel."

She marched Buttons out of the room, closing the door behind her before Tilly had a chance to say anything else. She heard Mrs. Pearce's continued chiding as they disappeared down the stairs.

Glad to be left on her own again, Tilly quickly changed into one of her cotton dresses, stepping out of the skirt she'd spent all day in, which, by now, was as wrinkled as a winter apple. She placed the silk freesias among the roses and violets in the vase on the windowsill and returned to her task of folding her undergarments and straightening the blankets, welcoming the familiarity of a simple, domestic task and the distraction it provided from alarming encounters in wardrobes.

As she bent down to grab the rest of the blankets from Buttons's hiding place, her eye was drawn to a slim wooden box nestling in the corner at the very back of the wardrobe. She presumed it must have been beneath the blankets before Buttons disturbed them. Maybe Buttons had left it there. Intrigued to see what it was, Tilly grabbed an edge and pulled it out, bringing a shower of dust with it.

She turned the box around in her hands, running her fingertips over the smooth surface of the wood. There was nothing particularly remarkable about it: just a simple dark brown box, the width of her lap, with a thin, lavender-colored silk ribbon tied in a neat bow across the lid. The ribbon personalized the box, suggesting that someone had cared about its contents. Tilly stood for a moment, wondering what to do. Maybe she should put it back? Forget about it. What if the box did belong to Buttons and she reappeared at any moment to claim it? The last thing Tilly wanted on the first day of her new job was to be accused of being a snoop. And yet, what harm would she be doing by taking just a quick peek inside?

Carrying the box over to the writing table, she settled herself at the chair. Taking a quick glance back toward the door, she listened for the sound of footsteps on the stairs. All was quiet. Reassured that nobody was coming, she carefully untied the ribbon. It fell aside easily, like a deep breath, gratefully exhaled. She lifted the lid, the perfume of violets intensifying around her as she did.

Inside the box was a small leather-bound notebook, its tan cover creased and worn with age. There was also a wooden clothes peg, a black button, a doll made of rags, and a postcard bearing a faded photograph of a group of young girls clustered around a display of flowers. The label at the bottom read, SHAW'S HOMES FOR WATERCRESS AND FLOWER GIRLS, 1883. Tilly lifted each item out of the box, wondering who they had belonged to. On the back of the postcard someone had written, *"December 1884. You will find her. I know you will. Happy Christmas. Lily B. x"* At the bottom of the box was a delicate lace handkerchief, stained and spoiled a little with age. Lifting it up to the light of the window, she saw the faint outline of shamrocks stitched into one corner. Her thoughts flashed back to the train. To Mrs. Ingram.

Walking over to the bed, Tilly spread the dusty items across the counterpane. It was a strange assortment of things. Why would somebody keep a peg—and a single button? But she was most interested in the leather-bound notebook. Opening it carefully, she read the inscription on the inside cover.

For Little Sister.
All flowers are beautiful,
but some are more beautiful than others.
I will never stop looking for you.
Flora Flynn

Tilly carefully turned the fragile faded pages, intrigued by the neat handwriting. The paper smelled musty and crackled as she turned more pages, the same, careful writing filling each one. As she turned a page toward the middle of the book, something fell into her lap. A flower. A pale yellow primrose, dry as an autumn leaf and paper-thin. She thought of her flower press at home, of all the beautiful wildflowers she had carefully placed between the layers of blotting paper: buttercups, harebells, bell heather, wild daffodils, summer snowflakes, bluebells, foxgloves, and marsh orchids. She remembered collecting them, each and every one.

Turning the notebook upside down, she shook it gently, sending several more flowers tumbling from their hiding places between the pages: purple hyacinths, pink carnations, primroses, violets, and pansies, each fluttering gracefully into her lap, like butterflies released from a display case.

She picked up each flower, running her fingers lightly over its delicate form. She held a violet toward the window, rubbing the stem between her thumb and forefinger so that it twisted back and forth, catching the light. It was almost translucent. She gazed at the skeletal structure of the leaf, every vein and cell of the petals. It was such a beautiful, fragile little thing. Looking back through the book, she saw that on each page from which a flower had fallen was the faintest of imprints, a shadow of the flower's image left permanently on the paper. Like a distant echo, the images spoke to her, whispering secrets of a forgotten past. Whose hand had placed the flowers here? Who had written these pages and pages of words?

As the surroundings of her new home faded into the background, Tilly settled herself against the pillow, turned back to the first page of the book, and started to read.

Flower Village. Clacton. June 18, 1880.

I been going to school these past years and learning my writing, Rosie, so as I can tell you what I been doing. Mother says my words is coming on grand. Mother is what we call the nice lady what looks after us here at the orphanage. It's by the sea. I watch the pleasure boats come up from London and think of us watching them leave Westminster Pier that day. That were four year ago, Rosie, and never a day passes that I don't think of you. I imagine you in the streets around Covent Garden, selling your cresses and violets. "Buy a flower off a poor girl? Oh, please, Miss. Do buy a flower."

I remember how ye'd sniff the sweet air of the flower markets, breathing it in like it was bringing ye back to life. And I'd tell you about all the different colors, what with you not being able to see them for yourself: the red and white roses, the pink peonies, the cream and lavender tulips, the purple stocks and hyacinths, and the reels and reels of shiny satin ribbon in every color of the rainbow.

Don't think I could bear to see it now, what with you not being beside me.

I ask Mr. Shaw about you when I see him. He says they

keep looking all around the markets and such, but that nobody sees a little girl with hair like flames. But she must be there, I tell him, she must.

But ye never are, Rosie Flynn. Ye never are.

Nighttimes are the worst. I wake, all cold and sweating like a cart horse, screaming and screaming for you, "Where are ye, Rosie? Where are ye gone to?" Mother comes to settle me then. Sometimes she lets me sleep in the spare bed in her room so as she can keep watch over me. She puts a damp cloth on my head to cool me. Tells me it'll be all right come the morning. But it isn't all right 'cause you're still not here with me, Rosie, sure you're not. You were just four year old and you were gone. Gone like a blown-out candle flame.

I know our bare feet was always frozen and we had an ache in our bellies with the hunger and we slept on doorsteps to avoid a beating from Da, even though we feared them dark courts and alleyways and the bad men who lurked there, but as long as we was together, it somehow seemed all right. Like shadows we were, me and you, Rosie, held together by a thread we neither of us could see. And now that thread is broken and I'm all unraveled without you.

There was something about the careful, childish handwriting, a desperate yearning captured within the words that seemed to lift from the page, reaching out to Tilly as she read. She remembered the motor cab driver and his tale of the Irish girl and her lost sister.

"Who are you, Flora?" she whispered, brushing her fingers across the faded writing. Her words hung in the small room, as if they expected an answer.

Tilly shivered as the room turned suddenly cold again. A

prickle ran along the soft, downy hairs at the back of her neck, the powdery scent of violets strengthening and then dissipating just as abruptly. Something in the atmosphere of the room had changed.

"Miss Harper! Miss Harper!" Mrs. Pearce was thudding up the stairs. "Miss Harper. Are you decent? We have visitors who would like to meet you. And there's tea in the pot."

Tilly slammed the book shut and jumped off the bed. "Yes, Mrs. Pearce," she called through the closed door. "I'll be right down."

Working quickly, while being careful not to damage anything, she gathered up the notebook, the delicate pressed flowers, and the trinkets, putting them all back into the wooden box before placing it in a drawer of the writing table. She smoothed her hair as best she could and hurried from the room, thoughts of a lost little girl, and a sister desperate to find her, settling like a fog around her heart.

Chapter 6

London

March 1876

Florrie

I think I'm eight year old, and Little Sister is half that. I'm not full certain, 'cause I don't know what year I was born, see. The passin' of the years don't make much difference to us street sellers, sure it don't. All I know about the years is it's primroses in the spring, roses in summer, lavender in autumn, and cresses in winter. That's all I know of the years.

I'm not stupid though. I know the Queen dresses in black since her dear Albert died, and I know how many pennies is in a shilling. I can spell my own name, too, so I can. I was at the Ragged School, but that were a while ago. Master walloped me for not paying attention, and Mammy said I weren't to be going no more.

Said I'd be more use selling the flowers and cresses and doing a bit o' sewing for a few pennies than getting my backside walloped. Anyway, one of the coster boys has been teaching me to read this last while, and I can say my ABCs well enough.

Mammy and Da come over on the steamship from Wexford when I were just an infant. Mammy's cousin had sent for us, see—said there was plenty of work in the factories. What with things being so bad in Ireland an' all, Da borrowed some money (Mammy never asked him where from, but I'm after thinking it was got by bad means). We took the boat to Liverpool before traveling to London. Da worked at the sugar factory in Whitechapel for a while until he got caught stealin'. Mammy said he was lucky not to be thrown in the gaol. She said if it hadn't been Christmas and people feeling charitable, he more'n likely would have been. Truth be told, I think Mammy would have preferred if he *had* been thrown in the cells. Could have stayed there, too, for all I care. Sure, that's a shocking awful thing to say about y'r own da, but that's the way of it. He don't have much of a likin' for me and I don't have much of a likin' for him.

After the sugar factory, he started out as a bone grubber, going round collecting old rags and bones and iron. He didn't have money for a cart, let alone a donkey to pull it, so he walked the streets with that greasy sack slung over his shoulder. Me and Mammy'd stay in our room at Rosemary Court and make our matches and wait for him to come back so as we could sort through everything he'd found. Stinking to make you sick, so it was, all that stuff he'd be after collecting—'specially them bones. We'd sort the colored rags from the white (the colored gets more pence, y'see) and the bones from the iron. Sometimes he'd set me to scraping at the cracks in the paving, looking for nails from the horseshoes—ye can get good money for horseshoe nails—and if I found a lost key, that was like finding real treasure, so it was. Good at finding the horseshoe nails I was, and it's better'n searching down at the filthy, stinking river like them mudlarks. Mammy said I was lucky not to be working at that business, standing on glass and rusted nails in my bare feet. She told me it's often a mudlark falls into the Thames at high tide and drowns, choking on all that shite that floats around in it.

I was glad when Mammy starting selling the flowers. I liked being away from Rosemary Court and its stinking drains. Preferred to be among them flowers in the market, I did, 'specially in the summertime, when the rains make the stocks and roses smell so sweet. And it turns out that I was much better at tying up the posies than I ever was at listening in the schoolroom. "Born to be a flower girl, so ye were, Florrie Flynn." That's what Mammy'd say to me. "Born and bred to be among the flowers, sure ye were."

We'd head out selling, whatever the weather—snows, rain, thick pea soupers, made no difference to the likes of us. Gen'lemen make the best customers—they often buy a posy to give to their lady friends. "Please, gen'leman, do buy my flowers! Poor little girl! Roses for love. Violets for faithfulness. Lavender for devotion." That's what I'd cry as the gen'lemen walked past or stood about chatting and smoking outside the theaters.

A kind lady once touched my face with her gloved hand—touched me, she did—while her gen'leman friend was buying a posy from me. Said I would be a "pretty little thing" if she could "scrub all that filth away." Then the gen'leman scolded her for talking to catchpennies and pulled her away as if I were nothing better than a mangy dog about to bite her.

Sometimes I'd forget I was supposed to be selling and would stand and gawp at the ladies' dresses, those green and purple silks, shimmerin' like the Thames when the sun pokes through the fog. Then Mammy'd give me a sharp dig in the ribs with her elbow. "Stop y'r gawping and start hawking," she'd snap and I'd get back to work, quick as you like 'cause Mammy had the sharpest elbows you ever felt.

It was always just me and Mammy, until she got the swellin' in her belly and I knew another baby was coming. It was hard for her then, and some days, toward the end, she couldn't go to market and I knew we would all go hungry if I didn't go on my own. So, I did.

I'll never forget the day Little Sister was born. Nearly killed Mammy, so she did, what with her coming out arse-ways first. If it wasn't for old Mrs. Quinn at the front of the house having delivered thirty-four babies in her time, they'd both have died then and there, sure they would. That's what Mrs. Quinn said. Seems like little Rosie Flynn was keen to have her life—and Mammy weren't ready to give up her own time on God's good earth neither. Not then, anyway. Not until the summer come along with all its disease. Then her time came all right.

Mammy knew she was dying. She made Da promise not to send me and Rosie into the workhouse ('cause there's nothing worse than the House, sure there's not) and she made me promise to look after Little Sister and not to be stealin' nor visiting the penny gaffs nor gin palaces. "And you're not to be falling in with them girls who sell *other* things to the gentlemen, as well as their flowers. Ye know the girls I'm talking of, don't ye, Florrie." I did know the type of girls she was talking about, and I swore on my life I'd never be fallin' in with them type, nor would Rosie, neither, when she was all grown up.

Before she died, Mammy gave me and Rosie a lace handkerchief each, what had been made by our granny back in Ireland. "Blessed with holy water, so they are," she said, "and with the shamrocks sewn on, for good luck." One of the nicest things I ever seen, that lace handkerchief was. Mammy told us we'd always be safe and have food in our bellies and flowers for the sellin' if we kept those handkerchiefs with us.

"You're to mind Little Sister now, Florrie," she said to me. "You'll be her mammy now. You mind her good 'n' proper, d'ye hear? Promise me ye'll mind her."

"Yes, Mammy. I promise. I promise I'll mind her."

"Ah, ye're a grand good girl, Florrie Flynn," she said. "A grand good girl, so ye are."

Those were the last words she spoke.

"MA'S DEAD," DA SAID the next morning. "Go in and pay your respects. She's still warm."

Made her sound like a loaf of bread, so he did.

Auntie May said it was a blessed release 'cause she'd suffered shockin' pain—"the cholera does that to you," she said, "eats a person up from the inside and drives them crazy with the thirst." Her lips and mouth were as blue as cornflowers when I finally found the courage to go and look at 'er, and then I took to bawlin'. She was my mammy, see, and she was dead and gone and me an' Little Sister were all alone. Da was still livin' and breathin'—more's the pity—but he didn't care tuppence for me an' Rosie. We might as well have been all alone, for all the use he'd be to us.

The blankets were put up again' the window and the broken mirror covered over. Mammy lay among us for a week, so she did. Lyin' there as we slept and ate our bread and pudding. I couldn't stop thinking about her dead body behind that old curtain. I kept a bunch of stocks 'specially, so as to mask the smell of her. I'm ashamed to say it, but I was pleased when she was carried out, feet first. Buried in a pauper's grave, so she is.

I tell Little Sister about Mammy all the time, about what I remember of her, 'cause Rosie never had the chance to see her alive—not so as she'd remember, anyway. And I've kept my promise—to look after Little Sister. Love 'er to pieces, so I do. Like my own baby she is. I sing the songs to her now, just like Mammy used to.

At early dawn I once had been
Where Lene's blue waters flow,
When summer bid the groves be green,
The lamp of light to glow—
As on by bower, and town and tower,
And wide-spread fields I stray,
I meet a maid in the greenwood shade,
At the dawning of the day.

She's all I have in the world. Don't know what I'd do if anything ever happened to her, sure I don't.

Chapter 7

London
April 1876

Rosemary Court ain't a good place to live, we all know that. Da says, "Beggars can't be choosers, 'specially not Irish ones." And there's no place else for us to be livin', sure there's not, so I don't grumble no more. What's the use?

You get to the Court down a long, cobbled laneway, just off Drury Lane, next to the oil shop. It's where lots of the Irish live. We like to keep ourselves to ourselves, see—don't be mixing with the English flower girls, sure we don't.

The Court is full of little lanes and alleyways so that you'd want to be knowin' y'r way around so as not to get lost. It's awful dark there, too, down the narrow lanes—the houses nearly touchin' each other and blockin' out the light. Some of the women upstairs can share a pipe of baccer or a smoke with their cousin across the street just by leanin' out the window. There are big, high walls either side of the Court. "Wide enough to fit a coffin through, and high enough to stop anyone escaping," so the saying goes.

Da says there's twenty houses in our court and two families in each, "which makes about as many Irish as there are left in the whole of Sligo." There's just the two houses at the end not lived in. They're nearest the busted drains—not a soul will live in 'em, not even the rats, the stink is so awful bad.

A family from Cork live at the front of the house—there's seven or eight of them—and we live in the room at the back: Da, me, Rosie, Auntie May (who suffers with her nerves), and my cousin, Kathleen. It's shockin' cold in that room. The walls are black with damp and the windows all cracked and rotten, letting in drafts that just about freeze your blood in the wintertime. The summers ain't much better, neither. We've lifted the floorboards at one side of the room, to use as a privy, and there's chickens roosting at the back of us. The smell from under those boards and from them chickens and the busted drains and the buckets of piss and rubbish that get thrown into the street at the back of the houses hangs about somethin' awful—it gets into y'r blood, into the back of y'r throat. In the summers it brings the bile up from y'r belly and the tears smartin' to your eyes. Even the Thames don't smell as bad, sure it don't. We pay two shillin' a week for the room. Da says the landlord should be paying *us* to live there, it's that bad.

We've no water in the house, just a standpipe in the middle of the Court that we all use. It comes up brown like mud. Sometimes me and Rosie take a drink from the pumps we use to wash the cresses down the markets—it's a bit better than the standpipe, but not much. Da says ye would never see brown water in Ireland. "Clear as glass," he says the water was back there. I think he's sometimes sad not to be livin' in Ireland still. He gets fierce angry when he's after taking the drink, and then he shouts, "Feck the robbin' bastards anyway." When he gets all maudlin and has a belly full of ale, I know a beating's coming for sure, 'specially if we don't sell our flowers and don't bring any pennies home.

They say not to drink the water now anyway, not until it's been boiled, for fear of the cholera coming back again, but we don't have money for buying fuel for the fire, so we've to drink it as it is, cholera or not. Sometimes I find some dropped lumps of coal on the street or walnuts—walnuts is grand for burning when they're dried out—and I gather them up in my skirts, and I know Da'll be pleased, but it's still not enough for a proper fire. Da says he'll more 'n likely have to burn the rest of the furniture this winter, just to get a bit of warmth, like. We don't have much furniture left anyway. He took most of it to the dolly shop for a few shillings. There's just a stool now for a chair, a tattered old rug by the fireplace, a penny tea canister that we use as a candle-stick for our light, and an old table what Da nicked from one of the other houses when old Mrs. Herrity died. It's on the pallets now, for legs.

Da sleeps behind the curtain, and I sleep with Little Sister on an old flock mattress in the corner of the room. I make up stories to tell Rosie, about travelin' on one of them fancy paddle steamers from the pier and heading off for a day trip to Gravesend. Rosie likes when I tell the stories to her; makes the nights less frightenin' she says. Poor little thing. Terrible afraid of the night-time she is—says she don't like it when the shadows go out. Lord bless 'er. She can only see shadows, y'see, what with her eyes not working proper: dark shadows and a faint glow from the gaslights, that's all Rosie can see. So, I keep her 'specially close to me at night and we say our prayers and sing the songs that Mammy used to sing to us.

We all know Rosemary Court is a bad, filthy place to live, but we've nowhere else to go, other than the workhouse. Even the cold nights and the street gangs and the bad men and the thieves is better than that. If they took me and Rosie to the House, I might never see 'er again, and that'd be worse than dyin', sure it would.

Chapter 8

London
April 1876

Turns out Mammy was right about them lucky shamrocks on the handkerchiefs, 'cause I know it was them for certain what brought Mr. Shaw to help me and Rosie at the Aldgate Pump. It was those lucky Irish shamrocks, sure as eggs is eggs.

Mr. Shaw stopped to help me, see, after some swell had knocked the flower basket clean out of my hands. Running for something that swell was—or from someone, maybe. Either way, he didn't even stop to say sorry, so he didn't. Right ruined they were—all my cresses and primroses—muddied and spoiled on the ground, and there I was, sobbin' and sobbin' as I tried to wash 'em under the freezing water, when up walks this great black top hat, soaring into the sky like the factory chimneys. 'Course there was a head attached to it, and a smart frock coat. Stopped to ask me what the matter was, that hat did—wanted to know why I was all weepin' and wretched.

Thought he was a copper's nark at first, come to arrest me for shouting after a gen'leman, but then didn't he pay me the money for the spoiled flowers and give me and Rosie a breakfast ticket for a room he has at the Garden. I known he was a good, kind man then. "He's a good, kind man, Rosie." That's what I told Little Sister when she asked who it was had stopped to talk to us. "A good, kind man with a great big hat. A good, kind man what prays to God and has given us a special ticket to get a hot drink and a slice of bread and butter."

We go to the Club Room each mornin' now. I give Rosie most of my bread and butter, and her cheeks get rounder each day and have a bit of color in them. And that hot cocoa feels just grand in our bellies after the cold nights and mornin's at the market buying our stock. Like a taste of Heaven, so it is. And when it's after raining, we get dry clothes to wear and some kind women read to us from the Bible, telling us about God's love. Sometimes they mend the holes and tears in our clothes and dip a rag in a bowl of warm water and teach us to wash our hands and feet and faces, telling how it stops the disease if ye stay clean. Sometimes we get given a blanket, and that's a grand thing to be given altogether!

Mr. Shaw is the name of the man in the hat who helped us. A good, kind man he is, and no mistake. And the ladies who help in the Club Room are good and kind, too. One lady, who Rosie has come to have a particular liking for, always stops to buy a couple of bunches when she sees us out selling on the street. She gave a silver sixpence once, when a penny would do. "Buy a mug of hot cocoa for yourself and your sister, and you'll still have plenty left to take home to your father," she said. And she'll sometimes pay for the violets, too, when they're all ruined and wilted by the late frosts.

There's lots of other flower sellers go to the Club Room. Some have a crutch, like me. Some have an arm missing or hands that won't work proper, and some are midgets, no taller than Rosie, though they're much older in years. One of them girls is after telling me that Mr. Shaw takes his Sunday School girls on a trip to the seaside at Clacton every summer and that they swim in the sea—putting their whole bodies in the water! I told her I don't think I'd dare to even put my toe in the sea—"Ye could drown," I say. But it would be a grand thing to walk on the sand, all the same, and they say the sea air smells as fresh as peas after the summer rains.

It's them shamrocks on our handkerchiefs for certain. It's them what brought Mr. Shaw to us—they're looking out for us, just like Mammy said. Even so, I know that good, kind men in chimney-pot hats and fancy frock coats can't keep me an' Rosie safe and warm forever. I still shiver till my bones rattle when we huddle together under a market barrow at night. I still keep my eyes open, watching for those bad men what lurk in the shadows. I can hear them, creeping in and out of the laneways, as quiet and menacing as a winter fog.

Chapter 9

London
April 1876

I do the washing and run errands for Da, and each morning he gives me a few coins and sends us out to the markets at the Garden to buy our stock for the day's sellin'. I have to bring Little Sister—"sure, minding babies is women's work," he says. I'd rather she was with me anyway. "A proper little mother ye are, Florrie Flynn." That's what Maura Connolly, down the market, says.

So, it's just me and Rosie now, sellin' the flowers. It's awful hard for me going about on the crutch, but Da says there's no hope of a cripple the like of me getting work in service, or in the factories, so sellin' the flowers and cresses is all I can do—other than stealin' or beggin', and that's not a good way for a person to live. We manage as best we can, me and Rosie, and there's no use blubberin' about what you can't change, is there?

It's fierce dark when we set out each mornin' so as ye can barely see where y'r steppin'. I trod on a rat last week, its tail all wiry between my toes. Screamed so loud you'd think my throat was being cut. I been longing for a nice, smart pair of boots ever since. Wouldn't care how many rats I was standing on then, sure I wouldn't.

We go down Wellington Street, off the Strand, and then along Russell Street. There's no noise like it when the markets is getting goin'. Sure, ye can hear the shouts and cries from as far away as Chancery Lane. It doesn't matter which way you're coming from 'cause all the roads to market—Southampton Street, Bedford Street, Long Acre, Bow Street—are stuffed to bustin' with the hawkers and costers, pulling their handcarts and barrows. Hundreds of men there are, balancing great baskets on their heads as they rush past, shoutin' and cursin' as they weave in and out of each other's way, past the carts and the knackered old donkeys. The greengrocers' wagons rumble past us, piled higher than an omnibus with their cabbage and sea kale, and I gawp at them funny-looking pineapples 'cause I never seen nothing like 'em. The wagons and carts make the road shudder under our feet. Me an' Rosie don't care about steppin' on the rotten cabbage leaves and we don't take no notice of the saucy dollymops who hang around the costers as they take their pint in the early taverns. We don't look at 'em, like Mammy always told us not to.

I take Little Sister along the back streets if it's getting too busy on the main roads. It's easy to lose people in all that busyness—and that's what frightens me more than anything else, losin' Rosie. I'd rather lose the use of both legs and not eat for a year, so I would, than lose Little Sister. So I hold on to her hand fierce tight, 'cause you never know who might be lurking round them corners: the natty lads waiting to steal y'r stock money, or wicked men waitin' to steal worse. You'd never know what, or who, was in them shadows, sure you wouldn't. So we go darting like rats down the narrowest alleyways, picking another way to the Garden, and when we turn in to the grand avenue and see the Floral Hall, all gleaming glass and iron, it's a nice feelin', familiar, like.

I know we're terrible filthy, we're hungry and cold all the days and nights, and I wish for a pair of sturdy boots for us both, but when the sun shines on the flower markets on a summer's morning, it can look real pretty; them baskets of violets shine like jewels. I tell Rosie how they reflect against the rain-soaked cobbles and turn the stones purple.

Sometimes, before we go sellin', we visit the Club Room. I make sure we pay our ha'penny and we wait as patient as our rumbling bellies will allow as the ladies ladle the soup or mutton out of great cooking pots. Spoonful after spoonful they pour into the bowls and that meaty steam all risin' up and the smell of that gravy getting up y'r nose is so good we can hardly wait a minute more. I never tasted nothing so good, sure I didn't. We both get an ache in our bellies from eating too quick. And then we sit around the kind lady who tells us all about noble and good people. I tell Little Sister that we should try to be noble and good, then we won't end up like that Nellie Byrne. Fell in with a bad lot so she did. Ended up at the bottom of the Thames. Only twelve year old. Lord knows what's to become of her brother and sister what she used to mind.

I don't think about food most days, it's easier that way, though it was hard not to think about them hot cross buns when the coster boys arrived near where we was selling on Shaftesbury Avenue on Good Friday. Little Sister said she wished we could stay there selling our flowers forever, just so as she could breathe in that delicious smell. Poor little Rosie. How I wished I could pay a penny for one.

Well, the luck of the Irish came to me then. Didn't one of them glistening buns fall out the seller's basket! Rolled right up to my feet, so it did. I grabbed it before he could notice and stuffed it into my pocket. Off we ran then, me an' Rosie. We hid behind a rag and bone cart on Haymarket. Stuffed that bun into our mouths quicker than you can say "one-a-penny, two-a-penny." It weren't stealing, sure it weren't, 'cause it fell on the ground and I just found it there and that's different from stealing from the basket, so it is. Sure, there's nothing nicer than a belly full of sweet bun and those spices were still on our lips when we went back to Rosemary Court. Best of all, Da was out Greenwich way, hoping to pick up some rag before the Greenwich Fair. Me and Rosie slept better that night than we had in months. I said a prayer and thanked Granny for her lucky shamrocks and slept until daylight.

But them nights of a good sleep don't come around often. When me an' Rosie is sleeping outside, I can't help thinking of the frightening men who walk around at night. I'm always glad to see the lamplighter come along with his pole and his light. I watch him from where we're hidden; watch him reach the pole up and then the flame starts. Like magic it is when the lamp starts to glow, and it's always nice to see that little puddle of light on the street. I can sometimes sleep for a while then, but mostly I keep my eyes open, watching out for danger, along with the cats and the rats and the scabby dogs who snuffle about near us looking for vegetable scraps. I start thinking on the stories the costers tell us then—the stories they're after reading in the penny dreadfuls. Scare your bones off you, so they would, with all their talk of murder and ghosts. So I don't sleep much. Can't. I lie awake, and wait for morning, and remember my promise to Mammy.

Chapter 10

London

May 1876

The late spring frosts are after making life hard. We ain't had flowers to sell for a week now—all ruined they are before they even get to market. The oranges and cresses are keeping us going, but only just.

Things are troublesome at home, too. Cousin Kathleen has run off and nobody's seen her for two week or more and Da's after taking ill with the consumption. Auntie May is minding him as best she can, but I don't think she's the full shilling herself these days and her nerves is playing up what with Kathleen disappearing. Auntie May says Da's sure to die before the month is out. I can't feel sad about it, even though I know I should, 'specially 'cause that'll make me and Rosie orphans, and most orphans get taken into the workhouse. Mammy's lucky handkerchiefs maybe ain't so lucky after all.

At least me and Rosie have Mr. Shaw's Club Room to go to—and we've got each other. Not like the little match sellers. Most of them are orphans—all alone—and some no bigger than Rosie. They come running like rats through the alleyways when they see the omnibus coming, the boxes of matches on the ends of their long sticks so as they can reach up to the passengers on the top deck. Rosie says they sound like a flock of birds with their little voices screeching all together.

More and more sellers come out as the months get warmer. We see the ham sandwich sellers, the coffee sellers, and the newspaper vendors who stand at the theater doors and the bridges and railway stations like us flower sellers do. Me and Rosie like the music of the nigger bands who play all the day in the summertime. It's nice to hear them when we sell around Oxford Street and Regent Street.

Sometimes we stop to talk to the midget who stands at the corner of St. Martin's Lane and Long Acre, selling his nutmeg graters. He's a dwarf and no higher than me. I thought he was just a young boy at first, but then I saw his face—a man's face in a boy's body. He has a sign hung around his neck: I WAS BORN A CRIPPLE. I know 'cause he told me himself what it says. The graters hang all around him on fraying bits of string, clinking and clanking whenever he moves. He fell over once and sent up such a great clatter. He wears a smart cap and a neckerchief of crimson red. Y'd know him if you saw him. He has sad eyes, so I try and remember to smile at him when we see him.

I don't care for some of the sellers, though. I 'specially don't like the lemonade seller on Westminster Bridge. Looks at you funny when he talks to you, so he does. His eyes are shifty and his teeth all rotten and fallin' out of his head, and he sneers when he looks at you. He stands all hunched over his stone barrel, his coat hanging about him and his hat balanced on his head. Maura Connolly says he looks like a monster. She says you could put him on the cover of a penny dreadful and have half of London terrified. "More frightening than Spring-Heeled Jack." That's what she says.

"Lemonade, buy your ice-cold lemonade fresh," he cries when we go past. "Halfpenny a glass, sparkling lemonade." He knows we ain't got a ha'penny to spare—cruel so he is to tempt us like that. But the glasses sparkle in the sun and it all looks so nice when you see the boys guzzling that drink down their throats without stopping. But I reckon the powder he mixes into the water ain't lemonade powder at all. Persian sherbet he sometimes calls it when he makes it turn red. Vitriol—I reckon that's all he's putting in there.

"Don't look at 'im, Rosie," I say as we scurry past. "Don't look in his eyes." 'Cause the coster boys say if you look into his eyes he hypnotizes you and takes little girls off to work for him, stealing and begging and pickpocketing.

So we dart and dodge among the ladies and gentlemen as they go for a stroll. We duck underneath the horses' bellies, making sure we don't get a kicking from them, and we crowd around the carriages, begging the pretty ladies to buy our flowers as they get in or out. The horses snort and paw at the ground, their coats all covered in white sweat, and I hold on to Little Sister's hands tight as I can. "Don't let go, Rosie," I tell her. "Don't let go."

Chapter 11

Violet House, London
March 25, 1912

A strange hush descended over Violet House as Tilly made her way downstairs. Each footstep she placed on the creaky steps seemed to emphasize the fact that she was a stranger here, that the house did not yet know her well enough to be fully at ease.

Wincing at the sound of each creak and crack, she wished she could spend more time in her room, reading the notebook. She wanted to know more about Flora and her sister, Rosie.

The knots in her stomach tightened at the prospect of meeting the "girls" who would be in her charge—some of whom, despite the affectionate name given to them as a group, were much older than her. She wondered whether they would accept her direction in place of Mrs. Harris's, whether she was up to the "demanding circumstances" facing her. She thought of her mother, of how satisfied she would be if Tilly were to fail, were to arrive home within a week, her great London adventure come to nothing. The thought made her stand taller. *Come along, Tilly*, she chided. *Pull yourself together. How difficult can it be?*

"Well, good evening, girls. And a fine one it is, too, without the rain to dampen our spirits."

Tilly's thoughts were interrupted by a loud, jovial voice downstairs.

"Good evening, Mr. Shaw," she heard the girls reply in unison.

He was here! Mr. Shaw was here. Tilly stopped on the landing, straining to listen to this man she had heard so much about, and for whom she already had so much respect and admiration, despite having never met him in person.

"And how are you today, Lorraine?" she heard him ask. "You're looking much better now, I must say. And Hilda, how's that sprained wrist coming along? We're hoping to see you back on the factory floor very soon—those orchids don't look quite the same without your delicate touch on the petals. Ah, Betty and Doris, I see you're planning to be first into chapel as usual . . ." On and on he went, naming each girl in turn, asking how she was, referring to some previous illness or problem, listening to them all, giving each of them his time and attention, like a doting father to his daughters.

Tilly hesitated, lingering on the stairs, not wishing to intrude.

"Well, are you going down to introduce yourself, or are you going to lurk on this staircase for all of eternity?"

Tilly jumped. She hadn't noticed Mrs. Pearce had joined her on the upstairs landing. "I just stopped to tie my lace," Tilly mumbled, bending down to fiddle with her boot.

Mrs. Pearce raised an eyebrow. She was not a woman who was

easily fooled. "And there was me, imagining that you were eavesdropping." She winked.

Tilly smiled. "I hear Mr. Shaw has arrived."

"Three Mr. Shaws, to be precise."

"Three?"

"Yes. Albert—and his nephews, Herbert and Edward. And all on account of coming to introduce themselves to a certain new assistant housemother, I believe." Mrs. Pearce tilted her head sideways, indicating that Tilly should start moving on.

Tilly made her way down the remaining stairs, each one creaking louder and louder, as if to announce her arrival to everyone gathered in the room below. Reaching the bottom, she brushed her hands over the front of her new white apron to smooth out any creases and tugged at the cuffs of her blouse to straighten them. Taking a deep breath, she walked to a door that was slightly ajar, knocked, and entered.

All eyes fell on her the moment she stepped into the room. She felt her cheeks redden as so many unfamiliar faces turned in her direction. Some of the girls smiled, some giggled, some frowned, some stood, some sat. Without exception, they stared.

"Hello." Her voice came out as a muffled whisper. She cleared her throat. "Hello, everyone." Better.

As the many pairs of eyes continued to gaze at her, Tilly looked around the room. It was softly lit by a gasolier suspended from a ceiling rose, the glass beading along the edge of the shade disturbed by a draft. The walls were covered with pretty rose-patterned wallpaper, and several pictures hung from the picture rail: watercolor landscapes and still-life paintings of various flora and fauna. A rag rug lay in front of the fireplace; to one side sat a built-in cupboard, to the other, a dresser, where numerous jugs and cups hung from hooks. In front of the window was a large mahogany table surrounded by Windsor chairs, where some of the girls sat. Another group sat huddled together, giggling, on a comfortable-looking couch. A butter-yellow budgie chirped happily in a cage hanging on a stand near the window, a collection of seed husks gathered on the floor beneath.

"And you must be our new assistant housemother! Welcome to our Flower Homes, Miss Harper! Welcome indeed!" A tall, dignified-looking elderly man, dressed in a smart suit and black frock coat, appeared from among the group of women. He held out a large hand in greeting, his voice reverberating through Tilly's chest. "Albert Shaw. It is a pleasure to meet you."

Tilly gazed up at him, somehow remembering her manners and holding out her hand in return. He took it, shaking it firmly but warmly. He was an impressive sight. Tilly guessed he stood over six feet tall. His face was dignified, with what her mother would describe as a "proud chin." Gray hair and sideburns added an air of gravitas. His eyes, a vivid cornflower blue, spoke of a man who possessed the qualities of passion and compassion in equal measure. He smiled at Tilly, a warm, generous smile that made the crow's-feet crinkle mischievously around his eyes.

"And these are my nephews, Edward and Herbert," he continued. "Twins—although you'd never believe it to look at them!"

Edward Shaw stepped forward. Much smaller in stature than his uncle, he carried nothing of the same air of distinction about him. His features were not unpleasant to look at, although there was nothing in particular to admire, either. He barely glanced at Tilly as he held out his hand to shake hers, but she noticed that he had the same striking blue eyes as his uncle. Edward's eyes, however, did not sparkle and dance like his uncle's, instead appearing empty and distant.

"Very pleased to meet you, Miss Harper," he mumbled, his voice barely audible as he tripped and struggled over almost every word.

"Likewise." Tilly took his hand. It felt weak and cool to the touch.

He nodded and shuffled back behind the girls as his brother stepped forward.

"Miss Harper! Herbert Shaw. Delighted to make your acquaintance."

Herbert Shaw didn't share his brother's awkwardness or hesitancy, and it didn't escape Tilly's notice that he was rather handsome.

"I'm very much looking forward to working with you all," she muttered, thrown by the feel of Herbert's hand in hers.

He smiled confidently, holding her gaze for a moment longer than was appropriate. She was quite captivated by his deep brown eyes, so dark they were almost black. The protracted and yet fleeting exchange between them caused a quickening of Tilly's heart. She hoped Herbert hadn't noticed the flush of color that she felt creeping up her neck and was relieved when he released her hand from his.

"I hear you've made quite the journey to be with us," he continued, "and by steam locomotive, I see." He gazed pointedly at Tilly's right cheek, offering a handkerchief from his pocket.

She winced, realizing that while she'd been busy poking around in other people's possessions upstairs, she'd forgotten to wipe away the smoke smudge she'd noticed earlier. She was annoyed with herself and even more annoyed with Herbert Shaw for pointing it out so unkindly.

"Thank you," she said, taking the handkerchief and putting it self-consciously to her cheek.

As he smiled—somewhat condescendingly—she decided that his lips were, perhaps, a little too large for the rest of his face.

"You're welcome. And you may keep that," he added, gesturing to the handkerchief before turning his attention back to the girls. He made a comment that Tilly couldn't quite hear, but which made them all giggle.

"The boys are showing quite an aptitude for the business side of our operation," Mr. Shaw added, giving Herbert and Edward each a hefty pat on the shoulder. "Which is just as well. With my dear wife insisting on producing daughters, I am forced to look to my nephews to take over the running of the charity when I am no longer able to see to things myself."

"I doubt anyone will be taking over for many years yet, Uncle," Herbert said as he turned back to Tilly. "My uncle has been blessed, Miss Harper, not only with the ability to save impoverished children from a life of destitution but also with the ability to continually deny the fact that he is not a well man."

Albert laughed. "And long may my abilities continue—on both counts!"

Herbert then excused himself, said he looked forward to seeing everyone at chapel, and left the room, his brother following quietly behind. Tilly was disappointed to notice that, of the two of them, it was Edward who gave her a brief backward glance as they departed.

"I hope you had a comfortable journey down to London," Albert continued after his nephews had left the room. "All the way from the glorious Lake country, I believe. Quite the distance traveled."

"Yes. It seems like a long while since I left this morning," Tilly replied. "But the train was very reliable and made good time."

"And Mrs. Pearce informs me that poor Mrs. Harris is incapacitated. I hope we haven't startled you too much by providing you with an immediate promotion to post of housemother! Although I'm sure Queenie can be relied on to help out, should the girls become too unruly."

Tilly nodded, wondering which of the girls Queenie was.

"Life here will be very different for you at first, Miss Harper," Albert continued, "but I'm quite sure that, with the support of the girls and the other members of our staff—and of course with the blessings of God—you will come to love London and family life with us, just as much as you do your own family and home."

His words weighed heavily on Tilly, as if they demanded an immediate acknowledgment of the truth: that she didn't love her home, or her family. Not anymore. Not since Esther had arrived to spoil everything with her perfect face and perfect manners and perfect white-blond hair.

Esther! Esther! Where are you? I can't see anything. Esther! Where are you?

The unfamiliar sound of the budgie chirping in its cage drew Tilly back from her thoughts. Albert Shaw stood in front of her, waiting for her to speak. All she could manage was an uninspiring "Yes. Thank you. I will."

"Very good. Now, I must go and prepare for my sermon." If Mr. Shaw had noticed Tilly's distraction, he chose not to draw attention to it. "I look forward to seeing you all at chapel, and"—he continued, lowering his voice and leaning down to be closer to the faces of the girls—"I have some *most* exciting news to share with you all, *most* exciting indeed!"

With that, he bid them farewell and walked out of the room, leaving the space of twenty men behind him.

Chapter 12

London
June 1876
Florrie

Da is dead. Dead and gone wherever the likes of men such as him go.

He didn't say nothing before he passed, just stared at me, though I don't think he was looking at me proper. It's awful to say, but I weren't even sad. I didn't cry—not one tear. I know he was my da, but I don't feel nothing for him like a daughter should. I don't miss him at all and that's the truth of it.

Auntie May's all me an' Rosie have now, and she's not well, neither. She talks to herself a lot and screams at me sometimes. "Get out of my house!" she shouts, jabbing her finger at me. "Get out, ye little tinker." Swears she's never seen me before and that

I'm after stealing things. Mrs. Quinn says it's syphilis. Syphilis can do that to a person, y'know—send them barmy. She'll end up in Bedlam with the rest of 'em, no doubt.

After Da was buried, I made Auntie promise not to send us to the workhouse. She says she won't, so long as we keep selling our flowers and earning some pennies, so I've been trying to sell as many bunches as I can.

At least we've the warmer days now and the start of summer. There's always something nicer about the summer. People are more friendly, and ye'll never get a lady or gen'leman refusing a posy on a fine summer's day, sure you won't. And them ginger-beer fountains that pop up all over the city—Lord! The best and fanciest I ever seen was in Petticoat Lane. Dark shining wood and gleaming brass on the pump handles, the glasses all shining in the sun, two handsome ponies to pull the machine—like something from Buckingham Palace it was. Oh, I wished I had a ha'penny to spare so as me and Rosie could have a taste of it.

All the sweetest flowers are in bloom this time of year, so we should have a decent trade, if the rains hold off. It's the violets and roses I like selling best. They look so pretty all tied up, and the violets with their leaves shaped like love hearts and the rose petals what feel so soft in my fingers I imagine I'm touching the ladies' velvet skirts. Smell good, too. It's nice to put them roses to your nose and forget about the stink of that busted drain at the Court. "God gave us roses in June so that we can have memories in December." That's what Mammy used to say. Loved the roses the best, so she did. Reckon that's why she named Little Sister after them. Dear little Rosie. Sweet little thing. All I have in the world, so she is. All I have in the world.

Chapter 13

Violet House, London
March 25, 1912

Now, girls, let's not forget our manners," Mrs. Pearce nagged. "I'm sure Miss Harper is keen to get to know you all. While Mrs. Harris is recuperating, Miss Harper will be in charge of the running of the house. Queenie, I suppose we should start with you, seeing as how you've been here the longest."

Moving around the room, Tilly was introduced to eleven residents of Violet House—Buttons had slunk off again while everyone else was fussing around the Mr. Shaws. Mrs. Pearce reeled off the names at an alarming rate: Doris, Lorraine, Betty, Hilda, Queenie, Alice, Edna, Bridget, Ivy, Maud, and Eileen. "And, of course, there's also Primrose. The budgie."

Tilly stared at the bewildering mass of faces. She guessed that the youngest girl, Hilda, was around sixteen, and the eldest, Queenie, around forty. She found herself relating each girl to her handicap, hoping that it would help her remember all the names. *Doris—blind. Lorraine—wheelchair. Betty—one arm. Hilda—crutch (one leg). Queenie—midget. Alice—wheelchair. Edna—blind. Bridget—wheelchair. Ivy—one hand. Maud—midget. Eileen—one hand.* Like a list of groceries, she mentally marked them all down.

Despite her reservations, everyone was perfectly polite. Only Queenie seemed to bristle a little at her arrival, paying less attention to her than the others and yet observing her far more intently than anyone else. Tilly tried to appear calm on the outside, even if her heart was pounding and her knees were shaking. She spoke briefly to each of them, telling them how much she'd admired the wonderful displays outside and how clever she thought them to be able to make such lifelike replicas. She was relieved to find that she wasn't too unsettled by the cumbersome wheelchairs and useless limbs that hung limply beneath cotton pinafores. Even the awkward stumps that some of the girls offered in place of a hand to shake didn't trouble her.

If anything, she felt a strange affinity with the girls. Although she had no physical limitations, she did know what it felt like to be pointed at and whispered about, to be the object of others' speculation and gossip. She knew how upsetting it was when people crossed the road so they didn't have to acknowledge you, unsure of what to say or how to act around you. For as long as she could remember, she'd felt like one of life's misfits. Maybe she had more in common with the girls of Violet House than they would ever realize.

When the introductions were complete, everyone readied themselves for the trip to chapel. Hats and coats were found, wheelchairs were navigated through the narrow door, crutches were matched to their rightful owners, and, finally, they were ready to leave.

Tilly helped one of the older girls, Alice, into her chair.

"Don't mind Mr. Herbert," Alice whispered. "He might be a handsome bugger, but there's a lot to be said for manners." Tilly smiled, grateful for the sentiment, although she couldn't stop thinking about Herbert's lingering gaze. "And as for the way he treats his brother . . ."

But Tilly didn't hear what Alice thought of the way Herbert treated his brother, because Mrs. Pearce arrived at her shoulder, chivying everyone along to make sure they wouldn't be late.

As they made the short trip to the chapel at the end of the street, Tilly noticed the easy harmony among the girls, each one compensating for another, lending an arm where there wasn't one, becoming the eyes for a girl who couldn't see. It triggered a rush of guilt within her as she thought about Esther.

"I hope you don't mind my asking, Mrs. Pearce," Tilly said as they walked, "but how did the girls become crippled? Was it factory accidents?"

"Some, yes. Those missing a limb will most probably have been involved in some manner of factory accident. Most of them suffer from diseases of the spine, bones, and joints—the result of tuberculosis. The blind, or partially sighted, are usually that way because of the scarlet fever. Others had rickets as young children. Of course, there are also tragic accidents. See Bridget over there? Her mother fainted and fell on top of her when she was just a baby. Paralyzed her from the waist down."

"That's terrible."

"It certainly is. Most of their stories are. How they manage to laugh and smile as much as they do is a wonder to me. Take Lorraine here, for example." She lowered her voice, indicating the girl whose wheelchair she was pushing. "Her father was out of work, so he moved the family to London from Bristol, hoping for a better life. Her sister went into service, and her brothers went to work in the factories. She was walking on unhealing fractured femurs since she was an infant. It was her Sunday School teacher who wrote to Mr. Shaw to ask if he could take her. Five operations on her legs—and here she is. Much improved, but she'll never walk or run as freely as you or I can."

Tilly walked on in silence, thinking about how difficult the girls' lives had been and how remarkable it was to see them all chatting and smiling, simply getting on with the business of living. She thought about Esther. She couldn't remember when she had last seen her smile.

"I know there are a lot of names to remember," Mrs. Pearce continued. "You might find it helpful to remember the girls by their appearance."

"Oh, yes. I started to do that already."

"Good. Take note of who wears spectacles perhaps, or the color of their hair, or their eyes, or the shapes of their faces. Physical features can help you remember who's who. It helped me anyway. Just a thought."

Tilly flushed scarlet with shame. She'd already labeled the girls to help her remember them, but not according to their appearance, only according to their afflictions. She said nothing to Mrs. Pearce and vowed to say a prayer for forgiveness in chapel.

AFTER THE LONG TRAIN JOURNEY, the erratic drive through London's streets, the drama of Buttons's appearance in her wardrobe, the discovery of the wooden box and notebook, and the fuss of all the introductions, Tilly was relieved to be able to sit quietly and absorb the serenity of the chapel hall.

She settled herself at one of the wooden benches alongside her new charges. Glancing around, she estimated there were at least three hundred people crammed inside the chapel to hear the evening sermon, including rows of girls from the Flower Homes. The black dresses and white aprons of the housemothers and assistant housemothers punctuated their group here and there. Tilly wondered if they had all felt as nervous when they'd first started their employment here.

As more people entered the chapel, Tilly recognized Albert Shaw's wife, Evelyn. She presumed that those who'd arrived with her must be her daughters, nieces, nephews, and grandchildren. She found herself scanning the faces for Herbert, despite the fact that she was still annoyed with him for embarrassing her earlier. Eventually, she spotted him sitting toward the front, his eyes fixed firmly on his uncle, his brother sitting quietly beside him with his head bowed.

Evelyn Shaw recognized Tilly as she caught her eye, mouthing a "Welcome" and offering a warm smile before settling herself beside Herbert at the front. Tilly was grateful to see a familiar face in all that was so new and strange. She was reminded of the letter Mrs. Shaw had sent to confirm the date and time of her interview. *We feel it is important for anyone taking a position at the Flower Homes to have the opportunity to meet with some of the girls and to see, firsthand, the work we do. It may not be desirable to all.* She also recalled how welcome Mrs. Shaw had made her feel when she'd arrived for the interview, a bundle of nerves and dread. It was hard to believe it was just a few months ago.

IT HAD BEEN a brief yet thorough meeting. The preacher's wife—a slim, elegant woman—had made an immediate impression on Tilly. Her silvered hair was tied into a neat bun at the nape of her neck, the soft shade suiting her pale complexion. Just a hint of blush colored the apples of her cheeks, and her blue eyes smiled as she talked. She wore fashionable London clothes, which Tilly had seen only in journals and newspapers. She smelled of rosewater and soap, and a small silver charm bracelet jangled at her wrist when she moved.

"The girls usually come to us at the age of fourteen or fifteen—no younger. It's at that age they would normally go into service, if they were able," Mrs. Shaw had explained. "We bring the inmates up from the orphanage when they reach the appropriate age and have finished their schooling. Often, we find a girl selling on the streets and bring her here directly. It takes two years or so for them to become really proficient in making the flowers, so by the age of sixteen or seventeen they are fully trained. Many of the girls move out of the homes then, to live with foster families, but many have continued to live and work with us as grown women. Even so, we still refer to them as our 'flower girls'—it's a name that's stuck, and of which they are all very proud.

"We prefer to use the term 'afflicted' rather than 'crippled.' You'll find them all extremely determined young women—fiercely independent. While they may have private thoughts and feelings about the physical challenges they face, they rarely complain or permit themselves any amount of self-pity. They've taught me much about the possibilities of the human spirit, Miss Harper. They've shown me that there is always an opportunity to display fortitude in the face of adversity, that it is not up to society to provide us with a sense of belonging and acceptance but rather up to each of us to allow ourselves to belong, to allow ourselves to be accepted."

Tilly had reflected on these words throughout that evening as dreams troubled her sleep on the long train journey back to

Grasmere. She'd thought of them often since and was reminded of them again now, as she returned Evelyn Shaw's smile.

AS THE SERMON BEGAN, Tilly picked up the small prayer book and focused on what was being said. She'd never been very good at reading her Bible, preferring to read the chapbooks and novels that the ladies at Wycke Hall sometimes passed on to her. It was her father who'd insisted they make the short trip to the local church every Sunday, to give thanks for their health and the food on their table. Tilly had prayed and said her amens only out of respect for her father.

She couldn't remember exactly when her faith had really faltered, but whatever small amount of belief she'd once held had been truly suffocated by the events that had torn her family apart. Yet, here, in this room full of strangers, Tilly found herself sitting up, listening attentively.

All eyes in the room were fixed on the orator at the front, all ears attuned to his words. Albert Shaw seemed different in his role as preacher—taller, if that were possible. And there was something else, something indefinable, otherworldly almost. Albert Shaw, as Tilly had quickly come to realize, was a man people took notice of. His words stirred strong emotions within her, a sense of compassion she hadn't felt for a while. She thought of Esther, of sea-green eyes staring blankly at her—through her—as if seeing a future she knew would never be hers.

At the end of Mr. Shaw's sermon, during which he talked passionately about the desperate plight of London's orphans and the need for the congregation to pray for those who suffered unthinkable hardships every day, he paused. There was much shuffling of feet and rustling of skirts, especially among the girls from the

Flower Homes, who knew that his much anticipated announcement would follow.

"With God's mercy, we have overcome many challenges and hardships—some physical, some emotional, some financial. But the work of our wonderful flower girls is not going unnoticed. We now supply many London homes and have even shipped our products as far afield as America and Australia. Indeed, the work of the girls is now so well known that we have been asked to produce something special—something very special indeed.

"Some of you will be aware that our Dowager Queen, Queen Alexandra, is—this June—to celebrate fifty years since her arrival in our country from her native Denmark. There is talk of a large processional drive through London to celebrate this occasion. The Queen has requested that the event be used in some way to help the sick and needy and to raise funds for our city's hospitals. It has therefore been decided that a 'flag day' will be held, to raise funds through the sale of artificial flowers on the streets of London. And we, here at the Flower Homes, have been selected to make the 'Alexandra Roses' that will be sold on the day!"

He had to stop talking then, as a great din of excited chatter erupted in the Chapel Hall. Tilly watched the girls, smiling at the excitement and joy on their faces. "The Queen," they kept repeating, turning to each other and to those who sat in front of or behind them. "We're to make flowers for the Queen!"

Mr. Shaw beamed like a proud father as he continued, projecting his voice to make himself heard again above the hubbub.

"It is wonderful and exciting news indeed! Never before has a charitable mission, such as ours, been asked to assist in this manner. That afflicted persons have been specifically asked to produce such important work is, most certainly, without precedent. But Queen Alexandra has heard of the excellent work being done by our girls, and of the wonderful flowers they make. She has therefore decided to honor our achievements by placing this order with us for her first Queen Alexandra Rose Day."

There was prolonged, spontaneous applause, which started somewhere in the middle of the congregation and moved outward in all directions, spreading like ripples across a lake. Tilly thought of her small church at home, so stiff and formal. There would be great consternation at such an outburst. She joined in, clapping enthusiastically, caught up in the buzz and excitement.

When the noise died down, one of the girls sitting alongside Tilly stood up. Tilly recognized her as a resident of Violet House.

Albert Shaw noticed her. "Yes, Eileen. Did you wish to say something?"

"Yes, Mr. Shaw. I was wondering how many roses we will be making for the Queen."

He laughed. "More than we've ever made before, Eileen. Thousands of them!" The girls gasped. "Yes, I know it sounds a lot," he continued, "but I am confident we can achieve what has been asked of us. Imagine how pretty the streets of London will look with everyone wearing a rose in their buttonhole!

"We have ample time to produce the blooms for the event, which will take place on the twenty-sixth day of June. We will be bringing some of the older girls from our orphanage in Clacton, to teach them how to make the flowers, and I will need every one of you to work to her best ability. With God's love and hard work, I know that we can do it. Let us all go back to our homes tonight with faith in our hearts and let us pray for those who do not have a home to return to on this evening, or any other."

Tilly joined in the final recitation of the Lord's Prayer before the congregation said their collective Amen.

With the sermon over and everyone's attention fixed firmly on the remarkable news about the Queen's roses, it took some time for Tilly and Mrs. Pearce to organize the girls and get them ready for the short trip back to Violet House.

While they gathered up their coats, hats, and crutches, Tilly found her eyes drifting toward the front of the chapel, where Mr. and Mrs. Shaw were chatting with people who were eager to leave some coins in the Flower Homes collection box or to pass on their regards in person. They really were an impressive couple. People gathered around, drawn to them and their infectious passion for their work and their faith.

As Tilly watched, she noticed Edward, standing quietly at their side, talking to nobody in particular. Her gaze then shifted to Herbert, who was chatting animatedly with a pretty young lady, who giggled and coquetted like a fool at every word he said. Tilly found herself quite unable to take her eyes off him, despite the fact that she had already decided she didn't care for him at all. Arrogant, that's what he was. As if he sensed her watching him, Herbert turned his eyes in Tilly's direction, staring directly at her over the young woman's shoulder. Tilly quickly looked away.

"Handsome bugger, isn't he?"

Jumping at the voice in her ear, she turned to see Mrs. Pearce standing behind her.

"Goodness! Mrs. Pearce. You gave me a fright!"

"Lost in daydreams of handsome young men, were you?" she teased.

Tilly blushed furiously, dipping her head. "Not at all. I was just admiring Mrs. Shaw. She's so elegant. Her clothes. And the way she dresses . . ."

Mrs. Pearce smiled knowingly. "She is indeed. Good-looking

family—all of them. 'Specially the nephew. Oh, don't worry. You're not the first to sneak a look at Herbert Shaw, and I'm sure you won't be the last!"

"Mrs. Pearce! Honestly, I was just admiring . . ."

But Mrs. Pearce had disappeared into the crowd, leaving Tilly with her flushed cheeks and her private thoughts.

She left as quickly as she could through the heavy wooden door, grateful for the light breeze that lapped at the edges of the evening air and cooled her cheeks. She resisted the urge to look back as she left the chapel. If she had, she might have noticed Edward Shaw watching her. If she had, she might have noticed the flash of anger in Edward's eyes as his brother entertained a group of women with a tale about a young girl from the north who'd arrived that afternoon, bringing half of the Carlisle-to-London express with her. If she'd looked back, she might have seen things a little differently.

Chapter 14

London
June 1876
Florrie

She's gone! Little Sister is gone—and I don't know where she can be!

Oh, I ain't never been so afraid nor so awful, awful sad in all my life. What shall I do? Oh, what shall I do?

Looked everywhere for her, I have, anywhere I can think she might be—the Garden, the Club Room, the doorways. Even looked down the sewers to check she weren't hidin' there, but she ain't nowhere to be found! She's not come home for three days and nights now. Just gone she is. Lost in the crowds. Oh, Rosie, where are you? What will I do?

We was on Westminster Bridge, see. We was selling the primroses and violets, and some of us was leanin' over the bridge to look at the boats leaving the pier. I was tellin' Rosie how nice they all looked when someone knocked my basket clean from my hands and kicked the crutch from under me. Fell to the ground like a sack of coal, so I did, and I felt her little hand slip from mine, and when I'd gathered myself together—oh—she was gone! Little Sister was gone!

"Rosie! Rosie!" I cried, over and over and over. "Dear God, Rosie Flynn, where are ye? Rosie!" I shouted and shouted her name as I grabbed at skirts and pulled at the ladies' fancy boots and shoes as they walked past me, my useless leg scraping against the ground; my crutch kicked out of reach. But they didn't stop to help, just carried on with their Sunday promenade, stamping all over my violets and primroses, what was strewn all around me. Too busy, that's what they were. Too busy to stop and help a crippled flower seller what had fallen and lost her little sister.

"Oh, please, Miss, please help me! Please, someone, help me find my sister! Rosie! Rosie!" I called and called and grabbed at them skirts but nobody stopped to help me.

The sellers were all callin' their wares—"Roses! Roses! Buy yer sweet red roses!"—and the crowds was all laughin' at the Silly Billy doing his clever tumbles, and nobody could hear me, or if they could, they didn't care nothin' for a wretched girl on the ground, sure they didn't.

I've walked the streets these last days and nights, desperate to hear Rosie's sweet little voice. Like the cock linnets, singing in their cages, that's what she sounds like. If only I could hear her sing. If only I could see that beautiful red hair. If only I could feel her little hand in mine.

Ain't slept once, so I ain't. Can't. Not till I find her, not till her hand is back in mine. She don't know her way around like I do, and, with her nearly blinded, she won't be able to find her way on her own, sure she won't. She needs to hold my hand, so as I can guide her—and I made a promise to Mammy that I'd look after her. I promised. I always told Rosie not to let go of my hand. "Don't you be lettin' go. You hold on good an' tight now." That's what I'd tell her. But it was me what let go of her, and now she's gone, and it's all my fault, all my fault.

Oh, please, can't somebody help me? Please! You have to help me find her. I beg you. I beg you. I beg you.

Chapter 15

Violet House, London
March 25, 1912

When everyone was back at Violet House, Tilly helped Mrs. Pearce to prepare a supper of bread and butter and hot milk. Tilly soon found her way around the small scullery, setting a saucepan of milk on the range, as Mrs. Pearce chattered on, telling her where she would find the firebox and the tea leaves and the mops and brushes for the morning. In the room down the passage, she could hear the girls talking about Queen Alexandra Rose Day. She smiled at their enthusiasm, despite her exhaustion.

After they'd all eaten their fill, the girls gradually peeled themselves away from the table in the cozy kitchen room, settling themselves to some sewing or a game of cards. Noticing that Tilly couldn't stop yawning, Mrs. Pearce insisted she go to bed.

"You look like death warmed up, girl. Go and get a good night's rest or you'll be fit for nothing tomorrow. I'll stay here tonight. I'll wake you at six and go through the daily routine with you then."

Tilly didn't argue, grateful for the opportunity to retire for the night. She filled a ewer with warm water from the kettle on the range, took a candle, and bid everyone a good night before trudging up the stairs. She sighed at the prospect of sweeping them the next morning.

Reaching her room, she washed her face and hands at the basin before changing into her nightdress. Despite the mild spring day, and the fire that burned in the small grate, there was a distinct chill to the room. She took a shawl from her trunk, wrapping it around her shoulders as she walked over to the writing table and opened the drawer. She was pleased to see that the wooden box was exactly where she'd left it. She was worried it might have disappeared—reclaimed by whoever owned it.

Lifting it out gently, she carried the box over to the bed, placing it to one side as she slipped under the covers, her toes flinching against the cold bed sheets. When she was settled, she lifted out the contents again, wondering whose possessions they were and how long they had been hidden away at the bottom of the wardrobe. She picked up the rag doll, noticing the word *Rosie* stitched neatly onto her little calico dress. She looked at the photograph, studied the faces. A collection of nameless girls stared back at her. One was holding a large spray of orchids. Placing everything else back into the box, Tilly pulled the candle closer, opened the notebook, and began to read.

June 24, 1880

It was Mr. Shaw what found me all those year ago.

I'd been sleeping nights on a bench at Westminster Bridge, thinking you might remember where we were that day and come back. But then I worried that you might have gone looking for me at Rosemary Court, or the markets, and what if you was waiting for me there and I was on Westminster Bridge? So I hobbled round the markets at daylight, wishing I could walk faster so as I could cover more ground and get back to the Court. I'd sit on that tatty old mattress and wait for you then, praying your little face would appear through the door.

But it never did.

It was a relief to see Mr. Shaw—Lord knows how he found me in that stinking room with Auntie May gone off someplace in her head, talking to the fairies. I wept and wept and told him all about you being lost, and he listened while I near choked on my tears and pleaded with him not to let them take me to the workhouse. I begged him to help me find you 'cause I promised Mammy I'd mind you.

He spoke some words to Auntie May, who wouldn't have known him if he was Jesus himself come to see her. Then he took me to the Club Room at Covent Garden. Do you remember it, Rosie? That hot cocoa and the good and kind ladies? We was happy in that room, wasn't we?

I was wrapped in blankets and given hot soup. A lady with kind eyes sat with me, not speaking, but rubbing the back of my hand so gently. It was like she was rubbing hope into my skin. "Don't give up," she told me. "You'll find her." But even with all the kindness and the soup and the hot June day and the blanket, I couldn't stop the shivering. The lady said it was the shock what was doing it to me.

Mr. Shaw sat with me for a long time, talking in that soft, buttery voice of his about our Good Lord and how He would be watching over you, keeping you safe. I remember looking into his eyes—bright blue, like cornflowers. I could only imagine the skies in Heaven could be as clear and true.

After I'd calmed down and had a belly full of soup, he took me in a carriage to a place called Violet House, in Sekforde Street. It's near Farringdon Market, where we sometimes sold our cresses. Do you remember how cold the water was at the pump, our hands and feet frozen blue as we washed those muddy bunches? I can still smell them, all peppery and musty.

Mr. Shaw told me all about the crippled girls who live in the houses on Sekforde Street. They used to sell their flowers on the streets like we did, but they make silk flowers now, in the chapel workrooms. He said I might make those flowers, too, when I was older.

I was washed and given clean clothes and boots and a bonnet. I don't remember much about my time in that house, but I know everybody was kind to me. They looked at me with sad eyes. They didn't need no words to say that they knew something of my suffering.

The girls in the house told me of the orphanage at the seaside, where I'd be taken good care of. Mr. Shaw said he'd spoken with Auntie May again and got some sort of sense from her. She'd agreed it best for me to go to the orphanage. "Everything will be all right, Flora," he said. "You've suffered enough now. You're not to worry anymore." He had a way of talking and looking at you that made it difficult not to believe him.

I didn't want to leave London, Rosie; didn't want to leave you, but Mr. Shaw insisted it was for the best. "You must try to be strong and keep well so that you'll be able to look after Rosie when she's found," he said. "I promise I'll keep searching. I'll look for her down every alleyway, on every doorstep, and behind every market barrow."

I had a liking for Mr. Shaw. Trusted him and his kind blue eyes, so even though I felt sick to my stomach at the thought of traveling so far away from you, I took him at his word.

After a few more days in Violet House, where I slept a little better and ate as much as my poor, puffed-up stomach could manage, we set out for my new home at the Flower Village in Clacton, on the south coast.

I took the only three things I had: a black button from Da's old coat (which I kept to remind me that, however bad things got, I was sure not to get a beating when I got home), a wooden peg what you used to play with as a doll, and the lace handkerchief given to me by Mammy when she was dying. I had a mind to leave that handkerchief in London, seeing as it had brought no good luck at all, but something made me take it. I hoped you had yours in your pocket, Rosie, where you always kept it. I hoped that it would keep you safe, while I could not.

I pray each night that you'll find these words one day, that you'll be able to forgive me for losing you. More than anything, I hope we can find each other, Rosie, because while you cannot be found, a part of me will always be lost.

Her eyes growing heavy, Tilly placed the notebook back into the box before returning it to the drawer in the writing table. She slipped back under the bed covers and blew out the candle. The room grew colder, the scent of violets drifting and swirling around her as she fell into a restless sleep, thoughts of the two sisters tumbling through her mind. She imagined a cool breath against her cheek, someone watching her, words whispered softly into her ear. *Find her. Find her. Please help me find my sister.* And then her dreams came . . .

The shrill blast of the whistle as the locomotive approached, the driver sending a warning to anyone who might be crossing the tracks or working on the line. The fog, thick and swirling, making it difficult to see any distance at all.

The nervous whinnies of the ponies.

"Listen, Esther! A train! Let's try and outrun it. Come on. I dare you."

Another blast of the whistle as the engine thundered past. One hand holding her hat on her head, the other pulling at the reins, urging her pony onward, faster and faster, chasing the carriages alongside the fence, her excited screams drowned out by the thunderous clatter of the locomotive until it raced ahead, around the bed and out of sight.

A momentary silence. Her heart pounding. Her breaths coming quickly with the thrill of the chase.

Hooves thundering past her. Esther's cries, fading into the distance, smothered by the fog, absorbed by the mountains.

A faint, sickening crack. A scream. Then, silence.

"Esther! Esther! Where are you? I can't see anything."

Thick, swirling fog, covering everything in a silent, misty shroud.

Digging her heels into the pony, guiding it first one way, then another. No landmark to work from; no landscape. Her senses blurred with panic and the blinding fog.

"Esther! Where are you?" Fear in her voice, tears streaming down her cheeks.

"Look after your sister," her mother had said. "And don't go too near the railway tracks."

"Yes, Mother."

"I dare you," she'd said to Esther. "I dare you."

Urging the pony onward in every direction. Where was she? Perfect little Esther, out there in the fog. Perfect little Esther, lost and alone.

She must get help.

Turning toward home, but which way? Which way? Galloping, galloping, galloping—each fall of the hooves on the soft, peaty ground taking her farther and farther away from her injured sister, farther and farther away from home, from help, from the life she might have known.

Tilly woke to the scent of violets and a pillow moistened with tears she couldn't remember crying.

Shivering, she stepped from the bed, her feet flinching against the cold of the oilcloth floor. Wrapping her shawl around her shoulders, she tiptoed across the room and looked out at the still-dark street. A cat prowled along the rooftops. A gas lamp guttered in the distance, the greenish light casting an eerie glow over the cobbles.

Lighting a candle, she settled herself at the writing table. She thought about the fragile pressed flowers, the heartbreaking entries in Flora's notebook, the faded photograph, the peculiar little trinkets—she was fascinated by them. They spoke to her of loss and remorse and of what it is to be a sister. Something about these simple things from a time past whispered to Tilly of her future.

Taking up her pastels and opening her sketchbook, she began to draw the blooms in the vase on the windowsill, her hands moving briskly over the page. She stopped every now and again, certain that she was being watched, that she'd heard a movement behind her. The hairs at the back of her neck prickled like nettle stings. Telling herself not to be silly, she worked on, until the first, pale light of dawn fell across her page. Closing the sketchbook she readied herself for her day.

She washed quickly, gasping as she splashed the cold water onto her face. Dressing in her undergarments and plain black dress, she tied the coarse apron around her waist before putting on the white crochet cap that had been provided for her. She tucked her unruly curls under the cap, laced her boots, and crept downstairs, flinching as each step creaked and cracked like ice beneath her feet.

Gathering everything she needed from the scullery, she set to work so that by the time Mrs. Pearce went to wake her at six, Tilly had already lit the fire in the range and the copper, set the kettle on to warm, cleaned the grates and fenders in the kitchen and parlor, swept all the downstairs floors, including the passage, and sifted the cinders from the previous day. The rooms were much smaller than she'd been used to at Wycke Hall, and she'd worked quickly and efficiently.

Mrs. Pearce was almost speechless, standing by the fireplace in the kitchen, sniffing the air. "And you sprinkled tea leaves on the floor to lay the dust before you swept?"

"Yes. Found the tin in the scullery."

"And you blacked the grate?"

"Yes, I found the blacking in the firebox."

"And you've shaken out the hearth rug?"

"Yes, and I laid a coarse cloth while I cleaned the fireplace," Tilly said, anticipating the next question.

Mrs. Pearce was clearly pleased with Tilly's work. "Well then. I suppose we should have a cup of tea before we lay the breakfast table. Then there'll be the chamber pots to empty. I must say, I'm very impressed, Miss Harper. Very impressed indeed."

Tilly smiled and followed Mrs. Pearce along the passage into the scullery. "To new beginnings, Mrs. Ingram," she whispered into the cool morning air. "To new beginnings."

Chapter 16

Sekforde Street, London
April 2, 1912

Tilly's father had always said that people cannot truly be happy in a place until they let it inside them. "Only when you know somewhere as well as the back of your own hand—when it gets under your skin and becomes a part of you—only then can you know you belong. The tourists who visit our beautiful lakes for a short holiday and spend the whole stay complaining about how it rains all the time will never truly understand what a joy it is to live here; they will never *belong*."

It was just over a week since Tilly's arrival in London. A week's worth of dust had been swept from the stairs of Violet House. A week's worth of bed linen had been stripped and washed. A week's worth of London grime had been scrubbed off her boots and the windows of the terraced house she now called home. She remembered her father's words as she stood now, in the middle of the new factory room, wondering when she would feel that she truly belonged here among the flower girls.

She looked around the vast space, her eyes drawn to the neat rows of workbenches where dozens of girls sat in deep concentration, surrounded by mountains of small pink roses. It was a scene of quiet industry and she felt a sense of deep pride spreading within her as she watched the girls at work. She was part of this now. In her own small way, she was contributing to this commendable operation. Apart from anything else, she was part of an organization that was working for the Queen. What would her mother have to say about that?

"It's very impressive, Mrs. Shaw," she remarked, her head tilted back, to take in the full scale of the building, which she was seeing for the first time. She stared at the high ceiling, at the electric light fittings suspended above the girls' heads and the long row of windows that ran along one wall, letting in great swaths of natural light. "It's so much brighter than I'd imagined. Not at all stuffy or cramped, like other factories I've heard about."

"I insisted that the rooms be bright and well ventilated," Mrs. Shaw explained. There was an irrepressible enthusiasm to her voice. "All standard factory acts and regulations are in force, just the same as in an ordinary trading factory. We even have a lift to help the girls move between the two floors—and that's something of a luxury, let me tell you!"

A low murmur of chatter from the girls was interspersed with ripples of laughter and the occasional scraping of a chair leg as someone stood up. They worked companionably, sharing their tools and taking pleasure in each other's handiwork as box after box was filled with the pink Alexandra roses. It seemed to Tilly not like a factory at all.

Most of the girls were so immersed in their work—their foreheads furrowed in deep frowns of intense concentration—that they barely noticed Tilly and Mrs. Shaw as they walked between the rows of workbenches. Some of the younger girls were more easily distracted, nudging each other and whispering before looking up and smiling at the two ladies as they walked past. Like her husband, Mrs. Shaw greeted them all by name.

Everywhere Tilly looked, the tables were piled high with the tools of the flower girls' trade: scissors, pins, spools of different-colored threads, pots of glue, wire, paintbrushes in all shapes and sizes, and endless boxes of paint. All the tables were adorned with flowers at various stages of completion: leaves without stems, stems without petals, petals without color. Here and there, partially constructed blooms lay flat, awaiting the next phase of their creation, while in other places completed flowers stood proudly in tall stands, thirty or more sprays arranged in each, running the length of the tables. Tilly also noticed that each girl kept a small book beside her.

"What are the books for?" she asked.

"Ah, those are for the girls to record the number of flowers they make so they can receive their due payment at the end of the week," Mrs. Shaw explained. "We make no secret of the fact that the girls are paid a fair wage for a hard day's work. The youngest girls, who are still learning and work more slowly, can make six or seven shillings a week when we're at our busiest. The older ones can make anything between thirteen and twenty-five shillings a week."

One of the girls in front of them stood up and rang a bell, producing a cheer and an appreciative round of applause from the others—except Buttons, whom Tilly happened to be standing near at the time and whom she overheard mumbling "show-off" under her breath.

"That signals one hundred!" Mrs. Shaw said, noticing Tilly's confusion. "Well done, Ada," she added, giving the girl a gentle pat on the shoulder. It was a gesture the girl clearly appreciated, beaming as she settled back to her work.

"As you can see, there are many, many stages to go through before a flower is complete," Mrs. Shaw noted as they stood to watch for a while. "First the petals and leaves are cut on the hydraulic press upstairs. We use different materials for different flowers—muslins, sateens, silks, velvets, and plush. Then there is a process of coloring and shading the material, then drying. At that point, the petals are given to the girls to form into shapes using goffers—the hot irons. The roses, and flowers with lots of petals, have to be formed carefully from the center outward. Then the hand painting takes place before the leaves and blossoms are attached individually onto stems with fine silk or with a paste. Finally, the mounters mount the flowers into sprays, or for dress trimming, headdresses, bonnets, hats—whatever is required."

With the recent announcement about Queen Alexandra Rose Day, most of the girls were working on little pink roses. Tilly watched as delicate pink petals were painstakingly glued and pinned together to form the flower heads, boxes and boxes of completed cherry-blossom-pink roses sitting on the workbenches. Some girls were working on larger roses for displays and others were working on regular orders, painting the dyed petals with the distinctive markings that would transform them into freesias, roses, and chrysanthemums. The colors of all the different flowers dotted around the room made for a wonderful sight, every color of the rainbow captured.

"I had no idea there were so many stages involved in making the flowers," Tilly said. "Or that it is such detailed work. It only makes me admire the girls all the more for seeing it."

Mrs. Shaw's eyes shone with pride.

"We did wonder, at first, whether the girls would be able to manage," she said. "As you can see, it's very intricate work. Even those of us fortunate enough to have the full use of our limbs and eyes would find it challenging. We shouldn't have doubted them for a moment. Actually, it was one of your Violet House girls, Queenie Lyons, who was among the first to come to the training homes. Lily Brennan was another. She went to live with a family member in the north, if I remember correctly. Lovely girl.

"Queenie and Lily took to the flower making like a duck to water—in fact, all the girls did. It's a curious thing, but they seem to have a peculiar aptitude for the work. Perhaps it comes from a life surrounded by flowers. Perhaps it's just sheer determination. I only wish we could let more people see the work they do," she continued, "then perhaps we would get more financial support and dear Albert wouldn't be forever worrying about funding."

She sighed before turning to Tilly. "But I mustn't trouble you with talk of such matters, Miss Harper. When we've shown our beautiful flowers to the whole of London on Queen Alexandra Rose Day, I hope we'll never need to worry about such things again! Now, come along, I'll show you the hydraulic press on the second floor. It might sound terribly dull, but it really is a fascinating piece of equipment."

As they walked toward the lift, Tilly stopped to speak to some of the girls from Violet House, admiring their work. She already felt a connection to them and missed them during the daytime, uncomfortable in the silence their absence left as she went about her work in the house.

"The girls are very fond of you," Mrs. Shaw remarked. "You've a certain way of interacting with them which they seem to respond to very well. It isn't always the case. We've had housemothers leave before their first week is out. Quite unable to settle. You seem to be fitting in very well indeed."

"It's very kind of you to say so," Tilly replied, delighted with the compliment and wishing her mother could be there to hear Mrs. Shaw speak of her in such flattering terms. "You've all made me feel very welcome."

"All the same, it must be difficult for you being so far from home. You must plan a weekend visit before the end of the summer. All the housemothers get a weekend off, once a quarter."

Tilly was caught off guard. "Oh, gosh. I don't think I could stand that long train journey again for a good while yet! My family certainly won't expect to see me this side of Christmas."

The truth of the matter was that she had no intention of returning home. Not at Christmas. Perhaps never.

"Well, let me know if you change your mind. It's important for us all to be among our own families from time to time—even if they do leave us reaching for the smelling salts when we leave!"

Tilly laughed to cover her discomfort.

After stepping into the lift, the two women were jolted up to the second floor, where Tilly was surprised to see Edward Shaw hard at work on a large hydraulic press. She and Mrs. Shaw stood for a moment, watching as he worked methodically, pushing levers with his feet to turn the huge metal drum onto which the stiff sateen cloth had been placed. From this, the shape of the rose petals was stamped out. The noise was deafening, but he was concentrating so hard he didn't seem bothered by it. He didn't even notice that he was being watched.

"These are for the Alexandra roses," Mrs. Shaw explained, leaning toward Tilly and raising her voice to be heard above the hiss and thump of the machine. "It's hard, repetitive work, but Edward never complains. He's a wonderful asset to us. He was involved in much of the planning and organization of the new factory. He shows a great aptitude for the work, and the girls like him very much. Of course, everyone presumes it will be Herbert who will take over the operation in the future, but it seems that Edward has my husband's favor."

"Really? But he seems so quiet." Tilly was amazed. She'd barely heard Edward speak and certainly couldn't imagine him running the Flower Homes and the orphanage with anything like the charisma of his uncle or his brother.

Mrs. Shaw laughed. "It's often the quiet ones who are the most intriguing, though. Don't you think?"

Tilly watched Edward as he worked. He wasn't handsome like his brother—not at all—but now that she considered him, there was, perhaps, something about him. His was a much softer face than Herbert's, his chin tapering into a narrow jaw. Strawberry-blond hair fell into his eyes as he concentrated on the press.

He looked up suddenly, catching Tilly's eye. She jumped, embarrassed to have been caught staring at him. He nodded at her, brushed the hair from his eyes, and continued with his work. She was relieved when Mrs. Shaw led her to a balcony area from which they could look down onto the floor below.

"Do you think they'll get the roses finished in time?" Tilly asked as they watched the girls hard at work.

"Oh, yes! Absolutely! We could make ten times the amount if the Queen required it! Roses for the Queen. Who would ever have believed it, Matilda?"

Mrs. Shaw stood for a moment, surveying the scene in front of her as if hardly able to believe that they had come so far. Tilly knew that for the Shaw family, and for everyone who was involved with the work, this wasn't just about establishing an efficient operation to make artificial flowers, or about a workforce that had been hired to produce work and receive payment in return. It went much deeper than that. This was a family—a religion all its own.

"You must all be so proud of what you've achieved, Mrs. Shaw."

"We are. Very proud indeed. There's a lot still to be done, though, and we cannot allow ourselves to rest on our laurels." She sighed. "I just wish Albert's health were better."

Tilly hesitated. "Yes, Herbert mentioned that Mr. Shaw is unwell. He seems so . . . vibrant."

"The stubborn old goat hides it very well, but he doesn't have the strength he once had. The filthy London air chokes his lungs. It really isn't good for him here. He'd love to spend more time in Clacton. That's where his heart lies—among the fields and the cliffs and the rolling sea. It captures your imagination, that place, holds you in its heart."

"It sounds delightful. I'd love to see it someday."

"Well, then you must go! We have the summer fete days to look forward to—oh, they're really such fun. The children do a wonderful job with their games and dancing, and the spectacle of the fire drill is something to see! Yes, yes, you must come. I'll mention it to Albert. You can accompany the girls from Violet House when they go. We'd be glad of your assistance."

Tilly was thrilled at the prospect. "That would be wonderful. Thank you. I'll look forward to it."

As the girls stopped for a tea break, Tilly excused herself.

"I really must be getting back to the house. The girls won't thank me if their supper isn't ready when they get home! Thank you for showing me around, Mrs. Shaw. It's been truly fascinating."

As she left, Tilly noticed a sign above the factory door: GIVE THE WORLD YOUR BEST, AND THE BEST WILL COME BACK TO YOU. She impressed the words onto her mind and resolved to try her best to abide by them.

TILLY ENJOYED HER EVENINGS at Violet House, with the exception of Mondays—washdays—when her hands were too raw and her body too exhausted to enjoy anything other than a soap-scented sleep. On other evenings, with the bulk of the day's work behind her and the coal scuttle filled, ready for lighting the range the next morning, she looked forward to sitting in the cozy warmth of the kitchen with a reading book or her sketchbook. She didn't even mind so much when a little sewing or mending was required, enjoying the chance to chat with the girls while she worked. She had quickly become familiar with their individual personalities and knew whom she could engage in conversation and whom she should leave in peace and quiet.

But her thoughts often drifted back to the drawer of the writing table in her bedroom and the wooden box hidden there. Although Tilly enjoyed the noise and companionship of the girls in Violet House, she also looked forward to the peace and solitude of her room, where she could read more of the notebook, without interruption. Flora Flynn's haunting words had stirred something in Tilly's imagination. There was something about Flora's desperate search for Rosie that resonated with her so that she felt somehow connected to the two sisters, as if they followed her, watched her, as she moved about the house with her buckets and brooms.

After her tour of the factory and a busy day of cleaning, she was relieved when the last of the girls went to bed. Locking and bolting the doors—as she did every night—she turned off the gas and climbed the stairs to her room, kicking off her shoes and rubbing her aching feet. In many ways, the work here was less demanding than the work at Wycke Hall—Violet House was far smaller for a start—but the added responsibility of the twelve girls weighed heavily on Tilly's shoulders. She didn't want to let anyone down; didn't wish to be found wanting in any aspect of her duties, of which she was constantly reminded by a large board that hung on the scullery wall (thanks to Mrs. Pearce, she suspected) setting out the routines of the house.

Standing up, she stretched her back and walked over to the window, resting her forehead against the cold glass. The street below was quiet and empty, lit by the gas lamps, which cast intermittent pools of light on to the cobbles. The view was becoming as familiar to Tilly as the moon rising above the jagged outline of the mountains back home. Still, she didn't think she would ever get used to not seeing the stars, obliterated as they were by the foggy London skies.

Settling herself at the writing table, she took up her pastels and sketchbook, working on a study of one of the dried violet flowers she had found in the pages of the notebook. Her body ached and her eyes soon grew heavy with the urge to sleep, but she moved her fingers deftly across the page, rubbing her fingers over the soft pastel, blending colors to add definition, shape, and form. This was Tilly's way of relaxing, of unwinding after a busy day. As she worked, the familiar scent of violets floated around her. She felt the atmosphere in the room change, as if the air had been disturbed, as if someone had brushed past her.

"Is that you, Flora?" she whispered. "Are you here?"

She sat perfectly still. Nothing. The scent of violets disappeared as quickly as it had arrived.

Eventually, unable to keep her eyes open any longer, she closed the sketchbook, climbed into bed, blew out the candle, and curled up under the counterpane. Then she waited for sleep and the dreams that she knew would soon follow.

Her father walking down the shale path in his soldier's uniform. A smile on his face, a twinkle in his eyes. He had come home!

She ran, shrieking with delight, ran from the cool of the scullery into the warmth of the sun to the warm embrace of the father she loved so much.

He stopped and sank to his knees as he saw her, his arms outstretched in welcome.

"Daddy! Daddy! You're home! You came home!"

Running, tripping, falling into his outstretched arms, throwing her hands around him, nuzzling into the sun-darkened skin on his neck, his standard-issue felt cap falling from his head.

"Yes, Tilly! Yes, love! I came home. I came back for you, my love . . ."

Chapter 17

Clacton

August 1876

Florrie

I could never in my life have imagined the sea was so big. Matron says it reaches all the way to France and if ye go the other way y'd be in America. I still don't like to dip more than my toe in the water, but I like the sound of them great waves. We sometimes leave the dormitory windows open at night—'specially when it's too warm to sleep—and there's never a better sound to soothe you to sleep than all them waves coming and going, sure there's not.

I'm in Buttercup House, which is closest to the cliff tops, and when the wind blows from the south, ye can taste the salt in the air. It's as different here from Rosemary Court as I think Heaven must be from Hell. Sometimes, the sky seems so big and bright I get an ache in my eyes with staring at it. I like to watch the clouds, too. Ain't never seen clouds like these ones, all fluffed up like a great bunch of cresses. And the grassy bits outside the houses, what the gardener calls "lawns," are as green as sea kale. They look so nice Lily Brennan says you could eat that grass, 'specially in the early morning, when the dew sits on it, sparkling like diamonds. There's gardens at the back, too, which is kept so nice looking, and the roses . . . the roses smell sweeter here than any I ever smelled before. If I shut my eyes and stand among them, I can pretend I'm back in the markets at Covent Garden. And I can pretend that Little Sister is standing beside me. Just for a moment, I can pretend that when I open my eyes there she'll be, smiling up at me.

But ye can't keep your eyes closed forever, can ye?

I like the meadow, too, just over the fence. There's poppies and cornflowers growing there, what we pick for Mother, who minds us in our house—and for Matron, who minds us all.

Some of the girls think she's fierce with her words, but I tell them they don't know what fierce is and that they should have met my da, then they'd think different. I think Matron's nice. She's as skinny as a bean and taller than anyone I ever seen, 'cept Mr. Shaw. Like a great stick, so she is, striding about the place. She keeps us all proper and right, though, saying we must be keeping ourselves clean and tidy in the black dresses and white aprons we all wear, and ye wouldn't want to be messin' when she gives you a job to do. Best to just get on and do it, that's what Lily Brennan says. Sleeps in the bed next to mine, Lily does.

Mother here at Buttercup is awful kind to us. I like it best when she reads to us at bedtime and I like when she tucks the bed covers so tight around me that I can hardly move my arms and legs and the blankets tickle my nose.

I help with the littlest ones when I can. There's eight little ones in our house, and there's the new home now, built 'specially for the little babies whose mammies and daddies don't be wanting them, or are after dying. I told Matron I was good with the babies after minding Little Sister, so she lets me help whenever I can, but only when I've my chores done.

I still wake a lot in the night, screaming Rosie's name. Matron says I'm after suffering from a shock and that it'll take a good long while to recover. I tell her I don't think I'll ever recover; that I don't want to, 'cause that would mean I'd stopped looking, and I'll never stop looking for Rosie, sure I won't.

Mr. Shaw tells me they're still searching for her up in London, but nobody's seen a sight of her in all this time, and I worry so much, so I do, and I'm after imagining something terrible has happened to her, so that I frighten myself. I don't know what's worse: to think that she's dying somewhere all alone or to think that someone's taken her and she's with people she don't know, scared out of her wits.

"Better to be lost than to be found dead." That's what Lily says. Maybe she's right. Lily has nobody in the world left living—or lost. All she has is her rag dolly she made, who she calls Mother. Takes that dolly everywhere with her, she does. Said I should make a dolly with the rags and call her Rosie, and that way I'll always have Little Sister with me.

I made that rag dolly.

But it's not the same.

It'll never be the same. Not till I find her.

Part Two

Pink Carnation (*Dianthus caryophyllus*)

I will never forget you.

London
September 23, 1880

Dear Mr. Shaw,

I must write, once again, to express my delight after attending the recent fete day at the Flower Village in Clacton. This is my fourth fete day and they never fail to impress. What wonderful displays the girls put on for us this year—the dancing, the singing, and the gymnastics were most impressive, not to mention the spectacular fire-drill display, which more than lived up to its billing. The smaller children were quite delightful, sitting at tea with their teddy bears and all so well-mannered and dressed so smartly in their cotton bonnets and white pinafores. They are a testament to the hard work and devotion of all the staff, who work tirelessly to make the children's lives so vastly improved.

The setting of the Flower Village is quite something. Such wonderful views over the meadows at the front of the homes and the sea just visible on the horizon. I must admit to finding the sea breeze quite invigorating—I am sure the children's health improves from the moment they take their first breath of that wonderful, clear air. My daughter attended with me this year. She was so taken with the place that she wept when it was time to leave.

Mr. Hutton provided a very informative tour of the

gardens. He has cultivated such beautiful displays, and the scent of the rose garden is unlike anything I have encountered before. He informed me that it is the sea air that creates such a wonderfully fragrant bloom.

I was also delighted to meet your president, Lord Shaftesbury. He speaks very highly of your mission and all the work you are doing on behalf of those who depend so entirely on the generosity and dedication of people such as yourself. It must be quite the boost to have the support of such an esteemed gentleman.

I hope to visit another display of the girls' work in the near future and will look forward to attending the fete day next summer. In the meantime, I hope the enclosed sum of one hundred pounds will be of help in making the necessary improvements to the Flower Homes, here in London and at the orphanage.

Yours in admiration,
"Daisy"

Chapter 18

London
June 1876

Rosie Flynn had known many bad things in her short life—cold, hunger, exhaustion, sadness, death, and cruelty—but she had never known terror like that which she felt as she ran to get away from the man who had grabbed her.

She ran and ran, darting wildly through the crowds, bumping into people, stumbling forward, then backward, a blur of grainy shadows and strange shapes all that she could make out. She had no idea what she was running toward. All she knew was that she had to get away from him. From the bad man.

She couldn't think. Couldn't breathe, almost choked by the panicked breaths that caught in her throat as she struggled to get away, struggled to understand what had happened.

She wanted to scream, to cry out, "Florrie! Florrie! Where are ye?" But she didn't, knowing that by shouting she'd only draw unwelcome attention to herself. So she stayed silent and kept running through the terrifying, shadowy world she inhabited.

Without her sister's hands and eyes to guide her, she quickly became lost and bewildered. A strange sound came from deep within her—a whine, like that of a frightened animal. She'd felt Florrie fall, felt her hand wrenched from her own. She'd heard the clatter of Florrie's crutch hitting the road, the mutterings of people inconvenienced by having to step over a child on the ground. She'd stood perfectly still, as Florrie had always told her to if ever they became separated. *"Stay right where ye are, and I'll find ye. It's best not to go wandering off."*

But within seconds of Florrie falling, strong hands had grabbed Rosie around her waist, whisking her away, her legs dangling in the air, a hand covering her mouth so that she couldn't scream. She'd smelled the sweet, sticky scent of lemonade on the rough, manly hands smothering her mouth and knew immediately who had taken her. *"Don't look at 'im, Rosie. Don't look in his eyes."*

Struggling and thrashing with what little strength she had in her frail body, she'd wriggled enough to make the man adjust his grip as he tried to get a tighter hold of her. That was when she'd grabbed a piece of his stinking, hairy flesh between her teeth, biting down as hard as she could on the back of his hand. Howling in pain, he'd lost his grip and dropped her. Scrambling to her feet, she'd started to run.

The usually familiar noises of a busy Sunday became strangely amplified in her terror, startling her at every twist and turn: hawkers shouting their wares—strawberries, hokey-pokey, gingerbread, knives to grind; the laughter and cheer of the crowd gathered around the Silly Billy entertainer; the lilting notes of the organ grinders and the chatter of their monkeys; beggars pleading with passersby; horses' hooves thudding past; dogs barking and snapping at her heels; children bawling in their perambulators. Twice, she was knocked to her knees by the thick legs of burly men who didn't notice a frightened child darting among them, running for her life. What would they care even if they did?

At first, the carriage appeared as just another indefinable shape, looming out of the passing blur of light and shade. Then she heard the familiar snort of a horse to her right, the bright jangling of metal from fastenings on reins and bridles and bits. Reaching out her hands, she stumbled toward the noise, detecting the distinctive, musty smell of horsehair and the rich scent of leather. Her hands fell first onto the wheel, her fingers tracing the spokes and the solid rim. Then she felt a step and the cool of a metal handle, which she used to pull herself up. The muffled noises from the street, the cool black shade, the smell of wood, and the gentle snorting of the horse told her she was inside a carriage.

Squeezing into the small gap beneath the seat—dust and cobwebs clinging to her hot, clammy skin—she curled into a tiny, tiny ball. She hardly dared to breathe, stifling her sobs of terror and panic as best she could to allow her to listen.

Had he followed her? Had he seen her climb inside?

"Rosie! Rosie!" She was sure she heard a cry from somewhere amid the noise outside. Was it Florrie, calling for her, or was it just a seller crying out her wares? "Roses! Roses! Buy yer lovely, sweet red roses. Two blooms for a penny." She didn't know, couldn't be sure. Too terrified to move, too terrified to shout back, she said nothing, rocking gently, retreating into herself as she felt a spider crawl slowly across her hand.

Everything became blank. She lay in a mute, paralyzed ball of fear, allowing nothing to penetrate the tiny space she occupied under the carriage seat. She was barely conscious of breathing.

Sometime later—she wasn't sure how long—a voice close by broke through the silence, a woman's voice, pleasant and gentle, wishing someone farewell. Then laughter, and the carriage door opening, allowing a welcome rush of light and air to fill the small space inside.

From her hiding place, Rosie listened to the rustle of skirts as someone sat down on the seat above her. She caught the sweet scent of damask rose. Perfume, not real flowers.

A woman's voice. "Back to the house, Thompson."

"Yes, m'lady. Right you are."

Rosie kept perfectly still as she listened to the two strange voices.

"And I do hope the river won't smell so terrible at Richmond. It really is quite something in this heat."

The man's voice again, shouting for the horse to move off. The crack of a whip, the creaking of wood and leather as the carriage rolled into motion.

A sense of panic. She was moving away, away from Florrie! "*Stay right where ye are, and I'll find ye. It's best not to go wandering off,*" her sister had said.

Should she jump out?

She listened to the steady rhythm of the hooves on the road beneath her, pressing herself farther against the back of the carriage. She was terrified of being discovered and thrown back onto the streets and just as terrified of the distance growing between herself and Florrie with each turn of the wheels.

Covering her ears, Rosie blocked out the thunderous rumble of the wheels as they rattled against the uneven roads. As the carriage rushed along, a breeze blew through a crack in the floor, tickling her bare toes. She drew her knees farther up into her body, shaking with fear, waiting for whatever was going to happen next. She didn't know where Richmond was, but she guessed that it was far away. How would Florrie ever find her there?

They traveled for some time, the noise of London's streets fading into the distance, the nauseating stench of the Thames dissipating with every rotation of the wheels. Occasionally, the woman readjusted her position, the fabric of her skirts rustling and the seat creaking as she did. Sometimes, she seemed to be rummaging in her purse. Each movement sent a fresh burst of rose perfume drifting through the carriage. It was the only familiar thing to Rosic in all that was so startlingly strange. She held that scent within her, locking it away in her memory as if it were the most precious of treasures; a trail of bread crumbs that would, one day, lead her back to Florrie.

Eventually, the carriage came to a halt amid the sounds of hooves and wheels crunching over gravel. A flurry of dust was disturbed from among the dry stones and blown through the crack in the carriage floor. The dust crept into Rosie's throat. The carriage door opened. The lady was standing up, stepping out. The dust tickled Rosie's nose. There was no way she could stop the violent sneeze.

The lady screamed.

Rosie screamed.

Footsteps came rushing to see what the commotion was. She felt hands pulling at her.

The driver's voice. "Well, I never did!"

She was discovered.

"It's a child, m'lady," he said, grabbing Rosie by the arms and dragging her from beneath the seat.

"A *child*?"

"A filthy little urchin. Well, I never did!"

Rosie was dragged out of the darkness of the carriage into the sunlight. She felt the change in temperature against her face. She kicked her legs against the driver's until he dropped her to the ground. Her feet crunched against the gravel. She crouched low, bundling herself into a tight, tight ball. "Florrie, Florrie, Florrie," she whispered. Where was Florrie? Where was *she*?

"But, but . . . what on *earth* is a *child* doing hiding in *my* carriage?" The lady's voice was high-pitched. Anxious. Breathy.

"I don't know, m'lady. But we'll soon find out." Rosie felt the man lean down toward her, blocking out the pale light. "Trying to steal from the lady's purse, was ya?" He dug a bony finger into Rosie's arm, his face so close to hers that she could feel his breath, warm and laced with tobacco.

She had no words. All she could do was cry fresh tears of fear and desperation, shaking her bowed head as she gazed blankly at the blurred edges of her feet against the stones. She sank to her knees, confused and terrified.

She heard the crunching of footsteps then, moving quickly, as another woman's voice joined them.

"M'lady! M'lady! Are you quite all right? I heard a scream and came as quickly as I could."

"Yes, Mrs. Jeffers. Thank you. I'm quite well. Just a little alarmed to find this child hiding in the carriage."

"A *child*!"

"Yes—and all the way from Westminster Bridge, no less. Just imagine what might have occurred had it been a young boy of ill intent!"

"My goodness! It doesn't bear thinking about. Would you look at the state of her?" Rosie caught the smell of bread and sweat as the woman—Mrs. Jeffers—walked a full circle around her. "She's filthy. *Filthy!* Street seller by the look of her. See, flowers in her hands. The cheek of it! Planning to rob you, most likely. Is anything missing, m'lady?"

"No. Nothing. I've checked. Everything is as it should be."

"She probably crawled in thinking it would be a good place to get some sleep. Lazy, good-for-nothing little so-and-so." Mrs. Jeffers tutted. "Well, she can crawl straight back in again and Thompson can take her back to where she came from. Carrying all sorts of infectious disease, I shouldn't wonder, and we certainly don't want any more of that."

Rosie sobbed as she listened to the two women and the driver speculate about what had happened and what might have happened and what they should do with her now.

"Yes, Mrs. Jeffers. Thank you." The lady from the carriage seemed a little calmer now, her voice measured and controlled. "Just look at her," she said. Rosie felt as though she were a pig being inspected at market, as footsteps moved around her. "She's nothing but skin and bone. And what unusual hair color—red—although it's difficult to tell under all that soot and dirt. Do you think she's Irish? What's your name, little girl?"

The words were spoken softly, almost whispered as the lady bent down. Rosie was enveloped by a strong burst of the lady's perfume and knew she stood close by.

"Don't get too close, m'lady," Mrs. Jeffers cautioned. "She might bite, and Lord knows what might be leaping around in that matted hair of hers. Goodness me, I never in all my days thought I would see such a thing, and right here on the carriage circle of Nightingale House, of all places!"

Rosie stayed on her knees. Silent.

"Why were you hiding in my carriage, child? Were you hiding from someone?"

Rosie listened to the lady's voice. It was different from other voices she'd heard. Musical, almost. She wanted to answer, wanted to blurt it all out, but she couldn't, limited both by her vocabulary and by her fear of what they would do with her. She glanced up, turning her head in the direction of the lady's voice, wishing she had the words to explain. Instead, she just nodded her head slowly up and down.

"You were hiding? Running away from someone?"

Again, she nodded.

For a while, this curious conversation continued on the sweeping gravel driveway in front of the grand Richmond Hill home. Had her eyes served her well, Rosie might have gasped at the sight of the carefully tended lawns, the pruned box hedges, the gleaming windows of the three floors of the house, the impressive Doric columns, and the ornamental pond, which shimmered in the sunlight and afforded the occasional glimpse of golden carp.

The lady continued to ask questions, and Rosie continued to answer with only a nod or a shake of her head. In this way, Rosie was able to let her know that she had been hiding from a man; that she had no parents, just a sister, whom she had lost; and that she was now frightened and all alone. But, above all else, she wanted to impress upon the woman that she was terrified of the workhouse.

"Not workhouse, Miss. Please, not workhouse."

Rosie was almost as surprised as the lady to hear these words fall from her mouth. If she could have seen the lady's face, she would have detected a softening in her eyes, a look of pity, the stirring of the memory of a child much missed. But she saw only shifting shadows and blurred shapes and a dark terror creeping toward her.

"She can't be more than four or five years old, poor little wretch. Look how she trembles, and still clutching her violets," the lady remarked. "*Violettes* we call them in France. Really, have you ever seen anything so pitiful?"

Mrs. Jeffers sighed. She didn't reply.

"Perhaps we should give her something to eat, and a warm drink. What do you think, Mrs. Jeffers?"

"Are you sure it's wise to encourage the child, m'lady? Surely, it's best to send her back with Thompson in the carriage and forget all about it. She'll only be telling the other urchins what a fine trick she played, getting a ride in a lady's carriage and going home with a full belly."

"Quite probably that *would* be the right thing to do, but then the right thing to do isn't always the *best* thing to do, is it?"

The question hung in the air above Rosie's head, circling and swirling in a light breeze that had sprung up. Conscious of the time that had already passed since she'd become separated from Florrie, she wasn't sure whether she wanted to be sent back to the city in the carriage to face whatever was waiting for her there, or whether it would be best to stay here and be given something to eat and drink. Her empty belly ached at the thought.

"It's only a little food after all. What harm can come of it?" Rosie listened intently to the hushed conversation between the two women. "Perhaps you could run a bath, Mrs. Jeffers, and give her a good wash," the lady suggested. "Ingram will be back from the factory soon, and I suspect it would be better for him to see the child clean and presentable, rather than in her current state."

"And what shall I dress her in?"

"She can use Delphine's clothes."

Rosie heard Mrs. Jeffers gasp. "*Delphine's* clothes? But . . . are you quite sure, m'lady?"

"Yes, Mrs. Jeffers. I am quite sure. Now, let's not dawdle. Thompson, you may take the brougham around the back and stable the horses for the time being."

"Yes, m'lady. Very well, m'lady."

Rosie heard the fading sound of carriage wheels on gravel as a soft hand clasped hers. How she wished it was Florrie's hand. She felt the absence of that familiar hand in hers as keenly as if she were holding a hot coal.

Too weak to protest, she allowed herself to be led toward a looming gray mass, which she presumed to be the house. For a moment she thought she might run after the carriage, driven by a desperate fear of never seeing her sister again. But the ache in her belly was too great and the thought of food too tempting to resist.

"What's your name, child?" Mrs. Jeffers asked as they walked.

Rosie remained silent.

"It's no use," the lady said, tightening her grip on Rosie's hand. "She's clearly too terrified to say anything, other than to plead for me not to take her to the workhouse. Poor little thing. It's unimaginable to think that a child so young and frail has been wandering the streets all on her own. And her eyes look infected. Perhaps Dr. Asquith will be able to prescribe a tincture or some drops. I'll have to ask him to come and take a look at her."

She stooped down so that her face was level with Rosie's. "My name is Marguerite. Marguerite Ingram. I'm going to take care of you."

Chapter 19

Nightingale House, London
June 1876

Thomas Ingram listened patiently to his wife's detailed explanation of everything that had happened that afternoon, trying to comprehend how, and why, there was a young girl eating bread and butter at the maids' table.

"And we know nothing about the child's circumstances?" he asked, his brow furrowed with concentration.

"No, darling. Nothing. She'll barely speak, she's so terrified. All I've been able to establish is that she's a flower seller—an orphan—who was hiding from someone. She indicates she has a sister, although I'm not sure whether they still lived together."

They were standing just outside the kitchen, in the maids' corridor, speaking quietly so that the child—and the maids—wouldn't hear them. They certainly didn't want to give the household staff any more reason to discuss their private matters. There'd been enough gossip about the Ingram family over the last few years; they were both acutely aware of that.

"Do we even know her name?"

"She won't say. I think she's worried I'll report her to the police if she gives me any personal details. It seems so unkind to simply refer to her as 'the child' or 'the girl,' as Mrs. Jeffers insists on doing. Honestly, darling, that woman can be so unfeeling sometimes. The child was carrying a bunch of violets when Thompson found her under the seat." Marguerite hesitated, pulling at the silver locket at her neck. "I thought Violette would be a pleasant name for her. For the time being."

Thomas Ingram was barely listening, his eyes fixed firmly on the child.

"Yes, dear. And you say she was already in the carriage when you got in? You're quite sure of that?"

"She must have been, darling, because we didn't stop between Westminster Bridge and Richmond Hill. Lord knows how long she'd been hiding there. She could have been there for days, Thomas, riding back and forth, cowering in the dust. Poor little thing. Oh, if you'd seen her . . ."

Marguerite stopped talking as Thomas placed his hand gently on her shoulder. She looked into his kind amber eyes. Studying his face properly for the first time that evening, she noticed that he looked unusually tired; the dark shadows under his eyes betrayed his many early mornings and late evenings. His ambitious plans to expand his sugar business, and to take on more factories outside London, were clearly taking their toll. She felt a pang of guilt at having added to his burden by bringing the child into the house. She knew he was trying his best to understand, to be patient with her. For Marguerite, this was not simply about a child seeking refuge in her carriage. This was about reignited memories of a daughter lost and a woman deprived of the chance to be a mother.

"Should *I* try to talk to her?" Thomas glanced toward the child, who seemed oblivious to everything other than the food on her plate. "She might respond more positively to the firm approach of a man."

"I'm not sure that's the best idea. She seemed particularly terrified when Thompson spoke to her earlier. Any male voice sends her into a panic. When Roberts spoke to her to ask if she'd like to go and see the horses, she cowered in a corner for twenty minutes and was still trembling like a lamb when Cook finally managed to coax her out with the promise of hot chocolate. I suspect she wasn't treated too well by her father. Probably gave her a beating if she didn't sell her flowers." She sighed and placed her hand over the locket at her neck.

"And we know nothing about her? Nothing at all?" Thomas's exasperation was now evident by the strain in his voice. He ran his hands through his thick black hair before leaning against the doorway. He resembled a puppet devoid of its strings.

"The only slight clue to her identity might be her hair color, and her accent. I'm sure I can detect a hint of Irish, although she doesn't speak very clearly at all."

"Irish!" Thomas laughed. "Well, that narrows it down then. We should have her back home before sunset!"

Marguerite flinched. "There's no need to be facetious, Thomas, and, please, lower your voice." She glanced anxiously at the maids.

"But there's half of Ireland living on London's streets, Marguerite. She may as well be invisible for all the help *that* gives us in trying to find out who she is. And you're certain she had nothing with her. Nothing hidden away in a pocket. A photograph? Anything that might help someone identify her—or help us to identify where she lives?"

"No. Nothing. Just the violets she was holding. Mrs. Jeffers insisted we burn her clothes to destroy any infectious disease they might be carrying." Marguerite took hold of her husband's hand, turning her eyes up to him. She tilted her head to one side, accentuating her slender neck. "Was that the right thing to do, darling?"

He nodded. "Yes. It was very wise of Mrs. Jeffers. This house has known enough disease."

They stood in silence, gazing at the child.

Marguerite wasn't sure why she chose not to mention the lace handkerchief Mrs. Jeffers had discovered in the pocket of the girl's dress. She wasn't even sure why, instead of permitting Mrs. Jeffers to burn the handkerchief along with the child's clothes, she'd quietly asked her lady's maid to boil it, dry it, and return it to her. Marguerite Ingram believed in destiny. She believed in the notion of trinkets bringing luck to a person. It hadn't escaped her notice that the handkerchief had a cluster of shamrocks neatly stitched into one corner. Perhaps the child and the shamrocks had been sent to her for a reason. Perhaps they would bring some good fortune to Nightingale House.

In any event, the handkerchief was now ironed, neatly folded, wrapped in tissue paper, and placed, for safekeeping, beneath Marguerite's prayer book in a drawer of her dressing table. It would remain there until the child was ready to return to the city. While Mrs. Jeffers had scrubbed the child clean of years of London filth, Marguerite had quietly taken the bunch of violets the child had carried and placed them in the flower press she kept in her wardrobe, along with all the other specimens she'd collected that year from her walks in Petersham Meadows: poppies, delphiniums, foxgloves, and pansies. She would keep the violets. They would be her secret, a hidden reminder of the little orphan girl who had come into her life, however fleetingly.

Thomas looked at his wife and back toward the child. He knew what Marguerite must be thinking as she watched the young girl, sitting at the table, eating bread and butter. It was such a simple, everyday scene, and yet he knew the emotions it would be stirring within her. She was remembering Delphine. He could guess the emotional leaps Marguerite was making; that she was already wondering what the child would look like at the age of eight, twelve, twenty. She would be running away with the future as she was always apt to do, until their future—their daughter—had been taken from them so cruelly. It was hard to believe that three summers had already passed since that dreadful day.

"I'm really not sure about this, Marguerite," he cautioned, pulling at the edge of his mustache, as he always did when he was troubled. "Perhaps it would be best if we inform the authorities this evening. Someone may be looking for her—a distant relative, or this sister she has told you about. She may also be lying through her teeth, of course—let's not forget *that* possibility. She may have a mother and father waiting for her at home. It isn't entirely impossible that she was sent here as part of a ruse, to see what we have that may be worth stealing. She'll run away as soon as she gets chance, report back to them, and the silver will be taken before the week is out. You mark my words."

Marguerite wrapped her arms around her husband's broad shoulders, resting her head against his chest.

"Oh, darling, please don't inform the police. Not yet. And who could possibly be looking for her?" Pulling back, she looked directly at him, tears forming in her eyes. "Look at her. She clearly has no one. If you'd seen how wretched she looked a few hours ago, you would know that for sure. I doubt whether anyone has looked for her—or cared for her—for most of her life. Oh, the poor little thing, Thomas. I didn't know what else to do. She was so terrified and filthy and wretched. How could I send her back? How could I sleep at night not knowing what had become of her? If she could just stay for a day or two, until her nerves are settled, she might start talking and then we can find out where she lives and Thompson can take her back. At least we'll know we did our best and didn't just abandon her to the streets like an unwanted dog."

Thomas listened patiently. He understood what was behind his wife's insistence on keeping the child. While he might have a reputation as a ruthless businessman, even *he* didn't have the heart to deprive his wife of the chance to be a mother again, if only for a day or two.

Against his better judgment, he gave his consent that the girl could stay until the end of the week. "At which point," he said, "if it transpires that she has nowhere she wishes to be returned to, or hasn't run away, I will make alternative arrangements for her. I'd also suggest that we keep the matter to ourselves for the time being—none of your gossiping lady-friends must know about this. I'll speak to Mrs. Jeffers about how we handle the staff, and I'll arrange for Dr. Asquith to come to the house first thing in the morning to give the child a thorough inspection. I also think it best, presuming she does start to speak, if she refers to us only as Mr. and Mrs. Ingram. We don't want her becoming overly familiar."

Marguerite threw her arms around her husband, planting soft, grateful kisses on his cheek. He was a good, good man. "Oh, thank you, darling. Thank you so much. This is the right thing to do. I just know it is."

He let out a deep sigh. "I do hope so, Marguerite. I do hope so."

DR. ASQUITH ARRIVED just after breakfast the following morning. He was greeted by frayed tempers and dark circles under the housekeeper's eyes. Everyone had been kept awake all night by the child's sporadic screams and the comings and goings of the maids to fetch things at Marguerite's request.

Despite the chaos, and the child's refusal to comply with anything he asked her to do, he continued with his examination until he seemed satisfied. Violette, as it had been decided she would be known, was then taken away by Mrs. Jeffers while the doctor addressed Marguerite with his conclusions.

"Clearly, she needs to put on a significant amount of weight, but I am sure Mrs. Jeffers and Cook's team in the kitchen will soon see to that. There is also quite a significant case of head lice to attend to, I'm afraid."

"Oh, dear." Marguerite sat upright in her chair, trying to appear unfazed by this announcement. She suspected that Thomas would have asked the doctor to take a note of her own health and general demeanor, as well as the child's. "And what should we do to address that, Doctor?"

"I would recommend that the girl's hair be cut short for a start and the head washed very thoroughly with soap and water. You might then apply a little benzene to the scalp—perhaps under a cap to confine the vapor. That should destroy all the live creatures. A pomade scented with oil of lavender should then be used to prevent their reappearance."

"Yes, Doctor. Of course. Although it does seem a shame to cut her lovely hair."

"Hair grows back, Mrs. Ingram." He stared at her from over his half-moon spectacles. "It is not for the sake of vanity that we should see the child suffer unnecessarily."

"No, Doctor. Of course not. We will see to it immediately. And at least there aren't any significant or life-threatening problems. I must admit, I was rather anxious that she would be carrying a chronic disease."

"Well, there is, of course, the other matter—which is rather more serious."

"The other matter?"

"Her eyesight, Mrs. Ingram. Surely you noticed her eyes?"

"Well, yes. I noticed they were a little clouded. I assumed she'd picked up an infection."

The doctor put down his notepad, crossed one leg over the other, and leaned forward. "I'm afraid it is rather more serious than that. The child appears to be completely blind in one eye and only has partial sight in the other. She may be able to make out light and dark and occasional shapes, but she is technically blind, Mrs. Ingram. This little girl will need more care than most."

Marguerite hesitated. "Blind? My goodness. No wonder she's so terrified. She can't even see us?"

"No. She will not be able to see any distinguishing features or colors. She was most probably born with the affliction, or perhaps suffered from the scarlet fever when she was an infant. It's very common among the poor. I'm afraid there is nothing we can do medically, unless she undergoes surgery, and I suspect that would be far too traumatic for her at the moment—not to mention terribly expensive. Given the circumstances under which she has arrived here, I would suggest that such drastic measures not be considered. Not for the time being, at least. Emotional and practical support is what she needs in the immediate future."

Marguerite nodded. Her heart was racing. She tried to appear unflustered. "Yes. Quite. I understand."

The doctor stood up, placing his instruments methodically into his black medical bag.

"And how are you feeling yourself, Mrs. Ingram, if you don't mind my asking?"

"I am quite well, thank you, Doctor. Of course, the summer months do wonders for a person's joie de vivre."

Even to her own ear, the words sounded forced.

"Well, I'm very glad to hear it. You will let me know if you require any more medication to help you sleep." She nodded. He paused and cleared his throat. "I hope you don't think it impertinent of me to say, Mrs. Ingram, but I do think it would be wise to give some thought to where the child might be placed—and sooner, rather than later. It could be confusing for her to remain here for any length of time. A foundling hospital may be appropriate, or I can recommend a number of very reputable children's homes, some of which specialize in the care of blind children."

Marguerite smiled. "Of course, Doctor. It has all been such a shock, as I'm sure you can imagine. It isn't every day one discovers a wretched child in one's carriage! Ingram and I felt it was our duty to give the child food and shelter for the night. Now that I have a clearer idea of the difficulties she faces, we will, of course, look into a suitable blind school, or somewhere that will be able to help her with her needs."

Standing up, she rang the bell to summon Mrs. Jeffers.

"Thank you again for calling at such short notice, Doctor. It was very good of you."

"My pleasure, Mrs. Ingram," he replied, shaking her hand.

"And again, do let me know if I can help at all with a suitable placement for the child."

"Her name is Violette. And thank you. Ah, Mrs. Jeffers. Dr. Asquith was just leaving. Would you be so kind as to see him out?"

LEFT ON HER OWN, Marguerite sat on the chaise for a while, absorbing the doctor's diagnosis. To discover that Violette was blind . . . She swallowed and tried to relax her hands, closing her eyes, imagining a life of darkness. It frightened her. Her head ached, her stomach flipped and tumbled. Perhaps Thomas and the doctor were right. The child needed to be taken into care. She wasn't their problem, after all. How on earth could they cope with a blind child?

You must show strength, Marguerite. Courage.

Standing up, she walked to the fireplace. She felt cold, despite the warm weather, and wished the fire had been lit. Lifting her face, she studied her reflection in the large, ornate mirror that hung above the fireplace. A wedding gift from Thomas's parents, along with Nightingale House. She'd never really cared for it—the mirror, finding it lacking in elegance.

Smoothing her chestnut hair, she ran her fingertips over her face. She looked pale and tired from the restless night. The once dazzling blue of her eyes was diluted, her cheeks pinched and deprived of the attractive flush of pink that used to reside there. Where was the confident, beautiful woman she used to be? Where was the vibrant young girl who'd arrived from Paris and fallen in love with the son of her father's lawyer? Thomas Ingram was a promising businessman dealing in sugar—white gold—and the most handsome man she'd ever met. What had happened to that ambitious, hopeful girl he'd married?

As she turned her face away from the mirror, her gaze settled on a photograph that stood on a table by the window. Her daughter. She walked over and picked it up, brushing her fingers over the glass. Beautiful, beautiful Delphine. Her wide, blue eyes, full of love and innocence. Her endless smile. The peach-soft feel of her skin. The scent of lavender that lingered on her hands from warm days spent in the gardens.

The room fell silent, just the gentle ticking of the carriage clock marking the passing of time. Marguerite stood still, lost in her grief, her arms heavy with the ache of her child's absence.

Her thoughts were disturbed by a nightingale that had settled on a branch of the oak tree outside the open window and struck up its familiar song. Clutching Delphine's photograph to her chest, Marguerite walked to the window, pushing it open farther. She closed her eyes, listening to the melodic song, remembering how Delphine loved to hear the nightingales sing, how she'd been enchanted by the fairy story Marguerite read to her about the nightingale whose beautiful song had restored the dying emperor's health.

As the little bird hopped and flitted among the dappled branches of the tree, Marguerite felt a flicker of hope stir deep within her. Discovering that Violette was blind did not lessen her affection for the child, it only increased it. There was no doubt in her mind that Violette had been sent to her to care for as her own daughter, and as the bird continued its joyous song, Marguerite's heart soared with hope. She knew that she could never send Violette away. The little girl was part of her life now—her very own nightingale—and she would treasure her as if she were made of a thousand precious jewels.

Chapter 20

Nightingale House, London
July 1876

Three days after Violette's arrival, Marguerite spoke to Thomas again, suggesting that the child remain with them a little longer, until she recovered her strength and returned to full health. Distracted by his business dealings, and happy to see his wife showing an interest in something again, he'd given his consent. As the days lapsed into weeks, still Violette resided at Nightingale House. With each passing day, Marguerite grew more and more determined to ensure it remained that way.

And yet, Violette's presence troubled her. She worried about what—or who—might be waiting for them when they returned from a long walk around the gardens. She wondered about the child's mother, whether she'd loved her little girl before she died or whether she'd died in childbirth, never knowing the joy of motherhood.

"Somebody may still come for her, Marguerite—a relative, or someone who knows of her," Thomas cautioned. "We are only keeping watch over her until we can find a suitable foster home. She must still call us Mrs. Ingram and Mr. Ingram—not Mother and Father. You do understand the importance of that?"

"Yes, dear. I know. I understand."

She could not have felt more constant dread if she'd stolen the crown jewels themselves. But whatever her worries and fears, and however much Thomas cautioned her against becoming too attached to the child, as she watched the roses in the gardens bloom, so she observed the child blossoming under her care. By the time the full heat of summer had settled over London, Marguerite found the prospect of living without Violette far worse than the consequences of living with her.

Whenever she felt suffocated by her worries, or by the memories of Delphine that lingered and whispered to her among the lofty rooms of Nightingale House, she took Violette for a stroll along the Terrace Walk. She held the child's hand tightly, describing the magnificent view to her as they took a rest on one of the wooden benches, looking out across Petersham Meadows toward the city.

"The finest view in all of London, they say. A patchwork of fields, in a dozen shades of green, spreading for miles to the river Thames. It's so far away, but I can see it clearly, glistening in the sun like one of the silver ribbons on your bonnet. It weaves toward the City, twisting and turning like an unpinned curl. And above the river and the fields I can see church spires and the Houses of Parliament and the clock tower. I can even see the dome of St. Paul's. And the deer are watching us, Violette. We must sit very still, my darling. If we make any sudden movement they'll hear us and run into the cover of the trees. Oh, it's so beautiful. How I wish you could see it with your own eyes."

As she sat with Violette, looking toward the impossibly huge metropolis, Marguerite wondered who was out there looking for the child. Did they feel the pain of separation as she had when Delphine lost her battle for life? Was there someone, at that very moment, looking across the London skyline toward the green fields of the suburbs, wondering where their dear little sister had gone, wondering whether she still lived? If she looked long enough, would their eyes meet? Would she see them staring back at her?

Tearing her eyes away from the view, she gathered Violette up into her arms, and began to make her way back to the house.

"Violette," she whispered as she held the child close. "My dear little Violette. Now you are loved and safe, loved and safe, loved and safe," rocking her, until she fell into a peaceful sleep.

IN THE FEW WEEKS since her arrival, Rosie had soon settled into the ordered routines of Nightingale House under Mrs. Jeffers's watchful eye. She explored the house, discovering favorite places where she liked to play with the toys Mrs. Ingram had given her. Sometimes she sat in a patch of light and warmth beside the windows, enjoying the feel of the sunlight on her face. Sometimes she preferred the cool, dark recesses of the library, or the space behind the ferns in the parlor, where she would play with the dollhouse, carefully moving the furnishings from one room to another, feeling the shape of each piece, walking her fingers along tiny corridors and rooms before deciding where to place them.

There was so much to occupy her, and so much food to eat, that occasionally she forgot that she hadn't always lived in this grand, comfortable house where people cooked meals for her, washed her clothes, and gave her toys to play with. Her life as a flower seller seemed like a distant dream, it was so different to the world she now inhabited. And when she forgot about the stench of Rosemary Court and the noise of the markets and the ache she used to always feel in her belly, she allowed herself to enjoy many things about her new life: the sensation of Mrs. Ingram's breath as she blew softly onto her cheeks, knowing how it made her chuckle; the gentle rhythm of the songs she sang to wake her each morning and the lullabies that sent her to sleep at night. She liked the way Mrs. Ingram smelled of roses and lavender and she liked to rub her fingers over the soft folds of silk on Mrs. Ingram's dresses and on the ribbons that tied her bonnets.

She especially liked the way everyone called her Violette. It was the prettiest name she'd ever heard, and when Mrs. Ingram addressed her it was as if she were singing. *Vee-o-lette. Vee-o-lette.* She copied the sound, repeating it to herself over and over again when she was alone. "Violette," she whispered into her ever-present gloom. "Violette, Violette," until the name Rosie became a distant echo, hidden away in some dark corner of her memory.

She also loved to spend time in the kitchen, while Cook prepared the meals. She liked to sit on a stool by the open window, breathing in the perfume of the jasmine and honeysuckle bushes that crept along the wall outside. She savored the delicious cooking smells and listened to the tantalizing crackle and spit of meat roasting and of spoons beating against bowls as Cook whipped up a delicious dessert. She felt the familiar gnaw of hunger in her belly, knowing that it would soon be full. She sensed that she was well cared for, that she was loved and safe, and yet she often felt a sensation of falling, of being pulled by an invisible thread that connected her to another life, to another person, far away.

"Is Florrie coming soon?" she would ask, as she walked with Mrs. Ingram among the flower beds in the gardens of Nightingale House. The smells took her back to the flower markets: lavender, mint, basil, hydrangea, hyacinth, lilac, jasmine, lily of the valley, rose. She imagined herself with Florrie, waiting to buy their stock for the day.

"Oh, now, don't you worry your pretty little head about that, darling. Mr. Ingram will be looking for her. London is a very large city. It might take a little time. Don't you worry, Violette. You must concentrate on getting healthy and strong. Your sister wouldn't want to find you unwell, would she?"

She often wondered if Florrie would be cross with her when Mr. and Mrs. Ingram took her back. Would she scold her for putting her through so much worry, or would she be excited to hear of her adventures at this big house and of all the toys and dresses she'd been given?

As the weeks progressed, she began to talk to Florrie, whispering to her when she thought Mrs. Ingram wasn't listening. She began to imagine that Florrie was always beside her; she had pretend conversations with her as she played or walked in the gardens. "Listen, Florrie, can you hear the nightingale? Sweet, ain't he?" Or "Can you smell 'em, Florrie? The roses. Buy a bunch, kind lady. Tuppence a bloom," and on and on.

Sometimes, Mrs. Ingram would overhear her secret whisperings. "Stop it, Violette!" she would snap. "Stop talking like that. It's silly."

And then she would close up like an oyster, refusing to speak to anyone, and the echo of Mrs. Ingram's weeping would drift through the vast rooms and corridors until it seemed that the whole of Nightingale House was weeping with her.

Chapter 21

Nightingale House, London
August 1876

As the searing heat intensified over London, so did the emotions within Nightingale House. Violette still asked regularly about Florrie, still whispered to her when she thought nobody was listening.

Marguerite couldn't bear it.

"It will pass," Thomas reassured her when she fell into his arms, weeping. "She'll soon forget about her previous life and her sister. She'll have to—there's no hope of finding the girl. Even if we did go searching among the slums of London's Irish—which I'm quite sure neither of us wishes to do—it would be like looking for a needle in a haystack. If you would let me make an appointment with one of the matrons of the children's homes, this could all be over. She would be well cared for and she wouldn't be our responsibility—or our problem—anymore."

But his words only upset Marguerite further. She didn't want this to "all be over." She didn't view Violette as a "problem." She was happy for her to be their responsibility. It could all be so perfect—if only the constant feeling of dread would leave her, if only Violette would stop whispering that name.

It nagged and it nagged at her, until she could ignore it no longer. For all that she longed to forget about Violette's past, she found herself unable to deny the feelings of guilt. The fact that she might be preventing the child from finding the sister she clearly adored and missed terribly preyed on Marguerite's mind. Although she was afraid of losing the child, she knew that she had to try to find Florrie.

She couldn't say anything of her plans to Thomas, knowing that he would absolutely forbid her to go anywhere near the slums of the East End, so she settled on speaking about it to her lady's maid—her longest-serving maid, whom she trusted—as soon as possible.

VIOLETTE LOOKED FORWARD to the evenings, when the nightingale sang in the oak tree outside her window. She'd never heard a sound so beautiful. She remembered hearing the cock linnets sing in their cages at market, but even those she'd hardly been able to hear above the cries of the sellers.

"Since you like the nightingale so much, I must read you a story about it," Mrs. Ingram said. "It was written by a Danish man, Hans Christian Andersen. I used to read it to Delphi—Well, let's just start, shall we?"

It quickly became a favorite. Violette asked for it every night, and Mrs. Ingram would fetch the big book, sit beside her on her bed, wrap her arms around her, and read.

She loved to hear about the Chinese emperor and his beautiful city and the palace and gardens. She loved to listen to the words of the story as Mrs. Ingram read. "*The nightingale sang so sweetly that the tears came into the emperor's eyes, and then rolled down his cheeks, as her song became still more touching and went to everyone's heart.*"

Violette pitied the nightingale, kept within a cage for her beauty, let out to fly only when tethered by a silken thread. She didn't think it was fair that the emperor kept the bird just for his own pleasure. She especially loved the descriptions of the artificial nightingale, covered all over with diamonds, rubies, and sapphires, and she worried when it broke and was only allowed to sing once a year. She wept when the emperor fell ill, and she clapped her hands with joy when the real nightingale returned to sing to him and made him better.

"*I will sit on a bough outside your window, in the evening, and sing to you,*" Mrs. Ingram read, "*so that you may be happy, and have thoughts full of joy. I will sing to you of those who are happy, and those who suffer; of the good and the evil, who are hidden around you.*"

And now, when Violette heard the nightingale sing outside her bedroom window, she imagined it was the emperor of China's nightingale, sent to tell her of what it had seen and of stories from far away. "*Florrie,*" she heard it sing. "*Dear Florrie. She looks for you. She waits for you.*"

It was while dressing for dinner that Marguerite gathered the courage to speak to Wallis—her lady's maid—about her plan to look for Violette's sister.

Several of Thomas's business colleagues were to be their guests that evening, to discuss the possible purchase of a number of sugar factories in the north of England. It was tedious business, and Marguerite was not looking forward to it. She fussed and fidgeted in her seat at the dressing table, while Wallis tugged and teased her hair, shaping it into a fashionable knot at the crown and pinning it tightly into place until her head ached.

"Wallis, I need to ask for your help with something. It's a highly sensitive matter and cannot be known by anybody else. Not even Mr. Ingram. Do you understand?"

Wallis stopped her pinning and looked at Marguerite, surprised by the seriousness of her mistress's tone.

"Yes, m'lady. Of course. You have my word. Are you unwell?"

"No, it is nothing to do with my health. Oh, Wallis. It is the most desperate secret. I must have you swear on the Bible that you won't tell anyone of it."

"Of course, m'lady. I swear. What is it?"

Marguerite stood up and motioned for her maid to take a seat beside her on the chaise.

"You're familiar with some of the poorer areas of London, aren't you? The places where the flower sellers live? The Irish, in particular."

"I know a little about them, yes. Most of the Irish are in Rosemary Court. That's where they gather."

"And do you think you could take me there?"

Wallis stared in astonishment. "Take *you* to Rosemary Court? But why ever would you want to go there, m'lady? It's a terrible place—riddled with filth and disease. That's no place for a lady like you."

Marguerite grabbed her hands. "But I need to try and find someone, Wallis, and I cannot ask anyone else to do it. It's in connection with the child—Violette. I suspect the maids all know the truth of the matter anyway, but her arrival here was not entirely as we would have had you believe. She came to us quite by chance. She isn't the daughter of my cousin. She's a total stranger we are caring for. I've grown to love her with all my heart, but she's missing her sister desperately and I think I must try to find her. Will you help me?"

The words came out in a rush, as if she would burst if she held the secret within her any longer.

Wallis was silent for a moment, unsure of what to say. "But, are you quite sure of this, m'lady? The markets are no place for a lady to be seen, and the slums would make your stomach retch if you get within half a mile of them. Is there no one you can ask to make inquiries about this sister on your behalf—one of the stable lads, perhaps? Or Mr. Ingram?"

While she may have shared some of her maid's doubts and fears, Marguerite certainly wasn't going to show it. Marguerite Ingram was made of stronger stuff than people gave her credit for. Her mind was made up, and nobody was going to change it.

She sighed and stood up, pacing along the Turkey rug.

"Why do women always expect a man to do everything for them, Wallis? Really—it infuriates me. Surely we are perfectly capable of taking a carriage to London and making a few inquiries among the market sellers. And what of the filth and depravity? Will it not simply make us more grateful that we have this wonderful house to return to at the end of the day? We have no need to drink the infected water and will be sure to wash thoroughly when we return home. Really, you seem so against the matter I wonder if I might ask someone else to assist me."

Marguerite could feel her cheeks reddening and grabbed her fan to try to cool herself.

"I'll gladly help you, m'lady. I just wondered. That was all."

"Well, please don't. Leave the wondering to me."

Marguerite settled herself back on the chaise and spoke to her maid in more detail about her plan. It was agreed that they would take the trip one morning the following week, when Mr. Ingram was due to be away on business. Wallis advised that it would be best to leave well before dawn, so they would arrive at Covent Garden early. She felt this would be their best chance of talking to the flower sellers, while they tied their posies. She didn't tell her mistress that she very much doubted they would be able to help them locate a young Irish orphan. It was like looking for a four-leaf clover in Petersham Meadow.

Over dinner that evening, Marguerite's thoughts were only with Violette. She left the men to their business talk for the first part of the meal, barely acknowledging Sarah Ross, their lawyer's wife, who was sitting opposite her.

"I hear you've agreed to take care of your cousin's daughter while she's recovering from an illness, Marguerite," Sarah remarked when there was a lull in the conversation. "Most admirable of you both. I was very sorry to hear that your cousin had fallen ill. I hope she recovers soon."

"Well, what more could one do for one's cousin? Violette will remain with us for the foreseeable future. She's a delightful little girl. Really, no trouble at all. We're enjoying having a child in the house again, aren't we, Thomas?" She smiled sweetly at her husband. Playing the part of doting wife and hostess over her husband's business dinners was something Marguerite had become very good at in the years of their marriage.

There was much shuffling of napkins and lifting of wineglasses as nobody quite knew what to say in response to Marguerite's remark; they were all too aware of the gaping hole left in the Ingrams' life by Delphine's death.

Thomas returned his wife's smile and sipped from his wine-glass. "Yes, darling. We are enjoying having Violette stay with us. And it is wonderful to hear the sound of a child's laughter in the house again. Truly, it is."

"And will she go with you when you move north?" Sarah continued.

"Move north?" Marguerite glanced at Thomas, demanding an explanation.

He coughed and dabbed at his mouth with a napkin. "Nothing is settled yet, Sarah. As you know, for some time now I've been discussing the opportunities available to us to expand the business in the northern counties: Yorkshire and Lancashire in particular. I'll be taking a business trip to the regions next week to assess the viability of certain operations."

Marguerite put down her glass, fixing her gaze on Thomas although her words were directed at Sarah Ross. "But of course we would take the child with us, Sarah. I made a promise to my cousin that I would look after her daughter for as long as she needs us to, and that is what I intend to do, regardless of geography. We consider Violette to be part of our immediate family now. Don't we, Thomas?"

"Yes, darling. We do. Very much so." He threw his wife a pointed look that told her to leave the subject.

Marguerite left the men to talk business for the remainder of the meal, chatting dully with the women about the successes and failures of the Season's debutantes. She was relieved when the footman showed the guests out.

Thomas approached her as she was making her way upstairs. "Darling, I was going to tell you. Nothing is certain yet and I . . ."

"It's quite all right, Thomas," she said, resting her hand on his shoulder. "You don't need to explain. I understand that it's just business. Let's talk in the morning. I have quite the headache."

AS VIOLETTE DREAMED of the nightingale and of her sister, Marguerite slipped quietly into her room and sat by her bed, watching her. The child looked so peaceful when she slept, free from the hardships she'd faced in life. Marguerite willed her to sleep and sleep, so that she could sit and watch her and pretend she was watching her own child.

Like the flowers in her window boxes, the child had blossomed under Marguerite's care. When she gazed at Violette's beautiful little face—her skin now as clear as glass, her lips like rosebuds, her cheeks glowing with health, and her newly grown, russet-red curls nestling around her forehead—she couldn't help but love her with all her heart. As she silently watched the steady rise and fall of the blankets, Marguerite wept tears of sadness for the daughter she had lost and tears of joy for the child she had found.

She thought about her husband's business plans. In the north, nobody would know anything about them. In the north, they could be whoever they wanted to be and, perhaps, if they were farther away from London, farther away from the memories, Violette might forget about her sister. This could be the perfect opportunity to start again, to establish themselves as a family from the outset: Marguerite and Thomas Ingram, and their daughter, Violette.

She would still visit London's markets, though, still try to find Florrie. She owed that much to Violette, at least.

Chapter 22

Covent Garden, London
August 1876

They left under cover of darkness, while everyone else in the house was sleeping. It was a cool morning, the sun still many hours from rising, when it would bring the stifling heat back to the city. The two women wrapped their cloaks tighter around their shoulders as the carriage rumbled out of the stable yard, jostling them around like rag dolls as the wheels crossed the cobbles.

As they pulled out of the driveway, Marguerite saw a glimmer of candlelight from the maids' quarters at the top of the house. She'd informed Mrs. Jeffers that she was taking Wallis to see her physician in London as the girl had been complaining of pains in her stomach. Mrs. Jeffers had merely looked at her and nodded in response. Marguerite was doubtful that the housekeeper believed her for one moment. Mrs. Jeffers was a perceptive woman, but Marguerite knew that she could also trust her housekeeper to say nothing, even if she had her suspicions.

Turning away from the light, she fixed her eyes on the driveway and her mind on the task ahead. Passing through the gates, the carriage rounded the bend at the top of the road and began the steady descent down the hill, London-bound.

"What will you do if we find this Florrie, m'lady?" Wallis ventured, her teeth chattering from the cold. "Will you explain about her sister? Bring her back with us?"

This was the one question that had kept Marguerite awake at night over the past week. What *would* she do if they found Florrie?

"I'm not entirely sure. Let's not worry about that until we find the child—*if* we ever do."

Marguerite knew that Wallis still harbored doubts, that she was certain a lady such as herself couldn't be at all prepared for the depravity she was going to encounter among London's slums. But they were on their way now. The wheels were in motion. There was no turning back.

After what felt like an age, Marguerite was relieved to see the black outline of the trees in Green Park. The driver kept a steady rhythm as they clattered along Piccadilly and on, toward the heart of the city. Eventually, he slowed the carriage, weaving and turning along the narrow roads leading to Covent Garden. Marguerite was glad of the posy of lavender that Wallis had insisted they take with them; the delicate perfume was a welcome relief from the sickening stench from the river Thames, which crept up her nostrils and settled at the back of her throat.

Peering through the window into the darkness, she could see that the streets were already choked with carts and barrows, donkeys and men, women and children—all jostling for position in a seething, sprawling mass. The noise was deafening.

As Thompson slowed the carriage, she faltered. Was she doing the right thing? What if she found Florrie? How could she bear to lose Violette now?

"We're here, m'lady," Wallis whispered, sensing her hesitation. "Should I ask Thompson to go on?"

Marguerite looked at her. "No. You might ask him to wait beside the theater. Tell him we may be some time."

"Very well, m'lady. If you're sure."

Marguerite wasn't sure at all.

Stepping from the carriage, the two women hurried across the cobbles, stepping around piles of rotting vegetable leaves and all manner of excrement—human or animal, Marguerite wasn't sure. She kept her nosegay to her face but almost retched with the stench all the same, her eyes smarting.

They found themselves standing at the North Hall and the covered flower markets. For a moment, all thoughts of Florrie and Violette were forgotten as they stared at the sight before them, every color and tone imaginable, represented by one bloom or another. Marguerite inhaled a deep, lingering breath, savoring the sweet scent of stocks, violets, and lavender. She walked around the edge of the cavernous space, keeping to the shelter of the columns and arches.

"Pretty, isn't it," Wallis said. "You'd never think a sight so lovely could exist among all the poverty."

"Yes," Marguerite agreed. "It seems a very cruel contradiction."

Soon their presence caught the attention of the flower sellers who were swarming around the vast displays like pollinating bees. They began pointing and whispering at the two ladies in their smart coats and hats.

"Come, Wallis. We don't wish to draw too much attention to ourselves."

Marguerite looped her arm through her maid's, and they walked then, around the cobbled square, toward the portico of St. Paul's Church, whose clock struck the hour of five. Several groups of women and children were already at work around the columns and steps, tying bunches of violets, primroses, and watercress by the flickering light of tallow candles dotted here and there. Wallis struck up an easy banter with some of the women. Too anxious to speak to anyone, Marguerite stood behind one of the imposing stone columns, watching as the first rays of the morning sun cast their pale, straw-colored light over the market.

Removing a glove, she placed the palm of her hand against the stone of the pillar in front of her. It was icy cold to the touch, as if the memory of a hundred winter mornings were stored within it. She imagined the bitter January winds being blown off the Thames, whirling around the frozen flower sellers, costermongers, and barefoot children who wandered in front of her. She leaned forward, allowing her hand to idle on the pillar. The solidity of the structure—the permanency of it—was reassuring.

Hidden from view, she stood silently, watching the market come to life. Closing her eyes, Marguerite allowed herself to absorb the smells and sounds and sensations, just as Violette would have done: the low rumble of the carts and metal of the horseshoes striking the cobbles as the hawkers made their way up the narrow streets; the ripe aroma of hops from the foaming tankards of ale, quaffed by the thirsty costers; the heat on her face from the hot coals of the smudge pot fires; the cries of "sparrow-grass, lovely green sparrow-grass" and "worter-creees" and "green gooseberries" and "cherries—round and sound" creating a wonderful melody of industriousness.

She opened her eyes, watching hungrily—reminded that she had missed breakfast—as steaming hot coffee and huge piles of bread and butter and hot shoulder of mutton were devoured by the hungry costers as quickly as they were produced by the women who worked the taverns and early coffee shops.

"You lost, love?" The voice made Marguerite jump. "It ain't often we see a lady round 'ere at this time o' day. Bunch o' violets was it?"

Marguerite studied the old crone who had spoken to her. Her face was as wrinkled as creased linen, her clothes muddied and torn, her mouth as toothless as that of a newborn infant, and yet her green eyes shone with the brilliance of a dozen emeralds, full of knowledge and spirit.

"Thank you," Marguerite whispered, unable to take her eyes off the old woman as she took the just-tied bunch of violets from her gnarled hands. "Here's sixpence for the bunch."

The crone smiled a toothless, gummy smile. "And one fer y'r friend?" she asked, holding out another bunch, sensing her opportunity to fleece the two women, who were clearly lost or uncertain as to the price of a bunch of violets.

Marguerite paid her another sixpence as the group of women sitting nearby joked and laughed among themselves. They were all dressed similarly: spotted scarfs tied around their necks, several shawls draped over their shoulders, ragged skirts, dirty white pinafores, black boots, and black straw hats adorned with garish bows and feathers. Their flower baskets and shallows were gathered in front of them, filled with the many bunches they had already tied. They worked with incredible dexterity, their stained fingers twisting and intertwining so rapidly Marguerite could hardly follow them.

"Actually, I was wondering if you might be able to help me," she said, bending down so that she was on a level with a cluster of women, the light from a candle illuminating her face and theirs. "I'm looking for a little girl. A flower seller. Irish. I believe her name is Florrie."

The group of women stared at her blankly before bursting into raucous laughter. Marguerite was unnerved.

One of the women eventually calmed herself and spoke up. "Florrie, you say? Irish?"

"Yes! That's right. Do you know her?"

"Oi! Charlie!" the woman shouted, addressing a group of young costermongers who were standing outside a nearby ale house. "You ever come across a young Irish girl? Florrie? Sells 'er flowers?"

The coster took a long drink of his ale, wiping the foam from his mouth with the back of his filthy coat sleeve, considering her question.

"Well, let me think now. I'm sure I knowed an Irish Florrie once—Florrie Butler was 'er name. And then there was Florrie Molloy. Oh, and old Florrie O'Grady and Florrie Dolan. Must be, what, about a hundred Florries round 'ere. What d'ya reckon. P'rhaps more?"

His response caused another great outburst of laughter among the women.

Marguerite stood up, glancing over to Wallis, who was standing beside a fire, shivering in the cold morning air.

"Come along. I don't think we're going to get much help here," she said, taking her maid's arm.

The two women began to walk across the cobbled square, toward their waiting carriage. Marguerite was angry with herself. She'd been a fool to come here.

"Wait!"

Marguerite turned. A younger girl, whom she hadn't noticed before, had stood up. She was dressed in a manner similar to the other women, but there was something different about her, a softness to her face.

"I knew a Florrie," she said. "Irish girl. Walked with a crutch."

Marguerite rushed back toward her. "Florrie? You're sure it was Florrie?"

"Yeah. My mam knew her mam. Had a little sister, if I remember right."

A shiver ran up Marguerite's spine. She took hold of the girl's hands. They were freezing cold. Even through the fabric of her gloves, they felt like ice.

"Used to go everywhere with her little sister. Rosie was 'er name. Think she were blind," the girl continued. "Never left 'er side, Florrie didn't, 'specially not after the mammy died."

Rosie. She was called Rosie.

Marguerite looked at the girl's face, at the dark shadows under her eyes, at her sunken cheeks and stooped shoulders. She had the appearance of an old woman, although she couldn't have been more than thirteen or fourteen years old. She hardly dared ask the question that hovered on her lips.

"Do you know her? Do you know where Florrie is?"

The girl sighed. "Ain't seen neither of them for a month or so now. I reckon they got taken to the workhouse what with them being orphans. I know she lived in Rosemary Court. You might find 'er there. Or you might not. I ain't promisin' nothin'. What you want 'er for, anyway? She in trouble with the law?"

"No! No. She's not in trouble. I just . . . I . . . I knew a relative of hers. That's all."

The girl looked at Marguerite in a way that suggested she didn't believe her.

"And where might I find Rosemary Court?" Marguerite asked.

"Off Drury Lane. Behind the oil shop."

Marguerite thanked the girl and pressed a silver sixpence into her hand, urging her to get herself something warm to eat. As she again pulled Wallis away from the group of women, a heaviness settled across her heart. What would she do if she found Florrie?

"I can't believe it," Wallis said as they walked. "I honestly thought you didn't have a chance of ever finding her. Perhaps Florrie is closer than you'd expected. Perhaps she's somewhere in this market, right now."

Marguerite could hardly bear to think about it. *And if she's here, she will be searching for her sister*, she thought, *searching and searching, brokenhearted and cold and hungry.* What if Florrie had seen her that day on Westminster Bridge as she'd climbed into the brougham and told Thompson to take her home. What if Florrie was looking for *her*?

As the chimes of the church clock struck the half hour, the two women walked back toward where Thompson and the carriage were waiting. Marguerite's attention was drawn to the many children she'd barely noticed in the dim pre-dawn light. Now she saw them clearly: some darting about like rats, some huddled under market barrows, some sitting with their mothers, others kicking a rotten apple along the cobbles. She gazed at a pair of half-starved toddlers, their hands held tightly as they walked across the piazza in their bare feet, standing in all the filth and dirt, their empty, glazed eyes seeing nothing of the dreadful conditions around them.

Some of them stopped to stare at the two ladies. A girl approached them—a pretty little thing, despite her ragged clothes and pinched cheeks. Her flame-red hair reminded Marguerite of Violette. She held a bunch of violets in her hand. She couldn't be more than four years old. "Buy a flower off a poor girl? Oh, please, Miss. Do buy a flower."

Marguerite stared at the child as a sense of unease spread within her like a fever. More than ever, she felt the burden of guilt at having taken something that didn't belong to her. The filth, the poverty, the reality of what she had done washed over her like an unstoppable wave so that she felt unsteady on her feet, grabbing at Wallis's sleeve as the stench of rotting vegetables and fish guts engulfed her. She doubled over and retched in the street.

"I can't stand this any longer," she gasped, pulling her maid along as she walked briskly across the cobbles. "I have to get away from here."

She almost ran down the slope of Southampton Street, across the Strand, and down the narrow alleyway toward the Victoria Embankment, Wallis running behind, calling for her to wait. Only when she was some distance from the market did Marguerite allow herself to stop and retch again, the bile burning in her throat, a cold sweat beading on her forehead.

"Mrs. Ingram! Good Lord, m'lady. Are you taken ill? Do you need to go to the infirmary? Oh, I knew this was a bad idea."

Marguerite stood upright, trying to catch her breath as she placed the violets to her nose to inhale their sweet fragrance.

"No. I don't need the infirmary. I will be quite all right." She stood for a moment, trying to regain her composure. "It's the smell of this place. It's enough to turn the stomach of the strongest of men."

"It is that, m'lady. Should we go back to Richmond now? I think, maybe, you've seen enough?"

Marguerite turned to look at her.

"No. Not yet. We came to find Florrie, and we still have one more place to look. We must go to Rosemary Court. Come along. We'll ask Thompson to drive us."

She stood for a moment, watching the strengthening morning sun as it shimmered on the Thames. The glare dazzled Marguerite's eyes, almost blinding her, so that she could make out only shadows and dark silhouettes of the boats on the river. She closed her eyes and said a silent prayer before she turned to walk back toward the din of the market.

Chapter 23

Covent Garden, London

August 1876

Alighting from the carriage at the corner of Drury Lane, the two women tentatively approached the entrance to Rosemary Court, the labyrinth of narrow alleyways quickly closing in on them, blocking out the sun. Marguerite shuddered, pulling her cloak around her shoulders. It was highly unconventional for a woman of her standing to be walking among these filthy, oppressive streets. She thought of how angry Thomas would be if he ever found out she had come here.

Turning a corner, they came across a group of women who were standing against a wall, smoking their pipes, their wrinkled faces partly obscured by their black bonnets. They stared at Marguerite and Wallis as they approached.

"You lost, love?"

Marguerite looked up to see a woman hanging her washing

from a window, two stories above her head. "Look like you don't belong round these parts. More likely it's the Palace yer looking for."

Her remark caused the other women to start laughing.

"I'm looking for someone actually," Marguerite replied, trying to suppress the nausea that was rising again in her stomach. "A child. Florrie is her name. That is all I know. She has a little sister, Rosie. They're Irish, I believe. I think they may have lived here."

"Well, you're in the right place if it's Irish yer looking for. There's a hundred Florries and Rosies living here, though, love. Don't fancy yer chances."

Marguerite sighed. "Well, thank you anyway."

Disheartened but determined to continue, Marguerite led Wallis along the dark alleyways until they were deep inside the Court. She'd heard of London's rookeries—the name given to the absolute worst of the slums—and wondered if this was one such place as her eyes darted from left to right, trying to take everything in. Chickens scraped at the ground, pecking between the cobbles. Emaciated dogs ran around her legs, barking at the geese, which scurried out of the way, flapping their wings and honking in fright. Barefooted, wretched children sat about in groups, some scraping at bundles of asparagus, some peeling walnuts, others minding infants who bawled with outrage at the indignity of it all. Empty baskets and shallows were dotted about the place, some with the remnants of unsold flowers from the previous day, withered in the heat. A dozen or so grubby, pale-faced children were gathered around a streetlamp, playing some sort of game with a long piece of rope. They stopped for a moment and stared blankly at the two women as they walked past. Everywhere they walked, they drew attention to themselves, despite the effort they'd made to dress in plain, dark clothes.

Eventually, they emerged into the center of the Court, where the early morning sunlight streamed over the tops of the buildings. Marguerite was glad of the light and the warmth, although she kept the posy of violets to her nose. They spoke to a group of women clustered around a small stall selling salt cod, who eyed Marguerite and Wallis suspiciously and told them they didn't know of a Florrie or a Rosie. And then another woman approached, whose words made Marguerite's stomach lurch.

"I knew a Florrie all right," she said. "Lived over there with her little sister, Rosie. Knew their mother, Nora, so I did, before she died. And there was an aunt—May, I think she was called—gone off to Bedlam or some such place. Ain't seen the littlest child for months now, though."

"And the eldest? Florrie?"

"Not seen her neither. Just disappeared one day, so she did. They're probably both gone to the workhouse. God love 'em."

Marguerite thanked the woman and led Wallis toward the house the woman had pointed to. It was one of two dozen single-story buildings, squashed into a small square, no more than fifty feet wide. Long wooden shutters were closed over most of the windows. In others, the frames were rotting, the glass cracked or missing; faded, yellowing newspaper used in its place. The most appalling smell came from a standpipe in the middle of the court, making Wallis retch as they walked past. Barking dogs, bawling babies, gruff-voiced men, and the shrill cries of women all mingled into a terrible noise that, to Marguerite's ears, sounded like Hell itself.

With her heart pounding, and the palms of her hands clammy, Marguerite continued across the small square to a dilapidated house in the center. Placing her hand over her nose and mouth, she peered in through the broken window, her eyes adjusting slowly to the gloom of the interior. She struggled to see, just able to make out a tattered mattress in one corner, a tabletop on upturned vegetable pallets for legs, and a fireplace—the grate empty. The walls were riddled with black mold from the damp.

Only when her eyes had adjusted to the gloom did she notice a woman looking back at her. She was almost invisible in the murky dark of the room.

"Oh! Oh, I'm so sorry," Marguerite gasped, jumping backward. "I didn't mean to intrude." The hollow eyes blinked at her. Marguerite faltered. She knew she had to ask the question, but it felt so wrong. "I'm very sorry to trouble you, but I wondered if you might know of a young Irish girl who lived here—Florrie?" The woman stared blankly at her before looking down at the infant suckling hungrily at her breast.

Marguerite pulled back from the window. "Let's go, Wallis. There's nothing here. Florrie isn't here." Her voice was weak; her knees trembled beneath her skirts.

They walked briskly away from the small square. She had done what she'd come for. Now, she just wanted to get back to the safety of her own home—back to Violette.

The two women twisted and turned, rushing down the maze of dark lanes.

"Which way is it, Wallis? Which way?" There was fear and panic in Marguerite's voice. "I don't remember the way!"

Turning a corner, she bumped into a little girl, almost knocking the basket of flowers from her hands.

"Oh, my goodness! I'm so sorry. Are you all right?"

The child stared at her. "Buy a flower, kind lady. Poor little girl. Buy a flower. Tuppence a bunch." It appeared to be the only thing she was capable of saying.

Despite her anxiousness to get out of the dingy streets, Marguerite didn't have the heart to say no. She reached into her purse for a coin, half a dozen other children flocking around her as she did, quick to spot the chance of a sale. They each held out their wares—posies, cresses, boxes of matches, horseshoe nails—imploring her to buy.

"Now, now, children. Give the lady some space."

Marguerite was startled by the sound of a male voice behind her. She turned around and was surprised to see a smartly dressed gentleman. He looked as out of place as she did, his frock coat and top hat striking among the depravity of the dark alleyway. He smiled at the children, patting them on their heads.

"Good morning," he said, extending his hand toward Marguerite. "Albert Shaw. I presume you are lost! We don't often see ladies around these parts of London."

Marguerite blushed, conscious of the fact that she shouldn't be there at all. She was relieved to have encountered the gentleman, nevertheless.

"Well, yes. We do seem to find ourselves a little lost. We were looking for Covent Garden theater."

"Well, you're not far away. It's so easy to lose your way in these little back streets. Perhaps you would permit me to escort you?"

"Buy a flower, kind lady?"

Albert smiled as another child thrust her flowers toward Marguerite. "Quite industrious, aren't they? You've got to admire their work ethic."

Marguerite felt her sense of panic subsiding in Mr. Shaw's company. "And how on earth could I refuse such beautiful flowers from such a pretty little girl?"

She gave the child half a farthing.

Albert clapped his hands. "Now, run along, children. You're not to be pestering the ladies again."

The children ran off, chattering like birds as they melted into the shadows.

"You seem quite at ease with the children, if you don't mind me saying," Marguerite remarked, as Mr. Shaw guided her and Wallis out of the alleyway. "It is admirable to see."

"Well, it takes a little while to get to know their ways. I have a small mission hall at Covent Garden. I encourage the children—blind and crippled flower sellers, mainly—to go there so that we can teach them about good people and read to them from the Bible. We provide a cup of cocoa and a hot meal. It's a small thing, but it can make all the difference to them. They are unable to find any other employment, due to their physical limitations."

Marguerite was reminded of the state poor little Violette had arrived in. She imagined the difference such a place would have made to her.

"And I assume the problem is widespread?" she asked.

"Unfortunately, yes. London is riddled with orphaned and crippled children. We can only begin to scratch the surface of the problem with the small amount of funding we receive, although I'm delighted to have the support of Lord Shaftesbury, who was recently appointed president of our mission. His involvement has made a significant difference. We take the older blind and afflicted girls into employment at a small workroom in Clerkenwell and the youngest go to an orphanage on the south coast."

Marguerite was enjoying the conversation. It provided a welcome distraction from the staring eyes that followed them as they walked back toward the entrance to the court. "It sounds quite fascinating. What employment are the girls engaged in at your workroom?"

"They make silk flowers, which we sell to wholesalers and to private homes. They're quite the thing nowadays."

"Yes. I've seen some of the silk flowers from Paris. They're very lifelike." Marguerite raised the posy of violets to her nose again as they passed a woman gutting fish. "And the children are able to manage such intricate work? Even the cripples?"

Mr. Shaw chuckled. "Yes! It really is amazing how adept they can become. One girl holds the paintbrush in her mouth to add the detail to the petals. I wouldn't believe it myself if I didn't see them hard at work every day. We are delighted to have been asked to decorate the Guild Hall for the mayoral banquet. The girls are quite beside themselves with excitement!"

"Well, it all sounds most commendable, Mr. Shaw. Most commendable, indeed," Marguerite remarked as they emerged onto Drury Lane.

"Ah. Here we are. Daylight!" Albert Shaw held out his hand. "I hope you won't find yourself lost in Rosemary Court again," he said. "It really is no place for a lady."

Marguerite felt foolish as she shook his hand. "Of course. We will be sure to stick to the main streets in future. Won't we, Wallis?"

"Yes, m'lady."

"Well, it was very nice to meet you, Mr. Shaw, and to learn of your work with the flower sellers. I will certainly look out for your displays."

Tipping his hat, Albert bid the ladies farewell before retracing his steps and returning to the dark alleyways.

It was only as Marguerite watched him walk away that it struck her. If he visited this area often, perhaps he knew of Florrie. Perhaps he knew a little girl whose heart was breaking because she was missing her sister.

She almost called after him, almost ran to him to explain everything that had happened—about the carriage and the little girl she'd found cowering within it. But she didn't. She merely stood in the middle of the busy London street and watched Albert Shaw, until he was engulfed by the shadows.

"Come along, m'lady. We should be getting back now," Wallis said, looping her arm through Marguerite's and guiding them both toward the theater where Thompson was waiting.

Their skirts and boots muddied, the smell of decay sticking to their coats like glue, the women were grateful to climb into the carriage. Thompson clicked his tongue and cracked the whip as he urged the horse to trot on. They were both glad to feel the wheels rumbling over the cobbles.

Lost in private thoughts about everything they'd seen and heard, neither of them spoke as the carriage followed the bend of the river, the chimes of Big Ben striking nine as they passed Westminster. As the carriage wheels turned, so, too, did Marguerite's thoughts. She closed her eyes and wondered.

She wondered whether Thomas's business trip would be successful and whether they might soon be far away from London, where nobody would ever know that Violette had once been a poor flower seller called Rosie. She wondered about the cruelty of life and why Delphine had been taken from her so soon. She wondered why a little girl had hidden in her carriage. She wondered whether the worry and guilt that pulled at her day and night would ever go away. She wondered about Albert Shaw's work with the flower sellers and whether there might be a way for her to repay some of her debt to Florrie, even if she couldn't find her. And she also wondered about the incredible power of love and hope, and it was that—love and hope—which she held on to. Then she locked those sentiments away, deep within her heart, as she resolved to do everything she could to make sure that the nightingales always sang for Violette, that her life would never again be one of cruelty and darkness but would be filled, always, with love and light.

Chapter 24

Violet House, London

June 1912

Galloping, galloping, galloping, the thundering hooves not going fast enough. The jangle of stirrups and bridle, the pony pulling at the reins. A fly in her eye. Wind rushing past her ears. Tears streaming down her cheeks. The thick, swirling fog distorting her senses.

Finally, the cottage, barely visible over the hill, never getting closer.

The crunch of gravel on the laneway. A tractor in a field somewhere nearby. Someone calling her name. "Good evening, Miss Matilda."

Running, running, running. The cat leaping off the doormat. The cool darkness of the cottage.

"Mother! Mother! Come, quickly. It's Esther! There's been an accident!"

Her mother's face, pale as a ghost.

"I told you to look after her, Matilda! I told you again and again to look after her!" Her eyes wild, flashing with fear. Screaming into her face, "What have you done to her? Where is she?"

She didn't know. Esther was lost. The fog had taken her.

Disturbed by her dreams, Tilly often found herself awake long before the rest of the house. At first, she'd felt uncomfortable in the dark quiet of her room, unsettled by the strange sensations that interrupted her sleep—a hand against her cheek, a cool breeze, the feeling of being watched, the scent of violets, a whispered voice. Dreams, or reality—she wasn't sure. As the weeks had passed, she'd grown to accept the unusual atmosphere in her room. Now, when she awoke early, she took the opportunity to sketch by candlelight, until the violet light of dawn crept in through the window, signaling that it was time for her to go downstairs to light the fire in the range.

As the cool air of spring made way for the cloying heat of summer, which stuck to the buildings and people like honey, Tilly began to relax into the routines of Violet House. What had seemed so strange and unfamiliar on that March morning, when Mrs. Pearce had reeled off the daily routine without stopping for breath, was second nature to Tilly now. With the bright, summer days to cheer her, the sashes thrown open to let in a little of the morning air, and a formal promotion to the position of housemother due to Mrs. Harris's continued absence, Tilly carried out her tasks with a newfound confidence.

She enjoyed the hush of the house as she crept downstairs, going about her work with efficiency and order: lighting the fires in the range and the copper; dusting the mantel and picture frames in the downstairs rooms; beating the mats and rugs in the backyard; scattering the tea leaves, before sweeping the carpets; washing the windows, which were always caked thick with coal dust from the factories.

She was grateful for the summer months, which meant no fires to clean and blacken and re-lay in the rooms. And although the warmer weather made the smell from the slop bucket much worse as she emptied the chamber pots in the girls' dormitories, she was glad that the pump handle was no longer freezing cold when she drew the water, and she took pleasure in hanging the starched and mangled bed sheets on the line across the backyard—even though they were often soot stained again by the time the warm air had dried them.

When the girls woke, the house was filled with the vibrant sounds of their chatter, and the thump and clatter of crutches and wheelchairs on the just-swept and polished floors. It was such a contrast to the hushed voices and polite conversations that had marked Tilly's days at Wycke Hall. While Lady Wycke and her daughters had lived a life as stiff and restrictive as the corsets that nipped at their waists, the flower girls filled Violet House with an infectious combination of noise and emotion. "Organized chaos," Mrs. Pearce called it.

There was no doubt that Tilly was growing fonder of the girls as the months passed. Like a real mother, she scolded them when their beds weren't made, settled disagreements about whose turn it was to help lay the table for dinner, found missing stockings and pinafores, and reminded the girls where they'd left the books they were reading or the packs of cards they'd been playing with.

After breakfast, she liked to stand on the just-scrubbed doorstep, watching like a proud parent as her girls made their steady progress up the street. She'd watch until the last girl entered the factory, then she'd close the door behind her and a strange hush would descend over the house once again until the daily round of callers started: the twice-daily delivery of milk; the baker's boy bringing the fresh loaves; the rumble of the coal cart; the bell and cry of the rag and bone man, "Bones! Any old iron! Bones! Any old iron!" She'd even enjoyed the drama of the visit from the sweep last month, despite the filth it had left for her to clean away.

But, between these pleasant interruptions, when the house was silent, Tilly thought about Flora and Rosie. Their story still intrigued her. There was such desperation in Flora's words that Tilly couldn't shake them. She wished she could reach into the pages of the notebook and help her. And while she read about the two sisters, she thought more and more of her own, of sea-green eyes looking at her, asking for her help.

While each new day in London brought a greater sense of belonging, Tilly's life back in Grasmere hung over her like a fog. Despite the passing of a season, there'd been no letter from home. She tried to ignore her disappointment when the postman made his deliveries and failed to bring anything addressed to her. Even the last delivery at night, past nine o'clock, would see her twitching at the window, wondering.

But nothing arrived.

No letter from her mother, asking how she was settling in; no telegram to wish her a happy birthday; no news of Esther. Even Mrs. Pearce, with all her charming lack of subtlety, had stopped inquiring, sensing Tilly's discomfort whenever she raised the matter.

As she swept and dusted, her thoughts often returned to Grasmere, picturing the simple blacksmith's cottage, the Coniston slate glistening from the recent rainfall, a thin wisp of smoke curling from the chimney. She imagined her mother standing in the doorway of her bedroom, staring regretfully at the unslept-in bed. She thought of Esther, sitting by the window, a blanket covering her legs as she read her novels about the wild Yorkshire moors and unrequited love.

Did either of them think of her at all? Would they ever understand? Ever forgive her? If only her father was alive. He would understand. He would want to hear about her life in London. He would care.

She adored her father, and he adored her. They went everywhere together: to the lakes, to the mountains, to the fells and the stone circle at Castlerigg, touching the cool stones and imagining whose hands had first moved those giant boulders. And when they weren't going anywhere in particular, Tilly loved nothing more than to just sit and watch her father as he worked, hammering and pounding at the white-hot iron as he molded it, the sharp hiss of steam and the billowing clouds of smoke obscuring him from her view as he cooled the horseshoes in the bucket of water. The heat of the furnace in the forge was stifling, and she liked to take him a tankard of ale. There *had* been happy times, before war came and changed everything. She'd even loved Esther once. If only for a while.

He woke her in the dim half-light of a fresh spring morning, excitement burning in his chestnut eyes.

"Tilly! Tilly, wake up. The baby's coming. Run down to the farm. Tell Dr. Jennings to come, quickly!"

"Yes, Father."

She was excited. For nine months, she'd watched her mother's belly grow. For nine months, "The Baby" was all anyone had talked about. Finally, "The Baby" her parents had prayed for, "The Baby," who would be the much-longed-for brother or sister for Tilly to play with, was coming.

She ran as fast as she could from the forge to the farm at the end of the lane, the long grass that grew alongside the hedgerows brushing her skin, her smock dress flapping at her knees, her petticoats wrapping themselves around her legs as if to trip her up, stop her bringing back the man who would make sure the baby came safely.

Tilly knew about babies dying. She'd had a sister once. For a few, fleeting minutes, their family was complete. But the cord was wrapped around her neck, taking her breath away before she'd even had a chance to taste the fresh Westmorland air. She was as blue as a bunch of cornflowers. The doctor couldn't get there in time. They'd called her Iris. Her mother had wept for weeks.

This baby would live. "The Baby" had to live.

Running past the fields of wheat and barley that swayed gently in the morning breeze, she raced the wispy clouds that drifted lazily across the sky. She was careful to avoid the potholes in the lane, jumping over the ruts from the tractors and plows and the indentations from horses' hooves, which were now murky puddles, filled with the rainwater of the previous night. She didn't stop until she saw the gate of the Jenningses' farm—didn't stop until she'd passed the butter churns and the chickens scratching for seed.

She could still feel her feet running as Dr. Jennings took her back in his cart, the great, lumbering shire horse trotting along as quickly as he could. *Please don't lose a shoe*, *please don't lose a shoe*, she repeated to herself all the way home.

They were in plenty of time.

The baby was still making its slow, difficult way into the world. Tilly stood in the scullery, covering her ears to block out the deep moans coming from her mother's bedroom.

"I think you're better off outside, love," her father said, resting his large, callused palm on the top of her head. She'd loved that sensation since she was an infant. It gave her a sense of stability. Sometimes, he would rest his hand on her head for so long that she could still feel it hours later, long after he'd gone back to work.

He gave her some plums from the garden, the end of a loaf of bread, a chunk of cheese, and kissed her on the cheek. "I'll come and get you when it's over."

She walked to her favorite spot by the lake, the mountains directly in front of her. She made piles of pebbles, balancing them, one on top of another, and watched the ripples from the fish as they caught flies from the surface of the water. It was a beautiful spring morning. She couldn't remember a day so perfect.

She enjoyed the plums, sucking every bit of their soft, juicy flesh from the stones, which she kept in her pinafore pocket to plant in the garden. Even when the breeze caused the goose bumps to bubble up on her arms, she didn't dare go home, afraid of what she might discover there.

It was noon when her father's footsteps came crunching along the shale path behind her.

"So, how would you like a little sister to play with?"

They were the best words she could have heard. She jumped into his arms. "Really? Everything's all right?"

"It was a bit of a struggle, but they got there in the end. Your mother is very keen to show her to you." He carried Tilly home on his shoulders, the breeze blowing around her hair, the gentle rocking motion as he walked almost lulling her to sleep.

From the outside, her home looked exactly the same: the bottle-green ivy creeping around the doorway, the pigeon-gray slate brightened from the light of the sun, the thin wisp of smoke twirling up from the chimney, the smell of woodsmoke in the air. But as soon as she stepped inside, Tilly sensed something different in the atmosphere—a sense of calm that hadn't been there before. It was as if The Baby's arrival had filled an invisible gap that she hadn't even known existed.

Her father took her hand and led her into the bedroom.

"Here she is. Your little sister," he whispered. "Come and say hello to Esther."

"Esther." Tilly tested the sound of the name. It was like a soft, breath of wind.

She tiptoed to the end of the bed, where her mother sat, propped up against the pillows, a perfect little baby girl nuzzling at her breast. She couldn't remember ever seeing her mother so content. She looked like a different person.

"Come and look, Tilly," she whispered. "Isn't she just beautiful?"

Tilly crept forward and looked.

She stared at the helpless infant, at her tiny fists curled into little balls, like rosebuds; at her impossibly small feet; at the tea-rose pink of her delicate skin. She stared and stared, and she knew that she loved her, very much.

"Do you love your new sister?" her father asked the next morning when he found her leaning over Esther's crib, staring at her.

"Yes, Daddy, I love her very much."

"And we love *you* very much." He wrapped his arms around her. "You know that, Tilly, don't you? We love you both."

She believed him. For a few precious, perfect months, she believed her father and she loved her sister.

But as the gentle spring rains gave way to the dry heat of summer, Tilly watched her mother from quiet corners of the cottage. She saw how she gazed so adoringly at Esther, fussing and cooing over her with such devotion. She soon tired of her parents talking endlessly about what Esther had done that day—her first sneeze, her first tooth, her first full night's sleep. She felt herself fading into the background, living in the shadows of her own family.

By the time the first storms of winter blew in across the mountains, Tilly didn't love Esther anymore. All she felt was envy. Or was it something darker than that? It was a feeling she hardly dared acknowledge. She shut it out, building a wall around herself.

And then Esther fell dangerously ill with a fever. For weeks, nobody noticed Tilly. Hannah Harper lost all interest in her elder daughter, caring only for the frail, much-longed-for baby, who had entered the world with a struggle and barely survived her first year.

Tilly became an irritation, a nuisance. Forgotten about, she retreated to the lakes and fells where she felt her anger stir within her like the iron-gray clouds gathering over the mountains.

She sensed a storm was coming.

Chapter 25

Violet House, London

June 1912

It was a week before Alexandra Rose Day. The girls had been working long hours to make the thousands of tiny pink roses. They were all exhausted but still the thrill of expectation buzzed around them as the day grew ever closer.

And as the real roses in the window boxes of Violet House bloomed, so did Tilly's fondness for the girls under her charge. She enjoyed their strange habits and quirky little ways: Edna's insistence on eating a boiled egg with every meal; Doris's eccentric collection of clothes—most of which she seemed to wear all at the same time; the little flowers that Alice carved out of bars of soap and left dotted around the bathroom; Buttons's tendency to go missing for long periods—particularly when it was time to attend chapel. Each had her own unique personality, which distinguished them far more than their physical afflictions, which Tilly hardly noticed now.

Of all the girls, she had developed a particular fondness for Hilda. Only sixteen, Hilda struggled, more than most, to accept her handicap—the result of an accident in her father's mill that had led to her right leg being amputated. With her mother dead, and seven older children to manage, Hilda's father hadn't been able to provide the care she needed. He'd reluctantly sent her to the Training Homes, where she'd quickly learned the craft of flower making. She was known affectionately by the other girls as "Lil," because of the talent she was showing for making the difficult lilies. As one of the newest arrivals at Violet House, Tilly had felt an affinity with her, although she found it strange that she looked so very like Esther.

Tilly had found Hilda weeping on the scullery floor that morning.

"Look at me," she wept, an upturned bucket of water soaking her skirts. "I can't even carry a bucket of water without ruining everything. I'm no better than those scrawny dogs you see down the markets, hopping around on one leg. I hate myself sometimes. Who's ever going to want to marry a girl with one leg?"

Tilly wasn't always sure what to say to make her feel better. She knew what it was to feel like a failure, to feel that you didn't belong, that you'd let everybody down. She knelt down, placing her arms around the girl's narrow shoulders.

"I know it seems as though life has been cruel to you, Hilda, and I can't blame you for thinking that, but you have a second chance here. Making your wonderful flowers, and for the Queen herself, and living here with the other girls—it's your chance to be part of a family. I know it can't mend your body, but perhaps it can mend something in here—in your heart. You're a wonderful girl, Hilda. You shouldn't hate yourself. You should be very proud of yourself. You all should."

Hilda smiled at her through her tears, her eyes so like Esther's.

"Did I ever tell you that you remind me very much of my sister?"

Hilda laughed. "No! I didn't even know you had a sister. You must miss her very much."

Tilly hung her head and wished she could agree.

As life at Violet House had become familiar, so London itself was beginning to settle more easily around Tilly. She almost didn't notice the bitter taste of sulfur that hung in the air over the city skyline and didn't balk quite as much at the heady mixture of industrial and human smells that crept into the back of her throat. For as much as London still suffocated her on occasion, it more often excited and delighted her. Mrs. Ingram was right, London did scrub up as fine as any lady when you got to know her.

Tilly especially looked forward to her monthly afternoon off, when she could enjoy the privacy of a few rare hours to herself, away from Sekforde Street, exploring the famous sights she'd heard so much about: the museums, the palaces and the royal parks. She took pleasure in discovering quieter, secluded squares and gardens, where she would sit, unnoticed, with her sketchbook.

Whenever she could, Tilly took Flora's notebook with her, reading snippets while she was certain of not being disturbed. She hadn't told anyone about the wooden box or the notebook—not even Mrs. Pearce, who'd become a good friend and confidante over the past months.

Most of all, Tilly liked to sit under the cooling shade of an oak tree by the Serpentine in Hyde Park. She observed the starchy nursemaids as they strolled past, pushing their perambulators, and watched the children playing with their sailing boats on the lake. Then she would take the faded old notebook from her pocket, immersing herself in the life of the two little flower girls. The more she read, the more anxious she was to discover what had happened to Flora—and to little Rosie. They'd become like real people to her, as if she could touch them if she reached far enough into the past.

JUST AS SHE HAD on her previous afternoon off, Tilly traveled now by omnibus, across London, to Hyde Park. The sun's relentless heat stuck to everything, casting a hazy shimmer onto the road. Red-faced street sellers cried their wares, as ladies, suffocating in their petticoats and high-collared blouses, sought shade beneath their white parasols.

Reaching the park, Tilly found a secluded tree some distance from the crowds that were gathered around the ginger-beer seller. Settling herself between the gnarled roots of the tree, she discreetly removed her shoes and stockings—abandoning all care for etiquette in the oppressive heat. She imagined how horrified her mother would be if she could see her, and smiled to herself, enjoying her small moment of rebellion, as she enjoyed the sensation of the grass between her toes. Tucking her feet beneath her skirt, she opened the notebook at the page she had left marked and began to read.

September 1880. Clacton.

It was June when I lost you, Rosie. June of the year 1876. Mr. Shaw tells me so. All the same, it's hard to believe it is four full year since I last seen you. It seems like only yesterday I felt your hand slip from mine. I still remember that awful

panic, like someone was after choking me, so as I couldn't catch my breath. Thought I would suffocate without you.

I didn't have the words to write back then, but I do now. I go to the school, see, where I learn my letters and numbers. I like school—it's nice to be able to read and write, and I don't get walloped like at that ragged school I went to.

The school mistress says it's good for me to write down my memories. She says it will help me remember you and that it will help with my writing, too. I try to be neat and tidy on the page, like she teaches us. And I plan to give this book to you, Rosie, when I find you. I know you won't be able to read the words, with you not seeing proper, but I'll read them to you so as you can understand how I never forgot you, nor stopped looking for you.

I'll tell you about my journey from London to Clacton, shall I?

I reckon most children would be thrilled to travel on a train to the seaside, but when I stepped off that platform at Fenchurch Street into the carriage compartment, I felt an awful sadness creeping over me. I was leaving you, Rosie. Leaving London.

The noise of the locomotive as it creaked out of the station scared me half to death, the smoke puffing out of the funnel like a great monster, the wheels clanking and the whistle screeching like a fishwife. I had to cover my ears it was so loud. Luckily, Mr. and Mrs. Shaw were traveling with me, to make sure I got settled into the orphanage. I remember staring at Mrs. Shaw's belly, which was as round as the moon, and her telling me she was to have another baby soon.

She lost that baby not a month later. Gone up to Heaven she is. Another angel.

I stared out the window as we left the grayness of London, and I gawped at the green fields we were soon passing. I'd never seen fields before. I'd seen nothing other than London. I liked the look of them fields—and the sky so big above them—but all I could think was that I was leaving you—every turn of the wheels, every blessed bit of grass taking me farther away from you, Rosie. I watched it all through my tears.

Mr. and Mrs. Shaw were awful kind. They tried to comfort me as them salty tears fell down my cheeks. I dabbed at them with Granny's lace handkerchief, what I kept scrunched into a ball in my hands till it was as sodden as the cresses after the rains. I wanted to jump out the window and run all the way back to Rosemary Court.

Mr. Shaw tried to take my mind off things, telling me about the villages we were passing and the sights we saw. "England is full of views like this, Florrie. Only cities like London are dark and crowded. There's no end to England's landscape." He told me of places I'd never heard of: the waterways of Norfolk, the lakes of Westmorland, the mountains of Wales and Scotland. I didn't have the heart to tell him I didn't care for any of it without you by my side.

After a long time, the train stopped at a place called Weeley, where a kind man, Mr. King from the local tavern, was waiting with his wagonette to take us to the orphanage.

As we rumbled along, I got a funny taste from the air—and a smell I didn't know. Mr. Shaw told me it was the salt, from the sea. I stuck my tongue out and lapped at it like a cat drinking milk. It tasted so nice, that salt.

Then we went round a bend and, Lor! There it was. The sea. Couldn't take my eyes off it. I sat, staring at that ocean for an age, all blue and twinkling like stars was caught in them waves. Ye'd have smiled at the funny noise of them seagulls, all screeching like a bawling baby. And that sea breeze, Rosie! I felt that it could lift me up by my petticoats and carry me into the clouds.

I soon got used to life here at the orphanage. I won't deny it is nice to wake up to that fresh sea breeze every morning. It makes me want to skip and run and laugh at them silly seagulls. Makes me feel like I am alive, that sea air does, and I'm happy enough here by the sea, but I think of you every day, Rosie, and pray to God that He will keep you safe.

When I'm after getting sad at night, Mother comes to comfort me. She tells me I mustn't worry about you. She says a person can never be truly lost, as long as someone is looking for them. And I'll always be looking for you, Rosie.

I'm keeping some of your favorite flowers what I found in the meadow and in the gardens that Mr. Hutton keeps so nice. One of the girls puts the flowers between the pages of her Bible. She says they dry out like paper if you leave them long enough and then you have them to admire all year round, even in the winter. She likes to put them onto card and make a picture of them. I'll keep my flowers here, in this book. Do you remember how I used to tell you about the flowers all speaking a language—that they all have a meaning? The gentlemen would buy flowers for a posy to tell their sweethearts of their love for them, and the ladies would choose flowers to send a message of sorrow to a friend whose sister had died. I hope you'll hear my flowers talking to you one day. I chose them especially.

Each year seems to pass quicker than the last. Is it really four full year since I first came here? Is it that long since I last saw you, my dear little Rosie?

There are lots of rules and jobs here, which I find dull, but Mother says it's good for a girl to learn how to behave with proper manners. She says, "A tidy home makes for a tidy mind," and that I shouldn't be grumbling about small jobs like turning out the cupboards and cleaning all the pictures and windows.

The food is grand, though, and there's always enough for seconds. I stuff my belly so full sometimes I think I'll burst—except on Wednesday's, when it's mutton. I don't care for that mutton—it smells like them bones Da used to collect. Do you remember how we'd sit and sort through the rag and hold a posy of violets to our noses to block out the bad smell?

When we all have our jobs done, we like to have a grand game of schools together, or play dressing up, or plays. Sometimes we have a picnic in the fete field with the Bluebells or the Daffodils (that's what we call the girls from the other homes). We practice the Greek dancing for the fete-day displays and play at games of hide-and-seek, blindman's buff, and skipping.

When it's warm enough, we go to the sea for a swim, with our bathing costumes. Some of the older girls swim way out, so their feet can't even touch the bottom, but I just like to stand up to my knees and jump over the waves. That's mighty craic, that is! You'd love the feel of it. When I think of how frozen and sore your little feet were and how warm and clean my feet are after standing in that sea . . . but I try not to let myself think of such things too much. It makes me too maudlin.

When it rains or when Mother says it's too cold to be outside, we stay in and make stuffed dolls with stockings and rags, and then we do needlework to make clothes for the dolls. We take the dollies to the hospital for the poorly children (there are three suffering from meezels this week, one from new moania, and seven from sore heads).

After tea we like to go into Mother's room to listen to the stories she reads to us. She also tells us about the orphange. We especially like it when she tells us about Isabella Hope Dearing. She was a little girl here who was looking forward to going home for Christmas, but she died of the consumption on Christmas morning. Before she died, she told the Mother she had seen an angel and that she wasn't afraid. "This is my going-home day," she said, before she died. We all cry when Mother tells us that part, and we bow our heads when she reminds us about the wreath of white lilies and snowdrops, made by the flower girls in the chapel workrooms in London for the little girl's grave. A wreath is placed in the gardens here, every year, in her memory. Isabella Hope Dearing is the nicest name I ever heard.

Today we had the Harvest Festival fete day—the last of the summer. It was great fun, and lots of people came to visit for the day. The adults played games of stilts and ran relay races, and there was a tug-of-war for the gentlemen. The children played wheelbarrow races and sang nursery rhymes and in the evening the older girls did their Greek dances and the hoop routine. The best event was the Grand Fire Drill display.

I was one of the children who had to be rescued from the pretend fire from one of the upper rooms. The gentlemen climbed up ladders and lifted us down over their shoulders. It was such fun!

I helped serve tea and lemonade to the guests. A kind lady told me I had the prettiest eyes she'd ever seen and that she liked my Irish accent. She told me she grew up in France. She was so pretty with her lace dress and parasol—we all gawped at her, like she was a princess in a fairy story. I saw her little girl from a way across the meadow. She had beautiful red hair, just like yours, Rosie. I wanted to run to her, to see if it was you. But I didn't. Of course it wasn't you. It was just a little girl, come to see the poor orphans with her mother.

But how I wished it had been you, Rosie, come to tell me you'd found me after all this time. Sometimes I find it hard to remember your sweet little face. And that scares me. What if I forget? What if I can't remember you, Rosie? What will become of you then?

"I'm sorry if I'm disturbing you."

Tilly dropped the notebook into her lap, startled by the voice. Putting her hand to her forehead to shield her eyes from the glare of the sun, she saw the silhouette of a man standing in front of her.

"Miss Harper, isn't it? The girl from the north?"

"Mr. Shaw! What a surprise." She daren't stand up, horribly conscious of her bare feet hiding beneath her skirts.

He grinned like a fool. "Still searching for a bit of green, I see! You country folk do make me laugh!" He bent down, took her hand in greeting and stood for a moment, not speaking.

Tilly felt his smooth skin against hers. A light breeze sent goose bumps running up her arms as he looked at her.

"Is it good?" he asked.

"I'm sorry?"

"The book." He gestured to the notebook Tilly was clutching in her other hand. "Is it good?"

She felt her heart racing.

"Oh, this? Not really." She let her hands fall to her sides, hoping that the folds of her skirt would conceal the notebook. "I picked it up from one of the stalls on the South Bank earlier—just passing the time really."

He smiled, his deep brown eyes sparkling like polished walnut in the sunlight. Tilly couldn't help but stare back at them.

"Well, it's a wonderful afternoon for some quiet reading. I should leave you in peace. I hear things are quite frantic in the workrooms ahead of next week. No doubt you're in need of a little solitude."

"It is a little hectic, yes! But the girls are working so hard on the Alexandra roses—and they never complain. Well, not very often."

"And I believe the Queen hopes everyone in London will wear a rose in their buttonhole on the twenty-sixth. Uncle Albert has all kind of plans to decorate the motor cabs that will deliver the roses out to the ladies who'll be selling them. He says he'll decorate the trams, too. There really is no end to his ambition!"

"It will be quite the spectacle, all right. There's such excitement among the girls. They're hoping Queen Alexandra will visit the factory."

Tilly felt awkward in Herbert's company. There was something about him that made her feel like a foolish schoolgirl, especially since he stood in front of her and she remained sitting on the ground.

"Well, it was very nice to see you again," she said, for want of anything better, hoping he might leave her in peace.

"Likewise. Perhaps we'll meet again soon. I've never visited the north of England. I'd love for you to tell me about it sometime." He hesitated, as if expecting her to say something else. All she could think about were her bare feet. "Well, enjoy the rest of the afternoon, Miss Harper—and mind you don't get too hot in this sun."

She wasn't sure whether she detected a smirk on his face as he tipped his hat in farewell and turned to walk across the grass. She watched him melt into the crowds, shielding her eyes from the sun, which cast a long shadow in his wake.

Chapter 26

Violet House, London

June 1912

Her father walking down the shale path in his soldier's uniform. A smile on his face, a twinkle in his eyes. He had come home!

She ran, shrieking with delight; ran from the cool of the scullery into the warmth of the sun, to the warm embrace of the father she loved so much.

He stopped and sank to his knees as he saw her, his arms outstretched in welcome.

"Daddy! Daddy! You're home! You came home!"

Running, tripping, falling into his outstretched arms, throwing her hands around him, nuzzling into the sun-darkened skin on his neck, his standard-issue felt cap falling from his head.

"Yes, Tilly! Yes, love! I came home. I came back for you, my love . . ."

"Do you miss your family?"

Tilly opened her eyes. She was sitting in her favorite chair, the warmth of the late evening sun having lulled her into a deep sleep. Looking up from the embroidery she'd been working on, she saw Queenie standing in the doorway, half in and half out of the room.

"Did you say something, Queenie? I think I nodded off for a moment."

"I did. Didn't realize you were snoozing. Thought you were concentrating on your sewing. I was just asking whether you miss your family. You've been here three months now, and I noticed you haven't had any letters. Three months is when most of the housemothers start to feel homesick, so I just wondered if it was bothering you the same way. That's all."

Queenie spoke in the same manner to everyone: direct, abrupt, and without the niceties other people placed around their sentences. At first, Tilly had put it down to her Yorkshire upbringing, but as Mrs. Pearce had explained, "Queenie Lyons is as short in manners as she is in stature. You'd do well to make a friend of her, rather than an enemy." Tilly had tried not to take Queenie too personally. It wasn't easy.

She bristled at Queenie's question and stood up, fussing with the cushions on the sofa—with anything—to deflect the attention away from herself.

"Well, yes. Of course I miss my family," she mumbled, "but I'm so busy, I hardly have time to think about them. And I consider you all to be my family now."

Hilda glanced up from the book she was reading. "That's a lovely thing to say, Miss Harper. Isn't it, girls? And we think of you as part of our family, too."

Sweet Hilda, not a bad word to say about anybody. She was as different from Queenie as it was possible to be.

Queenie persisted in her interrogation. "But you must miss your mother and father. It's only natural to miss your parents when you leave home for the first time. I just thought it seemed a bit strange that you hadn't mentioned them."

Tilly eyed Queenie suspiciously. While the others had all made Tilly feel very welcome, Queenie had watched from a distance, without ever showing any real interest. Tilly knew that Queenie had been at the Flower Homes the longest, having arrived as a young girl. "Queenie knows practically every girl who has ever lived or worked here," Mrs. Pearce had explained over the weekly wash. "She remembers almost every housemother and assistant housemother, and that gives her a sense of superiority."

Tilly stopped her plumping and tidying. The other girls in the room had fallen silent. Perhaps they'd *all* been wondering about her family life, perhaps they all had questions they'd like to ask.

Hilda sensed Tilly's discomfort. "Queenie, you shouldn't be so rude. You shouldn't be asking Miss Harper all these questions. Her family is none of our business."

"It's all right, Hilda, honestly." Tilly sat on the sofa. "I suppose it's only natural for you all to want to know more about me. I haven't said anything because I thought you'd all find my life back home boring. There's really not much to tell."

"What's it like? The Lake District?" Now Alice joined in, putting her cards down on the table. "Does it rain all the time, like they say? Sounds bloody miserable to me."

Tilly laughed. "Yes, Alice! It rains *all* the time! But when you see the mountains reflected in the lakes, and the shadows of the clouds racing over the summits—the colors changing from green to gold to purple as the sun catches the gorse and the heather—when you feel the mountain air blowing through your hair, it is truly magical. And the taste of the gingerbread from Sarah Nelson's shop—now that's something to miss, all right!"

She soon had a group of girls gathered around. They listened, wide eyed, as she told them about the lakes and mountains and wildlife, which, for those who had never lived anywhere other than the city, sounded like descriptions from a fairy story. Tilly found herself enjoying the opportunity to talk about home, although she said nothing about her mother or Esther, and nobody asked, not even Queenie.

THE NEXT MORNING was a glorious summer Sunday. It was now only three days until Alexandra Rose Day, and the girls were relieved to have a day off from the relentless pressure of making the little pink roses.

As they made the now familiar journey to the small chapel at the end of the street, Tilly found herself walking alongside Queenie. Or perhaps Queenie had made sure she was beside Tilly. Either way, Tilly sensed something different about Queenie. She seemed more relaxed, more comfortable in Tilly's company.

"I didn't mean to upset you yesterday evening, Miss Harper," she said as they walked. "I can be a nosy old cow at times. That's all."

Tilly chuckled. "That's all right, Queenie. I think we can all be accused of being nosy at one time or another."

"I didn't mean to pry. I just thought you might like to talk about home."

"Well, thank you. It was very thoughtful of you."

Although she didn't actually say the word *sorry*, Tilly understood that this was Queenie's apology, and she accepted it as such.

"You look a little tired, if you don't mind me saying. Are you sleeping well at night?" Queenie asked.

Tilly hesitated. She looked at Queenie, wondering what she knew.

"Reasonably well. Yes. I suppose it always takes time to get used to a new house—and a new bed. And, London is much noisier at nighttime than I'm used to."

"I knew the person who occupied that room before you."

Tilly stopped walking. "Oh?"

"'Course, it's been empty a good few years now. Nobody wanted to sleep in it after Flora—they all said it was too cold and depressing."

"Flora?" Tilly felt a shiver run up her spine.

"Yes. Flora—or Florrie, as I always knew her. She became housemother not long before she died. Preferred the girls to use her proper name: Flora. Thought it sounded more official or something."

Tilly couldn't believe what she was hearing. She wanted to pull Queenie to one side, forget all about chapel, and ask her about Flora. Maybe Queenie knew something about Rosie. She had so many questions.

"What was she like?" Tilly asked.

"Florrie was a natural with the flowers. One of the best. Came up from the orphanage at Clacton with Lily Brennan when they were both fifteen and finished with their schooling. Inseparable those two were—Irish, you see. Always stick together, don't they. They slept in beds next to each other in that little room at the top of the house and sat beside each other in the workroom. Became great friends. She had a good pattern hand, Florrie did—clever with the designs, you know, so she was always in demand. She was good with the girls, too. Understood them. She'd lived through hell and knew what it was like out there selling on the streets. She told me she never took it for granted being here, that she was thankful for it every day."

"She never married? She lived here all her life?"

"Yes. Couldn't get over all that business with losing her sister. Always looking for her at the markets and talking to the flower sellers in case one of them might know her, or even *be* her, grown up. That was her life: looking for her sister and making the flowers. Florrie always believed that Rosie was alive somewhere—but I wasn't so sure. What are the chances of a little blind girl surviving out there on the streets without anyone to mind her? Even if she'd managed to get away from the man who Florrie suspected of snatching her that day, I doubt she would have lasted more than a few days without food or shelter. Very sad. I think it was the not knowing that Florrie found so hard."

Tilly's thoughts drifted back to her room. To the wooden box. To Flora's notebook. To the scent of violets and the feeling of being watched.

"You must miss her," Tilly said, as they started walking again to catch up with the others.

"I do. She was a good housemother and a hard worker. Seemed to feel it was her duty to look after the girls. Said we were like her family, all of us, like her own sisters and daughters. I think she would have liked to have had children of her own. The Irish like a big family round them, don't they?"

Tilly smiled. "I wouldn't know. I don't know any Irish."

"What? With *that* hair?"

Tilly laughed, touching her rich auburn curls. "Ah, yes. *This!* Nobody knows where that comes from. Bit of a cuckoo, I am. One of those family mysteries."

They arrived at the chapel at the same time as Herbert Shaw.

Edward was trailing in his wake, as usual. Herbert held the door open for Tilly, making a grand gesture of doing so.

"Good evening, Miss Harper. I hope you are keeping well and bearing up under the dreadful heat of your first London summer?"

"Good evening, Mr. Shaw. I am enjoying the summer very much, thank you. At least the trees in the parks provide some welcome shade."

"Indeed. It would almost be tempting for a lady to remove her stockings if she were to find a secluded spot."

Her cheeks flared scarlet. She didn't think he'd noticed. He must have seen her stockings and shoes where she'd placed them among the tree roots. She wished she could melt away into the flagstones.

Thankfully, their conversation was interrupted as Herbert turned to greet somebody else.

Sensing Edward watching her over Herbert's shoulder, Tilly smiled and wished him good evening. He mouthed a few words in reply, but they were drowned out as everyone laughed at something witty Herbert had said.

Tilly slept fitfully that night, thoughts of home and of Flora at the forefront of her mind. She couldn't believe that Queenie had known Flora Flynn. She couldn't believe Flora had once slept in this very room—possibly in this bed. She wanted to tell Queenie about the notebook and the trinkets. She especially wanted to ask her about the pressed flowers—about what they might mean—but something held her back.

As she fell into a restless sleep, the familiar dreams drifted in, creeping around her troubled mind like storm clouds over the mountains. She dreamed of a hand resting on top of her head; of being watched; of the rich perfume of violets and roses swirling in the air around her.

After several hours tossing and turning, Tilly got up and dressed by candlelight. Peering out of the window, she could tell that it was still early—the lamplighter had not yet been to extinguish the gas lamps. She guessed it must be around four o'clock. She took Flora's notebook from the wooden box and turned to the page she had marked with the lavender ribbon, and began to read.

October 1883

I'm back in London now, living in Violet House, where I first came when Mr. Shaw found me. It's in the middle of the street, with Rosebud on one side and Bluebell on the other. I share a room with Lily Brennan at the top of the house. The room is nice—there's a big wardrobe at one end, where we keep our dresses and pinafores and boots, and there's a window, which lets in some light when the fog's not lurking. It's like a palace compared to that room we had in Rosemary Court.

The girls here are friendly and there's a few of us have come from the orphanage. Some of the other girls have been here years already. Queenie Lyons thinks she's in charge, telling us all what to do like a sergeant major. I don't mind her so much, though. I've met worse people than Queenie Lyons.

It's strange to be back in London, back among the streets we called home for so long. I miss the Flower Village—the sound of the sea and the blue skies. It's funny to think how sad I was to leave London all those years ago, not sure what life would be like at the orphanage. And now, here I am, sad to have left there.

London seems darker than I remember. Maybe it's because I got so used to the colors of Clacton. The sun shines so brightly there. I suppose it doesn't help that it hasn't stopped raining all day, and the yellow fog still hangs about, choking the sky and everyone beneath. Lily says she's worried about Mr. Shaw. Says she hears him coughing all the time.

I went back to the markets today, Rosie. It was so cold even in my nice boots and warm clothes—an east wind was blowing and a frost had settled in the night. Nothing's changed. Lots of the costers and sellers are still the same and the smells in the flower markets are as lovely as ever. It was strange to hear the cries of the sellers. "Lavender, sweet lavender." It felt so familiar.

I stood for a while, watching the catchpenny sellers down at Drury Lane and on the corner of Tottenham Court Road. I can hardly believe I used to live and work among them. If they could only see the waves crashing onto the beach—just once feel the sand between their toes.

I looked at all their faces for as long as I could, wondering if any of them was you, Rosie. I stared the longest at anyone with red hair. You'd be eleven year old now—I wonder what you look like. Do you look the same? I still can't believe you're not here with me, Rosie. I think about you every day, wondering where you are, wondering what became of you and what your life is like now—because I know you still live. I know you are here in London—somewhere—I am sure of it.

I went back to the room we had in Rosemary Court to see if you was still there, but it is taken by a family from Dublin. They tell me they know nothing of a little girl with pretty red hair. I walk the streets every day after I finish making my flowers. I look for you everywhere. I know you'll be changed with the years, but I would know you. I would know you, for certain.

If only I could find you, Rosie. If only I could know you are safe. It's the not knowing that's the worst of it—like a dark shadow that follows me everywhere.

Our working day in the chapel is long. We start straight after breakfast at eight o'clock, and we finish at six in the evening. The nights are closing in, so there's a darkness to the sky by the time we make our way back home. Queenie Lyons showed me around the workrooms when I first arrived and gave me some instruction on how to make the flowers. She told me I'd have three months to prove myself and if I wasn't any good I'd be sent back to the orphanage. I just ignore her when she's after saying things like that. I've a good pattern hand anyway—Mrs. Shaw tells me so. She says there'll always be plenty of demand for a girl who's good at designing the patterns, so Queenie Lyons can take that and shove it where the sun don't shine.

Mr. Shaw tells me he remembers you; remembers when we used to first visit the Club Room all those years ago. Do you remember it, Rosie? The good and kind people there. I tell Mr. Shaw that I hope you'll find your way here, to the crippleage, or that maybe you'll remember the chapel and the singing and the brass band you loved so much. I can tell Mr. Shaw is very sorry about you not being found. He doesn't say so, but I can tell that's what he's thinking when I look into his blue eyes. He told me once that he understands a little of how I feel about losing you, because of their baby what died. He says a loss of any kind is hard to bear. I asked him how he can still believe in God when He can let something like that happen. He says that there is a reason for everything, and even though we might not always understand the Lord's work, we should always try to accept it.

Which makes Mr. Shaw a better person than me, because I cannot accept that you are not with me, Rosie, and I will never understand why you were taken from me.

November 1883

The photographer, Mr. Matthews, came to see us again today. Mr. Shaw is keen on us getting our pictures taken for the postcards he uses to promote the Flower Homes. Mr. Matthews was only here a while ago—I remember, because Lily sat next to me for the picture. Queenie sat on the other side of me, holding a great spray of orchids she'd made for a display at the Guild Hall. I'm sure she was trying to block my face out of the picture, but I stuck my neck out to make sure you could still see me.

Lily likes to send the postcards home to her aunt in the north—an aunt she didn't even know existed until a year ago. She wrote on the back of one: "This is the big workroom but I am not in there I am in the better one with the girls and you no we don't get up to no tricks the lot of us. We are innocent little dears. I was making poppies last week and now I am making carnations. I am in the back row, in the middle, with Florrie."

Lily is cheeky all right. She has a fierce temper and can be bold when she puts her mind to it, but she makes me smile.

Lily looks as I imagine you must look now, Rosie; she has the same red hair, just like you.

Anyway, we all lined up again today for Mr. Matthews' photograph and we all jumped when the flashbulb popped—just like we did the last time. It's funny, isn't it, how the strange can become the familiar.

I think I'll be happy enough living and working here, but I do miss the orphanage and the sea air. I've set up the Forget-Me-Not Society, so that everyone who leaves Clacton will always be able to write to each other and keep in touch, wherever they go.

I wish that you could write to me, Rosie, wherever you are. I wish that you could remember.

January 1885

I haven't written in this book for a long while now. I sometimes don't know what to write, Rosie. What else can I say to bring you back to me?

I keep the notebook in a wooden box. Mrs. Shaw gave it to me as a gift for Christmas. I've also put my few trinkets inside. They're not much, but they remind me of the past. The black button from Da's coat, the wooden peg you used to play with as a doll, the rag dolly I made at the orphanage and the lucky lace handkerchief with the shamrocks stitched into the corner. I keep the box in the wardrobe and tie it with the lovely silk ribbon Mrs. Shaw also gave to me. I take the box out every now and again, to remind myself.

Lily left the Flower Homes last year. I miss her terribly. She went to live with her aunt in a place called Windermere, somewhere in the north of England. Lily says it is a nice place. She writes letters to tell me all about it and she sent a postcard at Christmas. It has one of the pictures on the front that Mr. Matthews took of us when he visited. She wrote on the back: "December 1884. You will find her. I know you will. Happy Christmas. Lily B. x." I'm adding it to the wooden box so I can always remember her.

She says there's lots of lovely lakes where she lives and huge, big mountains to climb. She tells me she's sweet on a young blacksmith's son who lives nearby and says she's always riding her aunt's horse on the rough roads, so as the shoes will need replacing. She reckons she'll marry that blacksmith's son one day. I hope he makes her happy if she does. Lily is a good girl. She deserves to be happy.

Everyone deserves a little happiness in their life, Rosie. I only hope that you found some in yours.

Chapter 27

Nightingale House, London
October 1880

Before she closed the lid of the last trunk, Marguerite walked over to her dressing table and settled herself on the stool. She looked around the room. It was strange to see it so empty—just a shell—nothing of herself or her life here visible anymore. Even her pots of cold cream, her lip balms, hairpins, bottles of fragrance and lavender water were absent from the places they had stood for so many years. Everything had been packed away, sent on ahead to the new house in Lancashire, where she and Violette would travel later that day.

It had taken much longer than either she or Thomas had hoped, but finally the right business opportunity had presented itself. Earlier that summer, Thomas had informed Marguerite that they would be leaving London and moving to a wonderful home in the north of England. "It's in a small village called Worsley," he'd explained. "I know you'll love it, darling. The gardens are stunning—the lawns running down to a lovely little stream—and the business prospects in Manchester are extremely good. This will be a wonderful opportunity for us. For all of us," he'd added, glancing at Violette, who was playing quietly with a new doll.

Marguerite melted when she saw the obvious affection Thomas now had for the child. Despite his reservations about the circumstances under which she had arrived, and his continuing belief that somebody was bound to come looking for her—nobody ever had. Violette was as lost as it was possible for anyone to be. And although she still spoke occasionally to her imaginary friend, as the years had passed, she had stopped asking Marguerite about finding her.

That Thomas had come to accept Violette as their own daughter made Marguerite's heart soar with a hope she had never thought she'd feel again. While there would always be an ache in her arms from the space left by Delphine, their family was, once again, complete.

More than anything, it was the thrill of watching Violette observe the world around her that filled Marguerite with so much joy. Several medical procedures had improved the child's vision beyond anyone's expectations. There was much to be grateful for. Even so, the chance to move away from the prying, inquisitive eyes of London society couldn't come soon enough.

Sitting at her dressing table now, Marguerite studied her reflection. There was color in her cheeks again. Her eyes were bright and hopeful where once they had been so dull and empty. There was a purpose about her. She sat upright, pulling her shoulders back, turning her head from left to right to catch her profile in the angled mirrors. This was the woman she remembered; this was the Marguerite Durant who had arrived in London as a temperamental teenage girl. This was the girl who had met and married a promising young businessman and become mistress of the renowned Nightingale House. She looked in the mirror and saw a woman who, despite everything, had endured.

The house was eerily quiet without the staff bustling about, without the clatter of tea trays and the comings and goings of endless callers. The only sound was the ever-present wind whistling around the eaves. Even the nightingale had stopped singing. She hadn't heard it for over a week now—perhaps it, too, had moved on.

Opening the drawer of the dressing table, she lifted out her prayer book, removing a delicate packet of tissue paper from beneath it. She hadn't looked at the lace handkerchief since placing it here, four years ago. Nobody but her had ever known it existed.

Having sat in the drawer all these years, the tissue paper was faded, but the handkerchief itself was pristine. She rubbed her fingers across the delicate lace, over the careful stitching of the shamrock leaves. She wondered about the person who had taken such care to make it. How strange that such a thing of beauty had survived among the depravity of Violette's former life.

Next, she took her flower press from the now-empty wardrobe—her dresses, coats, and furs having been packed and sent ahead with Wallis and Mrs. Jeffers. Opening the leather straps that held the press tightly closed, she removed the top page of thick card and carefully lifted up the delicate layers of blotting paper. She admired the simple specimens that she and Violette had collected on their many walks in the gardens and in Petersham Meadows: primroses, bluebells, daisies, pansies, ferns—all perfectly preserved where she had placed them. At the very bottom of the press was the small bunch of flowers that Violette had been clutching the day she was discovered in the carriage. Flattened now by the pressure of the press, the violets were as thin and fragile as tissue paper. Lifting them off the page, Marguerite marveled at their simple beauty. They hadn't browned or faded but were a perfect, paper-like representation of their natural form.

Seeing these insignificant little trinkets again made her so glad that she had kept them. Something about their simplicity had touched her all those years ago; some part of her had felt obliged to keep these small mementos of a life once lived. She planned to give the handkerchief and flowers to Violette on her twenty-first birthday. She would tell her the truth then, explain everything that had happened. With enough love in the intervening years, she was certain that Violette would understand. Perhaps then, Marguerite would finally be free from the guilt and doubt that she carried in her heart.

But that was for the future. Today's journey was about a new beginning; there was no need to spoil it by worrying about where it might end.

"MOTHER, THE CAR is ready!"

Marguerite jumped at the sound of Violette's voice. Her heart soared at the sound of that word: "Mother."

"Yes, darling. I'll be right down."

Wrapping the delicate violets in the tissue paper with the handkerchief and placing the fragile package into her purse, she took one last look around the room as the footman knocked and entered to collect the final trunk.

"Is that the last, m'lady?"

"Yes, Roberts. That's the last."

Marguerite stood up, took the flower press, prayer book, and purse from the dressing table and walked from the room. She was relieved to close the heavy wooden door behind her, to close out all the sadness, all the painful memories.

Holding her head high, she walked downstairs.

Violette stood, small and alone, in the vacuous space of the entrance hall, its size emphasized now that the ornate pictures and grand display vases had been removed. Marguerite studied her for a moment. She was dressed so perfectly, her auburn hair curled into wonderful, shimmering ringlets. With a deep breath, she walked the rest of the way down the stairs and took her daughter by the arm.

"Now, my darling, are we all ready for our big adventure?"

"Yes, Mother. We're all ready."

They smiled at each other as they stepped out into the dazzling sunlight of a glorious autumn day. Thompson was waiting for them on the carriage circle, the horses' coats gleaming like polished mahogany.

"Let us not forget this day, darling," Marguerite said as she helped Violette into the carriage. "My mother always said that every journey comes with either an end or a beginning. I think we should consider this journey a beginning. What do you think?"

Violette smiled. "I like that idea." She settled herself into the seat, having no recollection now of having once hidden beneath it, afraid for her life. "Will you miss the house, Mother?"

Marguerite considered the question for a moment. "A little. You?"

"I'll miss the nightingales. I'll miss them very much."

"Well, perhaps the nightingale will find its way back to you one day, like in the story."

Violette sighed and rested her head on her mother's shoulder. "I do hope so, Mother. I really do."

VIOLETTE SLEPT FOR MUCH OF THE JOURNEY, her head resting in her mother's lap. She dreamed of flowers: hundreds of flowers, the air around her heavy with the rich perfume of roses, lilies, peonies, stocks, and violets. It was beautiful. She took hungry, grateful breaths, inhaling the sweet scent, tasting it on her tongue. All around her, the familiar cries of market sellers, stirring memories held deep within her. A girl's voice, in the distance, rising above it all. "Rosie!" the girl cried. "Rosie! Little Sister, where are you?" She tried to call out in reply, but the words would not come and the image blurred into a mist, lost among the poppies and the meadows that stretched for miles, beyond the horizon and to the north.

Part Three

Primrose (*Primula vulgaris*)

I can't live without you.

A Note on Shaw's Training Homes for Watercress and Flower Girls (from *The Christian Magazine*, June 21, 1912)

It is with the utmost honor that I received a request from Queen Alexandra earlier this year, for the flower girls of our Training Homes in Sekforde Street to make roses for her inaugural "flag day." This flag day, "Queen Alexandra Rose Day," will be held on Wednesday, June 26. The flower girls have made—by hand—thousands of pink roses, which will be sold as buttonholes on the streets of London, by a small army of female volunteers. The money raised from the sale of the flowers will be used to support hospitals and other charitable concerns across our city.

I cannot express in writing the pride I feel when I see how hard the girls have worked to produce such an incredible volume of flowers—every single rose as perfectly made as the next. Indeed, I am sure that God Himself would find it difficult to reproduce such perfect replicas time and time again.

What started out as such a humble operation now sees us running some dozen homes at our orphanage in Clacton (housing over one hundred girls in total). We also have six homes, housing twelve girls each, here in London and are proud to have recently opened a factory, dedicated to the production of the flowers.

I have so often felt that my ability to express, in writing, the plight of London's orphans and street sellers is wholly inadequate. How does one explain the hunger, depravation, and fear that these poor unfortunates suffer, daily? It is quite impossible. I therefore felt it fitting to mark the occasion of Alexandra Rose Day with words, written some years ago, by one of the first flower sellers who came to the Training Homes, here in London.

I can only hope that those who read her words may be inspired to buy a rose from our sellers, and will, in turn, inspire others to do the same. By the end of the day, I hope that the man who never wore a buttonhole because he objected to making himself conspicuous will find that he makes himself conspicuous by wearing none.

Albert Shaw

Superintendent, Training Homes
for Watercress and Flower Girls

Sometimes, when I have a full belly and a clean bed to sleep in, it is easy to forget that I was once a starving little girl, living on the streets, selling flowers for a living. But I make myself remember, because I want to always be grateful for what I have now.

I first met Mr. Shaw when I was eight years old. He stopped to help me and my little sister, after a man had knocked my flower basket from my hands. When Little Sister went missing later that year, Mr. Shaw took me to his orphanage at Clacton.

It was like arriving in Heaven seeing those endless skies of the south coast. I don't know what would have become of me if he hadn't found me and given me a home there. When I was old enough, I was brought back to

London and trained to make the flowers with the other girls. I know that we are a source of astonishment and pity to many people, but we don't ask for sympathy. We just want to live and work as ordinary people—to do an honest days' work for an honest days' pay.

I can never thank Mr. Shaw enough for what he has given me, and the other girls of the Flower Homes and the Flower Village. He has been more of a father to me than my own flesh and blood ever was and I thank Mr. Shaw, and our Good Lord, for keeping me safe and for giving me a reason to hope, when I would otherwise have had none.

Flora Flynn, December 25, 1901

Chapter 28

London

June 26, 1912

Alexandra Rose Day arrived with a flurry of soft, white clouds and a whirlwind of excitement. Tilly threw open the sash windows, letting the sun warm her cheeks. She swept the stairs, scrubbed the front step, mopped the passage floor, and polished the mirrors until everything gleamed. She balanced on a chair at the window in the front parlor, hanging up the lace curtains that she'd washed especially for the occasion. She waved at one of the other housemothers as she walked by. The air fizzed with anticipation.

The girls could barely eat at breakfast—nerves and a steady stream of excitable chatter leaving no space for porridge or bread and butter, no matter how much Tilly reminded them that they needed their strength for the long day ahead.

"Come along now, girls," she nagged. "Try to eat a little of something at least. We can't have you fainting with hunger if you *do* meet the Queen."

But she was no more capable of eating anything herself, her stomach flipping and tumbling in great, giddy waves, so that it was all she could do to sip slowly at a cup of tea and nibble at a slice of toast. It felt like she was eating sawdust.

Mrs. Pearce had popped in early, to give Tilly a hand. She was her usual frantic self, rushing around like a dervish, fetching this, flapping about that, and chattering about the other.

"The men from the factory were up half the night, delivering boxes of roses all over London, ready for the sellers," she said as she slammed a pot of tea onto the table. "There's hundreds of volunteers going to be selling the roses. All of 'em highly regarded society ladies, and some of 'em friends of the Queen herself! Imagine. And they'll be selling *your* roses, girls!"

With rumors rife that the Queen planned to visit the factory, all the girls had washed their hair until it shone, and brushed their teeth until they squeaked.

When breakfast was over, Tilly helped to pack the last few boxes of roses into the cars and carriages that had gathered on Sekforde Street, ready to take fresh supplies out to the sellers. Just as they had on the day she'd arrived, the girls had decorated the street and the outsides of the houses, garlands and garlands of pink roses crisscrossing the street from the upper floors of the houses and adorning every window box and doorframe. The vibrant pink petals shimmered in the early morning sunlight. Tilly stood on the doorstep, admiring their hard work.

Mrs. Pearce joined her, stopping for a second to catch her breath. They stood together, admiring the scene.

"Beautiful, isn't it? Just beautiful."

"It is that, Matilda. It is that."

The excitement grew as the girls prepared to leave the house. They laughed over lost gloves and hats, fussing over each other as they pinned their own Alexandra Rose buttonholes to their pinafores. Tilly knew they were all waiting for the arrival of Mr. Shaw.

And then the alert they'd all been waiting for finally came.

"He's here! He's here!" Buttons shouted from the parlor, where she'd been watching at the window all morning. The parlor was usually reserved for Christmas Day, or when extra-special guests visited, but they'd been given permission to use the room today. Buttons's cries were accompanied by the blare of a car horn. "Mr. Shaw's here with the motor cab," she cried. "Come and see! Oh, come and see. It's beautiful!"

Tilly was nearly knocked off her feet as the girls rushed through the front door, spilling out onto the street. The girls from the other houses soon joined them. Tilly dropped her scrubbing brush into the tin pail, dried her hands on her apron and rushed to see for herself.

Mr. Shaw stood in the middle of the street, resplendent in his black frock coat and top hat. Beside him was a motor cab, although it was unrecognizable as any kind of motor cab Tilly had ever seen. Hundreds of tiny pink roses covered every inch of the vehicle. A special gauze frame had been placed over the windshield and decorated with roses that spelled out the words QUEEN ALEXANDRA ROSE DAY. On top of the car sat another gauze frame, more roses framing the edges, making a spectacular border for the magnificent A ROSE emblazoned across the front.

Tilly joined the others as they gasped and stared in admiration. Walking around the cab, she saw that each side panel had been decorated with roses spelling out the words PLEASE WEAR THE ROSE TODAY. Another large letter *A* was formed from roses at the back. On the driver and passenger doors were impressive crowns—made from roses—and all around the window frames, the wheel arches, and across the luggage rack, rose garlands were draped and twisted into stunning spirals. It was simply beautiful. The delight of the girls filled the street—those who could see describing in vivid detail to those who could not, and who felt their way slowly around the vehicle, seeing it through their fingertips.

"The motor cabs will take fresh supplies of roses from the factory to the sellers throughout the day, keeping them restocked," Mr. Shaw explained. "This is one of dozens of decorated cabs. What a sight to cheer London's dreary streets!"

If anyone had ever doubted the flower girls' ability to fulfill the Queen's request, they certainly didn't doubt it now. The displays were stunning, the roses were out on the streets, and the volunteers were ready to start selling.

Mr. Shaw called everyone's attention as he stood on an upturned crate to make an impromptu speech. "Today you can all be very proud. Today you do not need to hide in the shadows, afraid of what people might think of you. You have done an incredible thing. Be proud. Be jubilant, and let the work of the Training Homes for Watercress and Flower Girls be known by every person in London."

A loud cheer went up as the girls hugged each other. Even Mrs. Pearce couldn't resist, throwing her great arms around Tilly, enveloping her in flesh, as tears spilled down her cheeks.

"Oh, look at me," she laughed, dabbing at her eyes with the

corner of her apron. "It just gets to me sometimes. I couldn't be prouder of them if they were my own daughters. Daft, isn't it."

Tilly smiled. "Not at all, Mrs. Pearce. I feel exactly the same."

IT HAD BEEN ARRANGED that the girls from each house would travel to different areas of London to help the volunteers and to talk to people about the work of the Flower Homes. Arriving at their designated base at Hyde Park Corner, the girls of Violet House were met by an impressive display. Just outside the entrance to the park was a large table, draped with a Union Jack flag. To the right was a pagoda, standing some twelve feet high, decorated from top to bottom with garlands of pink roses and three large letter *A*'s at the front and sides. On the table were several framed pictures of a young Queen Alexandra and vases of roses and examples of the girls' work.

Tilly was delighted to catch her first glimpse of the ladies who were selling the flowers. A dozen or so were gathered in a group to one side of the display. Newspaper reporters were talking to them as photographers took their pictures, recording the event for their newsreels and newspapers. The ladies were all neatly attired in white organdy and muslin dresses, with striking red and white sashes bearing the words ALEXANDRA ROSE DAY proudly emblazoned across their chests. They wore white stockings, white shoes, and straw hats with garlands of the pink roses around the brims. Each of the ladies held a box full of roses, and small collecting tins hung from their wrists. Crowds were gathering around to look.

"White and red are the national colors of Denmark, the Queen's native country," Mrs. Shaw explained to Hilda, who had asked about the ladies' outfits. "They look wonderful, don't they? Every one of the volunteers is dressed the same."

"I hear there are titled ladies selling the roses today," Queenie whispered to Tilly as they watched the group have their picture taken. "Quite the society event this has turned out to be. Look, there's Lady Wyndham and Lady Bancroft. I heard that the Lady Mayoress has her own stall set up beside the Mansion House."

The sellers laughed and joked with passersby. One of the ladies ran after a man on his bicycle, calling to him until he stopped and bought a rose. The chatter and laughter and the rattle of coins being dropped into the collection tins made for a wonderful atmosphere. Unable to resist the temptation to join in, it wasn't long before Tilly picked up a box of roses and walked out into the gathering crowds to join the other sellers.

The roses were so popular that supplies soon began to run low, and the sellers and the Violet House girls were relieved to see one of the decorated motor cabs as it arrived with fresh stock. The word from the driver was that the roses were being bought by everyone.

The newspaper sellers at Hyde Park Corner proudly attached roses to their waistcoats, adding a cry of "Roses, buy y'r Alexandra roses" to their cry of the day's news. Shoppers stopped to look at the rose sellers, children tugging at their mothers' arms, encouraging them to buy a rose. The coal men, window cleaners, and road sweeps each paid his penny for a single bloom, proudly attaching it to his grubby clothing. Starchy-looking businessmen shoved their hands into their pockets looking for a penny. Some gave shillings, half crowns, and sovereigns. Someone even placed a five-pound note in Tilly's collection tin.

By noon, the volunteers and the girls were exhausted. Their feet ached and they were all uncomfortably hot under the midday sun. But their aches and pains were soon forgotten when word spread through the gathered crowd that the Queen's carriage was approaching.

Hilda was the first to see her. "Girls! Girls! Look! It's the Queen! The Queen is coming!"

They all rushed to the edge of the pavement, eager to get the best view of the procession.

The crowds cheered at the sight of their Dowager Queen's black carriage making its way along the road. The mahogany coats of the two horses at the front gleamed like polished wood in the sunlight. The clatter of their hooves against the road reverberated through Tilly's chest. Queen Alexandra smiled graciously as the procession passed Hyde Park Corner. She waved a white-gloved hand to the onlookers, who waved their handkerchiefs up and down in return, rejoicing at the sight of the Queen and Princess Victoria, who sat beside her.

Tilly stared numbly, trying to take it all in so that she would never forget what she was seeing. The Queen wore a beautiful black jacket and skirt, her clothing reflecting her status of mourning for the King. A heart-shaped headdress stood tall on her beautifully coiffed hair and a delicate veil fell across her face. The vivid blue of her garter sash was the only color about her other than the posy of pink roses she held in her hands. Her trademark pearl choker—worn, it was commonly believed, to hide a scar on her neck—glinted as it caught the sunlight, adding a soft luminescence to her face. The sides of her carriage were adorned with garlands of pink roses.

One of the lady sellers ran out toward the Queen's carriage, bowing as the horses clattered past. She offered her basket up to the Queen, who took a handful of the roses, throwing them like confetti to the crowds lining both sides of the street. Everyone cheered and applauded. Men threw their hats into the air.

Tilly had never seen anything like it. Her heart swelled with pride. She knew the girls who had made these flowers. She knew how tirelessly they'd worked to complete the volumes on time. She also knew how they cried into their pillows at night, frustrated by their physical limitations. But Tilly also knew of the deep-rooted affection they held for each other, for Mr. Shaw, and for their work, and she knew it was that which kept them alive inside.

She watched the joy and pride on their faces as the Queen's procession passed, and she thought about Esther—about the long, empty days she spent cooped up inside the cottage; nowhere to go, nothing to do. What was keeping Esther alive inside? She thought of those empty, staring eyes and for the first time in as long as Tilly could recall, she felt a sadness for her sister. It was like a rose petal, slowly unfurling within her heart.

By late afternoon, the girls and volunteers were still busy selling. Tilly was restocking her box when her attention was drawn to someone who had stopped to buy a rose: a slim, elderly lady, wearing a wide-brimmed hat. She stood with an attractive younger woman as they spoke to two of the sellers and admired the displays.

"They really are beautiful, aren't they," the older lady remarked. "It's hard to believe they were made by hand."

It was an accent Tilly had heard before, a face she recognized. Picking up her box—now full to the brim with the little pink roses—she walked toward the two women.

"Mrs. Ingram?"

The woman turned, surprised.

"Yes. That's right. Do I know you?" A flash of recognition crossed her face. "Well, I never! The girl from the train!"

Tilly was relieved that she had the right person. "Yes! We sat opposite each other on the London train. I was starting work at the Flower Homes that day."

"Yes! Yes! I remember. It's hard to forget hair *that* color! Miss Harper, isn't it?"

"That's right. Tilly."

"What a surprise!" She held out a gloved hand. "A pleasure to meet you again."

Tilly smiled and shook Mrs. Ingram's hand, detecting the scent of damask rose as she did.

"So, how is everything going?" Mrs. Ingram asked.

"Very well, thank you. Very well indeed."

"Delighted to hear it. And I believe it was the girls from the Flower Homes who made all these beautiful roses."

"Yes! They've worked so hard. Aren't they wonderful?"

"They certainly are. My daughter insisted that we come out to support the event. I must introduce you."

She led Tilly toward the younger woman, who was talking to one of the lady sellers.

"Darling, I'd like you to meet Miss Harper. She works at the Flower Homes with the girls who made all these wonderful pink roses. Miss Harper, this is my daughter, Violette Ashton."

Tilly shook the woman's hand. "Very pleased to meet you, Mrs. Ashton," she said, struck by the woman's beauty. She guessed that she must be in her late thirties—possibly a little older.

"Likewise," Violette replied. "It is always a pleasure to meet another person with red hair." Tilly laughed, touching her own hair self-consciously. Violette picked up a rose buttonhole from the display table. "Did you make the flowers yourself? They're very lifelike."

"Oh, no!" Tilly laughed. "I'm not one of the flower girls. I work as a housemother. I look after the girls and the running of Violet House."

"Ah. My namesake! Well, it sounds like a very worthwhile position," Violette remarked. "And the girls have done such wonderful work. You must be very proud."

"Yes. I am. We all are."

Violette opened her purse and took a small card from inside.

"Actually, I wonder if I might ask a small favor of you, Miss Harper," she said, handing the card to Tilly. "Perhaps you would be kind enough to ask Mr. Shaw to contact me. I'd like to arrange a regular supply of floral arrangements. My personal details are on the card."

Tilly read the card: *Mrs. Violette Ashton, Nightingale House, Richmond Hill, Borough of Richmond, London.* "Yes, yes, of course. I'll pass it on to him. Thank you."

Violette smiled. "You are very kind. Now, come along, Mother. We really must get going. We don't want to be late for the Lady Mayoress."

As she spoke, she took a handkerchief from her handbag, dabbing at her cheeks and the nape of her neck. "My goodness, the heat today is unbearable. Thank goodness these aren't real roses. They'd have died of thirst by now—as I think I might do if I don't get something to drink soon!"

Her voice faded into the distance as Tilly stared at the handkerchief. Lace. Neat stitching. A cluster of shamrocks in one corner.

"Well, good-bye, Miss Harper," Mrs. Ingram said. "It was lovely to meet you again."

Tilly mumbled a good-bye, standing absolutely still as she watched the two women walk away.

She didn't see her box drop to the ground, or the dozens of

tiny pink roses blown around her feet by the warm breeze. All she could see were shamrocks in the corner of a lace handkerchief and the face of a little girl with flame red hair lost to London's streets.

SHE LAY IN BED THAT NIGHT, still and silent, exhausted by the day and troubled by her thoughts. She glanced toward the writing table, thinking about the wooden box; about Flora and Rosie; about Mrs. Ingram and Violette Ashton; about a lace handkerchief. Tilly didn't believe in coincidence; she believed in fact and purpose. *There is a reason for everything, and everything has a reason.* Her father's words danced around her mind. *Keep a close eye on life, Tilly, and you will always know what that reason is.*

She'd always loved her father's wisdom, his ability to find just the right words to suit the moment: comforting words, thought-provoking words, inspiring words, loving words. How she wished she could talk to him now.

A steady stream of tears slipped down her cheeks as she crept around the edges of sleep: thoughts of Esther, of her father and mother, of Herbert Shaw and his quiet brother, Edward, tumbling and swirling around her mind like a hundred rose petals blown by the wind.

In her dreams, her thoughts turned to Flora. The young child's heart-wrenching words lifted from the pages of the notebook, whispering into her ear as if she stood beside her, talking to her now.

Please find her.

The sensation of a cool breath brushing against the delicate skin at the nape of her neck, the words spoken with absolute clarity.

Please find Little Sister.

Tilly sat bolt upright in bed, her heart pounding. It was unmistakable. The words had been spoken—it wasn't a dream.

"Flora? Is that you, Flora? Are you here?"

A distant sigh. The faintest sound of weeping, far, far away.

Tilly's skin fizzed and prickled. Was Flora still here, drifting between the edge of one life and another, lurking in the shadows of a past she couldn't release?

"I'll help you, Flora," she whispered into the cool dark of the room. "I'll find your little sister. I'll find Rosie." As she spoke, a glorious, intoxicating scent of violets flooded the room. "It will be all right now, Flora. I'll find Rosie. I'll bring her to you."

A prolonged sigh resonated around the room, as clear as a breeze sending ripples dancing across the surface of the lake. It wrapped itself around Tilly, like silk against her skin.

Her promise was made. She had to find Rosie. She had to reunite the two lost sisters, and perhaps, by doing so, she would find some absolution from the guilt that had surrounded her all these years.

As she lay back against her pillow, the scent of violets dissipated and a sense of peace settled across the room.

Chapter 29

Violet House, London
September 1912

"Will she live, Doctor? Will she live?"

Her mother's anguished sobs. The doctor's anxious face.

Standing in the shadows in the corner of the scullery. Forgotten. Unimportant.

"Life-threatening injuries," the doctor said. "Lucky to be alive. Difficult to recover."

Her mother sobbing at the table. "My little Esther. My child. My beautiful daughter."

Anger burning within her.

What about me? She wanted to scream, but the words wouldn't come out. What about me? I'm your child, too. I'm your daughter, too!

Hot tears falling down her cheeks. Fists balled in rage. Fingernails digging into the palms of her hands.

Why hadn't her father come home? He would have loved her. Why hadn't he come home? He'd promised he would come home . . .

As the final, honey-dipped days of summer slipped away, the distinctive chill of autumn settled over London. The golden and amber leaves on the trees in the parks illuminated the city like never before. The colors reminded Tilly of home, so that she found her thoughts returning there more and more frequently. It was six months since she'd left Grasmere, and still she'd received no word from her mother.

With the passing of the months, Tilly's dreams had only intensified, rather than fading away, as she'd so hoped they would. Often she awoke in the night, so alarmed by her visions that she was unable to go back to sleep. Other times, she would wake in the lavender-hued, dawn light—her dreams so real that she was momentarily unsure whether she was back in her bedroom in Grasmere or still in London. These were the dreams that stayed with her all day, troubling her, asking questions of her as she went about her work. "*Running away*, *running away*, *running away*," the train had whispered as she'd sped southward on that bright March morning. Whether running away or not, it was now clear to Tilly that for all she had gained from her new life at the Flower Homes, she hadn't been able to escape her past.

ALTHOUGH LIFE IN VIOLET HOUSE was calmer after the intense months leading up to Alexandra Rose Day, Tilly's days were still busy. She worked hard—harder than she'd ever worked at Wycke Hall—and was pleased when Mrs. Pearce, or one of the other mothers who'd called in for a cup of tea, commented on the sheen on the floors, the sparkle of the windows, and the neat corners she'd turned on the bed linen. And as her numbed hands turned the mangle in the backyard, or took frozen petticoats off the washing line—stiff as a board from an early autumn frost—erratic thoughts of Flora and Rosie, of Mrs. Ingram and Violette Ashton, clamored for space in her mind. She knew there was a connection between them all, but couldn't yet understand what it was. It nagged at her as she went about her work and as she walked through Farringdon Market to buy food for the evening's meal.

Tilly loved the atmosphere of the markets: the hustle and bustle of the wagons and donkeys and the cries of the sellers. "Chestnuts all 'ot, a penny a score," and the cry from the young girls who carried baskets of walnuts, their fingers stained brown: "Fine warnuts! Sixteen a penny, fine war-r-nuts."

She relished the feeling of the frost-tinted air on her cheeks as she walked past the fruit and vegetable sellers, their stalls covered in yellow onions, green broccoli, purple pickling cabbages, and crimson berries. She paid no heed now to the sickly looking hens and stick-thin dogs that wandered aimlessly around her feet.

Most often, she found herself watching the flower sellers, the little girls—no higher than her knee—slipping on walnut husks and cabbage leaves as they darted past, their baskets piled high with violets, watercress, and oranges. She looked at the faces of the older sellers, observing them as they went about their work. Were any of them Rosie Flynn? Did any of them remember a little Irish girl called Flora? Wherever she went, she just couldn't get the two girls out of her mind. Nor could she forget Mrs. Ingram and Violette Ashton. And yet, for all that her instincts told her there was some connection between them all, she couldn't find the courage to send the letter that sat in an envelope between the pages of Flora's notebook.

Dear Mrs. Ashton, she had written.

> *Firstly, my apologies for writing to you in such an unexpected manner. My name is Matilda (Tilly) Harper, and I am employed as housemother at Shaw's Training Homes for Watercress and Flower Girls in Clerkenwell. We were introduced by your mother on Queen Alexandra Rose Day last week . . . I know this will sound most unusual, Mrs. Ashton, but I believe you may be able to assist me in discovering the whereabouts of someone who I would dearly love to find.*

But each time she read the words, she doubted herself. The letter remained unsent. Rosie remained lost.

THE GIRLS OF Violet House were all looking forward to their annual trip to the Flower Village in Clacton. They had eventually settled down after the excitement of Rose Day, although they still talked about it frequently. To give the girls a chance to work on the increased orders for flowers that had come in over the summer (awareness and admiration of their work having spread across London after Rose Day), it had been decided that a Harvest Festival fete day would be held this year, instead of the usual summer fete day. Tilly was to accompany them, at Mrs. Shaw's insistence, and was delighted to accept the invitation.

The impending trip was all the girls talked about over supper.

"It's so wonderful there, Miss Tilly," Hilda said, as she helped to lay the table. "The smell of the salt in the air is something else, and the sea sparkles so beautifully in the clear light. Even the train journey is great fun!"

It was impossible not to get caught up in the girls' enthusiasm.

But before the trip to Clacton, more enjoyment arrived for Tilly, in the form of an invitation to dinner with Mr. Shaw and his family. They were celebrating the fortieth year of the Flower Homes and wished to invite the housemothers and assistant housemothers to a dinner party to mark the occasion.

Tilly's first thought, on reading the invitation from "Mr. Shaw and his family" was whether this would include Herbert and Edward. It had been some time since she'd seen the two nephews, apart from fleeting glimpses and brief, awkward exchanges at chapel on Sundays. While Herbert became more maddeningly handsome and flirtatious each time she saw him, Edward seemed to grow only more uncomfortable around her.

"Who do you think will attend the dinner party?" she'd asked Mrs. Pearce as they shared a cup of tea in the scullery—a familiar routine they had settled into as part of their morning's work.

"All the housemothers and assistants will be going . . . and I expect the nephews will be there. Looking forward to seeing Mr. Herbert again, are we?" Mrs. Pearce teased, winking at Tilly, who gave her a sharp dig in the ribs with her elbow.

"Honestly, I do *not* have feelings for Herbert Shaw! He may be handsome—granted—but he's incredibly arrogant. And as for Edward . . . I honestly don't know which of them is worse. I hope I don't find myself sitting next to either of them. I'd be embarrassed to death by one and bored to death by the other!"

Tilly's concerns about the seating arrangements were followed by the dilemma of what to wear. She didn't need to look in her wardrobe to know that she had absolutely nothing suitable. She was a girl of the outdoors, who liked nothing better than mud on her petticoats, the wind at her heels, and the fresh smell of rain in her hair. Dinner gowns were not something she thought about very often. All the same, she wanted to impress at the dinner party. Exactly *who* she wanted to impress, she wasn't quite sure.

Eventually, she confided in Mrs. Pearce, who offered to make a dress for her.

"Would you, really? Oh, that would be wonderful, Mrs. Pearce! Thank you!"

"Well, I doubt whether your housemother's wage will stretch to the shops in the West End." Mrs. Pearce chuckled. "It won't be an overly formal affair, so you don't need anything too fussy, but it doesn't do a young girl any harm to dress up for an occasion every now and again." She eyed Tilly with a knowing look. "I've some spare fabric. I'm sure I'll be able to put something acceptable together."

A week later, a black evening dress was unveiled to great drama and much approval from the girls, who had gathered in the kitchen to see Mrs. Pearce's creation for themselves. They all gasped as Tilly entered.

"Oh! Miss Harper. You look wonderful!" Hilda said.

Even Queenie agreed, in her own way. "Never knew you'd scrub up so well. You certainly look nice enough."

Tilly was surprised by how pretty she looked all dressed up. The beads and feathers—which Queenie had lent her for the evening—looked wonderful in her hair and added the finishing touch to her outfit. She twirled around, laughing, as the girls admired her. She remembered her father's words and felt a prickle beneath her skin. She felt as though she truly belonged.

ON THE NIGHT of the dinner party, when Tilly was ready to leave, the older girls—Queenie and Alice—were given instructions to take charge of the younger girls for the evening, and to fetch her if there were any problems at all.

"I'll make sure the girls behave," Queenie added, having gladly appointed herself housemother for the evening. "You don't need to worry about us."

Tilly walked with Mrs. Pearce to the Shaw's home at the end of the road. The other housemothers and assistant housemothers joined them, slowly emerging from their houses like nervous chicks emerging from their shells. They huddled together as they walked, gossiping and speculating about the evening ahead.

At the house, they were warmly greeted by Mrs. Shaw—a vision of elegance in cream lace and chiffon. Her soft, silvered hair was gathered in a neat pompadour style, which showed off her petite face and dazzling blue eyes.

"Welcome! Welcome, everyone," she enthused, ushering them in from the cool evening. "Come inside. We've a fire in the parlor."

There were eleven invited members of staff in total: two each from Bluebell, Rosebud, Primrose, Orchid, and Iris House, and Tilly from Violet House. Then there was Mr. Shaw, Mrs. Shaw, a gentleman called Mr. Hogg, who was introduced as the architect of the homes in Clacton, and finally, Herbert and Edward.

Herbert took great delight in entertaining everyone, reveling in the attention he commanded among so many women. He smiled as he was introduced to everyone, acknowledging Tilly in exactly the same way as the others. It was as if he had never seen her before, offering no glimmer of recognition, no spark of friendliness. It infuriated her. Did he not remember their unexpected meeting in the park? Did he not remember their conversations at chapel? It infuriated her even more when he took the seat beside her at the dinner table.

"Miss Harper," he said, sitting down and pouring himself a glass of wine. "What a delight."

She wished she could have kicked his shins with the toe of her new shoes. Instead, she managed a cursory "Mr. Shaw," picking up her own wineglass and allowing him to pour before she took a long sip. Mrs. Pearce caught her eye as she did so, winking in collusion. Mrs. Pearce had never believed Tilly's protestations about not being attracted to Herbert Shaw. Tilly barely believed them herself.

For a while, she enjoyed the good-natured envy that was clear in the eyes of the other women seated around the table. She knew they'd all hoped Herbert would take the seat next to them, and although she wished she didn't find him so attractive, she really couldn't attribute the racing of her heart to anything—or anyone—else.

As everyone settled to their meal, Tilly glanced around the table, noticing that Edward was sitting between two new assistant housemothers, chatting happily to both. Why couldn't he talk as easily to *her*? Why was he so awkward around *her*?

"So, Miss Harper, I trust you are enjoying your work here?"

Herbert's remark pulled her attention away from his brother.

"Oh, yes. Very much so. Everyone is so kind and helpful—and the girls are wonderful."

"Indeed they are. Still, it must be quite a change for you. Forgive me if I'm wrong, but you're originally from Yorkshire, I seem to recall?"

"Westmorland," she corrected. "The Lake District."

"Oh, yes." He laughed. "That's right. I always get confused when it comes to the north." He said "the north" as if it were some strange, mythical land that Mr. Dickens had created in one of his stories.

Herbert looked intently at Tilly as he spoke, a mischievous twinkle evident in his deep brown eyes. She really wished he wouldn't look at her like that. It made it difficult to concentrate on anything else. In any event, she suspected that he knew perfectly well where she was from and was just teasing her.

"So, if you're from the Lake District, you must know the famous Miss Potter—or perhaps Wordsworth is more your style."

"Beatrix Potter?"

"Of course."

Tilly was surprised that Herbert knew of Beatrix Potter, let alone where she lived.

"I can't say I know her personally, but I know of her. My father shoed her horse once, when she was passing through Grasmere on a summer holiday. She returned to illustrate the forge and father's horse for one of her books. She bought a farm at Near Sawrey, some years ago."

"Really! How fascinating."

Herbert took a sip of wine and asked Tilly to tell him more about her father's forge. For a while, he appeared to be genuinely interested in what she had to say, so that she ignored her usual reluctance to talk about home. Still, she was relieved when the conversation returned to matters of work.

"And how are you finding your employment here? I imagine it wouldn't be for everybody."

"It was a little overwhelming at first. But as I've got to know the girls I can honestly say that I hardly notice their physical differences. I don't see them as 'cripples,' I just see them as individuals, like you or I. It's the girls' personalities that really make them stand out. They're such characters! Really, I think they just want to be independent—to do as much as they can. It makes the ladies and gentlemen I used to be in service to look quite pathetic, with their reliance on others to do absolutely everything for them. I'd find it very hard to work in that type of household now. I don't think I could bear to assist a lady to dress when she is perfectly capable of doing it herself."

Herbert laughed.

"You're a very intriguing young woman, Miss Harper. Very intriguing."

Before she could respond, the dinner plates were collected and the conversation around the table became focused on the puddings that had been brought out: a very impressive blancmange and a jam roly-poly served with custard sauce. It all looked, and smelled, delicious.

Leaning across the table to help herself—as instructed—Tilly reached for the custard sauce. Edward reached for it at the same time, their fingers touching briefly as they both grasped the handle of the jug. Tilly pulled her hand away, as if she had touched hot cinders.

"My apologies," Edward said quietly. "After you."

He smiled, shyly—his face softening, the candlelight reflected in his blue eyes.

"It seems as if your custard sauce is as popular as ever tonight, Aunt Evelyn," Herbert joked, his eyes fixed firmly on his brother. "We'll be drawing straws next, to see whose turn it is."

His remark produced a titter of laughter around the table.

Tilly ignored him, smiling at Edward.

"Thank you," she said, taking the sauce and pouring it over the steaming pudding before placing it back on the saucer. She could still sense the light touch of Edward's fingertips on hers as she did and felt his gaze burn against her cheek as she started to eat.

With the wine and the enjoyable food, Tilly soon began to relax. She quite enjoyed Herbert's company, feeling more of an equal to him now that they were dinner guests around the same table. There was no flush creeping over her neck, and her heart had stopped racing. She glanced at him while he busied himself with the blancmange, suppressing the urge to laugh when a great dollop of it fell from his spoon and landed in his lap.

"And I presume your family will be traveling down to join us at the Harvest Festival fete day in Clacton?" he said, after he'd wiped the blancmange from his trousers.

Tilly bristled at the comment. "Oh, no. I don't think so."

"You surprise me, Miss Harper. *All* the housemothers invite their families. It really is a wonderful event. Would you not reconsider? I'm sure they would enjoy it."

Tilly wished he would be quiet. His voice was too loud, fueled by the wine. "No. It's such a long journey and—"

"But we've had people from the north before. Haven't we, Aunt Evelyn," he continued, grabbing Mrs. Shaw's attention. "I was just saying to Miss Harper about inviting her family to the fete day in Clacton and she thinks the journey would be too much for them. We had a family travel down from Scotland once, didn't we?"

Mrs. Shaw dabbed at the corners of her mouth with a napkin. "Oh, yes. The fete days are extremely popular, Tilly. It's a nice way for the housemothers to show their families what we do. You must invite them. Everyone else will."

"Exactly," Herbert agreed, turning to Tilly again, his voice grower louder with his drunken insistence, so that the rest of the guests fell silent. "You see, even my aunt insists!"

Be quiet, she thought, curling her fists into tight balls under the table. *Stop talking about my family*. She could feel anger rising within her, storm clouds gathering.

Herbert persisted. "You heard what Aunt Evelyn said. *Everyone* will be inviting their families. Surely you wouldn't want yours to—"

"My sister is a cripple," she hissed, unable to tolerate his ridiculous assumptions about her family any longer. "She is paralyzed and, besides, she wouldn't want to travel to Clacton, even if I wished her to."

She'd spoken much louder than she'd intended; her frustration with Herbert—and her temper—getting the better of her.

All eyes fell upon her, the clatter of a spoon falling into a bowl the only sound in the room.

The familiar sensation of guilt, of being the object of gossip and speculation, flared within Tilly. She stood up, placing her napkin on the table. Tears welled in her eyes.

"It was a riding accident," she whispered, her voice barely audible. "An accident. There was nothing I could do."

She ran from the room, ignoring the voice that called after her.

"Miss Harper! Wait!"

It was only later that she realized it was Edward who had spoken.

Chapter 30

London
September 1912

The day of the trip to Clacton dawned clear and bright. The chill in the morning air pinched at the girls' cheeks, giving them all a wonderfully healthy glow as they arranged themselves into the motor cabs and carriages that were to take them to Liverpool Street station. A great convoy of vehicles lined Sekforde Street, and the excited chatter of the girls filled the air like birdsong. For some, this was a regular event they had come to cherish. For others, the trip would be their first experience of the seaside—their first experience of anything beyond London. After a week of skulking around the house, ashamed of her outburst, Tilly felt buoyed by the positive atmosphere.

Since Mrs. Harris had announced that she would return to work the following week—her leg having healed well in Brighton's sea air—it had been agreed that Tilly would spend a full week at Clacton.

"It's a good opportunity for you to familiarize yourself with the work of the housemothers at the orphanage," Mrs. Shaw had said. "It is always useful for housemothers to be familiar with the routines of both the Flower Homes and the Flower Village. We never know when we might need to call on someone at short notice, if a mother is taken ill—or breaks her leg, like poor Mrs. Harris. And," she'd added in that wonderfully soothing voice of hers, "I thought you might be glad of a little time away from London—glad of a break away from . . . things."

Tilly was grateful for Mrs. Shaw's understanding. She'd felt horribly self-conscious since the dinner party, refusing to discuss the matter with anyone—even Mrs. Pearce—who'd given her a great big hug the following morning, told Tilly that her family was nobody's business but her own, and that there would be no more said about the matter as far as she was concerned. A week away at the seaside couldn't have come at a better time and Tilly hoped that when she returned, everyone would have forgotten about her little drama, having found something, or someone, else to gossip about instead.

Through the streets of Farringdon, along Old Street, City Road, and across London Wall to Bishopsgate, their convoy made quite the spectacle. Pedestrians, bicyclists, street sellers and shop owners, mothers and their children all waved and raised their caps and handkerchiefs in acknowledgment of the flower girls, whom they knew and admired for the success of Rose Day. The girls waved back enthusiastically. Tilly could not have felt prouder if she'd been in a royal carriage parade.

Reaching Liverpool Street station, and after a great deal of assistance and plenty of complicated maneuvering of people and equipment, the seventy-two flower girls, and the six members of staff, were seated on the train.

"It's a Pullman Express," Mr. Shaw announced, as the Violet House girls crowded into the compartment. "Quite the modern train. We'll be in Clacton in an hour."

Tilly noticed a flash of concern across a number of the girls' faces as he struggled to control a fit of coughing. She thought about Mrs. Shaw's words the day she had been shown around the factory workroom. *"He doesn't have the strength he once had. The filthy London air chokes his lungs."*

As the last of the girls settled into their seats, Hilda shuffled into a space beside Tilly, remarking on the décor of the second-class carriage.

"Can you believe it is fully lit and heated?" she said. "And look at the leather upholstery! Mr. Shaw said there's a ventilated parlor, a buffet car, and a smoking car. Imagine that!"

Finally, the great black locomotive made its way out of the station, the carriage compartments creaking and groaning under the strain as the wheels began to turn. The girls clustered around the windows, pressing their noses to the glass as they watched the drab gray of London give way to green fields and open countryside. For some, this was their first time on a train. For many, it was the first time they had seen green fields. For all, it was a thrilling adventure.

Just as she had a few months earlier, Tilly found herself watching the countryside flash by as the train wheels hammered and clattered on the tracks beneath, rocking her gently from side to side. How long ago that journey from Grasmere seemed, how distant the sense of doubt and uncertainty she'd carried with her that spring morning. "Is this an end or a beginning?" Mrs.

Ingram had asked. Tilly hadn't understood the question at the time. Now, perhaps, she understood the sentiment a little better, and found herself wondering which conclusion this particular trip would bring.

So much had happened in the months since she'd left Grasmere, so much about Tilly—about her life—had changed. She now felt part of daily life at Violet House. She'd made friendships with many of the girls: Hilda in particular—and even Queenie, with whom she had reached an understanding. She enjoyed their company in very different, yet equally important ways. She'd experienced the historic events of Alexandra Rose Day, she'd dined with Albert and Evelyn Shaw—two people whom she held in the highest regard—she'd even managed to fall in and out of lust with the most handsome, arrogant man she'd ever encountered, and without his knowing it.

But of all the events that Tilly had experienced since she'd knocked tentatively on the door of Violet House that March morning, she couldn't help feeling that the most poignant was the connection she'd made with a young Irish girl. Something had drawn her to Flora Flynn. Something had compelled her to keep reading the notebook, to discover Flora's words and the pressed flowers that had lain among the pages for so many years—hyacinths, carnations, primroses, violets, and pansies—their images having left an indelible mark on the page—and on Tilly.

As she listened to the excited hum of chatter in the compartment, Tilly thought about the lace handkerchief in the wooden box. It was an exact replica of the one Mrs. Ingram had used on the train journey to London all those months ago. An exact replica of the handkerchief she'd seen Violette Ashton use on Alexandra Rose Day. Surely coincidence alone couldn't explain something so strange, but she hardly dared believe that one of these women—Mrs. Ingram or Violette—had known Rosie, and might be able to tell her what had become of her.

Tilly also thought about the letter she'd written to Violette Ashton earlier that summer. Taking Flora's notebook discreetly from her coat pocket, she took up the envelope and removed the carefully folded sheets of writing paper.

Violet House
Clerkenwell
London

July 4, 1912

Dear Mrs. Ashton,

Firstly, my apologies for writing to you in such an unexpected manner. My name is Matilda (Tilly) Harper, and I am employed as housemother at Shaw's Training Homes for Watercress and Flower Girls in Clerkenwell. We were introduced by your mother on Queen Alexandra Rose Day last week. I had met your mother several months ago when we traveled on the same train to London. I had spoken to her then of the position I was about to commence at the Flower Homes.

After we were introduced, you passed me a card with your personal details. You wished for Mr. Shaw to contact you regarding floral arrangements for your home—which I believe he has done.

My reason for writing to you in person does not relate to the matter of the flowers, but is of a very sensitive and personal nature. I have sat at my writing table on many occasions to write this letter, but find myself unable to find the appropriate words. I know this will sound most unusual, Mrs. Ashton, but I believe you may be able to assist me in discovering the whereabouts of someone who I would dearly love to find.

It may be nothing more than coincidence, but I recently learned of a previous occupant of the room that I now reside in at Violet House, Sekforde Street. I discovered a box of her personal possessions: a notebook and several trinkets.

You may be wondering what this has to do with you, Mrs. Ashton. I hope I can explain.

Among the possessions was a lace handkerchief with a cluster of shamrock leaves stitched into one corner. In her notebook, the girl—Flora—describes how she and her sister, Rosie, each carried one of these handkerchiefs when they were flower sellers on the streets of London many years ago. She believed the handkerchiefs to be lucky talismans, given to them by their mother—their own grandmother in Ireland having made them. I couldn't help noticing that you carry a very similar handkerchief to the one I discovered in the box. It caught my attention when I met you on Alexandra Rose Day. (I had also noticed your mother use the same handkerchief when we traveled on the London train together.) I cannot help but wonder if your handkerchief, and the one I found, are a matching pair, given to those little girls many years ago.

Sadly, Flora became separated from her sister one day when they were out selling their flowers. She spent the rest of her life searching for her, but never found her. Flora died some years ago.

I do not wish to intrude, Mrs. Ashton, but with you having a similar—if not the very same—handkerchief as the one I discovered in the box in my room, I cannot help but wonder if you might have known Rosie, the missing sister—or if you might know someone who was connected to her in some way. Flora suspected that Rosie may have been taken into the workhouse, or died, unnoticed, on the streets. Perhaps the existence of this matching lace handkerchief suggests she survived?

If this means anything to you at all, I would be very grateful for a reply. Perhaps we could meet in person and I could show you the handkerchief and notebook and other possessions.

If I have things entirely incorrect and this is merely a strange coincidence, then please do excuse my intrusion. I felt that if I didn't write to inquire, I would always wonder. My late father used to say that fate is what happens to you but destiny is what you desire. Perhaps this is destiny, Mrs. Ashton?

Yours sincerely,
Matilda Harper

Folding the pages and placing the letter back into the envelope, Tilly sighed and turned her gaze back to the carriage window. She watched the undulating hills roll by as she searched for an answer among the hedgerows and fields.

Chapter 31

Clacton

September 1912

Long before they reached the coast, the salty air penetrated the narrow gaps at the tops of the compartment windows. Tilly breathed it in deeply as she closed her eyes, allowing the fresh scent to flood her body with well-being.

As Mr. Shaw had predicted, the train arrived at Clacton station just sixty minutes after departing from London. The girls were delighted to find a fleet of omnibuses waiting to transport them to the orphanage.

"Can you smell the salt in the air, Miss Tilly? Isn't it delicious?"

Tilly laughed at Hilda's excitement, watching as she and the other girls stuck out their tongues, tasting the fresh, brackish breeze that swirled around them, tugging at their hats and pinafores. The clear light and sense of space struck Tilly the most. After the claustrophobia of London, it took all her willpower not to run around in great, swooping circles like she had as a giddy child the first time she'd visited St. Bees beach with her father.

Although it took a while to move everybody from one mode of transport to another, nobody complained or fussed; everyone waiting patiently, despite their eagerness to reach their destination. They enjoyed the warmth of the generous autumn sun on their faces and the sensation of the fresh sea air as it filled their grateful lungs. The seagulls wheeled overhead, making the girls laugh with their peculiar cries.

Eventually, they were on the move again, the sparkling, turquoise sea ever present on the horizon as the merry cavalcade followed the coastline, weaving up a gentle incline toward the cliff tops.

Tilly's first sight of the Flower Village was the tops of several tall, red-brick chimney pots, soaring up toward the few clouds that dotted the sky. As the omnibus rounded a final bend, she read a large sign in black and white lettering, which stood proudly in a meadow alongside the road.

WELCOME TO SHAW'S FLOWER VILLAGE
ORPHANAGE AND HOLIDAY HOMES FOR AFFLICTED,
BLIND, AND CRIPPLED CHILDREN

Beyond the sign and the meadow stood a neat crescent of a dozen or so red-brick, two-story houses. Lace curtains swayed gently in the breeze that blew through the open sash windows. Just-reddening ivy crept over the fronts of the houses, while carefully tended gardens graced the fronts, before extending into lush meadows. Conifer and bay trees, hypericum berry and holly bushes skirted the pathways that snaked between the houses.

A group of children playing in the meadow heard the approaching omnibuses and ran, limped, and hopped toward the fence, cheering and waving. The flower girls waved back, leaning out of the windows to shout enthusiastic hellos.

"Isn't it perfect, Miss Harper?" Hilda said. "Did you ever see anywhere so pretty?"

"It is lovely," Tilly agreed. "Very lovely indeed."

In fact, it took her breath away.

As the convoy pulled up in front of the crescent of houses, Tilly was happy to see Mrs. Shaw waiting to greet them. She had traveled ahead the previous day to help with arrangements for the fete. She stood beside two tall, starchy-looking women in pale blue dresses and white aprons, whom Tilly presumed to be the matrons she'd heard so much about. Beside them stood a row of the sweetest little children, all smartly dressed in matching white pinafores and bonnets, their cheeks flushed pink with the pinch of the sea breeze. They resembled a line of toy dolls, neatly arranged by a careful child. They waved their chubby little hands in greeting as the omnibus came to a stop.

It was only then that Tilly noticed Edward, standing beside Mrs. Shaw. She was surprised at how pleased she was to see him—another familiar face from London—and only hoped that his dreadful brother wasn't lurking around somewhere to trip her up with his awkward questions and sarcastic remarks about "the north" or stockingless feet.

She stepped from the omnibus, helping the girls down after her, settling those who required them into their chairs, clambering back into the bus to retrieve forgotten crutches from beneath seats for others.

Edward quickly stepped in to help as she struggled with one of the cumbersome chairs that had been brought to the front of the house.

"Let me do that. Awkward things, these new chairs. Never seem to move properly, especially over gravel. Think I preferred the Bath chairs myself. Better wheels."

Tilly stepped to one side, grateful for Edward's help. She was struck by how relaxed he seemed. She'd never heard him speak so freely. Even at the dinner party, there'd been an awkward hesitancy about him, especially around her. Now, he spoke clearly and confidently, without the uncertainty she'd become accustomed to. And because he didn't look constantly at his feet when he spoke, he appeared taller. She noticed how his strawberry-blond hair glistened in the sun, how the blue of his eyes seemed accentuated under the clear autumnal skies.

"So, what do you think of our little Flower Village?" he asked as he continued to help Tilly organize the girls, whose nonstop chatter was like the drone of a beehive beside them.

"*Little!*" Tilly laughed. "It's amazing! I've heard so much about it, but it really is wonderful. Such a contrast to London's smog and narrow streets."

"And that's precisely why I love it here. London can be so suffocating, don't you think?"

"Yes. It can be a little . . . choking. It's lovely to breathe such clear air." For a moment, neither of them spoke. The hubbub of the girls' excitement swirling around them carried on the breeze. "And the gardens look so pretty."

"Ah, now that's all down to Mr. Hutton, our gardener. He takes great pride in his gardens."

Mrs. Shaw had joined them and overheard Tilly's remark. "Perhaps Edward could show you around the grounds a little later, Matilda," she said. "We'll be busy with the fete all day, but there should be a little time before supper. I'm sure Tilly would like to see the rose garden, Edward."

He looked at Tilly. She looked at Mrs. Shaw. It wouldn't usually be encouraged for a young woman to walk with a man, unchaperoned.

"I'm sure Edward will be the perfect gentleman," Mrs. Shaw prompted, sensing her hesitation.

"I'd love to see the rose garden," Tilly said. "If you're sure I'm not inconveniencing anyone."

"It would be my pleasure," Edward said. "The scent of the roses is quite something. Especially just before dusk. That's when they give off their best perfume—after a day being warmed by the sun."

Mrs. Shaw smiled brightly. "That's settled then. Miss Harper will be free by six. I'll leave you to make your arrangements." She looked pleased with herself as she turned to address Tilly directly. "Sarah is the matron in charge of Poppy House, where you'll be staying, Matilda. She'll show you around, and when the girls have eaten lunch we'll meet in the back gardens. The guests will arrive at two o'clock. Edward, don't forget we still have the fire drill to set up."

He smiled. "Yes, Aunt Evelyn. I hadn't forgotten."

"Good." Mrs. Shaw turned then, with an efficient swish of skirts and a hint of lavender water, and walked back into Foxglove House.

"Miss Tilly! Miss Tilly! Buttons has taken the seat I had chosen, and she won't budge."

Hilda was standing on the doorstep of Poppy House, the next house in the terrace. She looked cross.

"All right, Hilda. I'll come and sort it out now," Tilly called. She turned back to Edward. "I'd better go before a war breaks out."

He laughed. "Six o'clock in the rose garden?"

She nodded. "Six o'clock."

"And enjoy the fete, Miss Harper. It is quite the spectacle!"

They parted company as Tilly walked over to Hilda, her boots crunching noisily across the gravel. And no matter how much she tried, she couldn't stop the curl of a delighted smile that tugged at the edges of her lips.

TILLY'S TOUR OF POPPY HOUSE began on the top floor. Sarah, the senior matron at the Flower Village, proudly showed her the dormitory bedrooms. Crisp white sheets lay on the beds, blue candlewick blankets were tucked perfectly around the edges of the mattresses, and the windows were wide open, allowing the fresh sea air to flood the room.

"There are four cots for infants and twelve children's beds," Sarah explained, "which makes for a crowded room, despite its size. There are just over a hundred children here currently, varying in age from young infants to girls of fourteen or fifteen years. They leave us then, to go into service, or to the Flower Homes. Just as in London, each house is very much a 'home' under the care of a mother. Girls over the age of eleven are expected to assist with the younger children. All the rooms have views of the sea and are always well ventilated," she continued, throwing open more windows. "We've been inspected and measured by the sanitary officer of the district and certified to contain the requisite number of cubic feet of air."

Tilly had no idea what a cubic foot of air was, but she nodded in what she hoped was a knowledgeable manner.

Sarah chattered on as she tugged at sheets and plumped pillows. "A tidy bed makes for a tidy child. We encourage the children to keep everything neat and well organized. There's no point going to sleep in an unmade bed. That's where all the problems start, you know. Up here," she added, tapping her head with a stiff finger.

Tilly liked Sarah. Like Mrs. Pearce, she was strict and direct—as Tilly had expected her to be—but it was clear that she always had the best interests of the children at heart. She was a woman with exactly the right attitude to gain the respect of a hundred motherless children.

"On the first floor, at the front, there are two bedrooms. This one is Mother's," Sarah said, flinging a door wide open, "including, as you can see, a pretty little cot for an infant, and a child's bed, for whenever a child is unsettled. You'd be surprised at how often that bed is needed. Terrible dreams some of the children have. The other room," she said, opening a different door, "is used as a spare room. This is where you'll sleep while you stay with us. A week, I believe."

"Yes. That's right. Mrs. Shaw was very kind to suggest I stay on after the fete. She thought it might be helpful for me to get to know the work of the mothers here. I've been managing Violet House on my own, you see, after Mrs. Harris broke her leg and . . ."

She trailed off. Sarah wasn't listening. She was already striding on ahead, opening and closing more doors to show Tilly other rooms. She moved so quickly that Tilly barely had time to see what Sarah was referring to as she followed her downstairs, matching her step for step down the narrow staircase.

"On the ground floor there are two parlors facing the Old Clacton Road. One is used as Mother's, the other as a reception room for visitors. As you can see, there's a scullery and washhouse at the back. The ground-floor room is used as a kitchen, where the children take their meals. There is plenty of space for the children to romp about when they can't get outside. We also have a piano—the children perform musical drills. Good for their concentration. Some are becoming quite the little musicians. Now, here we are, back in the lunchroom. I'll leave you to your girls. I suspect they're all ravenous after the journey—and there's nothing better than sea air for stirring the appetite."

THE REST OF TILLY'S MORNING was spent with the girls of Violet House and Poppy House, who talked ten to the dozen, old friends catching up on life at the orphanage and new friendships being formed among girls who had never met before. She soon had a pounding headache and longed to sit down with a cup of tea, but, after much pleading, it was agreed that she and Elsie, the mother at Poppy, would take the girls down to the beach before the fete started.

Tilly and Elsie worked quickly to wash and dry the lunch dishes, sweep the floors, and wipe down the tables and chairs; then the boisterous group made their way to the shore. Fortunately, it was only a short distance down the cliff path to the dunes, which they navigated—somewhat awkwardly—before stepping onto the beach.

It was a vast expanse of golden sand. Tilly stood for a moment, listening to the crashing of the waves and the cries of the seagulls as the breeze tugged at her hair and ballooned her skirts out around her legs. She'd forgotten how much she loved the sound of the sea. She gazed at the rolling waves, the motion almost hypnotic.

"France is just over there," Elsie said, pointing directly across the water. "Hard to believe really, isn't it!"

Tilly knew instantly that she loved it here: the stiff breeze blowing her hair around her face, rushing past her cheeks; the endless sky above her; the enormity of the ocean and the endless possibilities it suggested. She felt alive, invigorated. And then eager hands were pulling at her to help remove stockings and shoes.

Laughing at the girls' enthusiasm, she set to work. Soon a great pile of stockings and black shoes were assembled on the sand, like rags waiting for the bone grubber to collect. Snow-white toes were dipped tentatively into the foaming water, the girls shrieking at the cold as the waves lapped around their skin and rushed up the sand, catching those who were hovering at the edge of the water, too nervous to step in. Those in chairs were lifted down one at a time by Tilly and Elsie, so that they could feel the refreshing water for themselves.

They splashed and laughed for a good while, Tilly and Elsie joining them. As they ran up the beach, shrieking as they tried to outrun a larger wave, Tilly noticed a man walking alone in the distance. She raised her hand to her eyes, shielding them from the dazzle of the sun. He raised a hand and waved as he drew parallel with their group.

Edward.

Tilly waved in reply before he walked on, back through the dunes toward the houses. She thought about how invisible he had been in London, always lurking in the shadows, always skulking behind his exuberant brother. She winced at the thought of Herbert's relentless barrage of questions about her family. As she watched Edward disappear, she remembered her father telling her that sometimes it is better to look at the shadows rather than be dazzled by the sun. She smiled to herself as she turned her attention back to her charges.

"Right, girls. That's enough messing about in the sea," she called, her voice whipped away by the breeze. "We have to go back now. The visitors will soon be arriving."

"Are you looking forward to the fete, Miss Harper?" Queenie asked as they made their slow progress back along the sand, stepping over the worm casts and pools of seawater gathered here and there in the ripples left by the tide.

"I am, Queenie. Very much so. After hearing you all talk about it so enthusiastically, how could I not be?"

But what she didn't tell Queenie was that she was looking forward to her six o'clock meeting with Edward even more.

Chapter 32

Clacton

September 1912

The lawns behind the houses were buzzing as the visitors walked around to admire the displays that had been prepared by the children of the Flower Village. Trestle tables had been put up to show the girls' needlework and knitting, handwriting and art. Other tables were covered with vibrant floral displays from the Flower Homes, made especially for the occasion. The youngest orphans sat with their teddy bears on a picnic blanket, while the toddlers ran egg and spoon races. The older girls put on impressive displays of hoop dancing and gymnastics. The warm afternoon sunshine added to the atmosphere, bathing everyone in a soft golden light as the giggles and chatter of the girls drifted through the air like music.

Tilly was kept busy in the scullery preparing refreshments for the visitors: patrons of the charity, would-be patrons of the charity, friends and relatives of the staff, and relatives of those girls who were lucky enough to have some family members still living, and willing to visit.

Carrying a tray of lemonade to one of the refreshment tents, Tilly couldn't help but stare at the ladies, admiring their fashionable lace blouses and skirts and tailored suits. She noticed that their gentlemen escorts had peeled off their jackets and hats in the unseasonal warmth. Everything was so much more casual here, as if society's stuffy restrictions had been blown away by the breeze.

Spotting Buttons and Hilda, she called them over to have a drink.

"It's the Greek dancing next, Miss Harper," Hilda said between gulps. "You must stay and watch. And the tug-o-war between the gentlemen will be after that, and that's always great fun, isn't it, Buttons?"

Buttons shrugged. She looked unimpressed. "I prefer the hoop display myself. But whatever takes your fancy, I suppose."

Tilly laughed. For someone so short in stature, Buttons lacked nothing in attitude.

Sarah asked Tilly to help serve refreshments at the tea tent. She was soon busy filling cups with lemonade for the thirsty girls and making endless cups of tea from the huge urn for the adults. She enjoyed chatting with the visiting families and supporters of the Flower Village and Flower Homes, taking pleasure in the opportunity to talk about her girls and the success of Rose Day. She hardly noticed the afternoon slipping away as the sun began to sink on the horizon.

It was while she was refilling a milk jug that she heard her name spoken.

"Well, if it isn't Miss Matilda Harper!"

She turned around to see who was addressing her.

"Oh! Mrs. Ingram! What a surprise!" Tilly's thoughts immediately leaped to the letter hidden between the pages of Flora's notebook. "How lovely to see you again."

She put the milk jug down, her hands shaking as she felt the color drain from her cheeks. She glanced around, looking for Violette Ashton. Was she here? The words of the unsent letter danced around her mind. *I know this will sound most unusual Mrs. Ashton, but I believe you may be able to assist me in discovering the whereabouts of someone who I would dearly love to find.*

"Are you not feeling well, Miss Harper?" Mrs. Ingram asked, staring at Tilly. "You look a little pale."

"Oh, no," Tilly bluffed, quickly recovering herself. "I'm perfectly well, thank you. Just a little weary. It's been a busy day."

"Yes, I can imagine. And more train travel for you to get here. You poor girl, you have my every sympathy!" Mrs. Ingram sipped from her teacup. "I must say, the girls have put on some wonderful displays. You might remember my daughter, Violette? She insisted we come to show our support. She's become a firm supporter of the Flower Homes since meeting Mr. Shaw on Alexandra Rose Day. We were fortunate enough to have tea with him at the Mansion House that afternoon, courtesy of the Lady Mayoress. Ah, here she is now."

Violette walked into the refreshment tent, three pretty, raven-haired girls at her side, ranging in age from ten to fourteen. The youngest walked with a crutch. Tilly hardly heard Violette speak as she introduced her daughters, missing their names entirely. She could only think about the letter concealed within Flora's notebook.

"It's quite the strangest thing, Mother," Violette remarked, "but I can't help feeling that I've been here before. There's something about the sounds and the smells—the sea, the salty air, the cry of the seagulls—it all feels so familiar."

"Really, darling?" Mrs. Ingram replied. "I can't imagine why."

Tilly's mind was racing. She remembered reading something in Flora's notebook, something about Flora meeting a French lady at one of the Clacton fete days. She'd said the lady had a child with her, a child with red hair.

Now it was Violette's turn to notice Tilly's distraction. "Are you unwell, Miss Harper? You look very pale."

"No, I'm fine, thank you, Mrs. Ashton." She pulled at the collar of her blouse. It was choking her. "If you'll excuse me, I need to go to fetch more lemonade. I'm sure the children will be glad of it."

Rushing back to Poppy House, glad to be in the cool interior, Tilly ran upstairs to the room she had been given for the week. Lifting Flora's notebook from her coat pocket, she removed the unsealed envelope. It was marked simply *Mrs. Violette Ashton.* Did she dare?

Placing the envelope in her skirt pocket, she walked back downstairs, making her way toward the scullery, where she took a jug of lemonade from the dresser. As she did, she noticed a pile of picture postcards. The image on the front was of a group of girls from the Flower Homes. They were arranged around a work table that was covered with displays of their flowers. She picked one up, reading the label at the bottom. SHAW'S HOMES FOR WATERCRESS AND FLOWER GIRLS, 1883. She recognized it as the same postcard she'd found among Flora's possessions in the wooden box. Placing the postcard in the envelope with her letter—which she quickly returned to her pocket—she began to strain the lemonade into a clean jug. The scent of the lemons made the back of her nose tingle and her eyes smart.

She was almost done when Edward rushed into the scullery.

"Miss Harper! I'm so sorry. I didn't know anyone was in here."

"It's quite all right," she muttered. "I'm just finished."

"We're about to start the tug-o-war and I need a ribbon to mark the center of the rope. Sarah said there should be one in a drawer here somewhere. You wouldn't happen to know . . ."

"Tilly! Are you in there?" Mrs. Shaw was calling for her now. "You're going to miss the gentlemen in the tug-o-war!"

She was flustered, as much by the sudden appearance of Edward as by the letter in her pocket.

"Coming!" she called back. "Sorry, Mr. Shaw. I have to go."

"Go!" He laughed. "Ah, here are the ribbons. And I look forward to six o'clock," he added as he rushed from the room.

Tilly blushed, straightened her skirt, and grabbed the jug of lemonade before making her way back outside, the slim envelope in her pocket weighing as much as ten men.

WHEN THE LAST OF THE GUESTS had departed, the last of the cups, saucers, and plates had been washed and dried, and the last of the many chairs and tables had been neatly stacked and removed from the gardens, Tilly wearily hung her apron on the hook at the side of the scullery door, smoothed her hair, pinched her cheeks, and stepped outside into the cool evening air. Her feet ached, her arms were sore from lifting and carrying, her hands were as dry as paper, her head pounded, and she still had supper to serve to dozens of hungry girls in half an hour, but the prospect of her six o'clock rendezvous lifted her spirits.

As she walked around the side of the house toward the rose garden, she watched the butterflies that flitted and danced among the purple buddleia. They replicated the fluttering in her stomach: whatever would she find to talk about with a man who'd barely said two words to her since she'd arrived in London six months ago? An unchaperoned meeting like this was most unconventional and although Mrs. Shaw seemed perfectly happy with the arrangement, Tilly knew her own mother would not approve. It was one of the reasons she'd agreed to it.

Edward was waiting for her, leaning casually against the red-brick archway at the entrance to the garden. Tilly watched as he ran a hand through his hair and took a draw on his cigarette. He saw her and smiled.

"Very punctual, Miss Harper," he remarked, checking the time on his pocket watch.

"Please, call me Tilly." Her voice caught in her throat, betraying her nerves. "Miss Harper sounds so formal. Clacton doesn't seem like the sort of place for formalities."

Edward laughed. "You are quite right. I'd be perfectly happy to dispense with the formalities. So, *Tilly*, shall we take a stroll in the rose garden. After you."

As Tilly walked through the narrow archway, the aroma hit her immediately, the air laced with the sweet perfume of the many blooms that had been warmed in the sun. It was delicious. The garden was abundant with different varieties and colors of roses that still thrived in the mild September weather.

"Mr. Hutton started the rose garden years ago, when there were only a few houses here," Edward explained. "It's always struck me how the garden has grown at the same rate as the orphanage, how the children have flourished just like the roses." He paused to pick at some aphids on an ivory tea rose. "I often wonder what the children make of it all here," he mused. "The contrast to their life in London could hardly be greater if they'd been removed to another world entirely."

"It's a pleasure to see them so vibrant," Tilly replied, "the orphans and the flowers. It really is a special place for children to grow up." She bent down to inhale the scent of a cluster of bright orange roses. "I've always loved the smell of roses. It reminds me of my grandmother."

She was transported back to her grandmother's garden as she savored the sweet scent. She recalled how her grandmother had comforted her after her father's death, how she'd held Tilly tightly as they'd watched the snow falling among the Christmas roses, as tears fell down her cheeks.

"I've loved flowers since I was small," she continued. "Granny had a lovely garden. She always took great delight in seeing the roses bloom. She said it was the first sign of summer."

As they strolled along the winding pathways, clusters of vivid pink rambling roses scenting their way, it struck Tilly how comfortable she was in Edward's company—comfortable enough to talk about her home and family. She felt free under the clear skies of the south coast, finding it liberating to be able to talk without feeling judged or anxious.

As Edward told her about the history of the orphanage, Tilly was also surprised by how animated he was. He really was a different person here. Perhaps it was being away from Herbert, or perhaps it was just the beauty of this place—the vast, open spaces—which allowed people to relax in a way that London never could.

Reaching a small wooden bench nestled beneath a canopy of rambling rosebushes, Tilly bent down to read an inscription on a small plaque on the back of the seat.

GOD GAVE US ROSES IN JUNE SO THAT WE CAN HAVE MEMORIES IN DECEMBER

"That's so beautiful," she whispered. "Do you know whose words they are?"

Edward stood at her shoulder. She could sense him next to her.

"It was one of the children. Apparently, it was something her mother used to say. An Irish girl, if I remember. Very poetic people. The matrons had the seat put here in her memory."

"It's very lovely."

Tilly stood in respectful silence for a moment, tilting her head to look up as a solitary seagull flew overhead, swooping and banking on the thermals.

"Do you like it here?" Edward asked, following her gaze skyward.

She turned to him. How had she never noticed how handsome he was: his hair always combed neatly to the right, his dignified nose—perfectly straight—and the slightest suggestion of a mustache that skirted his top lip? How had she not seen this before?

"Yes," she sighed. "Yes, I do. I like it here very much."

ALL TOO SOON, their brief time together had passed and Tilly had to return to the house to serve supper. They strolled amiably along the meandering pathways until they returned to the narrow archway.

"Perhaps I could show you the other gardens during the week?" Edward said.

"During the week?"

"Yes. You're staying on, aren't you? I'm sure Aunt Evelyn mentioned it."

"Yes. That's right. Mrs. Harris is back, you see, so she'll be able to mind the girls in London while I'm here. I'll be helping with the babies."

"I'm staying on a little longer also. Boring meetings with architects and accountants—that sort of thing."

Tilly laughed. "Then, yes. I'd love to see the other gardens."

He bade her good evening and walked back toward Mr. Hutton's cottage.

Lost in her thoughts of the rose garden and Edward's pleasant company, Tilly returned in a daydream to Poppy House, where thirty hungry and exhausted girls were waiting for their supper.

AFTER WAVING HER CHARGES OFF as the omnibuses made their way to the station for the return trip to London, Tilly climbed wearily upstairs to her room. She splashed water on her face, changed into her nightdress, and collapsed into the comfortable bed. Too exhausted to read Flora's notebook, she lay in the dark and listened to the sea. She'd left the shutters open and turned on her side so that she could look out at the millions of stars twinkling in the clear, dark sky. She'd missed the sight of them.

She wondered, for just a moment, about the envelope she'd given to Violette Ashton. She'd said very few words as she'd handed it to her.

"I thought you might like a picture postcard of the Flower Homes. It was taken a few years ago, but you might like it all the same."

Mrs. Ashton had simply thanked her and placed the envelope in her purse as the fire-drill display began.

Tilly wondered whether she'd read the letter yet. If she had, did it mean anything to her?

Lulled by the sounds of the sea and the ache in her limbs, she soon fell into a deep sleep, too tired even for dreams.

Chapter 33

Clacton

September 1912

Tilly's immediate love for the Flower Village intensified over the following days. She found herself charmed by the stunning seascape, by the breeze that rippled through the long meadow grass, and by the atmosphere of love and hope that oozed from every home, every room, every child at the orphanage. In particular, she developed a strong affection for the very youngest children.

Although she'd become accustomed to the afflictions of the older girls at the Flower Homes, Tilly found herself less able to accept the sight of the infants and toddlers, who were still struggling to adapt to their useless limbs and unseeing eyes. Elsie explained how some of them had suffered from polio when they were newborn, and Tilly's heart broke for them. Still, they made her laugh with their childish innocence and endless questions—excited by the chance to meet somebody new and ask her about the mountains and lakes of her home and about how the girls in London had made roses for the Queen. They loved to hear Tilly's stories, asking her to repeat them over and over again, especially the story of Alexandra Rose Day.

"It's quite amazing," Elsie said as Tilly shadowed her in her work and helped her fold endless piles of bed linen, "how children who will hardly speak or look at you when they first arrive can blossom before your very eyes. Sarah says they're like crocuses in the spring, the way they open up. They break your hearts when they leave to go into service, or to go to London to the Flower Homes. I don't think I'll ever get used to that, no matter how long I work here."

Amid all the usual routines of cooking, cleaning, and washing, Tilly found a new joy in her duties at the Flower Village. There was something less drab about scrubbing at small pinafores with carbolic while a pleasant breeze drifted through the open washroom window, and she almost took pleasure in hefting the heavy basket of mangled sheets out to the back gardens, where she hung them on long washing lines to snap and flap in the wind. The smell of the bed sheets when they were dried by the sun and the sea air was one of the nicest smells Tilly had ever known. She held the bundle of folded sheets to her face and breathed in deeply. Elsie laughed at her and said she must be cracked in the head if she took pleasure from the smell of folded bed sheets.

It was on the morning of her second full day at the Flower Village, while she was picking lavender for scenting the soap, that Tilly was startled by a cough behind her. She jumped and turned around, dropping the sprigs of lavender in the process.

"Mr. . . . Edward! You gave me a fright." She put her hand to her chest, her heart pounding.

"I can see that," he said, laughing. "My apologies. I didn't mean to startle you." He stooped to pick up the dropped stems and passed them back to her. "Looks like you've gathered quite a bunch there."

"Yes. For soap. But I think I might have gone a little over the top! It smells so lovely though, don't you think?"

He leaned forward to inhale the vibrant purple flowers, his face close enough to Tilly's that she could see the pale eyelashes that framed his eyes. She shivered, despite the warmth of the sun and the shawl around her shoulders.

Edward smiled and brushed his hair from his forehead. "I don't suppose you'd have time for a short stroll? I didn't get a chance to show you the walled garden yet. Mr. Hutton would never forgive me if he found out you'd returned to London without seeing his famous walled garden."

Tilly hesitated, glancing toward the house. "Well, I should really be getting back to prepare lunch . . . but I suppose a few minutes can't do any harm.

"So, how have your 'boring' meetings been going?" Tilly asked as they walked.

"Ha! Quite well, as it happens. It's so much easier to manage everything in person. There are so many little decisions that need to be made—windows to be put here instead of there, doors to open out rather than in. Progress is much faster when I'm here. And I'm always perfectly happy to find an excuse to stay awhile longer."

"Is it a new house you're planning?"

"Two new houses, actually. A convalescent home and a new cottage hospital. It's incredible, the pace at which this place has grown since the early days, when only Buttercup and Daffodil

Houses were built. There's still plenty of land available for more building, too. I suspect we'll eventually use it all. That's what my uncle plans, anyway."

Tilly stopped to shake a stone from her shoe before they continued walking.

"How is your uncle's health?" she asked. "Mrs. Shaw mentioned that he'd been feeling unwell recently and I can't help noticing how he coughs so dreadfully and struggles to get his breath."

"Hmm. He isn't the best, I'm afraid. Even a short stroll down to the beach yesterday caused him quite some discomfort. It's the smog in London. Irritates his chest. The doctors say he should rest and spend as much time here as possible, but Uncle Albert is a stubborn old swine, and he can't bring himself to leave London. He feels he would be 'abandoning his girls.' "

The sound of Mr. Hutton's grass mower grew louder as they neared the houses.

"Poppy. Foxglove. Freesia. Buttercup. Daffodil." Tilly read the names of the houses, etched into stone lintels above the doors. "Such lovely names. I believe it was Mrs. . . . your aunt's idea to name each house after a flower."

"Yes. She insisted that the orphanage be a place where the children could flourish. She always thought of the orphans as like little flowers that would blossom and thrive with the right care and attention. She was absolutely right."

"You can see it in their eyes," Tilly agreed. "There's a sparkle, a hope. And there's something about the space here. The meadow, the beach, the sea, the sky . . . I really can't think of a better place for any child to grow up—especially after all the darkness and horror of their terrible lives on the streets. No wonder they have such hope. How could you not when you realize the world is so vast and endless?"

They walked on in comfortable silence, the ever-present seagulls wheeling and crying overhead. They passed the rose garden and went on into the walled garden, where lavender, stocks, and sweet peas mingled to create the most wonderfully sweet scent. The high walls offered a welcome shelter from the cool breeze.

"I hope you don't mind me saying," Tilly ventured as they walked, their feet crunching on the shale path, "but you seem a lot more relaxed here than you did in London."

Edward was silent for a moment. "I think sometimes a place can bring out the best in a person, don't you? I don't know what it is, but I've always felt very comfortable here. I remember visiting as a young boy and loving the openness of it all, the rush of the wind in my ears. For the first time I felt I could run, laugh, and scream with the other children, free from the restrictions of a stuffy schoolroom. I didn't feel I had to be like . . . well . . . let's just say I felt as though I could be myself here." He stopped for a moment to admire a bush full of rose hips, the lush berries just turning from orange to their rich, distinctive red. "And, of course, my brother can't stand the seaside, so he rarely comes here."

Tilly understood the sentiment behind the words. Maybe her suspicions were right. Maybe there was a rivalry between the two brothers.

"It must be strange being a twin," she said. "I suppose you're always being compared to one another."

"No more so than any brother or sister is compared to the other, I suppose. At least we're not identical. People often don't even recognize us as brothers, let alone twins."

Tilly laughed. "That's just like me and Esther. People were always asking if we—" She stopped.

Edward looked at her, his eyes shaded with concern. "If you were what?"

"It doesn't matter. Would you mind if we sat for a moment?"

Walking toward a low bench set back slightly from the path and surrounded by wallflowers and delphiniums, they sat for a moment in silence. Tilly thought about how she would stare at Esther, wondering why they looked so very, very different: Esther with almost white-blond hair, and her with russet red. *I think there was a cuckoo at work in your family*, people would joke. *Minding someone else's eggs*. Tilly hadn't understood the reference, but she did understand why people remarked on their striking differences. It was a thought that had troubled her throughout her childhood. It troubled her still.

"I was very sorry to learn that your sister is paralyzed," Edward said eventually. "It must be very difficult for you all."

Tilly tensed at the words.

Edward sensed it. "Perhaps you don't wish to talk about it. My apologies. Let's talk about something else."

"No. No. It's all right. Really. I just . . . well . . . we were never that close you see and . . ." She hesitated, her fingernails digging into the palm of her hand.

"Would you prefer not to talk about your sister?"

Tilly smiled. "Yes!"

"Good. Because I'd prefer not to talk about Herbert."

They both laughed.

Neither of them spoke for a while then, happy to let the sounds and scents of the garden supplement any conversation. A bee buzzed idly around the sweet peas, a seagull cried overhead. Tilly watched a peacock butterfly settle on a leaf and fan out its wings, absorbing the sunlight. Without speaking, an understanding seemed to pass between her and Edward as they sat side by side. For all that Tilly had wondered about Edward's reluctance to talk to her when they'd first met, she now realized that, sometimes, words are simply not required.

Chapter 34

Clacton

September 1912

Running through the long grass, squealing with delight as her father ran behind, trying to catch her before she reached the gate. His strong arms, wrapped around her, scooping her up, spinning her around, the clouds blurring into a mass of white in the sky above.

Lying beside the lake, their backs warmed by the soft sand. Everything so perfect when it was just the two of them, Esther too young to join them on their nature walks and rambles along the mountains.

The screech of a pheasant hidden in the hedgerow, the hoot of an owl as dusk fell over the cottage, the cries of her baby sister.

The doctor's voice in the hospital. "She'll never walk again, Mrs. Harper. Her spine was crushed when the pony fell on her. I'm very sorry."

Her father walking down the shale path in his soldier's uniform. A smile on his face, a twinkle in his eyes. He had come home!

She ran, shrieking with delight, ran from the cool of the scullery into the warmth of the sun, to the warm embrace of the father she loved so much.

He stopped and sank to his knees as he saw her, his arms outstretched in welcome.

"Daddy! Daddy! You're home! You came home!"

Running, tripping, falling into his outstretched arms . . . falling into empty space.

There was nobody there.

He had disappeared; blown away by the breeze that knocked the conkers from the horse chestnut tree.

She stumbled forward, fell to the ground. His arms weren't there to catch her. He had never been there. He hadn't come home.

A brown paper package on the table. A standard-issue, felt cap. A letter for each of them.

Her mother weeping.

He wasn't coming home. He was never coming home.

Although her dreams still disturbed her sleep, Tilly settled easily into the routines of the Flower Village, and her love for the place soon extended to the town of Clacton itself.

While she ran errands to fetch cotton and buttons from the haberdashers, she liked to steal a few moments to walk along the pier, watching the paddle steamers coming in. She loved the gaiety of the brightly colored helter-skelter, the flags snapping and fluttering on top of the amusement stalls, the jaunty tunes of the organ grinders and the hurdy-gurdy, the cry of the toffee-apple sellers and ice-cream vendors. It reminded her of the day her father had taken her and Esther to Biggar Bank on Walney Island when they were young girls, how they'd gasped at the sight of the sea and shrieked with delight at the Punch and Judy show. It had been a pleasant, rare day when she'd enjoyed the company of her little sister, forgetting how much she envied her. She remembered the day so clearly, but mostly she remembered how delighted she'd been that it was *her* head, not Esther's, that had rested on their father's lap as they traveled home.

Tilly also enjoyed Elsie's company during her week at Clacton. They chatted easily, relaxed in one another's company as they went about their chores: making beds, sweeping sand from the floor, cleaning out and re-laying the fires, and repairing dozens of holes in dozens of pairs of socks and stockings. On sunny days they took their darning outside, laying out a blanket so that they could sit and watch the sea and the golden sand stretching around the great bay.

Tilly could sit for hours staring at the sea. She loved the way the color of the water reflected the weather: sometimes stormy and petulant, sometimes bright and fresh, sometimes calm and serene. It reminded her of how quickly the colors and reflections could change around the mountains and fells back home.

Elsie teased Tilly about Edward, whom they often saw strolling along the beach, his socks and shoes in his hands, his trousers rolled up past his ankles. It was a comical sight.

"Well, would you look? There's your Edward again, taking his morning constitutional."

"He's not *my* Edward!" Tilly protested. All the same, she was pleased when he looked up toward the cliff top and waved at them.

"You clearly enjoy each other's company. I've watched you walking together, and you talk about him all the time."

"I do not!" Tilly put down her sewing and stood up, her hands on her hips. "I barely ever mention him."

Elsie smiled. "Well, you can deny it all you like, but I can't deny what I see with my own eyes." She shook her head, laughing to herself.

"Honestly, Elsie!" Tilly didn't know what else to say.

"Oh, don't get all huffy. Come and sit back down. I think you're good for him anyway, a tonic. Poor Edward. What with all that business with Miss Johnson and Herbert it's a wonder he . . ." She trailed off.

"Miss Johnson? Who's she?"

Elsie lowered her voice, glancing around to make sure nobody was listening. "I shouldn't gossip. It was all very sad, really. Miss Johnson was Edward's fiancée. Some years back now, mind. And then didn't she fall for Herbert. Called the whole engagement off. Terrible business it was. Quite the scandal."

Tilly was shocked. "But, that's awful."

"That's not all. Miss Johnson contracted the scarlet fever and died not long after she'd left Edward for Herbert. Edward blamed himself, of course. Said that if he could have kept her happy, she'd never have gone to Herbert. And, of course, he blamed Herbert for not taking care of her—blamed him for her death. I don't think he'll ever get over it. Caused a dreadful rift between the two brothers, let me tell you."

Tilly was stunned. No wonder Edward was so subdued around his brother.

"Listen, I've probably spoken out of turn," Elsie continued. "Promise you won't breathe a word of what I've told you. Not to anyone. I shouldn't have said anything."

"I promise. I won't say a word."

Elsie packed up her sewing box. "Right, I'm all done. I'll see you at lunch."

She left Tilly alone with her thoughts and the ever-present sound of the waves rolling into shore. She thought about the despicable thing Herbert had done and she thought about what Elsie had said—perhaps she did talk about Edward a lot. But what Elsie didn't know was that, in quiet moments, while she darned a sock, or rubbed the soap along the hem of a skirt, or mixed the starch into the water in the copper, she thought about Edward even more.

WHILE TILLY MISSED THE CHAOS of London and Violet House and was looking forward to seeing the flower girls again, she was sorry that her time in Clacton was drawing to an end. In the week she had spent here, she'd fallen in love with the children and the orphanage and the sound of the waves crashing on the shore. She had also enjoyed her dusk walks in the gardens with Edward—a comfortable routine they had fallen into after the fete day.

After her conversation with Elsie, Tilly had thought about Edward more and more, how they would exchange a glance or a smile whenever their paths crossed as they went about their work, how she would sometimes observe him from a quiet corner, smiling at his funny little habits—the way he folded his handkerchief into a neat square before putting it back into his pocket, the way he lifted his glass of water to his eye, peering through the clear liquid to whatever was on the other side, the way he crossed and uncrossed his ankles, the way he rubbed his fingers along his lips when he was thinking, just like her father used to.

"WILL YOU COME back?" Edward asked as they strolled, his cigarette paper crackling as he took a long final drag. It was the evening before Tilly was due to return to London.

"I hope so. I feel so at home here. It would be a shame to think that this is all I'll see of Clacton."

"Has it really been that disappointing?" Edward teased. "I hoped our walks had been quite enjoyable."

Tilly blushed. "Oh . . . I didn't mean . . . It's just . . ."

They stopped walking. A bee buzzed around a honeysuckle.

Edward reached out to take Tilly's hand. Her heart quickened. Her breaths came quick and short.

"I have very much enjoyed my week, perhaps more than any other I have spent here." He pushed his hair from his eyes. "Tilly, do you think . . . when we get back to London . . . do you think . . ."

He hesitated at the sound of footsteps running along the shale path toward them.

"Oh! Tilly! I'm so glad I found you." It was Elsie, flushed and out of breath. "A telegram has arrived for you."

"A telegram? For me?"

"Yes. It's marked from Grasmere, Westmorland. It was sent to London, but they've redirected it here."

Tilly's mind raced. Why would there be a telegram from home? Why would they contact her now, after all this time?

"It must be Esther," she whispered. "Something must have happened to Esther."

She took the small brown envelope from Elsie, her hands trembling as she opened the seal.

Mother very ill. Come as soon as you can. Esther.

Chapter 35

Violet House, London
September 1912

Her mother's voice. "Your father's dead, Tilly. He's dead."

Standing in the kitchen, a chill winter wind blowing down the chimneybreast, her body shaking as she read the telegram from the War Office confirming that the Eleventh Battalion had suffered heavy losses at Tweefontein, and that Private Samuel Harper had fallen.

A small, brown paper package on the kitchen table—all there was to show for his bravery and sacrifice for his country. A standard-issue felt cap and three letters: one for each of them.

A silent whisper into the murky, gray light of morning. "What will become of me? What will become of me now?"

Tears falling down her cheeks, a cockerel crowing in the yard, a dog barking, the kettle whistling on the stove. Esther comforting her mother, her mother comforting Esther, Tilly standing alone. Everything as normal, when nothing would ever be the same again.

A brown paper package containing a felt cap and three letters: one for each of them.

Tilly woke with a start. It was still dark outside, the light from the gas lamps creeping in through the window, sending curious shadows dancing across the walls. It took a moment for her to remember that she was back at Violet House.

SHE'D PACKED IN A HURRY after reading Esther's telegram, sending a hasty reply from the post office in Clacton: *Will arrive in two days. Tell Mother I am coming. Tell her to wait.* Her farewells to Elsie and Sarah had been hurried and anxious, their kisses placed on her cheek along with a prayer that all would be well. She'd watched Edward turn and walk back into Foxglove House, her feelings confused, her heart full of hope and dread, as the carriage rumbled past the meadows where the children played so innocently.

The journey back to London had passed in a blur. The girls had greeted her with serious faces and words of support. She barely remembered being introduced to Mrs. Harris—a stout woman with a kind face and warm hands.

Her onward train north departed at nine o'clock the following morning.

With thoughts of her father racing through her mind, she lay perfectly still, waiting for the first hint of daylight to creep through the window. She remembered a line from *Wuthering Heights. I have to remind myself to breathe—almost to remind my heart to beat!* She'd never understood how it was possible to feel such despair, until the news they'd all been dreading had arrived in Grasmere, wrapped in a brown paper package.

She'd had to remind herself to breathe, remind her heart to beat.

Her father had always been a good horseman, teaching Tilly and Esther to ride when they were young. Because they were country girls, he taught them to ride like he did—legs astride—rather than in the traditional sidesaddle fashion.

Their mother disapproved. "How will anyone ever consider the girls for wives when they ride like a man? It's not right, Samuel."

He would laugh at his wife and kiss the top of her head. Tilly knew he adored her mother, even when she was fussing and criticizing, as she was so apt to do.

"Well, if any man is more worried about how the girls ride than what they know, or what they have read, or what interesting conversations they can hold, then I doubt we would want him for their husband, would we, Mrs. Harper?"

Tilly loved her father for that, how he always found the right thing to say.

But although he worked with horses, rode them whenever he could, and taught Tilly and Esther to ride as soon as they were able, nobody could have guessed that Samuel Harper would take his horsemanship to war.

Driven by the patriotic fervor that spread across England like a pox as the war in South Africa escalated, he'd taken an interest in the recruiting notice from the War Office. A second wave of volunteers was needed to join the Imperial

Yeomanry—experienced horsemen were required. By that stage of the conflict, married men were no longer discouraged from signing up.

"They're offering a wage of five shillings a week, Hannah. It's my duty to go. It'll be an honor to fight for Queen and country."

The day he traveled to Aldershot for his training, Tilly sobbed inconsolably into her pillow. Even the mountains and lakes couldn't help her this time.

It was a heavy, gray January morning when he left, the skies leaden with dense, dark clouds. Tilly watched him walk down the lane and knew that he would never come back, knew that her life would never be the same. It frightened her more than anything had frightened her before.

"I won't look back, Tilly," he'd said, his chestnut eyes smiling as he prized her hands, fingertip by desperate fingertip, from around his neck. "I'm going to walk away now, my darling girl, and I won't look back. I'll see you again—when it's all over."

She'd stood on the stone doorstep of their cottage, her mother's sobs audible inside, Esther standing quietly by her side. She so desperately wanted to run after him, wanted to scream and shout and wrap her arms around him so that he couldn't go. But she didn't. She stood perfectly still, trying to do what her daddy had asked: to watch him walk away from her with pride in her heart. He was going to fight a war for their country, and that was the bravest thing a man could do. That was what he'd told her.

"Look back, Daddy. Please, look back," she'd whispered.

He didn't.

If he had, she would have seen the tears streaming down his cheeks and the look of absolute terror on his face.

In letters that made their way slowly back to Grasmere from increasingly unfathomable distances, Tilly learned that after her father had turned the corner at the end of the lane, he'd traveled to Aldershot for his training (or what little training the hastily recruited soldiers were afforded). He'd passed all the necessary fitness and medical inspections, and because he was not a coward, a drunkard, or incompetent—as many of the other would-be recruits proved to be—Samuel Joseph Harper had set sail from Southampton on the SS *Avondale Castle* on March 14, 1901. He didn't write much about what happened during their time at sea, but eventually a letter reached home to say that he and the rest of his Battalion had arrived in South Africa by the end of April. Tilly's old schoolmistress showed her where South Africa was on a map of the world. To her young eyes, it seemed as though her father was as far away from the mountains and lakes of their home as it was possible for anyone to be.

After he survived several battles and the skirmishes near Rustenburg in September, Tilly's hopes that he would return to her increased with each letter. The government announced plans to decrease the number of Imperial Yeomen, each wave of returning soldiers providing fresh hope that he would soon be home.

But it was hope that came too late.

On Christmas morning, 1901, the Eleventh Battalion were attacked at Tweefontein, shot in their tents while they slept.

People told her that a quick, noble death was better than suffering horrific injuries or being taken prisoner, along with the six hundred others that day. He'd been a hero, they said. He'd fought as an equal in the army to which he had volunteered.

Their words were of no consolation to Tilly.

She had one photograph of her father. It had been taken during his too-short month of training at Aldershot. In it, he stood proudly, shoulder to shoulder with his new battalion. In his uniform—dark navy Norfolk jacket, breeches and gaiters, lace boots, and felt hat—he looked every inch the experienced soldier. But when she looked closer, she was sure she saw fear in those chestnut eyes.

Tilly was eleven years old. Her beloved daddy had left her.

She had to remind herself to breathe—almost to remind her heart to beat.

A BROWN PAPER PACKAGE on the table. A felt cap. A letter for each of them.

The letters!

It struck her with such force that she sat bolt upright in bed. The package from the War Office. Three letters—one for each of them. What had happened to them? They were never mentioned again, forgotten about in the aftermath of grief. Her father had written a letter especially for her. Where was it?

She stepped out of bed, washed, and dressed, her hands trembling in the dark chill of the room. Her train didn't leave for hours, but she would go to the station and wait. She had to get home. Even more than she needed to see her dying mother, she needed to read the words of her dead father.

Part Four

Pansy (*Viola tricolor*)

You are in my thoughts.

Open letter to "Daisy"
From *The Christian Magazine*, September 10, 1912

Thank you, once again, for your extremely generous donation to our cause. Without an address to thank you personally for your contribution, it is my hope that you will read this entry, which I write by way of our humble gratitude and thanks.

As you know, without the patronage of individuals such as yourself, we would simply not be able to carry on with the work of the Flower Homes and Flower Village. Since we have just taken on the rent of a seventh house on Sekforde Street, the additional sum of money you have provided is most welcome indeed.

As I am sure you are aware, Queen Alexandra chose our girls to make the ten thousand "Alexandra Roses" that were sold across the city on the inaugural Queen Alexandra Rose Day, June 26. The girls worked extremely hard to produce the volumes of roses required, but their efforts were rewarded with a brief visit to the factory by the Queen the following day. How their eyes shone with pride as she spoke to them about their work.

Some £30,000 was collected from the sale of the roses. The money will be distributed among various charitable causes throughout the city, including the Foundling Hospitals and Ragged Schools. I cannot find the words to express how this makes my heart swell with pride.

Our Flower Village in Clacton, Essex, is proving to be an extremely successful venture. We now have twelve homes—each named after a flower—as well as the Babies' Villa and a convalescent home. In total, we accommodate one hundred and twenty blind and disabled girls aged between two months and fourteen years. We recently finished construction on the new infirmary, which will accommodate twenty deserted children who are in most desperate need of medical help. We have named the building "Daisy Villa" in your honor. My nephew is currently working with architects to draw up plans to build a further six homes on land that has been obtained through generous donations of friends and supporters like yourself.

I still find myself shocked and appalled by the continual neglect of the poor children I see on the streets. It is a pitiful sight to behold. I fear that there will never be a lack of unfortunates requiring our help, but it is the many maimed, crippled, and blind flower girls—the worst afflicted—who need our help most of all. It is not our desire to "fix" them or change them in any way—simply to assist them in becoming self-supporting. Through the establishment of our factory, and the production of our artificial flowers, we are able to do just that.

We would welcome you to visit our flower factory in London or the Flower Village in Clacton. It would be my honor to show you what we have been able to accomplish with your generous assistance.

With warmest regards,
Albert Shaw
Superintendent, Training Homes
for Watercress and Flower Girls

Chapter 36

Grasmere, Lake District
September 1912

Tilly's stomach lurched as the branch-line train came to a stop beside the platform. She lifted her trunk from the overhead luggage rack, pulled down the window to open the carriage door, and stepped into the cool evening air. She was the only passenger to alight.

She jumped as the guard blew his whistle, great clouds of steam and smoke enveloping her as the train creaked on, toward its destination. She stood alone, pulling her hat down over her ears and putting on her gloves, the chill of the platform seeping through the soles of her boots and catching her breaths in a fine mist. Only when the last wisps of gray smoke had dissolved around her did she pick up her trunk and begin the short walk to her cottage. It had been only six months. It felt like many more.

Of any season that could have brought her home, she was glad it was autumn. This was when the real beauty of the landscape was revealed: the rich coppers, russets, and tans of the oak and horse-chestnut trees shimmering in the glow of the low evening sun, as if they were made of precious metals. The distant mountains were bruised with browned bracken and purple gorse. Haystacks dotted the fields like a row of paper dolls. The bushes and hedgerows were lush with elderberries, and sloes. *Ripe for the picking*, her father would say. *Perfect for making gin.* Fat blackberries hung from gnarled briars like brilliant black jewels; crimson rose hips clustered alongside hawthorn and holly berries. It was all so abundant.

But despite the landscape's familiarity, it struck Tilly how time had moved on. The last grip of winter had still touched the area when she'd left for London; the snow had clung to the mountaintops with a grim determination. The wildflowers—cowslips, buttercups, poppies, rapeseed—that she knew would have speckled the fields with glorious color during the summer, had been and gone. Time had slipped away, seasons had passed, regardless of whether Tilly Harper was here or not. It was a stark reminder that life had carried on perfectly well without her.

Her boots crunched over dry leaves, snapping the brittle, bare branches that lay underfoot. Despite the pounding in her chest and the knots in her stomach, she held her head high, allowing the honeyed light of the setting sun to brighten her face as she walked around the bend in the lane and caught the first glimpse of her home.

The cottage seemed smaller than she remembered, dwarfed by the mountains that soared in the background. The distinctive gray hues of the Coniston slate seemed dull against the myriad colors of the landscape beyond. A spiral of smoke drifted from the chimney; she caught the smell of woodsmoke—so familiar. She walked on, her eyes absorbing every detail: the wood stack by the side of the house, a spider web on the gate, gilded by the sun. Her home. The place that had harbored so many of her hopes and dreams. The place that now spoke to her only of sadness and regret.

Forcing herself to put one foot in front of the other, she progressed slowly toward the low front door, recessed slightly against two stone columns. The iron handle and knocker, forged by her father, lay against the oak, the wood weathered by years of harsh mountain weather.

She stopped. Took a deep breath. *A beginning, or an end?*

She knocked gently, pushed the door open, and walked inside.

"HELLO," SHE CALLED as she stepped inside, her voice small and nervous. The word hung in the musty air. There was no response. "Hello," she called again, placing her trunk on the slate floor of the scullery. Still, nothing.

She felt like an intruder, anxious and uncertain. She looked around: the black cooking pot hung across the fire; the horse brasses on the lintel above the fireplace; a milk jug on the table, a few sprigs of bell heather and hawthorn placed inside; the cat sleeping on a chair by the fireside, its nose buried in its thick, bushy tail. All was quiet. Even the usual rhythmic ticking of the grandfather clock in the back room was absent.

And then she heard the steady, familiar squeak of rubber on the slate floors. Wheels turning, slowly. It was a sound that set her teeth on edge. Esther's wheelchair.

For a moment, neither of them spoke. Time seemed to stop, the breeze outside seemed to still as Tilly studied Esther's face: pale and beautiful, her striking sea-green eyes so empty, so devoid of life or hope. The sight of her struck Tilly like a blow to the chest, stirring long-forgotten emotions deep in her heart. Was it pity? Was she, after all these years, feeling sorry for her sister? For the fact that she would never walk? For the fact that part of her had wanted this to happen?

As she looked at Esther, she suddenly knew why she couldn't hear the clock. It had been stopped.

"Is she dead?"

Esther nodded. "She heard the whistle of the train. She knew you were here."

Tilly blinked. She refused to let herself cry. Her legs trembled beneath her petticoats.

"She didn't wait? She didn't wait to see me?" The words came in a rush; anger in her voice, years of disappointment and resentment flooding out of her. "She knew I was here. That you'd be safe. She went without saying good-bye?"

Esther stared at her. "She'd waited long enough, Tilly."

She turned her chair around and wheeled herself back to her bedroom.

Tilly stood in the darkening silence of the cottage. She listened to Esther's muffled sobs, the sound running through her like a knife. She wanted to reach out to her, to embrace her, to tell her it would be all right—but she couldn't. The emotional brick wall built by her younger self was held together with so many layers of resentment that, even now, when their lives were crumbling around them, it was impossible to break down.

Unsure of what else to do, Tilly turned to what she knew best. She walked outside, to the mountains and lakes she loved so much, retreating into herself: the girl with the wind at her heels and a storm blowing in her heart.

As the amber sun sank behind the mountains, casting dusky shades of rose and orange onto the lakes, Tilly returned to the house.

Esther had calmed a little. Tilly persuaded her to take a nap while she saw to the necessities: drawing the curtains, covering the mirrors. Then she made the short trip to the Jenningses' farm to fetch the doctor, just as she had done all those years ago when Esther was being born.

Mrs. Jennings wept when Tilly told her the news, heartbroken to learn that her good friend had passed. She dabbed at her tears with a tea towel she was holding and hugged Tilly tightly, insisting that she make her a cup of sweet tea for the shock. Tilly politely declined.

"I don't want to leave Esther alone for too long," she explained. "If you could ask Dr. Jennings to come as soon as he returns from Oxenholme, I'd be very grateful."

"Of course, dear. He'll come as soon as he can. You poor dears. You poor, poor dears."

Only when she returned to the cottage, knowing that the doctor would soon be on his way, did Tilly go to her mother's room.

She thought about the last time she'd seen her. They hadn't parted on an argument or harsh words. Much worse than that, they'd parted under a cloud of distance and silence. For so many years they had fought and argued and condemned each other for their differing opinions and outlooks on life. When Tilly had left for London that March morning, it was as if they were simply too exhausted to continue their battle.

Tilly had thought about it as she'd made the long journey back from London that morning. As the train had sped northward, she'd felt a desperate need to fill the gaping hole of silence between herself and her mother. Even a blazing argument would be better than the blank nothingness they'd allowed to fester, like a sore neither of them was capable of healing. More than anything, Tilly wanted to tell her mother how she'd been accepted by the girls at Violet House, that she'd made a success of her new life in London, that she was cared for by many, many people there. She wanted Hannah Harper to know that her daughter wasn't the failure she'd always believed her to be. And the thought of never being able to explain this had bothered Tilly far more than the prospect of how her mother might receive her after all these months apart.

But she was too late.

Approaching the bedroom, she hesitated. She felt light-headed, her breaths coming quickly, her hands cold and clammy. Grasping the handle of the door to steady herself, she closed her eyes, took a deep breath, and pushed the door ajar.

She peered inside.

The room was shrouded in darkness, the curtains drawn across the small window. Other than a candle that burned on the windowsill, the space was gloomy. Shadows danced on the walls as the candle flame flickered, disturbed by a draft. As her pupils adjusted to the darkness, Tilly began to make out shapes, her eyes drawn to the bed in the center of the room.

There she was.

Her mother.

Tilly walked slowly toward the bed, her fingers steepled, as if in prayer, resting against her lips.

For an eternity, she stood in silence, looking at her mother, waiting for the rise and fall of the bedsheets.

All was still. The clock pendulum, motionless.

Who was this woman who had nursed her, rocked her to sleep, played with her, sung songs to her, made daisy chains with her in the fields? Who was this woman who, for six blissful years, had been her absolute world? How had it all gone so wrong?

"Why didn't you wait for me?" The whispered words tumbled from her lips. "You knew I was here. Why didn't you wait?" She stared at the lifeless face as frustration surged through her. "You knew I wanted to say good-bye—that I had questions only you could answer. Why did you deprive me of that?"

She fell to her knees, her body shaking.

"What did I do? I was just a child!" There was anger in her voice now. "I needed you to love me, and you pushed me away." She wanted to shake her, wake her up. "What did I do, Mother? What did I do?!"

Tilly felt a hand on her shoulder. She turned to see Dr. Jennings.

He spoke quietly, calmly. "You've had a terrible shock, Tilly. You both have. Come and sit down. Mrs. Jennings is making tea."

She stood up and allowed herself to be led from the room, her hands still trembling. But she refused to let the tears fall.

THE FOLLOWING DAY passed in a blur of arrangements, formalities, and tea as news spread in the village and people came to the cottage to pay their respects and pass on their condolences. Laurel wreaths were hung on the door, pennies were placed over lifeless eyes, candles burned.

Feeling suffocated, Tilly put on her coat and hat and walked the short distance to the village post office, where she sent a telegram to Mrs. Shaw, explaining what had happened and that she didn't know when she would be able to return to London. For now, she knew that she would have to stay in Grasmere, with Esther. Esther the cripple. Esther the invalid. Esther, the poor little girl whose pony had bolted after being startled by the whistle of a locomotive, whose pony had fallen on top of her, crushing her spine. Esther, who had lain lost in the fog for hours. Esther, who, like everyone else, blamed her sister for taking her so close to the railway track when she knew that the ponies would be startled, when she knew that her mother had asked her to take care of her sister.

Since the accident, Esther had been allowed to wallow in her self-pity. She'd had everything done for her. She rarely left the house, ashamed of her useless legs and her cumbersome wheelchair, afraid of the taunts from children who knew no better. She couldn't bear the pitying looks from people whom she'd once called her friends but who didn't now know what to say to her. A crippled girl! In Grasmere! They couldn't have felt more awkward if a Negro woman had come to live among them.

It struck Tilly how empty Esther's life was—so different from the lives of the girls at the Flower Homes. They didn't consider themselves incapable. They didn't wallow in self-pity. While they'd blossomed and grown, Esther had simply withered. Like a violet in a winter frost, she was slowly dying.

As Tilly returned to the cottage, she thought of Flora's desperate search for Rosie, and with a sudden clarity, she knew that she, too, had to try and find the sister she had lost many years ago.

EXHAUSTED FROM THE EMOTION of the day, she was relieved to fall into bed that evening. And yet, despite her aching tiredness, she couldn't sleep, her mind a whirl of questions and uncertainties. How she wished she was back in Clacton, sitting among the roses and the lavender with Edward. How she wished Elsie hadn't come running down the path with Esther's telegram. She lay in silence, staring through the window at the bright orb of the perfect harvest moon and the stars that glistened in the frost-filled sky. She thought of two sisters torn apart, of a brown paper package from the War Office, of a lace handkerchief, a cluster of shamrocks neatly stitched in one corner.

Perhaps she would have fallen asleep eventually. Perhaps she would have closed her eyes and stopped questioning, stopped wondering. Perhaps, if there hadn't been a faint knock at her bedroom door, she would have kept that brick wall strong and firm.

"I wish Mother had waited for you, too, Tilly. Really, I do." Esther's words, whispered through the darkness.

The sound of rubber squeaking on the slate floor, the steady rhythm of the wheels moving away down the passageway. The lonely sound of her sister's life.

Only then did Tilly let the tears fall freely. Only then did she allow the wall to crumble around her, until she could cry no more and the violet light of dawn crept quietly into the room, bringing the month of October with it.

"White rabbits, white rabbits, white rabbits," she whispered, as she always did on the first day of a new month.

Like the shamrocks on Flora's handkerchief, she could only hope that the words would bring her good luck.

Chapter 37

Grasmere, Lake District
October 1912

Tilly dug her hands deep into her coat pockets and shivered from the biting chill of the northeasterly wind as she stood on the station platform, awaiting the arrival of the five o'clock train from London. She was quite alone, apart from the marmalade station cat, which lay on a bench. As Tilly walked past, the cat glanced up momentarily before yawning, curled its tail around its nose, and went back to sleep, disinterested in the turmoil within Tilly's heart.

Pulling her woolen shawl tight around her shoulders, she shifted her weight from one foot to the other, stamping her feet to keep them from going numb. She felt for the telegram in her pocket, taking it out to read.

So sorry to learn of passing of your mother. Girls insist on sending flowers. Evelyn will arrive on five o'clock train to deliver them. Edward

That Edward had sent her a telegram was heartwarming enough, but the girls making a wreath for her mother's funeral was one of the kindest things anyone had ever done for her. She moved her fingers across the printed words, imagining Edward in the post office in Farringdon, dictating his message. Had he thought about her, she wondered. Had he thought about their pleasant strolls around the gardens? Had he pictured her face as often as she'd pictured his?

The distinctive hum of the tracks and the smoke billowing in great plumes above the tree line, told her that the train was approaching. She straightened her skirt and adjusted her hat, conscious of her country clothes. She knew Mrs. Shaw would be elegantly attired, as usual.

The great mass of the locomotive edged along the platform, the brakes emitting a deafening hiss that sent the birds fleeing from the surrounding trees. Black smoke surrounded Tilly, the cat, the stationmaster, and an elderly man who had just arrived out of breath. She waited for the train to settle, peering through the murk into the carriages as they moved slowly past, trying to catch a glimpse of Mrs. Shaw's face. Tilly was looking forward to seeing her, to reconnecting with her life in London. She saw a man's hand poised on the door handle through the open window, ready to unlatch it as soon as the train came to a stop. She couldn't see Mrs. Shaw.

When the train stopped, she watched as the elderly gentleman greeted a young woman—his daughter, perhaps. Tilly smiled at their lingering embrace. She watched the fireman step down off the footplate, his face blackened with soot and smoke. She watched the stationmaster unload a few packages from the mail carriage. Still Mrs. Shaw didn't appear. Wondering if she had the correct time, Tilly took the telegram from her pocket. As she was reading it again, a familiar voice spoke behind her.

"What beautiful landscape. I don't think I've ever seen such a glorious acknowledgment of autumn!"

Her skin prickled. The telegram fell to the ground. Her hands flew to her cheeks as she turned around and saw him.

"*Edward?*" Her voice was as faint as the wispy trails of smoke that snaked around her feet. "Edward! But . . . how . . . I thought . . ."

"I know." He smiled, taking her gloved hand in his, bringing it to his lips and kissing it tenderly in greeting. "You were expecting Aunt Evelyn. Uncle Albert had a bad night, so I offered to bring the flowers myself."

Tilly was too astonished to ask further after Mr. Shaw's health, too stunned by the sight of Edward standing in front of her, too enraptured by the sensation of his breath warming her skin through her cotton glove. She could do nothing but stand in silent surprise.

"I hope you're not terribly disappointed," he said, a shy smile at the corners of his mouth.

"No," she whispered. "No, not at all. It's just so unexpected!"

"Oh, and there's someone else who insisted on traveling with me, to keep me company."

Please, not Herbert, she thought. Please not Herbert.

Rising onto her tiptoes to peer over Edward's shoulder, she saw the stationmaster helping somebody—a child? It wasn't until he stood upright that she saw who it was.

"Hilda! Oh, my goodness!" A great smile spread from cheek

to cheek as she ran toward her friend. "Dear, dear Hilda! What a wonderful surprise!"

Tilly threw her arms around her. She was so delighted to see her.

"Hello, Miss Tilly!" Hilda beamed. "I hope we're not an inconvenience. I wasn't at all sure about coming, but Queenie said one of us should, to pay our respects. She said you'd enjoy seeing a friendly face."

"And she was right, Hilda. It's so *wonderful* to see you, truly, it is! I've missed you all so much! But . . . I can't believe you're both here!" She turned again to Edward, who had joined them. "It's so good of you to come—and all this way."

"It was important to us to give you these," Hilda said. "For your mother." She handed Tilly a brown paper parcel.

Tilly unwrapped it, revealing a beautiful wreath of snow-white lilies, ivory roses, creamy freesias, and white chrysanthemums, surrounded by green laurel leaves. The sight of it both delighted and appalled her—it was so lovely, but it was for her mother's funeral.

Her mother was gone; her questions would never be answered.

"Thank you," she said. "It's really beautiful."

"It was all Queenie's idea," Hilda explained. "She insisted that the Violet House girls make something. We worked into the night to get it finished so we could bring it on the train this morning."

"And we wish it was in less harrowing circumstances that we'd made the journey," Edward added. "We were all so very sorry to hear of your mother's passing, Tilly. It must be a very difficult time for you and your sister."

Esther. What would Esther think of her guests from London? What would *they* make of *her*?

Tilly turned her eyes to the ground. She spoke softly. "I think it was a release for her, in the end. She was taken ill with the influenza. Everyone expected her to make a full recovery, but she took a sudden turn for the worse. She died just before I arrived."

Edward looked at her. There was genuine sadness in his eyes. "That must be very difficult to accept."

"It is. I think we all wish to have the chance to say good-bye."

For a moment, the three of them stood quietly on the platform, Edward and Hilda taking in the view, listening to the calls of the pheasants and the birdsong from the hedgerows as greenfinches and robins picked at the ripe berries.

Edward stamped his feet, blowing onto his hands as he rubbed them vigorously, his warm breaths visible in the cold air.

"It's certainly colder than it was when we left London this morning," he said. "And Mrs. Pearce assures me that Lakeland water makes a wonderful cup of tea."

Tilly smiled. "Dear Mrs. Pearce. I hope she's well."

"She is. She's glad to have Mrs. Harris back, even though she isn't quite back up to full steam. Everyone misses you and looks forward to your return."

Tilly took Hilda's bag and placed her arm around her shoulder to help support her on her crutch. Edward picked up his luggage.

"I'm afraid there's no carriage to take us to the cottage," Tilly said. "It's only a short stroll. You might get your shoes a little muddied, mind."

"And don't they say that Lakeland mud is the best kind of mud?" Edward joked.

Tilly led them toward the lane that would take them to her home. "You must excuse the cottage," she said, wondering whether Esther had remembered to put more wood on the fire. "It's only very small."

Edward placed his hand on her arm. "We wouldn't dream of

imposing on you, Tilly. I've made arrangements for us to stay at the local tavern. The Blacksmith's Arms."

"Oh, no. Really. You must stay with us. I can't possibly let you stay in the village tavern when you've traveled all this way."

"Well, perhaps Hilda might prefer to stay with you," he conceded, "but as for myself, I insist on staying at the tavern."

"Very well. Mr. Lockwood will make you very comfortable."

"Good. That's settled then."

As they walked, Hilda and Edward commented on the stunning landscape, asking Tilly the names of the various mountains. She enjoyed pointing out the landmarks and explaining the geography of the area to them. Hilda told Tilly of a few incidents among the girls while she'd been away. Her stories made Tilly laugh and also made her realize how much she'd missed them all, even in the few days she'd been away in Clacton. It was comforting to hear everyone's names again and to learn that they were busy making Christmas cards to raise funds, along with hundreds of orders for Christmas flowers.

"It's so pretty here, Tilly," Hilda said as they arrived at the cottage. "It must have been very difficult to leave it all behind for the drab gray of London."

"Not as difficult as you might think, Hilda. Not as difficult at all."

Chapter 38

Grasmere, Lake District
October 1912

A week after her mother's burial, Tilly awoke to a cold, crisp morning, the windowpanes covered with a delicate lacework of a hoarfrost that had visited in the night. Opening the window, she breathed in the pure, clear air. It tasted so good. She closed her eyes, shivering in her thin nightdress, as the cool morning air sent goose bumps running over her skin. It was a day that spoke to her of clarity and certainty, the day when she and Esther would return to London. Together.

In the aftermath of their mother's death, the two sisters had sidestepped the issue of their futures, happy to let the arrangements of the funeral and the stream of visitors distract them from the unspoken questions that drifted around the cool interior of the cottage.

In the days following the funeral, Tilly had been increasingly grateful for Hilda and Edward's company. She'd found herself relying on Edward, asking for his advice on matters concerning the will, giving him small tasks to do around the cottage—odd jobs that had been neglected for some time. The first, tentative buds of emotion Tilly had noticed in Clacton began to bloom and flourish under the clear Lakeland skies. She felt a sense of quiet contentment whenever Edward stood near her, a calming of the storm in her heart—although it still raced when he looked at her with those cornflower-blue eyes.

Hilda, too, had proven to be an incredible help, spending time with Esther while Tilly dealt with the formalities and business affairs. The two girls seemed easy in each other's company, talking about their injuries, sharing their frustrations. Tilly watched them as they went about together, noticing how alike they were. They liked to sit in the garden, blankets wrapped around them for warmth as they enjoyed the autumn sun on their faces: two young girls doing what young girls do best—chatting and laughing and making sense of the world. Tilly couldn't remember when she'd last heard Esther laugh, and despite the fact that she knew Esther was grieving for the mother she loved so much, Tilly saw a difference in her eyes, as if a long-forgotten light had been re-lit within them.

Hilda especially enjoyed telling Esther all about the Flower Homes, and Alexandra Rose Day, and the beauty of the orphanage at Clacton. While Tilly listened, unseen, never letting the girls know that she was there, Esther absorbed everything Hilda told her.

"The Flower Homes sound wonderful," Esther said. "But how do you learn to make the flowers? Isn't it very difficult? I don't think I'd ever be able to make anything as perfectly as the flowers in the wreath you brought from London."

"Oh, but you would, Esther," Hilda replied. "It takes awhile to get the hang of it, but it's fascinating to see the flowers come to life in your hands. And when we put together the great displays—they're really something to be proud of, and to know that *we* did it, that *we* made every single petal and leaf . . . I think it's the best job in the world!"

As the seed of an idea grew in Tilly's mind, so she sensed something similar within Esther's. But she had to be patient. It just needed a few more days to blossom and grow under Hilda's care.

"Hilda's been telling me about the roses the flower girls made for Queen Alexandra," Esther said one evening after supper. "She says London never looked prettier than it did with the motor cabs driving around covered with garlands of pink roses. She told me that even girls without arms make the flowers—they hold paintbrushes in their mouths."

Having observed her sister closely for the past few days, Tilly wasn't surprised to hear Esther talking so enthusiastically about the Flower Homes.

"Yes, I've seen some of them paint with the brush in their mouth," Tilly said as she swept the cinders from the fireplace. "It's amazing. *They* are amazing."

"And Mr. Edward told me there have been a lot more orders since Rose Day. He said the girls can hardly keep up and that he's certain there would be plenty of work to keep one more flower girl busy."

Tilly's hand stilled. "Edward?" She'd had no idea that Edward and Esther had been talking about this.

"Yes. Edward. Your sweetheart."

Tilly felt the heat rise in her cheeks. "He's not my sweetheart," she said, prodding at the stubborn cinders with the poker.

"Then he *should* be. He's a very nice man." Tilly coughed at the clouds of soot and dust that were thrown up as she continued to brush the grate vigorously. "Anyway," Esther continued, "he said there would be a place for me, if I was ever interested in moving to London. He said I should mention it to you.

For a moment, Tilly said nothing. She continued to methodically sweep the ashes, the steady *swish*, *swish* of her brush the only sound. Even the stiff breeze that had blown down the chimney all day, momentarily stilled. It felt as though the mountains themselves were holding their breath, waiting to see what Tilly would say next.

"And would you?" she asked, without turning around. "*Would* you be interested in going to London? To the Flower Homes?"

Esther didn't answer right away, and then a whisper, a thin pipe of a voice . . . "Yes." It was just one, small word, a hesitant gesture toward a different future, and yet it held such weight, such importance. "Yes, I think I would. There's nothing to keep me here now, is there."

It was a statement, not a question. Tilly allowed it to settle into the air around them as she continued to work at the fire, lifting the charred cinders into the coal scuttle.

"What life is there for a crippled orphan in Grasmere?" Esther continued, her voice wavering. "There's nothing left here." She paused for a moment to compose herself. "I'm scared, Tilly. I feel lost."

The word struck Tilly like a blast of wild autumn wind.

Thoughts of Flora and Rosie rushed toward her. *A person can never be truly lost, as long as someone is looking for them.* Flora had spent her life searching for her sister; she had never forgiven herself for letting go of Rosie's hand. And what had she, Tilly, done for *her* sister, for Esther?

I feel lost.

Placing the fire tongs and poker on the hearth, Tilly walked to Esther, her heart pounding, her hands trembling. Kneeling down on the cold, hard floor in front of her, she took hold of Esther's hands, looking straight into her eyes. Those haunting eyes, the same color as the kingfisher Tilly had seen by the river that morning, a flash of turquoise-green. Those haunting eyes that had so often looked through Tilly to some distant, unreachable future.

Not today.

As Tilly looked into her sister's eyes, they didn't reject or repel her. They didn't look beyond her. They reached out to her, asking for her acceptance, asking for her help.

"I'll take you," Tilly whispered. "I'll take you to London, Esther, to the Flower Homes. We'll go back together."

She wrapped her sister in her arms, and they held on to each other, afraid to let go, afraid to let the moment pass. There was so much Tilly wanted to say, but she let the silence speak for her.

A quiet hush fell over the sisters, disturbed only by a breath of wind that rushed down the chimney.

The mountains had reminded them to breathe, reminded the heart of this small cottage to beat.

TILLY WASHED AND DRESSED before going to the scullery to prepare breakfast. She was surprised to see Esther already up, dressed, and sitting at the table, her gloves and purse lying expectantly beside her.

"I wanted to make sure we didn't miss the train," she said, looking at the table and not at Tilly. A hesitancy still lingered between them.

"We won't miss the train, Esther. I promise."

After breakfast, Tilly walked briskly into the village, leaving a note at the Blacksmith's Arms to inform Edward that she, Esther, and Hilda would be taking the ten o'clock train to London as discussed and hoped he would join them. She walked on then, toward the church, her breaths captured in the frosty morning air, her head held high, her gait strong and purposeful. She had nothing to be ashamed of, nothing to hide. People could look and stare and whisper to each other all they wanted. She didn't need their approval or affirmation anymore.

As usual, the church door was open, the grim-faced gargoyles keeping watch at either side. Stepping inside the dark interior, she walked to the altar, lighting two candles before bowing her head and saying a few silent words of prayer. Her whispered words echoed off the cold walls.

Hearing a muffled cough behind her, she got to her feet, nodding a solemn good morning to the vicar's wife, who was changing the floral arrangements. Tilly stopped to admire them—hypericum berries, bell heather, wheat, and lavender—before walking out into the pale buttercup light, following the gravel path down a small slope toward the cemetery gate.

Pushing the gate open, she walked straight ahead to the freshly dug mound of dark, peaty earth. Her mother's grave. No headstone yet to mark it, no loving words of remembrance. Several floral tributes lay on the mound, along with the wreath from the Flower Homes.

She turned then to read the headstone beside her mother's grave.

SAMUEL JOSEPH HARPER. 1860–1901.
IMPERIAL YEOMANRY. 11TH BATTALION
LOST AT TWEEFONTEIN, SOUTH AFRICA
LOVING FATHER AND HUSBAND
LOST, BUT NEVER FORGOTTEN

Tilly stood quietly. She thought about her past and her future. She thought about her father, carrying her on his broad shoulders, remembering how she had laughed with great squeals as he tickled her knees. She thought of her mother baking bread in the scullery, singing contentedly to herself as Esther kicked her fat little legs in the pram beside her. She thought of the storm, gathering in her heart, as she'd watched—unseen. She thought of the dark cloud that had settled over her as her father turned the corner at the end of the lane and disappeared from view. She thought of Esther's broken body being lifted from the doctor's wagon, thought of her mother's desperate sobs when she was told that her younger daughter would never walk again.

"Why, Tilly?" her mother had whispered. "Why?"

She'd known what she was doing—known that it was dangerous to take the ponies so close to the train tracks, that they would startle if a train came by..

She'd only wanted to give Esther a fright. She'd wanted to see fear in those perfect, sea-green eyes—just once. She'd wanted Esther to know what it felt like to be scared, to feel lost and alone. She'd wanted—just once—to see Esther's boots scraped and filthy, to see her hair muddied and imperfect, to hear their mother scold her for dirtying her skirts. "Thank goodness Tilly was there," everyone would say. "How brave she was bringing Esther safely home. You're a wonderful sister," they would say.

The shrill blast of the whistle as the locomotive rounded the bend, the sudden sound of hooves thundering past her. Esther's screams, fading into the distance, smothered by the fog. A faint, sickening crack, echoing off the mountains around her, and then silence.

Esther's foot had caught in the stirrup as the pony bolted. She'd been dragged through the gorse and the heather, through the mud and over boulders, before the pony had stumbled—tripped by a rabbit hole—and fallen, landing on Esther with its full weight. Her boots were scraped. Her hair was muddied. Her back was broken—irreparable damage done to her spinal column. She had lain for an age like a rag doll, lost and alone in the fog. Poor crippled little Esther and her spiteful, selfish sister.

Tilly made herself remember everything as she stood at her father's grave, and then she packed the memories away into the furthest recesses of her mind and threw her anger onto her mother's grave, along with a handful of dew-sodden earth.

"Yes, I wanted to hurt her," she shouted into the crisp, morning air. "But I never meant for this to happen, and I am sorry. I am so sorry."

Her cries startled the crows from the church steeple. They took off into the sky with a great cawing, a black mass gathered above her before they scattered into the trees.

"No more secrets," she said, brushing her fingertips over the lettering etched onto her father's headstone. "No more secrets."

Her words seemed to echo off the ancient slabs of the gravestones around her. *Secrets*, *secrets*, *secrets*, they whispered back. She turned to walk away, to leave it all behind.

And then she saw him. Silhouetted against the glare of the strengthening sun.

She walked slowly toward him, raising her hand to her eyes to block out the sun.

"Edward!"

He smiled as she reached him. "I got your message. It would be my honor to escort you and your sister back to London."

He held out his arm.

She took it without a moment's hesitation. She took it with a glorious abundance of hope, and as they walked back to the cottage together, Tilly was certain she could smell violets in the air around them.

Chapter 39

Violet House, London
October 1912
Florrie

She has returned to me, the girl with the almond eyes and the storm in her heart. I have been waiting for her, here in this room I once called home, and she has come back to me.

But something about her has changed.

There is a lightness to her soul, a vibrancy that was not there before. She sleeps soundly at night: no startled screams, no frightened cries. And yet, something troubles her. Letters remain unread, words remain unspoken.

From the veiled, distant world I inhabit, I come to her, watching as she sits at the window to draw her beautiful flowers: just budding roses, plump peonies, elegant lilies, simple little violets and their heart-shaped leaves.

"Tuppence a bunch," we would cry. "Please, kind lady,

buy a bunch from a poor child." That's what we would cry, Rosie and me.

"Find her," I say. "Please, help me find my sister!" But my words are as fragile and fleeting as snowflakes and she does not hear.

She draws the flowers so beautifully that I imagine they will burst into life, the petals and leaves unfurling, wandering across the page, filling the room with their wonderful scents. I stand beside her, watching her work. I try to reach out to her, but I cannot.

And yet, she senses me here.

She turns, suddenly. "Is that you, Flora?" she asks. "Are you here?" and I rush to her, breathing the scent of a thousand flowers across her face.

"Find her," I whisper. "Please find her."

She weeps as she reads the words in my notebook, wonders who I am as she lifts the paper-thin flowers from the pages, searching for me within their delicate petals.

"I will find her," she says. "I promise."

So, I watch and wait, and others watch with me. A woman comes to her, and a man in uniform rests his hand gently on the top of her head until she sleeps, a deep, peaceful sleep.

Chapter 40

Violet House, London

October 1912

As Tilly returned to London, so the mild weather departed—early morning frosts and cloying fogs lingering over the city in its place. To her relief, she found that everything at Violet House remained the same: the girls still squabbled over whose turn it was to help with breakfast, the flowers were still being produced at a phenomenal rate, Buttons still went missing, Primrose still chirped merrily in his cage by the window, and Queenie still bossed everyone around.

And yet, Esther's presence in London changed everything.

It had been agreed that she would live in Rosebud House, under the care of Mrs. Pearce. Rather than living under Tilly's care at Violet House, Tilly felt Esther would have a better chance of settling at Rosebud, where she would be treated just the same as the other girls—no special treatment, no allowances made for the fact that she was somebody's sister. She would be treated as an equal for the first time in many years.

"You'll be just next door to Hilda, and Mrs. Shaw says you can sit together in the factory," Tilly had explained as the train had carried them southward.

Esther was perfectly happy with the arrangements. Like a cloud moving away from the sun, a brightness was slowly returning to her.

"Some things change and some things stay the same, eh?" Mrs. Pearce chuckled as she hefted Tilly's trunk back up the stairs, just as she had done several months ago—glad to help since Mrs. Harris was assisting at a church fete for the day. "We're very glad to have you back, Tilly—and with your sister too! The girls missed you." Reaching the top floor of the house, she put the trunk down. "Oh, bugger it, *I* missed you," she said, engulfing Tilly in a great hug.

It was like being embraced by two huge hams. Tilly smiled, allowing herself to relax into it. "And I missed you all, too. I'm glad to be back, Mrs. Pearce. Very glad to be back."

"Well, I'll leave you to settle. Cup of tea?"

"That would be lovely. Thank you."

The small bedroom that had once felt so strange to her was now a welcome sight. She checked in the wardrobe, thankful that nobody was hiding there. She looked out of the small, sash window at the street below. The knife grinder trundled past with his cart. A cat stalked a pigeon on the rooftops. She opened the drawer in the writing table—the box was still there. She looked around the room and felt that she had come home.

It wasn't until she unpacked that she noticed the envelope on her bed. An envelope with a London postmark. There was only one person who might be writing to her: Violette Ashton. Settling herself on the edge of the bed, she took a deep breath, opened the small envelope and began to read.

Nightingale House
Richmond Hill
Borough of Richmond
London

October 1, 1912

Dear Miss Harper,

It is with some hesitancy that I write to you after reading the letter you passed to me at the fete day in Clacton.

I will admit that I was quite alarmed to learn about the poor little girl who was separated from her sister. How very frightening for both of them, especially with the child not having the benefit of her sight. I can imagine a little of how terrifying that must have been, as I was partially sighted as a young child. Unlike the little girl in your letter, I was fortunate enough to be given medical treatment and now have almost perfect vision. Even so, I still remember something of a life lived in the shadows.

How sad I was to read that the little girl was never found, that her sister was never reunited with her. My own sister died of the scarlet fever before I was born. Her name was Delphine. My mother still keeps a lock of her hair in a locket around her neck.

It is, indeed, a most unusual coincidence that the box you discovered in your room contains a lace handkerchief similar to the one owned by my mother—and now by me. It was only earlier this year that Mother gave me the handkerchief, along with a small bunch of violets that had been pressed between the pages of her Prayer Book for many, many years. Small trinkets that I had treasured as a child.

Miss Harper, while I do not know—nor have ever known—a person by the name of Rosie Flynn, I must admit that I found your letter most intriguing. There is something about the name Flora, and about the story of the two sisters, that seems somehow familiar.

As you suggest, it may be preferable to meet in person, to determine whether the handkerchiefs are, in fact identical. I would also be most interested to read the contents of Flora Flynn's notebook. Perhaps you could visit me at Nightingale House, Richmond Hill. I will be visiting relatives for the remainder of October, but will be home from All Saints' Day. Please send a telegram in advance to advise when it is convenient for you to visit.

I do thank you for writing to me, Miss Harper, and certainly would have done the same under the circumstances. There is nothing more likely to trouble the mind than the burden of an unshared secret.

With kind regards,
Violette Ashton

P.S. Many thanks also for the picture postcard that you included within the envelope. The girls in the photograph look so happy in their work. My mother spoke to a Queenie Lyons at the fete day in Clacton—Queenie happened to give my mother a copy of the very same postcard. Queenie is pictured in the center of the group, holding a large spray of orchids. It is wonderful to know that she is still at the Flower Homes. I wonder what became of the other girls who sat alongside her that day.

Tilly read the letter over and over. *There is something about the name Flora, and about the story of the two sisters, that seems somehow familiar.* Perhaps there was a connection after all.

She folded the page and placed it back into the envelope. She would send a telegram to Mrs. Ashton, advising that she would visit on her first afternoon off in November. It was several weeks away, but she would have to be patient.

Walking to the writing table, Tilly removed the wooden box from its hiding place in the drawer. She took out all the items from within, laying them out neatly on the small table: the notebook, the delicate pressed flowers, the wooden peg, the button, the handkerchief, the postcard and the rag doll. It was like a trail of bread crumbs spread out before her. Opening the notebook, she inserted Violette Ashton's letter between the pages, knowing that it had brought her that little bit closer to understanding what had happened to Rosie, understanding what it all meant.

Turning to the last few pages of the book, she settled herself at the chair and read on.

November 24, 1896

It is twenty years since I last saw you, Rosie, and yet I feel your loss as keenly as if you'd held my hand just yesterday. How can it be that so many years have gone by without a

word—without sight or sound of you? Where did you go to, Rosie? What became of you?

Most of the girls I once worked with have left the Flower Homes now—marrying and having children of their own. I am housemother at Violet House, and Queenie is still here. We share the responsibilities of looking after the younger girls and try to help the new girls as best we can. Queenie doesn't have much patience, but I remind her that we were just like them once—lost and afraid. Truth be told, I think Queenie is still afraid—afraid to leave, afraid to step out into the world. I understand her fear.

But it is not that which keeps me here.

I have dedicated my life to the Flower Homes and to the man who helped me step out of the shadow you left behind. I will never leave because I owe it to Mr Shaw to remain. He has given me, and the other flower girls, so much. And I don't just mean clothes and boots and a roof over our heads and food in our bellies. I mean purpose and confidence and hope, the things that can make more of a difference to a person than anything you can wear or touch.

There is a difference, you see, between living and existing. What me and you were doing on the streets was existing—and barely at that. What Mr. Shaw has given me is a life to live. And I am grateful for it, for the beautiful flowers I make, and the friendships I have formed.

I write in this notebook and I talk to Mr. Shaw and I have many blessings to be thankful for—but still, even after all these years, I cannot help but wonder what might have been. We knew nothing of what a comfortable life might be, knew nothing of warmth, clean water, or a father's affection. We

were lost little orphans, wandering the streets, gawping at the ladies who bought our flowers, wondering what it would feel like to wear a silk skirt or a bustle, to walk in elegant, heeled boots. But that was not the path life had chosen for us. We walked our path barefoot, with nothing but each other, and somehow, that was enough.

The girls ask me why I never married, why I never had children of my own. I tell them that even though it is sometimes easy to lose our past—especially when you have warm feet and a full belly and clean clothes—it is not always so easy to find our future.

Tilly found it difficult to adjust to Esther being in London—being part of the very world she had so carefully created to escape from her past, from her sister. Things were still awkward between them, a little forced. While location was easy enough to change, the two sisters accepted that their relationship would not be altered as easily. There were many bad feelings to excavate from the fragile foundations of their lives, and while Tilly's wall was coming down, brick by emotional brick, it was a slow and difficult process.

It was with much relief, then, that Tilly saw how inseparable Hilda and Esther had become since they'd returned to London together. She took great comfort from watching the two girls, who found such pleasure in each other's company. Tilly noticed how Hilda had also grown in confidence since meeting Esther, enjoying her role as instructor, tour guide, and confidante, despite the fact that she was the younger of the two. She'd noticed, too, how reliant Esther was on Hilda, turning to her for help and guidance, before she turned to Tilly.

The other girls of Violet House were intrigued to meet Esther and couldn't get over how similar Esther and Hilda were in appearance and how *dissimilar* Esther and Tilly were.

"Are you *sure* you and Tilly are sisters?" Buttons asked in her usual direct way, inspecting Esther as closely as if she was a puppy she was choosing from a litter. "You don't look anything like each other."

Tilly laughed. She didn't feel envy anymore; she didn't feel pushed out. She was simply glad to have been able to do something positive for Esther, to have found a way to begin to make up for the past.

DURING TILLY'S WEEK in Clacton in September, she had become increasingly aware of Albert Shaw's deteriorating health. It was with a heavy heart that she learned how his condition had worsened while she had been back home.

"He eventually relented and took the doctor's advice to spend time away from London. He'll spend the winter in Clacton," Mrs. Pearce explained as she and Tilly walked to the markets together. "It's where he stands the best chance of recovering."

"Is there a possibility that he might not recover?" Tilly asked.

"I'm afraid so, dear. I'm afraid so."

He was much missed among the flower girls. Even though they were busy with Christmas orders and distracted by dove-gray clouds that brought the prospect of snow, the absence of Albert's calming, reassuring influence was keenly felt. Every one of the girls at the Sekforde Street homes owed her present situation to him. Without him, many of them knew they might not be alive or, at best, would be living in terrible conditions, trying to make a penny or two from the sale of their frost-ruined flowers and cresses. He was their savior, their protector: a father to every single one of them.

"When will Mr. Shaw be back?" Alice asked as they sat around the table for supper. "Will he be home for Christmas? It would be nice to see him again."

"He'll be back as soon as he is well again," Tilly assured her. "And there's no better place to convalesce than Clacton. I'm sure he'll be back for his traditional Christmas sermon."

Her words were laced with doubt. They all ate their meal in silence that evening.

Tilly also sensed that the family was anxious. This was not merely a winter chill Albert had picked up; this was serious enough to produce a flurry of family meetings and furtive discussions behind closed doors. Tilly noticed the increasing regularity of visits from harried-looking men in business suits—lawyers, accountants, and clerks—carrying briefcases and hefty books under their arms, rubbing mist from their spectacles as the cold air lingered on the lenses. She recognized the process from her recent experience of her mother's death: they were putting Albert Shaw's affairs in order. They were preparing for the worst.

Mr. Shaw's worsening health also saw Edward and Herbert at Sekforde Street more than usual. While Mrs. Shaw had moved to Clacton to be with her husband, the nephews had been appointed to oversee the running of the Flower Homes in their absence.

Tilly did her best to avoid Herbert. She found herself looking at him in an entirely different light, wondering how she'd never noticed the way he laughed nervously all the time, or how he blinked rapidly when he was listening to someone talk. Perhaps it was the gray light of winter, but he also appeared far less handsome than she remembered.

Then, there was Edward, whose company she was delighted to find herself in more and more frequently, gladly accepting his offer to take a stroll or a carriage ride through the park. Mrs. Pearce would accompany them for appearances' sake, although she allowed them their privacy, being surprisingly discreet.

"How is your uncle this week?" Tilly asked as she and Edward walked in St. James's Park, enjoying the shrieks of delight from the skaters on the frozen lake.

Edward sighed, his breath captured on the cold air before being blown up to the snow clouds that hung overhead. He looked tired, the strain of his uncle's declining health showing in the shadows under his eyes.

"He's not much improved, I'm afraid, Tilly. His breathing is very labored. He doesn't leave the bed now, not even for the shortest stroll in the gardens. It's so difficult to watch a man who has been so active—so vibrant—be so restricted."

"And how is Mrs. Shaw managing? It must be a great strain on her."

"Aunt Evelyn is a remarkably resilient woman. She goes about with such purpose, always a smile for everyone, always time to stop and talk to the children. But I see the strain on her face. There's a weariness in her eyes. They don't shine like they used to."

"I miss Clacton," Tilly said. "I'd have liked to spend more time there, but . . . well . . . we both know why I couldn't."

Edward stopped walking, taking hold of Tilly's hand. "Then perhaps you could accompany me there on my next visit?"

"Really?"

"Yes. Really! You can discuss it with Mrs. Harris—we can work it around your quarterly day off." There was something about the way Edward spoke, an intensity to his words. It suggested to Tilly that this were more than just an invitation to travel to Clacton. "It would make me very happy," he continued. "Very happy indeed."

Tilly looked into his eyes, his kind, cornflower-blue eyes. Her heart soared at the feel of his hand on hers, his touch so tender, even through the fabric of her gloves. It was nothing but a whisper, and yet she felt it rush over her like a storm, over the nape of her neck, her back, every delicate hair on her skin responding to his touch. For a blissful, perfect moment, they stood in silence, the screams of the ice skaters muted behind them, lost in the distance.

Kiss me, she willed him. *Kiss me*.

His lips as soft as velvet upon hers; his hands so gentle as they held her.

She gasped with the unexpected thrill of it, breathing him into her soul, and her heart soared into the dusky pink clouds above, as the first fragile flakes of snow began to fall around them.

Chapter 41

Nightingale House, London
November 1912

Violette Ashton was not the type of woman to dismiss the notion of coincidence as mere folly. She believed in the possibility of life existing beyond what she saw taking place around her every day. She believed in the paranormal, in the spirit world, in the strange predictions of the fortune-tellers and the sideshow hypnotists and psychics.

Her mother scoffed at her.

"I don't understand why you would believe in such nonsense, Violette," she said, waving a dismissive hand. "It's all ridiculous. Quite ridiculous."

Violette disagreed.

Her whole life, she'd felt there was something missing, some inexplicable event that made her feel misplaced, off balance. It had started with a visit to a gypsy fortune-teller in a red and white tent at a local fair. Violette was mesmerized by the exotic scents seeping from the tent, by the wide, staring eyes of the dark-skinned woman sitting within. In strange, broken English, she'd spoken to Violette about flowers and a little girl crying—repeating a name over and over again: Rosie, Rosie, Rosie. It meant nothing to her, but it had captured her imagination all the same and stayed with her ever since.

While her father had always been a practical businessman, interested in machinery and industry, in how things worked—especially if they made him money—Violette had grown up full of wonder at the natural world. As a child, she would ask question after question. How does the sun stay in the sky? Why do the flowers all smell different? How do the birds know when it's time to leave for the winter—and how do they find their way back again?

Her naturally inquisitive nature had only been fueled further by regaining her eyesight at the age of twelve, when she and her mother had traveled from Manchester, back to London, to see Dr. Jeffrey, at Old St. George's Hospital. He was the best eye surgeon a successful factory owner's money could buy, and he'd performed a miracle, restoring Violette's sight to near perfect vision. The world was more beautiful, more magical, more mysterious than she could ever have imagined.

Hers had been a solitary, cosseted childhood, her mother overly protective, her father—although a perfectly kind and pleasant man—too busy to pay much attention to her. She'd spent much of her childhood playing with an imaginary friend, a girl of her own creation. They would sit on the lawns of the great house she lived in, making daisy chains or picking the wildflowers that she liked to tie into little posies. Everyone admired

Violette's posies. "Wherever did she learn to tie them so neatly?" people asked. She didn't know. She just went on instinct—often closing her eyes to feel her way around the flowers as she bound them into perfect little clusters. It was a happy childhood, albeit one lacking in close friendships. But despite all her privileges and comforts, Violette had always sensed that there was something missing. It was indefinable, unreachable, and yet there it was: an invisible hole that she often felt defined her more than anything she could see or touch.

The letter from Tilly Harper had stirred a memory within her.

THE DAY OF MISS HARPER'S VISIT arrived with the first snow flurries of the winter.

Gazing from the upstairs window of Nightingale House, Violette admired the views over Petersham Meadows sweeping down toward the Thames. She remembered seeing the view for the first time when she and her husband, Richard, had moved to this grand house, which her parents had once called home. She'd been a young woman when she'd first arrived here—just twenty-two—but as she'd looked across the fields, toward the London skyline, she'd felt a strange sense of déjà vu. She knew that view, knew the bends and curves in the river, the soaring church spires, the dome of St. Paul's. She saw it so clearly in her mind's eye.

She observed the same view now, admiring the expansive beauty. She watched as snow blanketed the bare branches of the elm and oak trees with a soft white dusting. Then she closed her eyes, listening to the wind as it blew around the eaves and gables; again, strangely familiar, as was the sound of the nightingales in the summertime. They were silent now in this wintry landscape, but she looked forward to their return in the spring.

"Excuse me, m'lady. There's a Miss Harper to see you."

She turned to address her lady's maid. "Thank you, Martha, I'll be right down. Could you show Miss Harper to the drawing room?"

"Very good, m'lady."

She checked herself in the mirror, straightening her skirt and smoothing her hair as she listened to footsteps crossing the marbled floor downstairs. Sometimes Violette felt stifled by the grand austerity of this house, longing to be back in the smaller home that she and Richard had lived in during their years in Harrogate. It had been his idea for them to come back to London, to Nightingale House. It was prime residential property, Richard had explained. It gave the right impression for a man in his position. Violette had reluctantly accepted that it was not her place to argue or disagree, whatever her feelings on the matter.

Descending the staircase and crossing the entrance hall—brightened by a spray of orchids from the Flower Homes—Violette walked purposefully into the drawing room.

"Miss Harper," she said, taking Tilly's hand. "You are very welcome." She shook the young woman's hand firmly. "Thank you so much for making the journey over. I hope the roads were not too treacherous."

"They were fine, thank you," Tilly replied. "It's really very pretty with the snow settling everywhere." She brushed a couple of flakes from her coat sleeve as the maid took it from her. A fire crackled in the grate, warming the room pleasantly. "You have a very beautiful home, Mrs. Ashton."

"Thank you. It was my parents' home before they moved north. My husband and I returned some years ago. I always felt it was a little too large for our needs—but I'll admit I am grateful for it when our girls go galloping about. They grow so quickly."

Tilly smiled shyly. Violette sensed that she was eager to dispense with the pleasantries and get to the real reason for her visit.

"Let's sit down. Martha will bring the tea."

They settled themselves into two comfortable Queen Anne chesterfields.

"So, Miss Harper, you've been working at the Flower Homes for some time, I believe."

"Yes, since March of this year."

"And you enjoy your position there?"

"Oh yes. Very much. The girls are so clever to make the flowers the way they do, and Albert Shaw is such an extraordinary man. Unfortunately he's unwell at the moment. He's recovering in Clacton. We all miss him very much."

"Yes, I was very sorry to hear that. My mother mentioned that he was unwell. She read about it in one of her religious magazines. I do hope he makes a full recovery."

"Thank you. We all do."

They paused as the maid set the tea tray onto the table beside them.

Violette noticed how Tilly's hand shook as she settled her teacup on the saucer, the rattle of china the only sound in the room for a moment other than the soft patter of snowflakes falling against the windows. Violette fussed with her own teacup, wondering how to bring up the subject of Tilly's letter. The tension in the room was unbearable.

"Would you like to see the handkerchief?" Tilly blurted out the words in a hurry.

Violette was taken aback. It wasn't very mannerly of the girl, but she was glad of it.

She set her cup down onto the table, pulling her shoulders up and straightening her back. "Yes. Yes, of course. I'd like to see it very much. I have my own here, so that we might compare them."

Violette opened her purse, removing the small lace handkerchief and the little bunch of pressed violets that her mother had given her during a brief visit earlier that year. She set the handkerchief out on the table, smoothing her hand over the light creases where it had been folded. She watched Tilly closely for a reaction.

"It's so strange," Tilly whispered, picking up Violette's handkerchief and studying it closely. "They're exactly the same. Look."

Tilly took the other handkerchief from her own purse, passing it to Violette, who ran her fingers across the stitching, turning it over and over in her hands before placing it on the table, beside the other one. They were identical. Undeniably identical.

Violette's voice was barely a whisper as she spoke. "How strange. They're exact replicas. Look, the shamrocks are embroidered with the same stitching. The pattern of the lace is the very same. And you say you discovered yours in a box in the bedroom of the house you live in?"

"Yes. It was in a box, under a pile of blankets at the bottom of the wardrobe. The room hasn't been used for several years, so I presume the box had been sitting there all this time, undiscovered. The notebook I referred to in my letter was also in the box—and these."

Tilly handed Violette a button, a peg, and a rag doll. She took them, holding them in the palm of her hand, considering each in turn.

The button meant nothing to her. She put it down on the table.

The peg, although so simple, seemed oddly familiar. She closed her eyes and felt around the object, tracing its contours with her fingertips. Why was it familiar? She placed it on the table beside the button and the handkerchiefs.

She looked at the rag doll next. It was composed of torn pieces of fabric—clearly made by a child. It was quite lovely in its innocence. "Rosie," she read, as she ran her hands over the clumsy stitching on the front of the doll's dress. "You said that was the name of the little girl who went missing."

"Yes. The older sister made the doll while she lived at the orphanage in Clacton. I think it gave her some comfort. Poor Florrie. She must have been so heartbroken."

"Florrie?" Violette felt the color drain from her face. She took a deep breath. "Did you say Florrie?"

"Yes. That was what she was called by the flower girls. Her name was Flora, but she was also known as Florrie." Tilly paused. "Are you quite all right, Mrs. Ashton? You look a little pale."

Violette nodded. "Would you excuse me for a moment?"

She stood up, her head spinning as she walked from the room. She felt suffocated. She moved as quickly as she could toward the front door, throwing it open, a rush of cold air blasting into the house.

"Good heavens, m'lady. You'll catch your death." Martha came rushing to her side, closing the door. "Are you quite well, m'lady? Can I fetch you something?"

Violette faltered. "I'm fine, Martha. Thank you. Perhaps another pot of tea for myself and Miss Harper."

"Right you are, m'lady."

Violette watched as Martha descended the stairs to the kitchens. Her breaths steadying a little, she leaned against the door, glad of the solidity behind her.

Florrie—the name of her imaginary childhood friend. Florrie—the little girl she had made her daisy chains and tied her posies with. Florrie—whom nobody else could see. She remembered how her mother had become so upset by her constant reference to Florrie, remembered how she would snap at her, telling her not to be so silly, that there was nobody sitting next to her, nobody else to set a place for at the dinner table, nobody else making the daisy chains.

Florrie.

So many questions raced around her mind. She needed to speak to her mother.

Regaining her composure, she returned to the drawing room, where Tilly sat patiently, sipping her tea.

"I am so sorry, Miss Harper. Please forgive me. You must think me quite rude."

"Oh no. Not at all." Tilly stood up. "I should probably leave. I've taken up enough of your time. I thought this might all mean something to you, but I can see that it is not the case. I'm very sorry for troubling you, Mrs Ashton."

Violette sat down. Her hands trembling in her lap. "I'd like to talk to you a little more, if I might, Miss Harper. This is all quite strange, but there is something to these objects. I'm not entirely sure what, but there is something familiar about them. You mentioned a notebook?"

"Yes. Flora—Florrie—wrote quite extensively. It is fascinating—terribly sad, but fascinating nonetheless."

"I wonder if I might be able to look at the notebook. To read the entries. I will, of course, return it to you."

Tilly hesitated for a moment before passing the small, leather-bound book to Violette.

"Thank you," Violette said. "I'll take great care of it."

"You'll notice a very faint image of a flower on some of the pages," Tilly said. "There were several flowers pressed between the pages of the book—hyacinth, carnations, primroses, violets, and pansies. I think they might have meant something to the two sisters."

"Really? How lovely. I'll look out for them."

"Well, I must be getting back. The girls are very busy with Christmas orders and they come home with a tremendous appetite each evening. They would not be impressed if supper was late!"

"Of course." Violette stood up and rang the bell to summon Martha. "And thank you so much for coming to see me, Miss Harper. It has been quite . . . interesting, although I'm not entirely sure that I've been of any use in finding your missing flower girl. Perhaps if you give me a week or so to make some inquiries, I may be able to shed some light on the matter."

Tilly smiled. "That would be wonderful. Thank you, Mrs. Ashton. Thank you very much."

Violette watched from the drawing-room window as Tilly climbed into the carriage. She waited until it had disappeared from view, and only then did she rush to her room, clutching her lace handkerchief and the notebook. She was certain that the revelations that lay between the pages of the faded old book would create more questions than they provided answers.

Violette Ashton was not the type of woman to dismiss the notion of coincidence as mere folly, and as she opened the pages of Flora's notebook and began to read the simple account of two little flower girls struggling to survive on the cruel streets of London, she felt an invisible hole being filled, felt that some indefinable thing she'd been missing all her life had finally been found.

Chapter 42

Violet House, London
November 1912

Heather Farm
Grasmere
Westmorland

Dear Tilly,

I hope you and your sister are both keeping well, and that Esther is settling into her new life in London. It is very strange to see the cottage so empty—no smoke rising from the chimney or washing hanging on the line. Dr. Jennings and I think about you both often, and say a prayer for you each time we walk by the cottage.

Winter has taken hold of the mountains, and we struggle to keep ourselves warm. Dr. Jennings suggests the damson gin may help. Do you remember how you used to pick the berries for us? It seems so long ago now.

As you asked, I returned to your mother's cottage and emptied the contents of any cupboards and drawers that you didn't have time to see to yourself. I have passed any clothing to the vicar's wife for the church Christmas fete. It is strange how quickly the possessions of a person's life can be removed, don't you think?

My reason for writing is to send on a small package that I discovered in the bottom of your mother's wardrobe. It is marked "For Matilda and Esther Harper." I don't know whether it contains anything of interest or importance to you, but I didn't wish to pry, so I have sent on the entire parcel.

Please thank Esther for the wonderful buttonhole she sent for me to wear at Christmas Mass. It is beautifully made—from a distance, there would be no way of distinguishing it from a real Christmas rose.

With all best wishes,
Annie Jennings

Tilly sat in the pale winter light of her bedroom. The air around her stilled. She wondered.

Her hands shaking, she untied the string that bound the nut-brown package, carefully easing open the neatly folded edges.

A standard-issue felt cap.

The last thing she'd seen of him, just visible above the hedgerow, as he'd turned the corner at the end of the lane and disappeared from view.

She lifted it from the parcel, its shape imprinted onto the paper it had sat within for so long. She turned it around in her hands, put it to her nose, breathing in deeply. It smelled of him, of the flaming furnace, pipe smoke, musty straw. She closed her eyes, shutting off all her other senses, inhaling the familiar smells, feeling the hat that had rested on her father's head, just as his hand had rested, so often, upon hers.

Opening her eyes, she noticed two envelopes, the paper yellowed and water-marked, the writing smudged. *Tilly* was written on one, *Esther* on the other. Her father's looping, sprawling handwriting. Where had he been when he'd written this? Was it written in haste as he realized death was imminent, or had it been written long before he'd reached the battlefield—ready to be sent back to Grasmere when the inevitable time came?

For a long while, she sat on the edge of her bed, holding the envelope in her hand. Everything was perfectly still, perfectly silent. She was suspended on an invisible thread, hanging between her past and her future.

Carefully, she opened the envelope, lifting the paper from inside. It was neatly folded into quarters, so thin and worn that the creases almost tore as she gently unfolded it.

Rustenburg, South Africa

September 1901

My darling Tilly,

How can I possibly write this letter? How can I ever say good-bye?

I know you didn't want me to go to war. I know you don't understand why I left you to come to this faraway land, to fight against other men. I can only hope that, in time, you will understand, will see things differently.

I try to picture you reading this letter; I see your beautiful face, the tears in your almond eyes—and I am so sorry, Tilly. I am sorry that I did not come back to you, that I didn't walk down the lane, didn't watch you running to me, your hair streaming like flames behind you. That is what I have dreamed during the dark nights here, as the sound of musket fire fills the black sky. I picture you reading these words and I worry that I will never feel you in my arms again, my darling girl. Still, I want you to know that I would not have changed my mind. I would still have come here, to fight for the Queen.

There are so many things I want to say to you, Tilly—too many. It is easy to tell you that I love you with all my heart, to tell you that you are the most wonderful daughter any father could hope for. Your thirst for adventure, your love of books, your gift as an artist—there are so many things I admire in you—and you have so much still to learn and discover. I know you will have a very bright future.

But there is something I need to tell you, Tilly, and this is where it becomes so difficult to find the words. I'd hoped that we might sit together, on the breezy top of Catbells, so that I could explain everything while I looked into those eyes of yours. I am sorry that I cannot hold your hand as I tell you this.

Before I met your mother—Hannah—I was married to another woman. She'd come from London to live with her aunt in Windermere. We met at a village fair, and I loved her instantly. We were married after a long courtship, and she fell pregnant within a year of our wedding day. I could not have been happier. But fate was not kind.

The birth was complicated. While the child survived, my beautiful wife was lost. I was heartbroken. Without the child, I do not know how I would have found a reason to keep living. That child—my daughter—was you, Tilly.

I raised you with the help of my parents—your grandparents—who loved you as much as it is possible to love anyone. You grew into a wonderful, happy child. You were two years old when I meet Hannah Blake. You needed a mother, Tilly, and I needed a wife. Hannah was a wonderful woman, and we were soon married. We made a happy family, but Hannah longed to have a child of her own. For years we struggled. Many babies were lost. And then Esther arrived.

I know you sensed a distance growing between you, that you felt your mother didn't love you as she loved Esther. She tried, Tilly, she really did try to love you, and in her own way, she did. She had loved you for many years, but when Esther was born, something changed for her. She'd felt Esther grow within her, she'd felt her kicks and tumbles. There was a connection between them, a thread that bound them together. It broke her heart to know that she couldn't feel that way about you. I watched the cracks appear, and the storm clouds gather around the three of you, and it saddened me beyond words.

I know it will be hard for you to hear this, but I only ask that you try to find it in your heart to forgive your mother. She meant no malice. She struggled to understand her emotions, to understand the space which she and you inhabited. Please try to understand, Tilly. Please try to forgive her. I know that if you could, it would allow her to live the rest of her life with some peace. Per-

haps we all deserve a second chance? Perhaps we are allowed to make one mistake which can be forgiven?

I also want you to know what a wonderful woman your real mother was. She was raised as an orphan at a home for blind and crippled children on the south coast. She worked, for a short while, at a place in London where she made flowers in a chapel workroom. She is in the back row of the enclosed photograph, in the center. I have marked her for you, so that you can see her. It is the only photograph I have of her—and I wish for you to have it. The note on the back was written by her.

Before she became Lily Harper, your mother's name was Lily Brennan. She was the most beautiful girl I'd ever seen and you look just like her, Tilly. You are your mother's daughter. The enclosed silver locket also belonged to her. The picture inside is of me as a younger man. She wore it every day, to keep me close to her heart, she said. I hope that you will wear it now to keep me—and her—close to your heart.

Lily loved all flowers, but violets were her favorite. She loved their sweet scent and had chosen Violet for a middle name, if her baby was a girl. I kept her wish in naming you Matilda Violet.

Be happy, Tilly. Wherever life leads you, be happy. Be the strong, independent girl I remember and know that you are much loved, if even from afar.

I will be waiting for you—somewhere in the future.

Daddy

x

Tilly carefully folded the pages of her father's letter and picked up the picture postcard. An arrow pointed to one of the girls. Her mother, Lily Brennan, Flora's closest friend. She was pretty. It struck Tilly how much she looked like her.

Turning the card over, she read the words on the back: *Me and Florrie after we were making the violets. Florrie is on my left.*

Her mother's writing. Her mother. She looked at the picture again—Lily and Florrie, side by side, their distant gaze reaching out through the years, whispering to her.

Overwhelmed with emotion, she clutched the silver locket in her hand and lay down on the bed, curling into a tight ball, hugging her knees to her chest, her heart bursting with grief for her father, for her real mother, for Hannah, for Esther—for everything. "Daddy. Daddy," she whispered, clutching his letter as the tears fell—tears of relief, of regret, of hope—tumbling down her cheeks.

HOURS PASSED. Her tears eventually subsided. Drained of energy, she fell into a deep sleep. It was dark when she awoke to the sound of the girls returning from the factory.

She sat up, rubbing her eyes, gritty and swollen from her tears. She looked at the picture postcard again; studied the face of her young mother.

"I look like you," she said, smiling as she traced her fingers over the edge of her mother's face. "I look exactly like you."

Almond eyes, narrow chin, the arch in her eyebrows—there was no mistaking the resemblance.

She read the label beneath the photograph: SHAW'S HOMES FOR WATERCRESS AND FLOWER GIRLS, 1883.

Turning it over, she read her mother's words again. *"Me and Florrie after we were making the violets. Florrie is on my left."*

She remembered Queenie's words: "Florrie came up from the orphanage at Clacton with Lily Brennan . . . Inseparable those two were—Irish, you see, always stick together, don't they. They slept in beds next to each other, in that little room at the top of the house . . . Became great friends."

Tilly looked around the room. She was sleeping in the same room her own mother had slept in as a young woman.

Her skin prickled as a light breeze sent a shiver through her. The familiar perfume of violets filled the room—powdery, sweet, and aqueous—and from some distant place, she heard a gasp, a sigh, as if someone was weeping far, far away.

Chapter 43

Nightingale House, London
December 1912

It was the roses Violette noticed first. Long before the muffled voices in the hallway, the soft footsteps ascending the stairs, or the gentle knock on her bedroom door, it was the familiar scent of damask rose that announced her mother's arrival.

Her heart raced. This wasn't her mother's usual flamboyant Christmas visit, arriving with a trunk load of presents for the girls, producing squeals of delight as they felt the shapes of the packages, guessing what might be inside. This wasn't about singing favorite carols around the piano.

This visit was different.

Everything was different.

Violette had read Flora Flynn's notebook, and like a winter morning mist clearing from the windowpanes, it had all become so clear to her. Like those first days after her eye surgery, when blurred colors and shapes had gradually become more distinguishable, the truth of her life had emerged from the pages of Flora's book. She'd chased her memories back over the years: the birth of her children, the move to London, her home in Harrogate, her marriage, meeting Richard, her schooling, her emerging eyesight, distant memories of the wind in the eaves and a nightingale singing outside her window, her imaginary friend, the cries of the street sellers, her hand in someone else's, her bare feet numbed by the cold, a song she remembered, "*I meet a maid in the greenwood shade, At the dawning of the day.*"

SETTING DOWN THE NOTEBOOK, which she'd clutched in her hands all morning, she turned to face the door. Her mother's footsteps were assured, purposeful, yet gentle. She carried herself with such elegance. "You can take the lady out of Paris," she'd once said, "but you can never take Paris out of the lady."

Who was this woman she called Mother?

It all made sense to Violette now—the air of anxiety she'd sensed about her mother when they'd spent time together in London earlier that year. She'd arrived on the pretext of visiting her eldest granddaughter for her birthday, but often, when the two women had sat together, the conversation felt forced. "Is there something you want to tell me, Mother?" Violette had asked on more than one occasion. "You seem distracted. Is everything all right?" But despite the awkward pauses, her mother had dismissed the notion, busying herself with trips to the zoo and the theater. But Violette had sensed something lingering in the air between them. She'd heard secrets whispered on the wind, heard stories from the nightingale that sang at her window.

She jumped at the sound of three brisk knocks on the door.

"It's open. Come in." There was an edge to her voice.

The door creaked as her mother pushed it open, the scent of roses filling the room as she entered.

"Violette, darling! How wonderful it is to be back."

They embraced. Violette absorbed the sensation of her mother's arms around her, the feel of her hair as it brushed against her cheek—just as it had when she was a child. How she'd loved her mother's warm embrace. How safe it had made her feel. She savored the familiar scent of her perfume, the scent of her childhood.

And yet, a hesitancy passed between them, its presence in the room as real as a living thing.

Violette pulled away, turning her head to the window, wondering how she could ever ask the questions that burned within her, how she would find the courage to demand the truth.

"New coat, Mother?" she asked, trying to distract herself from the thoughts that troubled her mind.

Marguerite laughed. "Yes! Wonderful, isn't it?" She twirled once, catching her reflection in the mirror. "Do you like the color? Peacock blue."

"Yes. It suits you. Very much."

Pleasantries, niceties, insignificant chatter.

"I know I shouldn't have, but I saw it in Whiteleys window. Well, you know me, I couldn't resist. Not that I have much need for it in here," she added, undoing the buttons and removing her gloves before commencing an exaggerated fanning of her face with them. "My goodness, it's so stuffy in here, Violette. Get some fresh air into the room. You'll faint in this heat."

Violette settled herself at the window seat, waiting patiently for her mother to fiddle with the awkward lock on the window. Eventually, it relented, allowing a welcome breath of cold air to enter the room. Perhaps the maid had banked the fire a little too high that morning.

"Much better." Marguerite stood at the window, allowing the chill air to wash over her. "I think it's being cooped up on that dreadful train for so long. I suppose I should be thankful that we made good time—the most annoying woman sat next to me. She spent the entire journey telling me about her ailments. I'm sure I would have been in danger of contracting something myself if I'd listened to her a moment longer."

Violette observed her mother as she spoke, watched her as she walked around the bedroom, picking things up and replacing them—perfume bottles, pots of face cream, brushes and combs—adjusting the curtains, rearranging the pillows on the eiderdown. Her mother. Marguerite Ingram, the beautiful girl from Paris, the wife of a wealthy factory owner: sugar, cotton—everything he turned his hand to, a success. Her mother—and yet, not her mother.

Violette watched her as she walked around the room without a care in the world, and she felt herself drowning, as if years of pretense and fabrication were washing over her, smothering her beneath a wave of confusion and anger.

"Oh, do be quiet, Mother!"

Marguerite jumped, startled by the sharpness of her daughter's words. "Violette! Whatever is the—"

"Please. Just stop chattering on about nonsense. It doesn't matter. None of it matters."

The words caught in her throat, emotion overwhelming her. She gripped the edge of the window seat, her fingernails digging into the plush fabric to steady herself against the rocking and reeling of these strange, uncharted waters she was sailing.

"But, Violette. Darling, I don't—"

Violette walked to the drawer of her dressing table, removing the lace handkerchief and the pressed violets.

"These," she said, holding her hands out. "These belonged to me."

She glared at her mother, watching her for any sign, a flicker of remorse, a look of regret as she took them from her daughter. She saw none.

"Yes, darling." Marguerite crossed the room, perching on the edge of the bed. Her face paled. "Yes. Of course they are yours. Remember, I gave them to you when I visited in the spring—little trinkets from your childhood."

"My childhood! My *childhood*?" Violette walked back to the window seat, resting her cheek against the cool glass.

"Darling, is everything all right? Is anything the matter?"

"And at what part of my *childhood* did I have these trinkets, Mother? As a baby?" She could almost feel the words as they tumbled from her lips, they were so important, so laden with emotion.

Marguerite sat perfectly still, staring at the violets and the handkerchief. They were such delicate, fragile things, and yet so appallingly substantial.

She turned her face to Violette's, her eyes clouded with tears. "You know." Her voice so faint, so brittle the words would surely break before they were heard. "You know. Don't you?"

They gazed at each other in silence, frozen in a moment neither of them could bear to move on from,; one afraid of hearing the answer to the question that hung in the air between them, the other afraid of providing it. The only sound, that of the wind whistling through the eaves.

Violette walked toward the bed and handed the notebook to her mother. "Yes. I know. I know everything."

"What is this?" Marguerite looked at the faded, cracked book in her hands.

"My life," Violette replied, her voice as icy as the blast of air blown through the window. "It is the story of my life. My *real* life. Mine—and my sister, Flora's."

"But . . . but, I don't understand."

Violette watched as her mother leafed through the pages, noticing names and dates. "Where did you—"

"It doesn't matter." Violette sat down again, staring numbly at the frosted grass on the lawns in front of the house. It glistened like diamonds. A single tear slipped down her cheek. She refused to scream or shout, refused to wail or sob uncontrollably. She just wanted to understand.

"Why?" she asked, turning to face her mother. "I just want to know why."

Marguerite, her powder-blue eyes soft, compassionate, looked at her. Her shoulders dropped, as if a lifetime's burden had been lifted from them. "Because I loved you. Because I saw your terrified little face and your bare, muddied feet and your tiny hands clutching your tattered flowers—and I loved you." She dabbed at her tears with the lace handkerchief. "I loved you," she repeated, walking to her daughter and grabbing her hands. "I *love* you."

She waited for Violette to speak. Violette had no words. Marguerite continued.

"I can't expect you to understand—can *never* expect you to understand. I don't deserve your understanding—or your forgiveness. It's so hard to explain. You were hiding in my carriage. You were hiding from someone. You were so terrified, my darling. So utterly lost and terrified. I couldn't bear to send you back. You were a street urchin, a little dot of a thing—four years old at most. We took you in, nursed you back to health. I couldn't let you go. How could I let you go when I loved you so, so much?"

"Violette isn't my real name, is it?"

"No. It isn't. You couldn't speak. You were so afraid, you couldn't tell me your name. I called you Violette after the violets you held in your hand."

"I was Rosie Flynn," Violette said. "And my sister was Flora—Florrie—Flynn. We were orphaned flower sellers living in Rosemary Court in London. I was almost completely blind and Flora looked after me until we were separated on Westminster Bridge. She thought that a man who sold lemonade had tried to snatch me. It's all there, written in the book. And then you found me—and Flora spent the rest of her life looking for me."

"I knew nothing of your circumstances before I found you, darling. All I knew was that you needed a mother—and I needed a daughter. Somehow, we found each other." She dropped to her knees, her eyes searching, beseeching. She shook her daughter's cold hands. "I am so, so sorry, Violette. So sorry for keeping it a secret from you. I should have told you a long time ago, but I was afraid."

"Afraid of what?"

"Afraid of losing you. Afraid of losing another daughter."

Violette knew she was referring to Delphine, the girl she had grown up believing was her sister. She'd almost forgotten about her in all the revelations from Flora's book.

"So, Delphine wasn't my sis—"

"She died when she was four years old. The scarlet fever took her from me. She died before I found you."

Violette looked at the locket hanging around her mother's neck. She didn't deny her the grief she felt for Delphine. She couldn't deny her that.

"But what about my real sister? Flora. Did you never think of her?"

"I thought about nothing else. I never stopped thinking about her, wondering who she was, where she was. I looked for her. I went to the places you'd lived and worked. I asked for her. You were children of the shadows, you and her—she was as lost as you were."

Violette looked down at her mother. She had been a good, kind woman. She had given her the best of everything: her time, her love, her passion for nature and music.

"She spent her whole life looking for me," she sighed. "Her whole life, wondering, waiting. It's so sad, Mother. So very sad. I think I remember her—very vaguely. She used to sing to me. She was very kind to me. *She* loved me, too."

She wept then, wept for her sister.

"I may not have given birth to you, darling," Marguerite whispered through her tears, "but I do not know how it is possible for a mother to love a child any more than I have loved you."

There was nothing else either of them could say. They sat together, bound by grief and sorrow, until the grandfather clock in the hall chimed six.

Time passed.

Life moved on.

MARGUERITE STOOD UP. She walked to the window and pulled it shut.

"Could we take a walk in the garden? We used to have such lovely times together walking in the gardens, admiring the view over London from the Terrace Walk."

Violette considered her. She didn't feel anger anymore, she felt only numbness and pity.

"But it's dark outside, Mother. And cold."

"Then let's put on our coats and hats and mufflers. I would like to see the lights of London."

THEY WALKED IN THE DARKNESS of the December night, their breaths captured by the cold air as they gazed over the pitch-black meadows toward the London skyline. The gas lamps of the city illuminated the winter fog that lurked over the church spires and chimney tops, giving everything a peculiar, yellow hue.

The two women stood in silence.

Violette looked at the city sprawling in front of her, and she wondered. She wondered about the privileged, happy life she had lived, and she wondered what it might have been, what might have become of her if she'd lived her life on the streets, beneath the fog.

Without speaking, Violette looped her arm into her mother's. The gesture spoke a thousand words.

A lone deer watched, unnoticed, within the shadows of the trees, before turning and disappearing into the blackness of the night.

Chapter 44

Violet House, London

December 1912

"Do you think she's found her, or found something out about her?" Queenie asked. She was helping Tilly decorate the parlor for Christmas. "Surely, she wouldn't have sent the telegram to ask if she could visit if she didn't have some news."

"Maybe she just wants to return the notebook," Tilly replied. "I'm not sure."

"When is she coming?"

"Today. Three o'clock."

Tilly's stomach flipped as she said the words.

Since Tilly had returned to London after her mother's death, Queenie had been surprisingly supportive. "I know what it feels like to be without a mother or father," she'd said. "It doesn't matter how young or old you are when you lose them, it still leaves you feeling just as lost."

Tilly found Queenie's empathy very touching. Surprising, but touching nonetheless.

So much had happened in the past month—the revelations in her father's letter, the visit to Violette Ashton, Esther coming to the Flower Homes—that Tilly began to feel overwhelmed by it all. It was Edward who had encouraged her to talk to Queenie. He knew how desperate she was to ask Queenie about Lily Brennan, to talk about her mother with someone who'd known her.

She'd finally plucked up the courage and told Queenie everything.

Queenie was speechless, but she was glad Tilly had told her and promised to tell her everything she could remember about Lily Brennan. It gave Tilly immense comfort to talk to Queenie about her.

"What was Lily like?" she asked.

"She was a very kind girl. Had a fierce temper, mind, but you'd expect that with the red hair, I suppose. Everyone liked Lily Brennan—and she was very talented at making the flowers. Violets were her specialty. Loved the violets. She liked to draw flowers, too—real ones as well as the ones we made in the workrooms."

Tilly fizzed with excitement at these snippets of information. Slowly, the fog was clearing. She could finally see who she was, where she'd come from.

"How did she get placed at the orphanage?"

"Her parents died when she was a baby—within months of each other apparently. Consumption, I think she said. An aunt arranged for her to go to Clacton when she was only a few months old. She was one of the few girls who didn't have any physical limitations. She came to the Flower Homes when she'd finished her schooling. It was always intended for her to go into service, as all the able-bodied girls did, but she had her heart set on coming to work on the flowers. She told Mr. Shaw that she had such admiration for the work the girls did, that she felt it was more important than fetching and carrying for some rich folk. She was like that, Lily—down-to-earth, practical, keen to help others." Tilly absorbed the words hungrily, taking in every detail of her mother's life. "Then she left—all of a sudden. Went up north to stay with the aunt, who was sick," Queenie continued. "Flora missed her terribly. 'Course, we weren't surprised when we heard she'd met someone and married. Last we heard, she was carrying a baby. Never heard from her again. We all thought she was just too busy with the new baby to write. Turns out that wasn't the case, eh?"

Tilly had also told Queenie about the notebook and the flowers and trinkets she'd found in the box in the wardrobe. She asked Queenie about Flora, and the time they had spent together in Clacton and London.

"I remember her scribbling away in that notebook," Queenie said. "We used to tease her about it at first. We shouldn't have, though. It was something she needed to do. Said it made her feel that she was talking to Rosie. 'Course, she wrote less and less as the years passed, but she took good care of that wooden box. Mrs. Shaw gave it to her one Christmas, if I remember. I'd forgotten all about it, to be honest."

Queenie had also explained how it had been Flora's idea to set up the Forget-Me-Not Society.

"It was for the flower girls who moved on—who left the orphanage and Flower Homes. She wanted to find a way for everyone to keep in contact, wanted to make sure we didn't lose each other after spending so many years together. It was a nice idea. She didn't like the thought of losing anyone after all that business with Rosie, see."

Tilly enjoyed Queenie's company as they hung paper chains around the picture frames. They chatted about the Christmas traditions in the Flower Homes and both hoped that Mr. Shaw's health would improve.

As it approached noon, they stood back to admire their work. They both agreed that the swags and garlands of little red silk roses finished off the room perfectly.

AT THREE O'CLOCK there was a faint knock on the door. She was exactly on time.

Tilly put down the sampler she was working on as a Christmas gift for Mrs. Pearce, removed her white apron, and smoothed her skirt. She took a deep breath. The house was perfectly quiet—the girls having gone out for their Saturday afternoon off and Mrs. Harris having gone on some errand or other.

She removed her white cap, scrunching it up and shoving it into her pocket as she opened the door.

Violette Ashton stood on the doorstep, a bunch of snow-white tulips in her hands. She looked pale, as fragile as a china teacup.

"Mrs. Ashton!" Tilly said, taking her hand in greeting. "Thank you so much for coming. Please, come in, out of the cold."

"Miss Harper! So lovely to see you again," she replied, smiling and shaking Tilly's hand in return as she stepped inside the narrow passage. The scent of the cold air entered with her, captured in the fabric of her hat and coat. "I hope I haven't come at a bad time."

"Not at all. Please, come inside." Tilly showed her into the parlor. It was the best room in the house, reserved for the most special occasions, but still, Tilly was conscious of how humble it was after the grandeur of Nightingale House. She gestured to a chair by the fire. "Please, take a seat. I'll make tea."

Violette perched on the edge of the chair. Tilly noticed how she clasped her hands tightly on her lap, how she fidgeted and fussed with her hair as she admired the flower garlands around the walls.

Tilly rushed off to the scullery, quickly spooning the tea leaves into the pot before lifting the heavy kettle from the range and pouring in the hot water. She set everything onto a tea tray and carried it back to the parlor. Her heart thumped in her chest. Her hands shook, rattling the cups and saucers.

She set the tray down on the sideboard, noticing that Flora's notebook had been placed there.

"Thank you for returning the book," Tilly said. For something so small, it had a profound effect on the atmosphere of the room.

"You're welcome," Violette replied. "I enjoyed reading it." She fell silent as Tilly poured the tea, the crack and spit of the fire the only sound. "What a charming little room," she remarked, looking around. "So neat and cozy. I must admit that it feels a little strange to be here, in Violet House, after reading so much about it."

"I imagine it must be," Tilly said, willing her hands to steady as she passed Violette a cup of tea.

Violette thanked her, resting the tulips in her lap as she took the cup and saucer.

"It was so very heartbreaking to read of Flora's desperate sorrow," she said. "So very sad . . . I . . ."

Her words trailed off. She didn't know what to say.

They sat for a while, drinking their tea, talking about the weather and plans for Christmas—about anything other than Florrie and Rosie Flynn, and while an undeniable sense of anticipation stung the air around them, Tilly felt far more relaxed in Violette's company here than she had in the austere surroundings of Nightingale House.

She studied Violette's face as they chatted. She looked tired. There was something different about her. She seemed distant, displaced—as if a taut thread had been suddenly released to unravel into a dozen strands.

They talked and talked until Tilly could bear it no longer.

"So you found the notebook interesting?"

Her words seemed to get caught among the dust motes, floating around in a shaft of pale winter sun that peered through the window.

Violette swallowed. She set her teacup down onto the table beside her.

"I did," she said. The words were spoken quietly, carefully. "Yes, I found it very interesting." She paused, tugging at the choker around her neck. "Miss Harper, I wonder, if it isn't too impertinent of me to ask, whether it would be possible to see the room that Flora—Florrie—lived in, when she was here. It really would mean a great deal to me."

Tilly understood. Part of her had been expecting Violette to want to see Flora's old room. She was glad now that she'd taken the extra time and gone over the floors twice and dusted all the surfaces thoroughly that morning.

"Of course. Please, follow me. It's quite a climb to the top of the house, I'm afraid."

Ascending the stairs, Tilly remembered how nervous she'd

felt when she first arrived here, following Mrs. Pearce, not knowing what would be waiting for her when she reached the top. She felt the same trepidation now.

Reaching her room, she opened the door and stood to one side.

She spoke quietly. "This is it. This is the room that Flora Flynn called home. She shared it with another girl for some years, but it was just hers for the final years of her life."

She wanted to tell Violette about Lily Brennan, about how she'd only just discovered the identity of her real mother, about how Lily and Florrie had been such good friends, but as she watched Violette step into the room, she noticed her face change. She stood to one side and said nothing.

Violette was completely silent. She stood on the simple rag rug in the center of the room, her eyes closed. Tilly hovered in the doorway. She felt the temperature in the room drop, detected the scent of violets around her.

After a while, Violette spoke, her whispered words—charged with emotion—filling the small room like electricity, fizzing in the air.

"What a palace, Flora. What a beautiful palace you found to call home. I remember, Flora. I remember you. I remember the flowers and the cries of the sellers."

She paused for a moment to catch her breath, dabbing at her tears.

Tilly stepped into the room. She waited by the door.

Violette closed her eyes again. "She's here. She's still here, isn't she, Miss Harper? Do you sense her, too?"

Tilly nodded. "I wasn't sure for a long while, but as I read more of the notebook, the sensations became more noticeable. The room cools very suddenly. I sometimes get a sense of someone brushing past me. It never frightened me, though. It's comforting in a way." She walked over to the bed, perching on the edge. "Do you smell the violets, Mrs Ashton?"

"Violets?"

"Yes. Every so often I smell violets, although there have never been any in the room."

"How funny," Violette said. "And yet all I smell are roses. Wonderful, sweet roses. Her favorite." She breathed in deeply. "Perhaps there are others who linger here, too, Miss Harper."

Violette took another breath and began to sing softly; her voice as clear as a nightingale's.

"At early dawn I once had been
Where Lene's blue waters flow,
When summer bid the groves be green,
The lamp of light to glow—
As on by bower, and town and tower,
And wide-spread fields I stray,
I meet a maid in the greenwood shade,
At the dawning of the day."

Tilly sat on the edge of the bed, plaiting the fringe of the counterpane. She felt as if she was intruding. She waited until the song came to an end.

"Would you like to be alone, Mrs. Ashton?"

Violette walked over to the bed and settled herself beside Tilly, taking hold of her hands, grasping them tight, as if she might fall if she were to let go.

Tilly looked into her eyes. They burned with so much intensity it was hard to believe that they once couldn't see.

"It is me, Miss Harper. Rosie. Little Sister. *I* am Rosie."

She let out a huge sigh as she spoke, a thousand memories tumbling from within her.

A cool breath of air rushed between them. Goose bumps bubbled all over Tilly's skin. She couldn't speak.

"Florrie? Florrie, is that you? Are you here?" Tilly watched, frozen, as Violette spoke into the pale midwinter light of the room. "I feel you," she continued. "I remember you. It is me, Florrie. Rosie. Little sister. I am found. I have come back to you, Florrie."

A distant sigh, like a breath of wind in the treetops.

Tilly felt hot tears prick her eyes. "I can't believe it," she whispered. "I can't believe it is you. I can't believe I found her."

Violette continued to speak, lost in her memories. "I remember the flower markets, Florrie. The wonderful scent of the flowers—and the noise of the hawkers and costers. I remember your hand in mine—always in mine. I don't blame you, Florrie. It wasn't your fault. I hid in the carriage of a lady who found me and took me in as her own daughter." She paused, her words broken by tears.

Tilly held her hands to her mouth, immobilized by what she heard.

"She has explained everything to me," Violette continued. "She only meant for the best. She didn't mean to deprive you of your sister, didn't mean to break your heart. She is a good woman and has been a wonderful mother to me. She is so sorry for taking me from you, truly, truly sorry. I have forgiven her, Florrie—and you must forgive yourself. You must let yourself go on now—toward the light."

Tilly could smell roses now; an intense perfume of a hundred roses, filling the room.

Violette stood up. She walked to the window and laid the white tulips on the windowsill.

"For you, Florrie," she whispered. "White tulips for forgiveness. You don't need to search for me anymore. You don't need to wait. You can go. Be at peace."

A gasp. Tilly heard it so clearly. A woman's gasp. And then a sigh, a long, gentle sigh like the faintest breath of wind, blown in from the sea.

And then silence.

Chapter 45

Nightingale House,
Richmond Hill,
London

December 15, 1912

Dear Mr. Shaw,

I write to tell you how very moved I was to read your most recent entry in The Christian Magazine. *You write with such eloquence, such dignity. And I quote: "To those who are blest with the riches of this world and who may chance to read these observations, I earnestly commend the cause of the Waifs and Strays and Homeless little ones, hoping that they will assist in providing the funds necessary to carry on this Institution, and so help in providing a Home for the homeless."*

I applaud your continued commitment to this most worthy of ventures.

With the Festive season upon us, I would like to donate a further sum of three hundred pounds to the Institutions. It is my only hope that this may assist in providing some poor, wretched child a home for Christmas and a brighter future for the New Year and beyond.

I hope that your health is much recovered after your period of convalescence in Clacton. I was fortunate to visit the resort earlier in the year and must admit that I found it uncommonly pleasant and quite difficult to leave behind when it was time to return to London.

You may recall that I first wrote to you some years ago, after seeing a display of the flower girls' work. I was keen to support your work, and have always made my donations under an anonymous name. But the truth of the matter is a little more complicated than that.

My support of your work is driven by a deep sense of obligation to do whatever small thing I can to support the lives of London's crippled and blind children. While the reasons for my obligation cannot be easily explained, it gives me great comfort to know that your wonderful work will prevent the needless suffering of other children.

With God's blessings for a wonderful Yuletide and peace and happiness to you and all your family—including the flower girls and orphans you have dedicated your life to. I once heard you say that you think of them all as your daughters. They could not wish for a more devoted father.

With fondest regards,
Marguerite Ingram ("Daisy")

Chapter 46

Clacton

December 1912

As the icy grip of winter brought everything in nature to a creeping halt, Albert Shaw's health continued to deteriorate. Despite his insistence that he was perfectly well, there was no denying the fact that his rasping cough had worsened and his breathing was increasingly labored. From her room in Foxglove House, Tilly heard his continual struggle for breath. There was no escaping the sound of his pleurisy, the illness he had carried for many years. It frightened her.

True to his promise, Edward had arranged for Tilly to accompany him on a day trip to the Flower Village. He had some matters to attend to before the Christmas festivities commenced in full and insisted that she would be a great tonic to his aunt and uncle while he was taking care of business. With Mrs. Harris happy to hold the fort in London, it was settled. "And, it would certainly cheer me to be greeted by *your* smile each day, rather than Sarah's," Edward had joked. "She can be quite fearsome sometimes."

"Dear Edward. You are too harsh. Sarah wouldn't harm a fly. She may be all starch on the outside, but her heart is made of pure velvet."

It was agreed that Mrs. Pearce would accompany them, since she needed to make arrangements for some of the older girls from the Flower Village to be moved up to the Flower Homes in London. While Tilly wished she could make the journey with Edward alone, she knew that Mrs. Pearce's presence would keep matters more "appropriate."

Tilly had told Edward everything about her life. She'd wept hard, gulping tears of guilt and remorse as the words and emotions she'd kept locked within her for so many years spilled from her as easily as milk from a dropped jug. Through all her revelations about Florrie and Rosie, Violette Ashton and Mrs. Ingram, Lily Brennan and Esther's accident, Edward listened and understood. He didn't judge or condemn her—just embraced and loved her. And she loved him in return. Truly loved him, with all her heart.

Before they left for Clacton, Queenie, Hilda, and Buttons gave Tilly a beautiful wreath of white lilies and snowdrops. "It's for the little girl," Queenie explained. "Edward will know what I mean."

There was so much Tilly wanted to say to the girls, whom she saw now as friends and family, as well as her charges, but how could she ever begin to thank them for everything they had given her? They would never know the difference they had made to her life since she'd arrived in London that spring.

Although it was only to be a short trip, she packed some spare clothes in her small carpet bag just in case a snowstorm saw them stuck in Clacton. She added a few personal possessions, things she liked to have with her always—her sketchbook and pastels and her favorite reading books. She'd given the wooden box, and everything in it—the button, the peg, the rag doll, the pressed flowers, the handkerchief, the postcard and Flora's notebook—to Mrs Ashton. She was delighted with the box of trinkets but said she would discard the button—that she didn't like the feel of it.

And then there was Esther. Tilly was relieved to see how much her sister was flourishing under the watchful eye of Mrs. Pearce and the flower girls in Rosebud House—and the special bond she had forged with Hilda. When she looked at her sister now, she saw life and hope burning in those kingfisher eyes.

Esther had listened quietly while Tilly told her everything about the letter from their father.

"I'm sorry for how everything worked out," she said. "I wish Mother could have loved you."

"Me, too," Tilly said. "Me, too."

Esther had also shared the content of their father's letter with Tilly. Her letter hadn't contained any startling revelations or shocking truths, just words of love for the daughter he and Hannah had longed for, and words of encouragement for the life she would lead. *Your sister is a good person*, he'd written. *Try to understand her. Try to follow her advice. You may be very different, you and her, but there is much that you have in common. Reach out to her, Esther, and I am sure that she will let you in.*

Some of the bricks still refused to fall from Tilly's wall, no matter how hard she pushed at them, but she could now see a way through at least. She hoped that, in time, there would be nothing standing between her and her sister. For now, she was content that they were building new foundations, forming a new relationship. *Perhaps in the spring*, she wrote in a letter she pushed under Esther's dormitory door before she left for Clacton. *Perhaps we'll be able to start again in the spring. Daddy always said springtime is the best time for renewal, for starting again. I hope we can nurture the little bud of friendship we've discovered. Perhaps we'll see it flourish by the summertime.*

As Tilly walked arm in arm with Edward through Mr. Hutton's frost-dusted gardens, she looked at the stark outline of the oak trees against the pale winter sky. Their branches were bare, their leaves withered on the ground. So much in nature was coming to an end—a quiet pause before the vibrancy of the spring—and yet she felt the love between her and Edward blooming as brightly as cherry blossoms in April.

They strolled on, through the rose garden, Edward carrying the wreath sent from the flower girls in London.

"There are lots of little symbols of remembrance for children who lived here and who, sadly, died here," Edward explained.

"I remember this bench," Tilly said, stooping beneath the gnarled branches of the rambling rosebush to read the words again. "*God gave us roses in June so that we can have memories in December*. Such lovely words."

She remarked on the patterns left by the frost in the delicate folds of the petals of the Christmas roses. "Just like sugar frosting. It's as beautiful here in the winter as it was at the end of summer."

"Look, over here. This is the one we're looking for."

Tilly followed Edward toward the back of the garden, to a lilac tree, its branches now bare. She read the small plaque set into the earth. IN MEMORY OF ISABELLA HOPE DEARING, WHO WENT HOME ON CHRISTMAS MORNING, 1872.

"The flower girls send a wreath every Christmas," Edward said. "To remember her. She was the first child to die here. My uncle tells a story of her every Christmas, and the mothers here read it to the orphans."

Tilly leaned forward and placed the simple white wreath on the ground, saying a silent prayer.

They stood in respectful silence. Tilly thought back to how she'd watched the snowflakes gather in the corners of the cottage windows after the letter had arrived from the War Office. They hadn't been able to bury her father—his body interred thousands of miles away. She thought of the memorial headstone they'd placed in the churchyard, a place she would go often to remember him.

"It's a funny thing, grief, isn't it," she said. "It brings about a great change in people, makes them forget about the little things they had time to fret and worry over the day before, like the fact that they've an ache in their tooth or a missing button or a new hole in their boot or that it's raining for the fourth day in a row. Grief washes all that away." She brushed a tear from her cheek. "They tell you it will pass, that there'll be a day when you wake up and your heart doesn't ache, a day when you don't cry, but laugh and smile and remember the person you've lost with great fondness. You can't believe that day will ever come. But it does, doesn't it? Somehow, it does."

Edward placed his arm around her shoulder. She let her head rest against him.

"Sleep well, little angel," she whispered as they left the memorial place. "Sleep well."

They walked then, down the cliff path, through the meadow toward the sand dunes, a trail worn into the grassy sand by so many footsteps over the years. A chill wind blew, whipping around them, pulling at their coats and hats, nipping at their noses that soon turned as red as holly berries. Tilly had missed that sea breeze and the crash of the waves. She held tightly to Edward's arm as she watched the clouds race across the low winter sun.

"Let's walk barefoot," she said as they reached the sea. "Let's see how cold the water is."

Edward laughed. "Dear Tilly. Are you insane? We'll freeze to death!"

But she was already removing her boots and stockings, bundling them under her arm, driven by a wonderful, wind-fueled recklessness she hadn't felt for some time. She didn't care how shocking it was for a gentleman to see her bare feet and ankles, didn't care how cold the wet sand was against her porcelain-white skin. This was Edward. This was Clacton—two things she loved more than anything in the world. "Come on," she laughed, running ahead toward the water. "It'll be fun!"

Tilly shrieked and leaped backward as the icy-cold water lapped between her toes. Soon, Edward joined her. They fooled around in the water for a while, before standing quietly to watch the white-tipped waves far away in the distance.

Turning her back to the sea, Tilly looked across the sand to the houses of the Flower Village, standing proudly on the cliff top like shining beacons of hope and safety—a lighthouse for all the lost little children who had found their way there.

"It really is a very special place, isn't it?" she said, holding her hair back from her face.

Edward stood beside her, their shoulders brushing against each other. "It is," he said. "Quite, quite special."

"Do you think your uncle understands what he's done for all the children he's helped?"

Edward considered the question for a moment. "I don't think it's possible for anyone to fully understand the difference this place has made to them. Until you've lived their life, walked on frozen cobbles in bare feet and felt hunger pains in your stomach, I don't think any of us can ever know what it really means to them—or how much Uncle Albert means to them."

They stood, quietly. Looking. Thinking.

"You realize he's dying, don't you? That he won't recover."

Tilly let Edward's words swirl around her in the breeze before answering, softly. "Yes. I know."

"Do you think you could love it here as much as he does, Tilly?"

"I think I already do."

Edward turned her to face him. She looked into his gentle, blue eyes, their color accented by the sea and the sky. The breeze tugged at the fabric of their clothes—Tilly's skirts ballooning out, reaching to Edward, his coattails stretching out like fingertips toward her. She felt her heart swell with endless waves of love.

"Dear Tilly," he whispered, his mouth so close to hers that his breath moved across her lips.

The freezing water lapped around her toes, but Tilly felt nothing but warmth. As their lips met, the seagulls wheeled in jubilation above them and Tilly Harper knew, with absolute certainty, that she was loved. That she mattered. That whatever had happened in her past was behind her. She closed her eyes and saw the rest of her life stretching endlessly before her, like the vast, beautiful sea.

Lost for a moment in their embrace, they were disturbed by a faint voice, high on the cliff tops, the words carried toward them on the wind.

"Mister Edward! Miss Tilly!"

Tilly opened her eyes. It was Sarah. She was standing on the path, her white hat flapping in the breeze, waving her arms, beckoning them to come—not wildly, but insistently.

And they knew.

Turning from the sea, Tilly linked her arm through Edward's and they walked quietly along the sand. They didn't stop to put on their stockings, socks, and shoes. They didn't care about the rivulets of freezing water they had so carefully sidestepped a few moments ago.

They walked peacefully up the worn path toward Sarah, whose ashen face confirmed their fears—that the man who had made all of this possible, the man who had given so many lost souls a life, had, finally, lost the battle for his own.

The world had lost a wonderful man, and hundreds of little girls had lost a dear father.

Chapter 47

Grasmere, Lake District
March 1913

March 1, 1913

Dear Daddy,

I've been drawing these pictures for you ever since the day the packet arrived from the War Office to tell us the news we had been dreading. I simply could not believe you weren't coming home, so I continued my sketching, illustrating the hole your death left in my life. I always imagined that one day you would return, and I would give them to you.

I have to accept that I will never again run to you and fall into your open arms, as I so often dreamed I would. So, I am giving my drawings to you now—leaving them where I know you will find them, here at the lake, nestled within the mountains we loved so much.

I want to thank you for raising me on your own, for always believing in me. Fate may have led my mother, Lily, to you, but I believe it was destiny that brought me back to her. I see her in the photograph you sent with your letter. I look so much like her! How I wish I could have known her.

I wear the silver locket around my neck and I sometimes sense your hand resting on the top of my head. It comforts me to know that you are still here, watching me, guiding me. My husband tells me I still have the wind at my heels, but I feel a peace in my heart now. The storm has passed.

There are so many other things I want to say to you, but words seem so inadequate. I will let my sketches, and the beauty of this place, speak for me.

Sleep well, Daddy.

Until the next life.

Your loving daughter,
Tilly
xxx

Tilly had wrapped the sketchbook and her letter in a paper parcel. She placed it now on a large piece of driftwood and pushed it out into the lake, watching as the current took it. She followed it as it moved slowly toward the center, where it was lost in the early morning mist. As she turned to walk away, she caught a flash of a white rabbit in the distance, scurrying into its burrow. "White rabbits. White rabbits. White rabbits," she whispered.

It was just dawn—the sky streaked with shades of violet, lavender, and bluebell. It was the first day of a new month, and a sense of spring laced the air.

Taking her husband's arm, she leaned her head gently on his shoulder.

"Thank you, Edward. Thank you for coming back with me one last time. I feel at peace now. Let's go back home—back to Clacton."

As Tilly watched the brilliant orb of the sun rise in the sky, a ray of hope and happiness spread within her. She had been lost for so very long. Now, she was found.

Epilogue

March 25, 1932

I wait in the silent, early morning light. It is the first day of spring. The primroses will be in this morning, I tell her. Let us run to get the best of the blooms. "Rosie," I call. "Rosie, I am here."

I sit by her bedside, watching her slow, irregular breaths. Her once flame-red hair, now grayed with the passing of the years, fans out on the pillow around her. Her frail hands rest on her chest, rising and falling with each breath.

She senses me near her—I know she does. Sometimes she opens her eyes, looking around to find the cause of the cool breath she feels against her cheeks. She speaks of roses. "I remember," she whispers. "Buy my sweet roses. Tuppence a bunch. Poor little girl. Buy a bunch, kind lady."

"Take my hand, Rosie," I whisper. "Don't let go."

She reaches out, her touch like silk. A dazzling white glow surrounds us, the air enriched with the scent of a thousand blooms: roses, violets, lilies, and lavender.

I hold her hand, tight in mine, and we rush toward the beautiful, beautiful light.

Acknowledgments

It is an absolute pleasure to start by thanking two ladies in particular: my amazing agent, Michelle Brower, for all her sage advice and hard work (I must remember to send her more tea), and my incredible editor, Lucia Macro, who—from the moment she read the manuscript—was as passionate about my little flower sellers as I was. I'm so grateful for her enthusiasm and support and consider myself very lucky to be under her guidance and expertise.

To my publisher at William Morrow, Liate Stehlik, and everyone in New York who has worked on this book—thank you! Special thanks to the eagle-eyed copy editors who spot my bloopers and spare my blushes, and to the brilliant marketing team—especially Jennifer Hart and Molly Birckhead—who wave their wands and tell the world that a new book has been born. A big thanks to my wonderful publicist Megan Schumann who, quite frankly, I don't know what I'd do without, and thank you also to Nicole Fischer for her terrifying efficiency and for answering the questions only a newbie author would ask. And to Diahann Sturge, thank you for the beautiful design work. To the team at HarperCollins360 in London—Karen, Ellie, and Helena—thank you for taking me on board your exciting new venture! I am so thrilled to be working with you all to bring this book to the UK and Ireland.

Writing historical fiction poses its own peculiar and fascinating problems. While I had endless amounts of information about London's flower sellers, Alexandra Rose Day, and John Groom's organization, I sometimes struggled to find smaller, essential details about the minutiae of Tilly's life in 1912. Many people—most of them volunteers—answered my cries for help with astonishing enthusiasm and detail: Peter Robinson at Cumbrian Railways Association, Roger Kennell at Frinton & Walton Heritage Trust, and Guy Marriott at the London Transport Museum. It really did matter to me that I knew the exact train routes and how much Tilly's motor-cab fare would have cost, so thank you all! Pat Cryer's website 1900s.org.uk was also a wonderful source of period information for writing the scenes set in Violet House.

Without the support of Kildare County Council's bursary, I couldn't have made the much-needed research trip to the London Metropolitan Archives. Opening those dusty archive boxes in the hush of the reading room was a very moving experience, and a pivotal moment in the development of the book and my belief in myself as a writer.

I don't know how I can ever properly thank the amazing Philippa Gregory for giving me (me!) her time and invaluable feedback on the early chapters. After meeting her in Dublin in September 2012, I had a sense that somehow a door had opened—I could never have guessed how far. The e-mail she sent late one evening, offering her thoughts on my chapters, could not have made an exhausted mummy and frustrated writer any happier. I will never forget her support and generosity.

Closer to home, I must thank my amazing friends, fellow writers, and family who cheer me on, "Like" my Facebook updates, wave pom poms at appropriate moments, make very kind offers to accompany me on trips to New York (Tanya, Sheila—I'm looking at you!), and generally live through the long gestation period of my books. Special thanks to my sister, Helen, for telling me about *Goblin Market* and for reading early chapters and saying kind things (even when they were terrible) and, of course, the biggest thank you of all to Damien, Max, and Sam for putting up with me, especially when I go into editing lockdown and become the crazy lady in the attic. I love you all, and yes, you can have sprinkles on your ice cream.

I must also thank a wonderful teacher at Driffield School—Michael Knight—who is sadly no longer with us. It was through his brilliant production of My Fair Lady, and his casting of a much younger me as Eliza Doolittle, where the idea for this novel really started.

Finally, to my wonderful readers—thank you all. I simply couldn't do it without you.

Hazel x

About the author

About the book

Read on

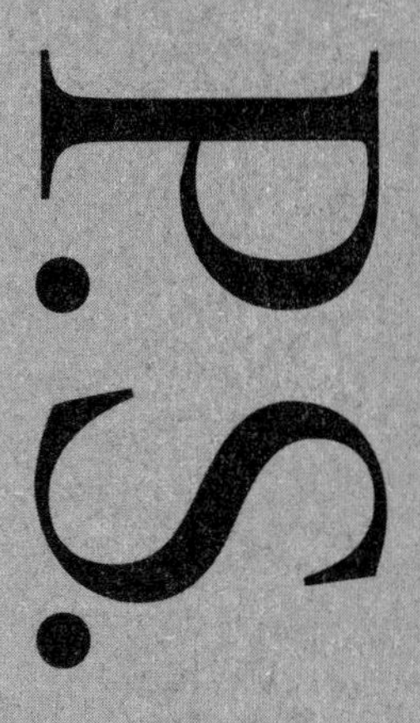

Insights, Interviews & More . . .

About the author

Meet Hazel Gaynor

Deasy Photographic

HAZEL GAYNOR is an author and freelance writer. Originally from Yorkshire, England, she now lives in Ireland with her husband, two children, and an accident-prone cat. Contact Hazel on Twitter @HazelGaynor or visit hazelgaynor.com.

The Memoirs of Albert Shaw

Extracts from the Memoirs of Albert Shaw

1842–1912

The first time I encountered the two wretched little Irish girls was on an April morning in the year 1876, at the Aldgate Pump. This is the point at which Leadenhall and Fenchurch Streets meet and where, they say, the City stops and the East End begins.

The older girl, Flora (who, I subsequently learned, also goes by the name of Florrie), was sobbing as she tried to rewash her cresses and rearrange her posies of primroses after "a swell" had knocked the flower basket clean from her hands as he rushed past. "The swells ain't got a bit o' heart, Mr. Shaw," she wailed, after I tried to calm her and introduced myself. "They pushes us out of the way if we ask 'em to buy a flower. They're a bad lot, sure they are!"

What a sorry sight she made, weeping and complaining about the ruination of her stock, "and the sun barely risen and hardly tuppence earned." I noticed how her hands shook as she worked, numbed by a combination of the freezing water and the lack of a decent meal in Lord knows how long.

I eventually calmed her by paying her the value of her spoiled stock and handing her a breakfast ticket for her and her sister to use at the Club Room at Covent Garden. How her sullen eyes ▸

lit up at the prospect of a hot cup of cocoa and some bread and butter—such a simple pleasure for many children, but such unexpected treasures for street urchins like these two ragged little girls.

I spent a little time with them at the Club Room, where I was able to talk to Flora further and discover something of her circumstances. Surprisingly, she was quite happy to talk—so many of the girls are shy, nervous creatures and will barely look a person in the eye, let alone speak with them. Perhaps it is the Irish gift of the gab that made her speak so openly. Perhaps it was just want of a friendly soul to hear her speak. In any event, I was glad of my notebook and pencil so that I could record some of what she told me. I find that it is only through the girls' own words that I can ever truly express—to the more fortunate—the real plight of these poor souls. I always hoped that if I might capture something of these "conversations" in our fund-raising pamphlets and *The Christian Magazine*, benevolent, kindhearted folk would learn something of the pitiful conditions these children live in and might, as a consequence, donate generously to our cause.

The girls were so dramatically different in appearance that I was surprised to learn they were sisters—born of the same "Mammy" and "Da," the elder assured me. The only common feature between them was the color of their eyes—a curious shade of emerald-green, which, I am sure, only the Irish would be capable of producing. I did notice, during my first encounter with them, that the younger child, Rosie, suffered from some problem with her eyes. She wouldn't hold my gaze long enough for me to inspect this more closely, but I suspected that she did not have her full vision.

Other than the eyes, the girls were as different as winter and spring. The elder had a pinched, haunted look about her, the deep hollows around her eyes making her look many years older than she was. No doubt she gave the lion's share of any food to the younger girl, who had a more rounded look to her face, even though it was smeared with filth. While Flora's hair was as pale as a primrose, Rosie was blessed with the red hair of her native Ireland.

The girls, like all the street children I encountered, wore what could only be described as rags—tattered, dirty frocks, which hung off their undernourished bodies, and meager shawls draped about their hunched, narrow shoulders. They both went about barefoot, as is common among the poorest street sellers and orphaned children. It never failed to amaze me how oblivious they seemed to the rough cobbles and filth they walked over with every step. It was a sight to make one dreadfully conscious of one's own comfortable boots, cleaned and polished every morning.

Although Flora spoke with a clear Irish brogue, she was not so difficult to understand as some of the Irish who come from the County of Cork, or the Midlands. Hers was a much softer accent, and seemed to have been somewhat tempered by shades of the local dialect when she used certain words or phrases. The younger child didn't speak much at all, and I had reason to wonder if she might be deaf and dumb. Nevertheless, she was a pretty little thing, and her occasional shy smile spoke more than any words she may have carried in her head.

In addition to the girls' pitiful appearance, it saddened me greatly to hear the elder speak in such an adult, wearied manner, her tone more like that of a grown woman who has known all the struggles of life. All that they have in the way of toys is an old peg that the younger girl plays with as a doll, and the occasional rotten apple to kick down the street.

Perhaps it was my dear wife Evelyn's pregnancy that had my emotions running particularly high (a pregnancy that, although surprising, was considered a great blessing—an unexpected gift from God, which we both embraced with all our hearts), or perhaps I found myself becoming more intolerant of the desperate human conditions I encountered every day, but after meeting those little Irish girls, I remember that I returned to Sekforde Street more determined than ever to raise the necessary funding to expand our work and to help more children like them. I recall how I hoped that I would encounter Flora and her "little sister" again, as I found myself quite unable to stop thinking about them.

I often wonder how many more children are hidden away ▸

in the darkest corners of our streets. Perhaps it is better not to know, for there are surely not enough bricks in all of London to build houses enough to give them all a safe, warm home.

It is late now, so I will extinguish the candle and retire. And even though my heart may be heavy with the burden of all that I have seen and heard, it is also filled with hope and faith as, once again, I find that my appeals for funding have been heard. I plan to write tomorrow to our architect, Mr. Hogg, to request that he draw up plans for a Children's Hospital and for the Babies' Villa, to be added to our Flower Village for the orphans in Clacton.

I suspect it is this dreadful cough I have developed that has me feeling so particularly desolate this evening. Of course, Evelyn insists on mixing me a terrible concoction to ease the discomfort in my chest. How I ever came to deserve such a dear and patient wife is truly beyond my means of comprehension.

• • •

I came across many "little mothers" as I walked the streets. This is the name given to the young children who raise their younger siblings in the absence of any parents. Yet there was always something uniquely compelling about young Flora's devotion to her sister. I cannot recall (with the exception of my own wife) when I had seen any mother as dedicated to the task of raising a child as she was, and I was always struck by the manner in which she addressed her, as if mimicking the mothers she'd observed around her, copying them and their "motherly" voice, singing the songs she'd clearly heard her own mother once singing.

While it was terrible to see such an absence of "childishness," I cannot deny that I found it admirable to see the girl take on her responsibilities and seek to fulfill her sense of duty to her sister. She told me that she had made a promise to her deceased mother that she would mind the younger child. The father was still living at that time—a rag and bone man, if I recall correctly. Although much of his day was spent seeking escape from his life at the bottom of a bottle of liquor. He relied on his daughters to go out to earn some sort of a living for the family.

It was situations such as this that never failed to galvanize me in my efforts to expand the work of the mission—to continue to seek ways in which we could remove these children from the dreadful conditions they lived in before they became further statistics on the child mortality charts. It was children like Florrie and Rosie Flynn who inspired me to place further advertisements in the newspapers to alert people to our cause and to seek further funding for the homes and for the orphanage at Clacton.

Yet every time I put pen to paper, I found myself struggling to find the right words to convey just how desperate the situation was. How could any man portray in writing—on a page cluttered with advertisements for malt drinks and soap—the sorry sights I witnessed every day? How could I begin to express the horror of the dying mother I encountered at a tenement slum in a dark court at The Dials who, in the last stages of consumption, begged me to take her child to the orphanage. "For the Lord's sake," she begged, "take her into the home. Please—take her."

I always asked myself: How can anyone truly comprehend why we have established this operation, unless they have seen such poverty and human suffering with their own eyes?

As I write these recollections, I pray, once again, for a miracle, and I pray, also, for a mild spring and an early summer. There is nothing better than a dose of warm weather to cure a cough such as mine. Either that, or the fresh sea air, and I am looking forward to my next visit to Clacton for precisely that purpose. Happily, Evelyn's pregnancy progresses well. She is in good health and insists that she will be perfectly fine without me if I do visit the south coast.

• • •

I was very touched to know that the girls were visiting chapel—and to hear young Flora speak so fondly of our Club Room at Covent Garden. When I met children like Flora and Rosie, and especially when I heard their desperate tales, it felt like such a small, insignificant thing we did for them—the occasional cup of cocoa and a mended tear in a dress could hardly make much of a difference when there was so much wrong in their lives. Yet, my dear wife often reminded me that when your existence is as unforgiving as theirs, cocoa and stitching can become very large and significant things indeed. Perhaps, beyond anything physical we could provide, the most important aspect of our work was simply giving the children a sense that somebody cared about ▸

them. Being loved and cared for should be the absolute right of every child, should it not?

Nevertheless, being the "restless, intolerant, stubborn fool" that I am (my dear wife's words—she, I might add, loves me dearly despite these rather unattractive attributes), I could not help but feel that more could be done.

I was most pleased when it was agreed by our board members that we would rent several more houses on Sekforde Street, to provide more family homes for the flower sellers. Offering the training to make artificial flowers was proving to be very successful—and although the small workrooms in the Chapel Hall hardly met our needs, they sufficed. I always sensed, though, that it would be only by housing the girls, removing them permanently from their life on the streets, and providing them with a proper purpose, that we could ever make a real and lasting difference to their lives. Happily, our pamphlet drives and prayers for funding to enable us to rent the additional Sekforde Street houses, and to expand the orphanage at Clacton for the youngest children, both proved to be extremely fruitful.

Undeniably, the greatest boost to our cause was the generous contribution from Lord Shaftesbury, who happened to come across me as I assisted a crippled seller in Piccadilly Circus one summer morning. She'd been knocked off her crutches by a hansom cab, and Shaftesbury was quite concerned by the girl's plight. After speaking with me for some time and visiting the Mission Hall, he promised a generous sum and assured me that he would use his contacts to assist in raising further funding.

I still find it quite remarkable that I ever found myself corresponding with such an honorable gentleman as Lord Shaftesbury! When it came to the welfare of the children, my capacity to mix with gentry and royalty appeared to know no bounds. "Stubborn fool" as I was, I was inclined to believe that with the generous support of such patrons, and with God's good will, we may just achieve our aims.

On a less positive note I am to visit the doctor tomorrow at Evelyn's insistence. This infernal cough will not improve, and she insists that I am keeping our unborn child awake at night.

• • •

As I write down my recollections, it has struck me how Florrie made very little reference to her own, or her sister's, afflictions. It was almost as if she had forgotten that they did not possess the means with which to move about and behave in the same way that normal people, such as you or I, might do. There was never a word of complaint or self-pity—and this was by no means a characteristic unique to the two Irish girls.

In all the flower sellers I encountered—the afflicted, blind, and orphaned—there was never a suggestion of feeling sorry for themselves, such as a gentleman may feel if he is deprived of a woman's affections or of his evening brandy, finding that the bottle—emptied on some previous occasion—has been put back into the cabinet. These children displayed the greatest of human spirit, and I suspect it was this, rather than the few mugs of cocoa and blankets from our mission, that kept many of them alive.

Florrie remained resolutely focused on her duty to generate a living for herself and her sister. Although she was tall for her years and able to stand quite upright while resting on her crutch, there was a noticeable stoop to her shoulders and back. I can only conclude that this was a result of all the bending and lifting and carrying she had done for almost her entire life—the young, pliable bones of her body bent and twisted out of shape before they'd had a chance to form the natural shape that the Good Lord intended.

Despite her hardships, she had a bright enough face, and her eyes seemed to hint at an inner soul that might someday, if recovered in time, become a jewel to somebody. I was of the opinion that she could be a reasonably clever child if she were given the chance to attend school.

Perhaps the thing that struck me most about Florrie was the continual air of concern and worry that hung about her, a seriousness that was truly sad to see in one so young—and all born of her duty to care for her sister. They really were inseparable, like living shadows of each other.

Often, after spending time chatting with the young flower sellers, I would leave them to tie their posies and walk among the alleyways that open up off Drury Lane. As I walked, I would see group after group of ghostlike children huddled together ▸

on filthy staircases—their staring eyes not really looking at me, but through me. I am not ashamed to admit that I would shed a few tears as I returned—with a heavy, guilt-laden heart—to the warmth and comfort of my own home. I have often found it difficult to sleep at night, unable to forget the haunting faces of those children, who would sleep where I left them while I tossed and turned in my comfortable bed.

At such times when I experienced this melancholy, I took much comfort from the developments of our mission—particularly from the confirmation that the Earl of Shaftesbury was to become president of our little society. I knew, without any doubt, that with his esteemed name attached to our affairs, we would have much greater success in continuing to raise funds. Construction on the Babies' Villa in Clacton commenced immediately, and plans were drawn up for an infirmary to add to the ever-growing Flower Village. Given the physical plight that some of the poor little orphans came to us in, it was a much needed facility.

On a more current note, I am delighted to report that I felt the first kick from Evelyn's belly today. Quite some kick it was, too—almost visible to the naked eye! Evelyn insists that it doesn't hurt, although I find that hard to believe and insisted on her retiring early to get some rest, despite her protestations that she felt quite energetic and well. The creation of life really is a miracle that dumbfounds me every time I experience it, and I pray to the Lord for the continued health and well-being of my wife and our unborn child.

• • •

I'm not sure at what point I decided to take the two Irish girls into the Flower Homes. They still had an aunt living with them, but the more I spoke to Florrie, the more apparent it became that this aunt would be better off in Bedlam. It became clear to me that she had no more of a mind to care for those two little girls than she did to pour a bottle of gin down the drains.

While I would sit, late at night, in the warmth and comfort of my study, where I was supposed to be recording the minutes of a board meeting that our new president, Lord Shaftesbury, had attended, I often found myself procrastinating, unable to get the pitiful faces of those two little girls out of my mind.

And so I set my mind on talking to Florrie about the matter of herself and her sister going to our orphanage homes at Clacton. I was certain that the prospect of regular meals, sand between her toes, and the fresh sea air in her lungs would be sufficient to tempt Florrie to leave London, although she was always a fiercely independent young thing, and I was afraid she would decline and insist on continuing to sell her flowers here.

It never failed to amaze me how afraid the waifs and strays could be of a change in their circumstances. Many a time I saw how difficult they found it to adjust to a conventional life—struggling to sleep in a proper bed (having never experienced the luxury) and even finding that they missed their life on the streets. Within the first month of many a girl's arrival at the homes, she would be restless and want to go to the streets again. I suppose it is the same with any human being; they are more often happier with what they know and what is familiar to them than they are in unfamiliar circumstances—however much improved those circumstances may be. How strange it seems that a proper bed and a regular working day of six in the morning until eight in the evening, week in, week out, may be a more frightening prospect to some than a life of sleeping with the vermin on filthy doorsteps and not knowing where your next meal is coming from.

In any event, I resolved to talk with young Florrie the next time I saw her on the streets or at the Club Room. And once I set my mind on this, part of me desired to go to Rosemary Court immediately and locate her that very night. I remember how I almost suggested the idea to Evelyn, but thought better of it. She is a sensible human being after all—unlike me—and I knew that she would only tell me what I already knew: that it would be impossible to find the girls at that hour of the night, not to mention a dangerous and foolhardy enterprise.

So, I settled to my paperwork instead and prayed that the girls had a peaceful, safe night—if it is possible to have such a thing out there amid the cruel streets of our city.

• • •

In other matters I am delighted to report that Evelyn's belly continues to swell with child. The physician is happy with ▸

The Memoirs of Albert Shaw *(continued)*

her health, and that of the infant. He is, unfortunately, not so impressed with my own health. I should perhaps confide in my wife the extent of my illness, but I do not wish to worry her, especially in her delicate condition. So, I will continue to pray for us all. There is, perhaps, never a more worrying time for a man than that during which his wife is with child and in which he also finds his own health in a state of decline.

• • •

It is with some difficulty that I write these words, knowing that if I had taken the girls under my care sooner, as I had felt compelled to do, a most tragic incident would not have occurred. Dear Evelyn tells me I must not blame myself in any way, insisting that it was a terribly unfortunate event that nobody could have prevented. But she didn't see the look in Florrie's eyes when I found her. It is a look that will haunt me for the rest of my life on God's good earth.

I had become anxious to see the girls after deciding on my plan to place them in the orphanage in Clacton, and having not seen them about for several days, I will admit that I had begun to worry for their welfare. So I took it upon myself to seek them out, and after much wandering, I eventually found the child Florrie in a room at Rosemary Court, utterly distraught and bereft. Her little sister, Rosie, was gone. Lost. Disappeared.

There was nothing I could do or say to console her. She looked as if she hadn't slept or eaten in days. It was quite, quite heartbreaking to see her so desperately sad and to be so helpless to remedy the situation.

She pleaded and pleaded with me to help—to go with her and look for Rosie (which I did—both with the child and when I was alone). I knew that there was no purpose to informing the police. With there being so many lost and deserted children roaming the streets, it is hard to tell one from another. In any event, I suspected that the harsh reality of the matter was that the poor little girl would not have survived long on her own. There are all kinds of ill-intentioned people in this city of ours who will prey upon a lost and bewildered child and take them in to use to their own advantage. I suspected that someone would already have her making matches or pins or be teaching her how to pick pockets. Perhaps a worse fate had befallen her—although I prayed to the Lord to keep her safe.

As for Florrie, I spoke to her aunt, who agreed that I could take the child to the care of the housemother at Violet House in Sekforde Street. I knew she would be well cared for there until she had built up her strength, and then I planned to house her at the Flower Village in Clacton—once I was happy that she would be able to tolerate the journey.

I felt so utterly helpless, but there was nothing I, nor anyone else, could do to help the poor child who had gone missing. I tried to forget that she was not yet five years old and did not have the full use of her sight, for there is surely nothing more frightening than to be alone and lost and not be able to see where you are, or to know who may be walking a few yards behind you.

I did, of course, ask our missioners—who walk the streets every day looking for children to assist—to be especially vigilant and to look out for the child. I hoped that her distinctive red hair might prove to be of some assistance in locating her. Other than that, I knew that only Almighty God himself could intervene, so I prayed and prayed that the child was unharmed and that some kind, benevolent person had happened upon her and taken her somewhere safe. I recall how I sat weeping in bed, clinging to my dear wife. "There must be some good people left among this world of villains, thieves, and swindlers, Evelyn. Surely, there must."

December 1912
Somebody once told me that all flowers are beautiful, but some are more beautiful than others. I forget who it was said those words to me, but they have always stuck with me. And yet, as I sit here in my bed at the Flower Village and smile at the sound of the girls' laughter while they decorate the Christmas tree, it occurs to me that this does not ring true of children. To my mind, all children are beautiful, without exception.

I have been blessed to father three healthy children, all of whom have gone on to have children of their own. And yet, there was a fourth child, our dear little girl, whose breaths would not come once she left the warm cocoon of her mother's belly. ▸

No matter how much we prayed for her, she could not stay with us. Our little Violet was needed elsewhere, to bring light to others.

My heart is heavy this late winter's afternoon. I know that my health fails more with each passing day. I remember how I watched the autumn leaves as they dropped from the great oak trees around Mr. Hutton's carefully tended gardens and found myself wanting to wither and fall with them. And yet, I go on. I endure, despite all the doctor's grim warnings.

And while I find that I am too weary to extract much in the way of joy from the quiet moments that fill my days, I find that this gives me time to reflect on the good and purposeful life I have known. I have much to be grateful for, much to be thankful for—especially since my lasting prayer has, finally, been answered. Little Rosie Flynn has been found. After all these years, she is found, safe and well.

The young woman, Miss Harper, who came into our lives and our homes earlier this year, has found her. After all these years of hoping and praying, after all the nights when the shadow of that lost child darkened my heart, Rosie has been found, full of health and life and with her eyesight fully restored and three children of her own. It is surely a miracle and one that swells my heart with happiness. I only wish that dear Flora could have seen her sister once more. How proud she would have been of the woman Rosie Flynn has become.

As I rest here and write these words, I find a wonderful sense of completeness—a calm settling within—and I wonder. I wonder if I might soon slip quietly away, with just the sound of the children's laughter and the gentle hush of the sea to carry me onward, to the brilliant light that beckons.

Copy of a Letter Written by Albert Shaw in The Christian Magazine, *September 1876*

Open Letter to "Daisy"

I must thank you, "Daisy," for your most generous donation to our cause. I hope that you will read this entry, which I submit by way of humble gratitude.

Just yesterday, I visited our orphanage in Clacton and was

much inspired to see how the health of so many of the children has improved since being taken there. One little Irish girl, who weeps every night for her lost sister, has gained so much in weight that Matron is busy making new dresses for her! While the child's heart may still feel the pain of her sister's absence, I am encouraged to see how her cheeks glow with vitality.

Nevertheless, I cannot help but feel that we can do more. As such, our board members have agreed that we will rent several more houses in Sekforde Street, to provide more family homes for these poor, afflicted flower sellers. Providing the training to make flowers is also proving to be a very successful enterprise. By removing the girls permanently from a life on the streets and providing them with a proper purpose, we can hope to make a real difference to their lives. Happily, our recent pamphlet drive and prayers for funding have both proved to be extremely fruitful.

I thank you again for your support and generosity and pray for a mild autumn so that for all those flower sellers we cannot reach, their cresses do not freeze and their violets will not spoil in their baskets.

With gratitude,
Albert Shaw
Superintendent, Training Homes
for Watercress and Flower Girls

The Language of Flowers
The Lost World of Floriography

In writing *A Memory of Violets*, I was constantly struck by the cruel contradictions of the lives of the flower sellers. Here were some of the poorest women and children in society, living the harshest of existences, and yet every day they were surrounded by the beauty of the flower markets. Black-and-white images and shaky newsreel footage taken during the late nineteenth and early twentieth centuries give a fascinating glimpse into market life in London, but it is difficult for us to imagine what these scenes would have looked like in full color. Oddly beautiful, perhaps.

Research for the novel also led me to understand more about the wonderful world of floriography—the term given to the Victorian tradition of the language of flowers. Of course, the Victorians were not the first to use flowers and herbs to express meaning. The symbolism and "language" of flowers and herbs goes back much farther, with many ancient civilizations using this manner of expression. But the Victorians and their almost obsessive passion for all things flora are best associated with the language of flowers.

At a time when social etiquette meant that a declaration of love was tricky (to say the least), flowers could express everything that a person could not state more explicitly. This very formal and reserved society used the powerful language of flowers to express their strongest passions and emotions—love, grief, devotion, and jealousy. Sometimes the interpretations were quite dramatic. "I attached myself to you but shall die if neglected." No pressure there, then!

It is quite something to think that all this could be expressed through a posy of flowers, bought, perhaps, from impoverished street sellers such as Flora and Rosie. How fascinating to think that the simple arrangements made by the women and children on the steps of St. Paul's Church at Covent Garden by candlelight were so important to the everyday lives of the ladies and gentlemen who paid their tuppence for a bunch of violets or a tussie-mussie (a small bouquet of flowers, presented in a lace doily, tied with satin).

With so many varieties of flowers and herbs and so much riding on the correct translation of their meaning, it was important for Victorian women and men to familiarize themselves with the language of flowers. As a result, a number of beautiful books—flower dictionaries—were written, to explain the meanings of hundreds of varieties of flowers and herbs. How many hearts must have raced beneath corsets as young ladies pored over the pages of these little books to decipher the messages contained within the carefully selected posies sent to them by secret (or not-so-secret) admirers!

With flowers being paired or used in a bouquet to add a more ▸

The Language of Flowers ***(continued)***

complicated meaning, with the size and shade of the flowers and even the direction in which the flowers faced, all resulting in slightly different meanings, these flower dictionaries must have been very well used. Far from being simple lists of meanings, most flower dictionaries were beautifully illustrated with color plates showing flower combinations and their meanings, and many were accompanied by poetry.

One wonderfully titled Victorian flower dictionary from 1852, *Flora's Lexicon: An Interpretation of the Language and Sentiment of Flowers; with an Outline of Botany, and a Poetical Introduction,* outlines the importance placed on the language of flowers in this evocative opening paragraph:

> The language of flowers has recently attracted so much attention, that an acquaintance with it seems to be deemed, if not an essential part of a polite education, at least a graceful and elegant accomplishment. A volume furnishing a complete interpretation of those meanings most generally attached to flowers, has therefore become a desirable, if not an essential part of a gentleman's or a lady's library. In the manual now offered to the public, an attempt has been made to comprise all that is important in the way of interpretation in a

reasonable compass, and to adorn this part of the work with such quotations from the best poets of our language, both native and foreign, as have a direct and graceful reference either to the peculiarities of the flowers, or to the sentiments which they are made to express. The outline of Botany placed at the end of the volume will be found to contain a sufficiently clear exposition of the Linnean system to explain fully the scientific terms and the classification used in the body of the work.

On the occasion of her marriage to Prince William, in April 2011, the Duchess of Cambridge, Kate Middleton, used the traditional language of flowers to select the combination of flowers and herbs for her bouquet. The main component of the bouquet, lily of the valley, represents that which is "trustworthy." Myrtle, another flower selected for the bouquet, has traditionally been included in royal wedding bouquets since Queen Victoria's daughter Princess Victoria carried it in her wedding bouquet in 1858. The myrtle in Kate Middleton's bouquet was picked from a tree planted by Queen Victoria at Osborne House on the Isle of Wight in 1845. Myrtle represents "hope and love." And the sweet william in her bouquet? I think we can guess why she chose that! ▶

The Language of Flowers ***(continued)***

Although we still use certain flowers to express emotions—red roses, for example, being the ultimate expression of love—the language and meaning of flowers has largely been forgotten. Where we might now go to the florist's shop and select a bouquet based on color preference or how a particular flower looks, the Victorians selected their flowers so very carefully. In an increasingly hectic world where social media is such a dominant form of communication, there is a part of me that mourns the loss of the hopelessly romantic notion of floriography. Through writing *A Memory of Violets* and sharing the meaning of the flowers hidden among the pages of Flora's journal illustrated so beautifully at the start of each "part" of the novel, I hope that I have reawakened a little piece of history and have given the flowers a chance to speak once again.

Some popular flowers and herbs and their meanings:

Pink carnation—I will never forget you
Red carnation—my heart breaks
Daffodil—new beginnings
Daisy—innocence
Purple hyacinth—please forgive me
White hyacinth—beauty
Ivy—fidelity
Lavender—mistrust
Lilac—first emotions of love
Lily—majesty
Lily of the valley—return of happiness

Mignonette—your qualities surpass your charms
Michaelmas daisy—farewell
Moss rose—confession of love
Oregano—joy
Pansy—you are in my thoughts
Peony—anger
Primrose—I can't live without you
Red rose—love
Pink rose—grace
Yellow rose—infidelity
Rosemary—remembrance
Snowdrop—consolation; hope
Stock—you will always be beautiful to me
Violets—faithfulness ❧

Extract from Flora's Lexicon *taken from Catharine Harbeson Waterman, Chatsworth Vintage (Boston: Phillips, Sampson & Co., 1852).*

Flower meanings from Mandy Kirkby, A Victorian Flower Dictionary: The Language of Flowers Companion *(Ballantine Books, 2011).*

The Story Behind the Book

WAY BACK IN 2010, I had a notion to write a book about flower sellers in London. Perhaps it was driven by my love of Eliza Doolittle (I did, after all, play Eliza in the school production of *My Fair Lady* at the tender age of seventeen). Perhaps it was those lazy Sunday afternoons spent pottering around Covent Garden when I lived in London. Whatever the reason, I was drawn to the lives of the flower sellers—but it took a while to discover my story.

After dabbling in some research books and online sites about everything Victorian, I discovered the work of the social researcher Henry Mayhew. I found extracts from his writings online and was immediately drawn to his transcribed interviews with London's street sellers. I picked up a copy of *London Labour and the London Poor* and found myself folding down the corner of every page because I wanted to go back to it and read more. As I read the account of two orphan flower sellers—sisters—my heart leaped. I knew immediately that it was their story I wanted to tell.

From there, I followed the trail of bread crumbs to the fascinating life of the Victorian philanthropist John Groom and his incredible work to support the watercress and flower sellers who worked around his Clerkenwell home by giving them an occupation that would remove them from the streets. Discovering the history of Groom's "Crippleage" and the blind and disabled girls and women who produced artificial flowers for a queen was like finding buried treasure.

In 2012 I visited the London Metropolitan Archives in Clerkenwell, where a vast amount of information about John Groom and Alexandra Rose Day is held. I returned home to Ireland with a head full of stories and characters. It was simply incredible to see photographs of the young children at the orphanage in Clacton and the girls and women in the flower workrooms in Clerkenwell. To see their handwriting on the simple postcards Groom produced to promote their work, to read accounts of their daily routine and their work, to walk the street where they'd lived, to hold one of the pink Alexandra roses that had been made a hundred years earlier—it was all very humbling and hugely inspiring. *A Memory of Violets* was under way.

With the exception of Albert Shaw, who was based on John Groom, the characters in the novel are fictional. Florrie and Rosie were inspired by the many heartbreaking accounts of street children whose harrowing tales are recorded, in their own words, in Henry Mayhew's "masterpiece of personal inquiry and social observation" and in numerous other accounts of Victorian street life.

The inhabitants of Violet House are drawn from my imagination and from stories told in two fascinating pieces of work: *Reminiscences of a Flower Girl* ▸

and *More Than One Mountain to Climb.* Both were written by former flower girls who had lived and worked at John Groom's Edgeware estate from the 1930s onward. They provide a fascinating insight into how these incredible women lived and worked together.

Way back in 2010, I had a notion to write a book about flower sellers in London. I simply had no idea of the amazing stories that were waiting to be told.

P.S. The name Albert Shaw was derived from Queen Victoria's much-loved husband, Albert, and the surname of the Irish playwright George Bernard Shaw, who wrote *Pygmalion*, in which he created the unforgettable character of Eliza Doolittle, the most well-known flower seller of all.

John Groom: The Real Albert Shaw

My character Albert Shaw is based on John Groom, a man who deserves to be acknowledged in his own right.

John Groom grew up in Clerkenwell, London. Raised in a happy Christian home, he had a strong faith and, despite his apprenticeship as a silver engraver, always felt he had another calling.

In the streets and markets around his home, John was regularly exposed to the lives of the young watercress and flower sellers, many of whom were disabled or deformed. Many were born this way as a result of diseases that were rife amid the unsanitary conditions of London's slum housing. Others had worked in factories as very young children and suffered terrible accidents. Unable to take up other occupations because of their disabilities, the children turned to selling on the streets, as this was the only way to make a living without begging or stealing.

At the age of twenty-one, John started his own engraving business from his home on Sekforde Street, but he still knew his calling lay in helping the street sellers. When he was invited to become superintendent of a local Christian mission, visiting people in his district and offering practical and spiritual help, his life changed forever.

From the humble beginnings of a hired room at Covent Garden, where he would provide hot cocoa and bread and butter to the street sellers, John's ▸

John Groom: The Real Albert Shaw
(continued)

ambitious plans led him to the idea that the flower sellers could make artificial flowers. From 1866 in small workrooms in Harp Alley, to Woodbridge Chapel Hall, to a dedicated factory on Sekforde Street, the Watercress and Flower Girls' Christian Mission (initially known as John Groom's Crippleage) was formed. With the support of patrons such as Lord Shaftesbury, the mission went from strength to strength. In 1890 John's attention turned to helping London's orphans, and the Flower Village at Clacton was established.

In 1912 the work and recognition of the flower girls reached new heights when they were asked to make roses for Queen Alexandra Rose Day. On June 26, thousands of society ladies took to the streets carrying baskets of roses. Over thirty thousand pounds was collected for the hospitals from the sale of the roses. This was the first charitable "flag day" of its kind—the forebear to all the familiar events we see today, such as Daffodil Day, Poppy Day, and other charitable collections days.

After his death in 1919, John Groom's name continued to be associated with assisting the disabled. In 1932 the organization moved to a new premises at a large estate in Edgeware, North London, where the flower girls continued to live and work. During the war years in the 1940s, they even turned their skills to producing munitions and rivets instead of flowers.

John Groom's legacy continues as the organization Livability, the United Kingdom's largest Christian disability charity, which aims to provide disabled and disadvantaged people real choice about how they live their lives. Her Royal Highness Princess Anne, the Princess Royal, is the charity's patron.

The Alexandra Rose Charities also still operates today. Since 2013 its aim has been to work with the London Food Board in an attempt to bring about positive change in food-related issues affecting lower-income families. The charity's patron is Princess Alexandra, the Honorable Lady Ogilvy—great-granddaughter of the charity's founder, Queen Alexandra.

John Groom's impact on the lives of the watercress and flower sellers and on London's orphans was profound. He was a true pioneer in his work to assist those least fortunate in society, and it is testament to his vision and dedication that his legacy continues to this day.

Reading Group Discussion Questions

1. The role of the "little mother" was very common among London's poor, with the eldest siblings (often no older than six or seven years themselves) taking responsibility for younger sisters and brothers. What was your response to reading about Flora's life and her relationship with Rosie? What are your thoughts about the lives of child street sellers in Victorian England?

2. The unique relationship between sisters is explored throughout the novel. To what extent do the relationships between Tilly and Esther, and Florrie and Rosie differ? Are there any ways in which they are similar?

3. Marguerite Ingram is determined to raise Violette as her own child. Do you think she is justified in her conviction that this is the best thing for the child? Is she right to keep the truth from Violette for so many years?

4. While Tilly's mother cannot find love for her in the same way she does for Esther, Marguerite loves Violette almost instantly. Why is this? How have their different experiences of motherhood influenced the two women's emotions?

5. The novel is written in alternating periods, Tilly's story in 1912 and that

of Florrie, Rosie/Violette, and Marguerite from the late 1800s. In what ways do the two story lines reflect each other and in what ways do they differ?

6. One of the main themes of the novel is forgiveness. Do you think Violette should forgive Marguerite for hiding the truth about her past? Should Tilly be forgiven for her feelings toward Esther? Should Esther forgive Tilly for the accident? Should Tilly forgive her step-mother for her feelings toward her?

7. There are many other themes in the novel—second chances, hope, family bonds, overcoming adversity. Which themes resonated with you the most?

8. Disability was very much a hidden or ignored part of society in Victorian London. The Flower Homes and the orphanage were pioneering approaches to assisting those who were disadvantaged. Now that you have read the novel, what are your thoughts about attitudes toward disability in Victorian England? How have attitudes toward disability changed?

9. The language of flowers was well known among the Victorians, and the flowers hidden within Florrie's journal convey very specific messages and emotions. What are your thoughts about the "language of flowers"? ▶

Reading Group Discussion Questions
(continued)

10. Landscape plays a large part in the storytelling of the novel, with the settings moving from the cramped streets of London to the mountains of the Lake District and the open seascapes of Clacton. How do these landscapes reflect the emotions of the characters?

11. Through flower making, the girls and women of the Flower Homes were given a way out of hardship and a way to become independent. Why did Albert Shaw insist on the girls working for a living, rather than simply providing them with charity?

More from Hazel Gaynor

Read on

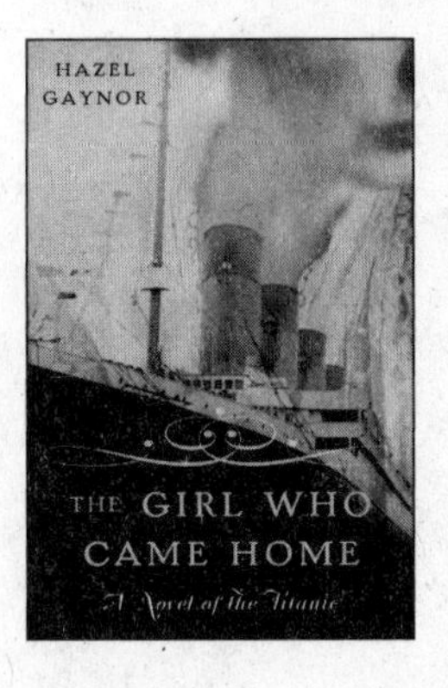

THE GIRL WHO CAME HOME

Ireland, 1912 . . .

Fourteen members of a small village set sail on RMS *Titanic*, hoping to find a better life in America. For seventeen-year-old Maggie Murphy, the journey is bittersweet. Though her future lies in an unknown new place, her heart remains in Ireland with Séamus, the sweetheart she left behind. When disaster strikes, Maggie is one of the few passengers in steerage to survive. Waking up alone in a New York hospital, she vows never to speak of the terror and panic of that fateful night again.

Chicago, 1982 . . .

Adrift after the death of her father, Grace Butler struggles to decide what comes next. When her great-grandmother Maggie shares the painful secret about *Titanic* that she's harbored for almost a lifetime, the revelation gives Grace new direction—and leads both her and Maggie to unexpected reunions with those they thought lost long ago.

Inspired by true events, *The Girl Who Came Home* poignantly blends fact and fiction to explore the *Titanic* tragedy's impact and its lasting repercussions on survivors and their descendants.